Thirty

Days

to the

Unimaginable

Dominique Darley

To Debbie
Happy Christmas
love Joan.
x

DDarley
x

Field Mouse Publishing

First published by Field Mouse Publishing, 2021

Cover illustration by Tristan Van der Linden
Jacket design by Antony Wootten
www.antonywootten.co.uk

Contact details for Dominique Darley:
dominiquejdarley@gmail.com
Twitter: @DarleyD_Author
Instagram: dominiquedarley_author

ISBN: 978-1-7398153-0-1

for my parents

Minus Eleven

The late summer heat hung heavily. It was after two in the morning and Henry was awake. Content, staring through the darkness into the small room, he made shapes out of the distorted shards of amber light projected in by the street lamp, enjoying the patterns dancing on the wall as the billowing of the thin lace curtain played with the early morning breeze.

Unable to sleep, he was happy in the Parisian bed of feathers and white sheets he shared with his wife, Lorna, letting his mind recapture the events of the past week and thinking about what had made him choose Paris for the Small-Space Theatre Company's first international performance...

An obscure English play, performed in a backstreet theatre in Paris, did not initially strike Henry as a sensible idea. Such plays had fallen out of favour in recent years as more mainstream work enticed the less discerning theatregoer. But, luckily for Henry, there was still a niche market for plays such as his and, after visiting the city with Lorna, he became convinced that this play, with its unconventional plot and intriguing characters, would be brilliantly suited to a harshly critical French audience. After looking around at several small 'alternative' venues, they had fallen in love with a dingy, intimate space above a bar with dark green walls and murky lighting. It had kooky seating made up of old pews, springless sofas and mismatched metal chairs. It was perfect. They could imagine themselves there, with the audience leaning forward in their seats inches away from the stage, smelling the sweat of the actors and feeling their breath on their faces.

Before arriving in Paris, the play had spent three weeks previewing in small theatres in the UK, beginning in Cambridge and travelling up the east coast to Norwich, Hull and Newcastle before heading into Scotland and settling in Edinburgh, the city of Henry's birth, for the first two weeks of the festival. Having drip-fed the media with carefully selected reviews from each performance as they moved from theatre to theatre, by the time they reached Edinburgh, their two-week run was sold out. Five-star reviews and outstandingly positive press coverage from the festival were further shared with the arts editors of the Parisian papers, so that when they transferred to Paris for an intense seven-day run, they were fully booked and could banner the theatre with 'Les billets ont ete vendus'.

Now here Henry was, on closing night, imagining what it would be like to give up his 'proper' job as a maths teacher, so that he could tour the theatre company all over the world. Congratulating himself, he smiled, enjoying the cool breeze that wafted in through the sash window and the light show, which provided entertainment for his insomnia.

~

To a passer-by, looking in through the Edinburgh factory window, the sight of a millionaire lying on his back beneath a huge industrial machine in the early hours might stop them in their tracks, make them clear the night rain from the glass, and look a little harder. For Sebastian, being under the machines was all part of a day's work. It was imperative they kept running, vital they were not hindered in their output by bits of detritus. So, when the nightmares came and he couldn't sleep, Sebastian would drive to the factory and spend time with them, watching their every move, listening to their nocturnal voices, making sure they were working at peak efficiency. Some of the machines were over twenty years old.

The company had been running at full capacity for a long time and required significant investment if it was to continue to compete with cheap imports which were sniffing ever closer at its door. But, heading into his twenty-fourth trading year, Sebastian had decided he was not the man to take it in the direction he believed it needed to go. Tatch-A UK had a brilliant future ahead of it, but he had achieved what he set out to achieve and had made a good income along the way. Now he wanted to sell it while he was still young enough to do something else.

Although he employed a capable team of skilled engineers, some of whom had been with him since the early days, no one knew the nuances of the machines as well as Sebastian who had helped build them. Like old friends, he knew them intimately and with the keenest ear was able to hear the smallest of changes as each one performed its task. He knew when things didn't sound right long before things didn't look right, and over the years this had saved the company hundreds of hours of downtime. He often felt at his most productive when he was beneath the machines.

Scrabbling out, covered in dust, Sebastian sat on the floor. Tall and broad he sat awkwardly, looking around the factory, remembering how he felt the day he and Paul, his best friend and formidable negotiator, had visited it for the first time.

Sebastian and Paul had, more or less, grown up together, and Paul was right by Sebastian's side when the company was in its embryonic stage. An experienced accountant and financial advisor, with an ability to get everyone to see his point of view, Paul was a good man and Sebastian trusted him implicitly. So when Paul had turned to Sebastian and nodded that day, Sebastian knew that the factory would become so much more than the empty space they had first seen. He loved it, especially at night, with its dim lights and familiar noises, when production continued churning away quietly, with little human interaction.

In the distance, from one of the rooms opening onto the factory floor, he could just make out the sound of a telephone ringing. He looked at his watch. It was 1.25 a.m. He ignored the ringing and it eventually stopped, but a minute later it started again. Standing up, he brushed himself down, grabbed his jacket and walked over to the office.

~

It had long been an unwritten rule in the Campbell family that 10 p.m. was the latest time for telephoning without causing undue concern. The only justifiable reason for a late-night phone call would be to summon help to aid a cow or ewe in distress whilst giving birth, but that hadn't happened too often in recent years since Elspeth and William Campbell had semi-retired and run their East Lothian farm, Taligth, down to just a few hundred animals. So, when his mobile phone rang at 1.15 a.m. UK time, Henry knew there must be something wrong.

'Hello?' he whispered anxiously into the phone, his heart in his mouth after seeing his mother's number come up on the screen. Motionless, Lorna continued to sleep beside him.

'Henry, is that ye?' came his mother's familiar voice, her jumbled Scottish-English dialect, thick with heavy accent, speeding off her tongue. 'I'm tryin' to get hold of yer brother, d'ya know where he might be?'

'Why? What's happened?' Henry asked anxiously, running his hand though his mop of blonde hair as he sat up, tucking the sheet around Lorna's sleeping form.

'Yer da's had a fall.'

'At quarter past one in the morning?'

'No Henry!' she said sternly. With a tough Scottish farming heritage, Elspeth was a forthright matriarch who did not mince her words. Despite her small, rounded stature, she was a force to be reckoned with. Strong in physique and with a formidable temper, she could floor any ill-considered comment at twenty paces. Firm but fair, would be the way she would describe herself. 'Yer faither had a wee fall this afternoon. He tripped over something in th' piggery. I dinnae know what, but he can trip over his own shadow when he's nae lookin'.'

'Is he okay?' Henry asked, sitting hunched and naked on the edge of the bed, his thin body exposed to the cooling breeze.

'Obviously nae Henry, else I wouldnae be callin' ye!' she said brusquely. 'T'was a harder fall then he let on, so determined was he to watch th' bloody cricket!' she tutted. 'So we're at th' hospital and I'm needin' yer brother to come and pick me up. Where are ye?'

'Paris, Mum.'

'Och aye, of coorse, how's it goin'?'

'Fine,' Henry said, anxious to get back to finding out how his father was. 'Is Dad badly hurt?'

'Well, he's broken a couple of bones in his shoulder, 'n' one in his wrist as he tried to save his-sel from landing head first into Betsy's trough. Ye know what th' piggery's lik', trip hazards everywhere. Luckily, Betsy wasn't in there otherwise we might have had them both wi' broken bones.'

Betsy was William's favourite sow and at nearly eighteen years, she was an old lady. After a lifetime of producing hundreds of piglets, she had been spared the slaughterhouse and allowed to stay on the farm to live out the rest of her life in comfort. Each morning and evening, William would go to her pen and make a fuss of her. Sometimes one animal can find a special place in an old farmer's heart, and Betsy had wormed her way into William's the first day he brought her, as a tiny squealing piglet, onto the farm.

'That doesn't sound good, when did it happen?' Henry asked, getting increasingly concerned.

'Like I said, this afternoon! But ye know what yer faither's like, he thought he'd just bruised his-sel. Despite my suggestion, he didnae want to get checked out. He was quite happy resting in front o' th' tellybox. But it was clearly bothering him. Then, with th' excitement of th' test match he raised his arms in delight and 'crack', one of his bones snapped,' Elspeth explained, 'so, at teatime he decided he should go to th' hospital. Tell ye something Henry, Saturday night in A&E is a sight to behold!'

'Are you in the Edinburgh Infirmary?'

'Aye, that we are. He's been x-rayed and his wrist's been plastered. He needs a wee operation on his shoulder, which they'll do in th' mornin'. He's perfectly happy. I could just do with gettin' hold o' Sebastian to come pick me up. I dunae know how come I cannae get hold o' him.'

'He'll be at the office, Mum. You know what it's like for him at the moment.'

'Aye, of coorse he will, he's like yer faither, he never stops, he'll drive his-sel into an early grave if he's nae canny.'

'Did you get an ambulance to the hospital?'

'Would ye believe your faither insisted on driving over in th' Land Rover, with a broken shoulder! He can be so headstrong and there's no way ye'll get me drivin' it back, so it's stuck in th' car park.'

Henry laughed. His father was one of the most pertinacious men he knew. Although he was easy going and good-natured on the whole, if he did or did not want to do something there was no way anybody could persuade him otherwise, even Elspeth, whose temper he had learned to handle. He always thought he was right, even when he knew he was wrong.

The farm Land Rover was an ancient beast held together by bodywork that was more rusted holes than metal. It was temperamental and Elspeth had long since given up driving it, preferring to run around town in a smaller, more reliable car.

'Don't worry about the Land Rover, leave it where it is and we'll get someone to collect it.'

'Well, that's good, 'cos of coorse there's no way I can take it without yer faither telling me how to drive th' bloody thing!' she quipped.

Henry smiled. Every journey they had taken in the Land Rover his mother had complained to his father about his driving, but if he ever did the same to her he would get short shrift and she would stop the car and tell him to either take over or get out.

'Where's Dad now?'

'He's here, do ye want a word?'

Taken by surprise, Henry laughed. His mother was the only person he knew who could talk about people as if they were not in the room. He heard the muffled sound of the phone being passed over and his mother telling his father which way up to hold it.

'Hello there you,' came his father's booming voice, bright and breezy. His father had the wonderful ability to instantly lift Henry's spirits. William was an Englishman, and although not born into the farming world, he had happily accepted Scotland as his home from the day he married Elspeth and had worked the fields for over fifty years. His deep love for both his wife and the farm had glued him to his adopted country, and for better or for worse, he and Elspeth had weathered some storms and kept some secrets no couple should ever have to keep.

'So, what's all this fuss you're causing?' Henry asked, relieved to hear his father's voice.

'Yes sorry about this, but you know what it's like. The cricket had stopped for tea...' William laughed.

'How are England doing?'

'Very well. It's going to be close I think.'

'Excellent. Hopefully, I'll be around to watch some of it with you when I'm up next week. So, what happened?'

'Like your mother said, I went to see to Betsy just after lunch, taking the unused veg out. I opened the gate, put the veg down and as I turned to come out, over I went.'

Henry imagined his father falling. Although William was not a particularly tall man, he was weather-hardened and had enormous strength. It took a lot to knock him off his feet. 'Sounds like a hard fall. Which shoulder and wrist?' he asked.

'My right.'

'That'll put you out of action for a while.'

'It will, what a shame when it's getting to the exciting part in the cricket. Right, I'm going to hand you back to your mother.'

'Oh, okay, bye then, Dad.'

'Bye Henry,' William answered, as the passing over of the phone was accompanied by the muffled tones of Elspeth telling William to 'be canny wi' it'.

Not excluding William, Elspeth treated all the family like children. Nancy, at fifty-three, was the eldest, but had not been seen for years. At forty-nine, Sebastian was the middle child, and Henry, the youngest, tucked in behind him at forty-eight.

'Tis me darlin,' Elspeth said into the phone.

'He sounds in good spirits.'

'Ye know what yer da's lik'.'

Thinking of his father, Henry smiled. 'Right, I'll get hold of Sebastian and call you back.'

'That would be perfect. Tell him not to rush, just to hurry and get here as quick as he can, if he wouldn't mind.'

'Will do,' Henry laughed, 'I'll call you in a...'

'Hang on, yer faither wants to ask something...' Henry could hear his mother's short exchange with his father. 'What is it William?' she asked, impatiently. 'Hurry up, I'm wantin' Henry to cal' Sebastian for me...' The phone went quiet as Henry tried hard to listen to William's muffled request. 'Och, right ya are... Let me tel' Henry... Are ye still there Henry?' she asked, turning her attention back to the phone.

'I am.'

'Yer da says could ye borrow a pair of Sebastian's pyjamas for him please...' she relayed. 'Nae that they'll fit him, they'll be fancy ones, ye know what Sebastian's lik',' she said, 'but he can have a go I s'pose, though I imagine it'll be lik' squeezing an inflated balloon into th' neck of a boattle,' she laughed, making Henry laugh too.

'I'll see what I can do.'

'Thank ye, my bonnie laddie,' Elspeth said, signing off abruptly.

~

Wondering who could be calling in the middle of the night, Sebastian picked up the phone.

8

'Seb, it's Hal.'

'Hal!' Sebastian exclaimed, looking at the clock on the office wall, 'is everything okay? Where are you?'

'I'm in Paris. Listen I've had Mum on the phone. She's trying to get hold of you.'

'Is she? Why?'

'Don't panic, but Dad's had a fall this afternoon and they're at the infirmary. He's fine, but he's broken his shoulder and his wrist.'

'Shit! What happened?'

'He tripped over something in the pigpen apparently. He needs an operation tomorrow to pin his shoulder, so they're keeping him in. The Land Rover's at the hospital, but Mum won't drive it home. You know what she's like.'

'She must have driven it there.'

'No, Dad drove it.'

'Typical!' Sebastian exclaimed, sighing heavily, checking his pocket for his keys. 'Is he okay? Have you spoken with him?'

'I have. Don't worry, he's fine. I'm just sorry this one's landed on you. I'd be there like a shot but...'

'Don't worry about it; I'll head over now. How's it gone?'

'It's been incredible.'

'Do you think this is it? Goodbye to teaching?'

'Not sure I'd go that far but who knows, it could be.'

'God! My brother a 'writer and international theatre director' and there was I thinking I was something special,' Sebastian laughed. 'Right, I'll give Mum a call and see what she wants me to do.'

'Just to warn you, she's stressed.'

'Has she gone all 'Bonnie Prince Charlie'?'

'I could hardly understand a bloody word she said!'

Elspeth's broad Scottish accent had been diluted over the years she had lived with William, a well-spoken Londoner. But at times of stress or rage, or when she was with her relatives, she would quickly slip back into the depths of her mother tongue. Having been to an English university and then living in Newcastle all his adult life, Henry had more or less lost his accent, or at least it had morphed into a strange, individual mix of Scots and Geordie, whereas Sebastian had held onto his, albeit not as thick as his mother's, unless he was terribly drunk.

'Can you let me know what's happening?' Henry asked. 'Don't worry about the time, I can't sleep anyway.'

'Of course,' Sebastian replied.

Saying goodbye to Sebastian, Henry felt the bedroom become strangely quiet. He sat on the edge of the bed thinking about what was happening back 'home' and, deciding to go down to the late-night bar for a nightcap, he searched in the darkness for the clothes he had dumped on the old wooden chair in the corner of the room.

A heavy sleeper, Lorna had not stirred during Henry's hushed conversation and, choosing not to wake her, he quietly put on his jeans and a sweatshirt. Slipping his phone into his back pocket he crept silently out of the room.

The small, family run hotel they had been staying in for the past ten days had become their home and the hotel owners their friends. After trotting down the narrow wooden staircase, Henry entered the bar, which was dotted with locals accustomed to starting their evenings at midnight. The air was thick with conversation and hung heavily with the smell of alcohol.

'Henry!' Gustav called, seeing Henry come in shoeless and half asleep, 'you look like you need a drink. What can I get you? Your usual?' he asked, his English almost perfect, tiredness in his dark eyes giving away the long hours he spent running the hotel. Well past retirement, Gustav was as energetic as he had been the day he and his wife bought the rundown building just after they got married, but his old bones were starting to ache and he was feeling everyone of his seventy-two years.

'Yes please, Gustav.'

'This was your last night was it not?' he asked, busying himself with Henry's order.

'It was,' Henry said sighing.

'You have done good, yes? I read good things in the newspaper.'

'Praise indeed. If I can crack you tough Frenchies I can crack anything.'

Gustav laughed. 'Ah, non, we are pussycats,' he smiled, his grey moustache twitching, 'will you be back soon I hope?'

'I hope so Gustav, and when we are back we would like the same room please.'

'It is yours! I save it for you always, my favourite English writer friend. When you are famous you must not forget who gave you free drinks. Here, on me, as a 'see you soon' parting gift,' Gustav said, placing a coaster on the counter accompanied by a large brandy.

'Cheers,' Henry said, picking up the drink and raising the glass, 'I will not forget you, I promise.'

'You make sure. Cheers,' Gustav replied, wiping down the old wooden counter with a tea towel, before tucking it into the waistband of his stained white apron.

~

Switching off the factory lights and turning to look into the black space illuminated by the nightlights, Sebastian listened to the rhythm of the machines repeating their melody; all seemed harmonious.

Back at his car, he called his mother who updated him on what was happening at the hospital. He was surprised to hear that in the past half hour things had changed. The right surgeons happened to be in the building and his father had been taken into the operating theatre.

'No, I'll stay and wait, if ye dinnae mind,' Elspeth said when Sebastian suggested he pick her up and take her home.

'Do you want me to come and sit with you?'

'No thank ye,' Elspeth answered emphatically.

'Well, I'll stay in the office then, just call if you want me.'

'Will do, thank ye Sebastian,' Elspeth replied, sounding tired.

Heavy in thought Sebastian got out of the car and walked back into the factory where his office was on the second floor. There was plenty for him to be getting on with whilst he waited. Switching on the bright foyer lights, he thought about his father in the operating theatre and smiled to himself knowing how, had he not been anaesthetised, he would be asking a hundred and one questions about all the different pieces of equipment in the room, wanting to know what each one did and how it worked, how much it cost and how long it lasted. He would be fascinated... if only he were not asleep.

Although he was now a farmer, William was first and foremost an engineer and Sebastian could not have started Tatch-A UK without him and his extensive knowledge, advice, hours of patience, encouragement and, more than anything, his money. William had had such faith in the potential of his son's idea that he had financially supported him for the first few years when the business was getting off the ground. It was a major investment for which he never asked anything in return.

The idea for the company had come after a throwaway comment Sebastian's wife, Matilda, had made one cold morning in their then, rundown, unheated flat on the outskirts of Edinburgh. She was turning a hair bobble into their seven-month-old daughter's thin, blonde hair...

'Oh for goodness sake!' Matilda exclaimed.

'What is it?' Sebastian responded to what seemed an overreaction from Matilda as she held up a snapped elastic hair bobble.

'That's the second one that's done this.'

'Right,' Sebastian replied, wondering why Matilda seemed so upset by a ruined hair accessory belonging to Isla, who was sitting in her high chair happily oblivious of her mother's angst.

'They were expensive, Seb!' Matilda snapped at his obvious lack of compassion.

'Why, how much were they?'

'I'm not telling you. They were just expensive that's all.'

'How expensive?' Sebastian insisted.

'Twenty-five pounds.'

'Twenty-five pounds? For a hair bobble?' Sebastian exclaimed. 'Someone's making a lot of money!'

'For the pair.'

'Oh, that's all right then, although I didn't realise we had twenty-five pounds to waste on hair bobbles!'

'We don't. Lucy bought them.'

'Your sister's got more money than sense.'

'The annoying thing is that it's just the elastic that's snapped, the thing on top's fine.'

'Show me,' Sebastian said, sticking his hand out. He could hear Matilda's disappointment in losing what appeared to him to be an insignificant piece of accessorised elastic, but to Matilda the hair bobble meant something.

'Twenty-five pounds for *this*?' Sebastian was shocked. 'How can something so small and cheap-looking cost so much and then be ruined by the malfunction of something even cheaper?'

'What would be good,' Matilda said as Sebastian examined the snapped elastic, 'would be if you could buy detachable accessories for hair bobbles.'

'Go on,' Sebastian said, suddenly interested.

'Well, it's not the elastic I'm bothered about. It's the fact that now it's broken, the little doll has to be thrown away, and that's the bit I like. I can't see how it can be attached to another elastic, can you?'

Sebastian sat thinking. 'So, the 'doll' part of the bobble needs to be detachable,' he muttered. 'Then you could attach it to any old elastic and if the elastic breaks you've still got the 'doll'... oh my god Matilda, that's it!'

'It is?'

'What a brilliant idea! So bloody simple! Someone must have thought of it already,' Sebastian said, suddenly dashing his own hopes.

'If they have, I haven't come across it.'

'Not until now you haven't,' and excitedly Sebastian grabbed his little girl from her high chair and held her tight. 'You, my little princess, will have the most beautiful hair bobbles you could ever wish for. If you want sparkles, you can have sparkles! If you want dollies, you can have dollies!' And she squealed with delight as Sebastian held her tightly and whirled her around their tiny kitchen. It was the 'eureka' moment he had been waiting for and his idea of the 'Tatch-A' brand was born.

Sebastian's first calls had been to his father and Paul and, with their joint mathematics and engineering expertise, they sat for weeks discussing Sebastian's ideas and working on different designs for the 'claw' that needed to attach a variety of small ornaments to hair elastics. After months of research, late nights and considered and then discarded ideas, they finally arrived at what they believed to be the perfect designs. With Paul, his soon-to-be Financial Director, securing brilliant deals on factory, warehouse and office space, and supported generously by William and Elspeth, Sebastian took his first step into manufacturing, creating a successful company born from an off-the-cuff comment by Matilda and a note written on the back of a ripped formula box.

Having met in their first term at university, Sebastian and Matilda had been together several years by this time. Although they had gone through periods when their relationship was tested, especially when Matilda became pregnant in Sebastian's final year, they made a good team. They chose to keep the baby and with William and Elspeth desperate not to miss out on their grandchild, Sebastian and Matilda moved back to Scotland where Taligth became their home until they could afford to rent somewhere of their own.

Returning to live at Taligth had not been easy for Sebastian. Although he loved being back with his parents and enjoyed the freedom of working in the fields, he found it difficult to settle back into a house where he was unable to shake off indelible memories. Keen to get a place of their own, accepting as much work as they could, he and Matilda got dead-end jobs, saving every penny they earned. It put enormous pressure on their relationship and they were both emotionally exhausted by the time Ewan, their first child, was born, three weeks early, which coincided with them moving out of Taligth into a tiny, one-bedroomed flat which they rented on the outskirts of the city. Without the need to be asked, his father and Paul had helped Sebastian make the place habitable before Matilda and the baby moved in. It was at this point that Sebastian knew, despite his harrowing memories, being back in Scotland with his family and friends was where his heart lay.

Settled, Sebastian's first 'proper' job was with a firm making plastic components for machines used in the food industry. Paul, who worked in the financial department at the time, had introduced him to the company. It was interesting, and good to be working with his friend, but Sebastian was growing impatient. When Isla was born, less than two years after Ewan, the company was sold and it was at this point Sebastian's desire to have his own business strengthened.

It had been on a beautiful day when all they could do was stare longingly out of their fourth-floor window at the children lucky enough to be playing in their own gardens that Matilda was turning an expensive hair bobble in Isla's bunchy.

Three years later, Tatch-A UK moved into larger premises on the outskirts of Edinburgh. By now Matilda was the company's Environmental Director, with Paul, alongside them, as Financial Director. With an experienced sales team, hungry for business and eager to get the company on the map, they worked tirelessly, united in the sole purpose of making the 'Tatch-A' brand a household name, and it didn't take long before little girls had drawers full of Tatch-A-Bobbles, Tatch-A-Hairbands, Grips and Slides. Venturing into the clothing market, numerous other Tatch-A-accessories were developed, including Tatch-A-Button and Tatch-A-Zip and soon they were making good headway into footwear with Tatch-A-Lace and Tatch-A-Buckle. The opportunities were vast and Sebastian had forged his way into every sector he could, exploiting the unchartered waters with skill and determination.

So now, whilst they were still expanding, they were selling to an American group who bought companies such as Tatch-A UK with 'Made in Britain' ethics to compete in the international market. Sebastian was all too aware that cheap imports were an increasing threat to a British manufacturer of integrity.

Unlocking his office door, Sebastian called Henry.

~

Alone, nursing his brandy, watching the gesticulations of a couple of very old French men sitting on tall stools at the bar, Henry answered quickly.

'I've spoken to Mum. Dad's in surgery,' Sebastian told him.

'What? How come?'

'An operating theatre became available so they decided to do the operation tonight.'

'That's good I suppose,' Henry said, feeling concerned. 'So what's Mum doing?'

'She's going to wait around for him to come out. I offered to go over but she said she would prefer to call me when she's ready. I'm still at the office so I'll hang around here and then go home for some pyjamas. I doubt they'll fit but he's welcome to try.'

Smiling, Henry conjured up the image of his father in Sebastian's pyjamas. Due to his father's penchant for whisky, he was sporting a rather large stomach in his old age and, Sebastian, the tallest and the broadest of them all, was very slim. Against Henry's rather malnourished appearance, Sebastian was well defined after working out in his gym every day. Henry was short and naturally skeletal and no amount of pumping iron would build muscles that were not there in the first place.

'It's going to be a long night,' Henry said.

16

'I've got some work to do.'

'Well, I'm in the bar soaking up a brandy and the last of the atmosphere, so let me know when you head over.'

'Will do.'

'How are you feeling about Tuesday by the way?' Henry asked. 'Are you ready?'

'Getting there, though now Dad's out of action, I'm wondering whether I should go. Mum can't manage the farm on her own.'

'I'll be there. I can help Sam and Ade, plus there's Finlay who works for them sometimes and Brodie, who owes Dad big-time after he helped dig his tractor out. Dad's not broken his legs, he'll still be able to make sure the place is kept in order,' Henry said knowing how important the trip to New York was to Sebastian. 'Dad will want you to go, Seb.'

'You're probably right. You should go back to your room. I'll call you as soon as I leave.'

'Call whenever, I'll be awake.'

The phone went silent and Henry sat thinking, tipping his brandy glass and examining the remains of its contents. He stood up, downing the last mouthful. Leaving the glass on the bar, he waved to Gustav who was in deep conversation with an attractive woman sitting at the end, and headed back to the room, acknowledging the night-man at the desk as he passed. With leathery, olive skin and the gaunt look of a man who sat in the sun too long and smoked too many cigarettes, the night-man looked how Henry felt; knackered.

Henry quietly unlocked the door. The warm room had taken on the stale smell of sleep joined by the waft of alcohol, which had crept up the staircase behind him. Sliding the window up further, Henry let the fresh, early morning breeze dilute the air.

Aware of the change in atmosphere, Lorna stirred. Looking to see whether she was waking, Henry thought back to when they had first met on the set of his second production...

17

His first professionally performed play, in a repertory theatre just outside Derby, had been well received by the sum total of 157 people over its seven-night run, half of whom had been family and friends.

'You've got to start somewhere,' had come the voice of reason from his best friend and financial backer at the time, Frank, who had lent him £10,000. Frank, a fellow teacher, had great faith in Henry's ability as a writer, and supported and encouraged him when it became obvious that being a maths teacher was not Henry's vocation. 'Don't expect much in the early days,' he said. 'You need to get your work out there. No one's going to know what you have to offer until you show them.'

But the ticket sales for his first production had not even covered the rent of the theatre, let alone the actors' wages and the technical team costs, so Frank's money was soon swallowed up. Watching from the sidelines, Sebastian had offered sponsorship for Henry's second production, but Henry did not want to lean on his brother's generosity any more than he did Frank's; he wanted to do it on his own, sink or swim, without financial gift horses. But employing a professional team did not come cheap, so Henry asked the bank for a loan for his second play and to repay the money Frank had so generously lent him for his first.

Recruiting good people in an overcrowded industry was not easy. One of his best finds was a couple of technical guys who knew more about sound and lighting than anyone Henry had ever come across. They were nerdy and knowledgeable and he intended to keep them, if he could afford them. He had kept the team small by giving himself the task of sourcing props and costumes and, as he also wrote, directed and produced the plays, he was able to keep costs down. Despite this, it was still expensive for someone with a very limited budget. With the little money he had, he employed the actors, the tech guys, a stage manager, a set designer and a couple of young stage hands who spent most of their time lying on the set rather than moving it, but they were nice, and more importantly, they were recruited through a government training initiative so they were, more or less, free.

It was at this time that Henry met Lorna. Henry needed a set designer and when he asked his friends in the industry for a recommendation, Lorna's name was at the top of everyone's list. A pretty, thin, mouse-like creature, Henry had been attracted to her the moment they met and her set designs were the best he had ever seen. Having studied Fine Art in Liverpool, during her student years she had worked for some of the best theatres in northern England.

Married for twenty-two years they had one grown-up daughter, Lilith.

~

Henry sat on the deep, worn oak window seat looking out as the sun started to peek over the clay-tiled rooftops of the city. With sightseeing tours booked for the afternoon, they had planned to stay one more day, but in light of his father's accident, Henry decided to bring the flights forward and get back to the UK as soon as they could.

Knowing he would struggle to sleep in the final hour before sunrise, he sat watching the sky lighten and the city wake up. As he did, his phone rang. Answering, he looked at the steeple of the church to which his attention had been drawn by the sound of bells peeling across the city, welcoming in the dawn of a new day.

'Just to let you know Dad's out. The operation went well apparently. Mum's decided to stay with him; she's told me to go to bed!'

'Now she tells you!' Henry laughed, the bells tolling 5 a.m.

'I've stayed up half the bloody night and can't even be helpful. Are you back in your room?' Sebastian asked.

'I am. I'm sat on the windowsill soaking in the Parisian dawn.'

'Is the hotel nice?'

'You'd hate it, not a pane of glass bigger than a book.'

'Sounds horrible.'

'Not from where I'm sitting,' Henry said.

Having said goodbye to Sebastian, and feeling happier knowing his father was out of surgery, Henry sidled back into bed. He marvelled at the way Lorna could sleep through anything. It was a skill she had perfected when Lilith was a baby, leaving Henry to do the majority of the night feeds.

~

Sebastian continued working. There was still a lot to do and, although they were all exhausted, he was pushing everyone hard to prepare the company for sale. He was not going to let this one slip through his fingers.

Patrick McCarthy Inc., known as PMaC, had not been their first choice for a buyer. They would have preferred to sell to a British company. Their first offer, made by a large, well-established manufacturing business in Cardiff with a wealth of experience in the international market place, had been ideal. The Welsh company had wanted to expand their portfolio of products and services with the idea of taking successful British products like Tatch-A UK's into stable regions such as Europe, America and Australia as well as highly competitive regions such as China and South-east Asia. Their mission was to retain a British manufacturing ethos with British values and quality whilst exploiting the overseas market in the face of competitors. There was a growing international market for British-made goods even in countries that might have once considered them too expensive.

The sale had been progressing and the future for the company and its employees looked bright but, with a sudden change of fortune, the buyers unexpectedly pulled out and the sale collapsed, crushing Sebastian and his plans. Luckily, however, the news reached the ears of another interested party, Patrick McCarthy.

The son of immigrants, Patrick McCarthy was a shrewd Irish-American businessman. Having just celebrated his seventieth birthday, he had a wealth of acquisition experience. He had grown his multi-million dollar company off the back of his parents' small leather goods shop, which they had opened in downtown New York. The leather goods they sold were cheap but of good quality and, as a young man, Patrick had seen a marketing opportunity to rebrand and repackage them and to sell them on. It brought a small return and had ignited in Patrick the understanding that, in some cases, people would pay more for quality products and services.

He had watched Tatch-A UK for a long time before instructing his team to approach. To him, the most important aspect of any company he acquired was the person or people behind it, and he had been impressed by how the middle-aged Scotsman had grown the business.

~

Henry was slowly drifting off when his phone startled him awake.

'Seb!'

'Hi, I've spoken to Dad. He's doing fine but Mum's been sick. She's been up all night. I'm going to go and get her and take her back to Taligth.'

'Oh my god! Is she okay? Have you spoken with her?'

'Yes, she's okay, she's just exhausted.'

'Where are you?'

'I'm still at the office.'

'Have you slept?'

'No, but I'm all right. I'm going home for the pyjamas on my way to the hospital, so I'll catch up with you later.'

Lorna started to stir. By the time she was properly awake and asking what was happening and why he had not woken her, Henry had booked two flights to Newcastle for later that morning. The rest of the team would travel home in the van with the equipment and go back to their real lives before heading into rehearsals once more.

Packed, ready to leave, Lorna and Henry headed to breakfast. The smell of coffee and fresh pastries met them as they walked into the bar, where Henry had been served a large brandy only hours before. With full plates and espressos in hand, they took up their seats at their favourite table.

The sun was streaming in through the window and Henry and Lorna watched the square come to life. Sunday was the slowest day. Street sellers casually pushed their carts into position and café owners unfurled awnings and put out chairs and tables dressed with tablecloths and vases of twiggy flowers. Dog walkers ambled past and a few tourists, having read the menu on the wall pondered whether to sit outside or go into the warmer breakfast rooms.

Quietly observing, Henry and Lorna talked about the people they watched. 'So that lady over there, sitting with the older man,' Lorna said, spotting a young woman dressed in a pretty summer skirt and cardigan with open-toed high heels and a Galeries Lafayette store bag by her side, 'they're having an affair. He's an American businessman who flies to Paris once a month to see her.'

'And what brings you to that conclusion?' Henry asked, looking out of the window at them.

'Look around, no one else is dressed like her, or him come to that, not on a Sunday, and the bag she has is very expensive, something he bought her yesterday no doubt.'

'So how will she explain that to her husband?'

'She's not the married one. Her American friend is.'

'How do you know he's American?'

'His boots. Only American men wear boots like that with smart trousers.'

'And what does this American friend of hers do?'

'I'm not sure.'

'Perhaps he's an oil tycoon?' Henry suggested.

'Too obvious. I think he's a lawyer. He looks rich.'

'They both look rich. I don't blame him coming to Paris to see her.'

'Really?' Lorna asked, curious, 'so, what is it about her that lures him across the Atlantic?'

'She's British and lives in Paris...'

'No way is she British. Look at her!' Lorna protested.

'Italian then.'

'Clichéd, but I'll take Italian.'

'And she's lived in Paris for ten years, and she works...'
Henry paused, thinking. What job would he give a character
that looked like she did? She was beautiful, but not pretty,
and elegantly tall and slim with a dark complexion, nipped-
in waist and particularly thin legs. 'She's a model,' he said.

'Clichéd!' Lorna said again, looking at Henry cheekily,
knowing how irritated he got when she read a new script of
his and described some of the characters in that way. Henry
looked at her – she was being naughty.

'That's twice you've said that,' he observed, 'I'm not
sure I want to play this game anymore.' Lorna took a sip
from her coffee. 'Okay,' he conceded begrudgingly, 'so if
she's not a model, what is she then? And perhaps you should
be the playwright instead of me!' Henry's lack of sleep made
him a little unreceptive to Lorna's playfulness. 'Anyway,' he
said, standing up, 'it's time we were heading to the airport.
Come on, eat up. Let's get going.'

Having not finished her breakfast, Lorna looked at
him. He was so like his father. She finished her last mouthful
of coffee and tucked a croissant into a napkin, thinking she
might be grateful for it later. 'Do you want me to pop one in
for you?' she asked.

'Go on, it'll save paying airport prices.'

Sporting a croissant in each pocket, like a double
gunned Billy the Kid, Lorna waited outside for the taxi as
Henry checked them out of the hotel, saying goodbye to
Gustav and promising to return.

The taxi was old and the driver took little care as he
bumped kerbs and cut corners through the narrow streets.
By the time they arrived at the airport, Henry was feeling
sick. He despised travelling and the taxi ride and thronging
airport did not help. He hated the experience so much that
before his father's fall, he had offered to drive the van back
and let one of the crew take his seat on the plane.
Unfortunately for Henry, no one had wanted to swap with

him. They were planning on taking the scenic route via a couple of distilleries, so no matter what, Henry had been stuck with flying home. To his relief the flight was uneventful and after landing in Newcastle, he called Sebastian, leaving him a message.

Looking at his phone, Sebastian saw Henry's missed call. Leaving Elspeth in the kitchen he walked into the yard, looking over the gate at Betsy as she snuffled about in her pen. 'Hi,' Sebastian said returning Henry's call. 'I'm at Taligth and as ever, the signal's crap. Are you back?'

'We are. How are things? How's Mum?'

'She's okay, but imagine the scene...' Sebastian replied, clearly irritated. 'I got to the hospital, where it's impossible to park...'

'You didn't get a ticket did you?'

'Of course I did.'

Sebastian had acquired hundreds of parking tickets in his lifetime and had paid only a handful, believing payment to be optional. If he felt justified parking where he did because there was nowhere else to park, the ticket would go unpaid. If, however, he felt the parking ticket was fair then he would stump up the cash - after a while. In the majority of cases, he believed his parking misdemeanour to be justified and he refused to pay. How he had avoided anything other than a strongly worded letter was anyone's guess.

'I finally found Mum and Dad. Dad was happily sat in bed tucking into a bowl of cornflakes and a cup of tea whilst Mum was sat there looking absolutely terrible. She's seventy-five for fuck's sake, but because she's not the patient they just ignored her.'

Sebastian had found it inconceivable that his mother had not been offered anything to eat or drink during the hours she had been waiting, and to his parents' embarrassment, had made his feelings known to the nursing staff as he and Elspeth left. William and Elspeth were not ones to cause a scene.

'That's bad. How's she feeling now?' Henry asked.

'Tired, but she'll be okay. I've made her a drink and some toast and she's perked up a bit. I'm just about to head home. Sam and Ade are going to pick up the Land Rover and they'll look after things here whilst Mum grabs some sleep.'

'How's Dad?'

'He's absolutely fine,' Sebastian laughed, recalling his father joking with the nursing staff about soggy cornflakes.

'Did he get into your pyjamas?'

'You should have seen him, Hal! The bottoms are far too tight and long for him and the buttons of the top don't meet, but he insists they fit perfectly.'

Henry laughed. 'I'll grab a pair from Mum when I come up tomorrow.'

'I'm still not convinced I should be going to New York,' Sebastian said.

'Well it's up to you, but for what it's worth, I think you should. Believe it or not, I'm perfectly capable of helping out at Taligth.'

Henry knew Sebastian would find it difficult to leave. Despite the demands and pressures on him, Sebastian had always suffered tremendous guilt if he wasn't around when his parents needed him, and he hated the idea of not knowing what was going on first hand.

'Let's see how things go today,' Sebastian said, feeling torn.

'Okay, but I'm coming up tomorrow whether you like it or not. I need somewhere quiet to finish my script and you promised I could borrow your place for a week. So, with all due respect, I could do with you guys buggering off. If you decide to stay however, feel free to book into a Travelodge.'

Sebastian laughed. 'I'm not sure you're going to find it all that quiet. Panda's mad.'

'I'm a teacher remember, I can cope with a puppy!'

Whenever he was on the phone with Sebastian, or their parents, Henry felt close to Taligth, the farm on which he had grown up. As they talked, he could visualise the farmhouse kitchen and the fields with the sheep and the highland cattle rough grazing as far as the eye could see. He could visualise the people his mother talked about, often family and friends, and the ones she met at McGregor's garage, which doubled up as the village shop. But when the phone line went quiet, and the connection between them dropped, Henry could feel every one of the one hundred and twenty-four miles between them. When his parents needed extra hands he was always too far away.

He was looking forward to going back to Edinburgh and spending time on the farm with them. He needed to get out into the fields, his most valuable source of inspiration.

Minus Ten

Finally back in his own bed after several weeks away, Henry had a restless night. Not due to his father or dreams of the multiple 'Olivier Awards' he was bound to win for 'Best New Play' or 'Best Director' after his successful Paris run. Instead, he was tangled up in vivid night terrors about an empty swimming pool. He had been plagued with nightmares since childhood after discovering an abandoned swimming pool in the middle of dense woods near a derelict school when he was out playing with Nancy and Sebastian one day. He remembered peering over the edge, looking into the deep murk of rancid water, with decaying leaves and dead animals rotting in the blackened sludge. He remembered the animal's empty eyes staring up at the overhanging trees, their decaying bodies exposing ribs and teeth. He remembered seeing broken tiles, old tyres and mounds of discarded rubbish mixed with fur coats that no longer protected bones, and he remembered seeing the gradual slope of the pool as it headed into the deep end. Then he remembered the 'push' and the feeling of the fall as he descended, landing hard amongst them, swallowing the festering slime. He had never forgotten how he heaved at the taste and smell of the decaying mass or the feel of it on his skin as he scrambled on his bloodied knees, slipping and sliding back to the shallow end. Crying as he reached the steps, which had mostly disintegrated, he clambered to get out, and he remembered Nancy, pointing and laughing at him.

When he wasn't dreaming, he was awake, dwelling on what lay ahead; staying at Sebastian's, the urgency of getting his next play finished, and his father. His father's fall had made Henry worry about what would become of Taligth should anything happen to his parents. He knew how much it meant to them and, although it was nowhere near the size it had been in its heyday, it still had hundreds of animals; cows, sheep, goats and Betsy, keeping it a vibrant, working farm that took a lot of looking after.

It was the first time Henry had given it serious consideration. What would they do with the place when their parents were no longer able to manage it? What do people do in such circumstances? He assumed they sold off the animals, the land and the house bit-by-bit to pay for their care, or perhaps they sold it as a going concern, although it required a lot of work if they wanted to bring it in line with modern farming standards. It was not something he could imagine his parents ever considering. In their mid-seventies, William and Elspeth showed no sign of hanging up their tractor keys anytime soon. They were in good health and didn't seem to want to retire from what they loved. When asked about what might happen in the future they would shrug it off and say they would deal with it 'as and when', and that would be the end of the conversation.

Taligth had been in Elspeth's family for generations, and although Sebastian and Henry had loved working in the fields and spending time with the animals as they were growing up, neither they, nor Nancy had ever shown any interest in taking it on full-time. Elspeth lived in hope that one of them may come around to the idea one day. Not knowing the farm's destiny worried her, but she also accepted that her children had their own lives to lead and if that did not involve the farm then so be it, and Taligth would move out of the family once both she and William were gone. The farm had been all Elspeth had ever known. She was an only child, so when her father died, seven years after her mother, the responsibility had naturally passed to her. She was young and had been learning fast, looking after the place almost single-handedly during her father's long illness. It was hard work and a lonely existence, until she met William.

28

As an apprentice with a national engineering company that specialised in the manufacture of components for all manner of farm vehicles, William had often travelled to Scotland as part of his training; spending days visiting the farms, mending and servicing their machines. That was how he and Elspeth met, him beneath one of her tractors and her asking him about what he was doing in order that she might understand and be able to mend them herself. In the early days, William found any excuse to travel to Taligth, and then as the company grew and the opportunities for work expanded, it was easy for him to relocate his job to Edinburgh. Over the fifty-five years they had been married, his engineering skills had saved their bacon on more than one occasion. Having never worked on a farm before, it had taken him some time to get to grips with the long hours and lack of sleep, but he loved it enough to give up his job and take it on full-time. He enjoyed being outdoors and liked nothing more than donning his boots and trudging out into the fields in the middle of the night to help a ewe in difficulty, or to catch a cow who had escaped the confines of the fence, or to watch, in wonder, as Betsy gave birth, seemingly effortlessly, to yet another squealing litter.

Keeping the machinery working was time-consuming and expensive. To have any of them out of action would cost them dearly. William had learned a lot from his apprentice days. There was little he did not know or could not mend, and what he could not mend he would learn about for next time. His mechanical skills became well known amongst the local farming community and he could often be found beneath a neighbouring farmer's tractor, a pie and a pint at their local being all the reward he needed for his labours.

~

Sebastian and Henry had talked about helping out more, or the possibility of employing a manager to keep things going when their parents showed signs of slowing down. Sam and

Ade were good workers, but they could not deal with the calving or lambing in the way William and Elspeth could.

'What do you think?' Sebastian had asked Henry a month before their father's fall, over a late Monday afternoon beer whilst enjoying their annual family holiday to Norfolk. 'I don't know how they'll cope as they get older. I suppose, once I've sold the company, I can help them out.'

'Do you want to do that?'

'Not every day, but I do love it when I'm there.'

'You never used to.'

'That was a long time ago,' Sebastian replied sharply, ending the conversation.

The reason they were talking was that earlier, sitting in the vast kitchen of the house they had rented for the week, Elspeth and Henry had discussed the farm's future over breakfast. Unusually for Elspeth, she had been the one to bring the subject up.

'Och, I do worry aboot it,' she commented, busily lashing her toast with butter and honey.

'Of course you do, but there's no point worrying about it until something happens.'

'Tis definitely goin' to happen, Henry, one day,' his mother replied, a little sharpness in her tone, which was unlike her, especially towards Henry.

'Yes, but we don't know when, so there's no point in worrying about it now is there?'

'I suppose not,' his mother conceded.

With Sebastian and the younger members of the family taking an early swim and Lorna and Matilda still getting ready, the house was quiet. William was sitting with his tea and toast, reading the paper, listening to Elspeth and Henry going around in circles, again... 'Looks like it's going to be lovely out,' he interrupted. 'We should head down to the beach.' But Elspeth was not listening, and they all sat silently eating breakfast, thinking about the same thing.

~

Henry got out of bed and jumped into the shower, which ran cold; Lorna had got to the hot water before him.

'You had a bad night,' she stated when he came downstairs into the hall. 'Swimming pools?'

'As usual,' he replied, playing with Mabel, their little dog, as she jumped up at him.

'So what are your plans?' Lorna asked, watching Henry reorganise the bag out of which he had lived for the last few weeks.

'I'm still going. Seb and Matilda need to go to New York.'

'Where will you stay?'

'Seb's, I can't concentrate at Taligth. It'll do them good to get away, they've had so much crap this year, and they could do with a bit of a holiday once they've had their meeting. God, I hope the sale goes ahead this time. Have you seen my laptop charger?'

'It's in the study, isn't it?

'Are you going to be okay here on your own?' Henry asked.

'Of course I am, I've got tons to do and anyway, I'm not on my own. I have Mabel to keep me company,' Lorna replied, picking Mabel up and ruffling her soft, chocolate brown curls.

Mabel was the source of the majority of Henry and Lorna's happiness and, other than Lilith, and Henry's plays, was the subject of most of their conversations too. For as long as they had been together, they had wanted a dog and had talked themselves in and out of it for years. Like having children, there was never a good time, so they had decided to just get one and deal with the consequences as and when they happened, which they did, often, but they wouldn't want to be without her.

Getting Mabel had coincided with Lilith leaving for university. In fact, Lilith's bed was barely cold when the pup arrived. In the early days, Mabel, a scruffy, mixed breed, kept Henry and Lorna on their toes; it was like having a toddler in the house again. No one warned them that puppies would

31

wee and poo all over the place, that their needle-sharp canines could make mincemeat out of best suit trousers or that they were adept shredders with the ability to rip up thirty-one maths exercise books in the time it took to make a cup of tea.

Now older, Mabel had mellowed into a relaxed, loyal dog who enjoyed little more than having her tummy scratched and a tennis ball thrown for her in the back garden. She was a real companion, and Henry and Lorna adored her. It was Mabel's arrival that had inspired Sebastian and Matilda to get a puppy. Panda, now eight months old, was just finding her feet... and her teeth! She was a very active, insanely sweet, black and white cocker spaniel.

'Have you heard from Seb? Anything from your mum or dad?' Lorna asked, following Henry into the study, with Mabel at her heels.

'Nothing yet,' Henry replied, leaving the study and going into the kitchen, 'I'm going to go to Taligth to check Mum's okay and then I'll head to Seb's. Hopefully, Dad'll come out today, but we'll see.' As soon as Henry uttered that phrase, his phone rang; it was Sebastian.

'Hi,' Henry answered.

'Is that Seb?' Lorna mouthed. Her question went unanswered as Henry turned away, trying to listen to Sebastian. 'What's he saying?' she asked.

'Hang on a minute, Seb,' Henry sighed, turning to face Lorna. 'Yes, Lorna, it's Seb. He's just saying he's spoken with Dad this morning. Apparently, they're going to keep him in for a few days.' Going back to the phone he continued speaking with Sebastian as Lorna put the breakfast dishes in the sink. 'Right, yes, that's great, thanks Seb. See you later.'

'So?' Lorna asked, pulling on tight yellow washing up gloves. 'What's happening?'

'Dad's staying in. That's all I know. Right, I'm going to make a move.'

'Okay. Let me know when you get there.'

'Will do,' he said, gathering up the last few bits. 'See you in a week or so,' he said to Mabel, as he stroked her head, 'be good for your mum.'

'She's always good,' Lorna said.

'And you be a good girl,' Henry said, going over to the sink and giving Lorna a kiss.

Henry set off, not realising that this was to be the first journey of many he would be making to Taligth over the next few weeks.

~

'For Christ's sake!'

'What on earth's the matter?' Matilda asked, watching Sebastian empty his bag for a second time. Panda was sitting on the bed seemingly fascinated by the game Sebastian was playing before she became distracted by a large, furry moth that had fluttered into the bedroom.

Sebastian was attempting to travel light, but he needed so much stuff he was struggling to get it all in the bag he was determined to use. 'Why the hell won't it go in?' he exclaimed. 'Panda!' he snapped as the puppy knocked his neatly piled papers.

He had stopped being surprised at how, in these digital days, there was still so much paperwork associated with the sale of a company. Along with the documents he needed for the meeting, he had decided to pack just one suit, a couple of shirts, a tie, cufflinks and one decent pair of shoes. He would have the clothes he travelled in and a couple of casual things for when he and Matilda took time out to explore New York, but the bag was too small for the number of items he was desperately trying to squeeze in.

'This is only an idea, but why don't you use a different bag?' Matilda suggested. Sebastian was in no mood and continued to take everything out once more. 'As I said, it was only an idea,' she sighed, watching him get more and more enraged. Panda continued to chase the moth, dashing along the pillows in a crazy attempt to catch the poor creature.

Matilda was ready for the trip, and her small suitcase was neatly packed with outfits to cover all eventualities. As she was not needed in the meeting, for her this was a proper holiday, and she was looking forward to relaxing for a few days. Selling the company, the past months had been particularly stressful.

Having jumped off the bed, Panda was now running around the bedroom chasing the moth. Playing hide and seek, it appeared to be enjoying the chase and started fluttering inside the bedside lamp, which came crashing to the floor after Panda leapt up in the vain hope of catching it.

'Panda!' Sebastian shouted, recovering the lamp from the floor and putting it back on the bedside table.

The moth flew to higher, safer ground and Panda followed it by jumping back onto the bed, inadvertently rearranging Sebastian's neatly piled clothes.

'For fuck's sake Panda!' Sebastian snapped again, pushing the puppy so that she toppled off the bed.

'Seb!'

'Look what she's done,' he said, gesturing.

'For god's sake Seb, calm down! You're being ridiculous! It's not her fault you've chosen to pack the smallest bag you own. Why don't you use one of the bigger ones?'

'Because I want to use this one!'

'But it's too small.'

'It isn't!

'You're so stubborn!' Matilda responded, kneeling down to cuddle Panda. Sensing there was more to Sebastian's irritation than met the eye, Matilda tried to talk to him. 'Are you nervous about the meeting or worried about your dad?' she asked, having made sure Panda had suffered no ill effect from her tumble.

'A bit of both, I suppose. It seems wrong to be going away when Dad's in hospital.'

'He'll be fine, Seb,' she said, reassuringly.

'You don't know that!'

'You heard what he said this morning. It's only his shoulder they're concerned about.' Having said her piece, Matilda went quiet. She knew Sebastian well enough to know when to stop speaking.

In the silence, Sebastian got lost in his thoughts. He was very close to his father. He thought how, as a child, he would ask his father to sit with him to help him work out various unfathomable mathematical problems. They would sit for as long as it took to get it right, never once giving up. 'If a job's worth doing it's worth doing properly' was William's mantra. It was from his father that Sebastian had got his dogged determination, and from his mother, his quick rise to temper.

One of the toughest lessons William taught him was when Sebastian was first learning to ride a bike. He fell so many times that he chucked the bike onto the grass and stood, head down, arms folded across his chest refusing to go any further, insisting his father push it back home for him. 'What sort of an attitude is that?' his father asked a sobbing Sebastian. 'So, this is how it's going to be is it? The first time something becomes a little challenging or doesn't go the way you want it, your answer is to give up and chuck it on the grass?' he continued. 'That's not how things in life work, Sebastian. Quite the opposite. When it gets difficult, that's when you've got to take control, dig deep, and go at it all the harder! We Campbell's most certainly do not give up!' The sternness in his father's tone was enough to draw him up, and with bleeding knees, still sobbing, Sebastian silently picked up his bike and mounted it. They did not speak a word on the slow, wobbly cycle home but Sebastian was determined he was not going to fall off his bike ever again. He never forgot that lesson.

His father practised what he preached and worked hard. If a job needed doing he would do it. Nothing was beneath him or too much trouble. If he needed to sleep out with his cows when they were in labour he would do so. If he needed to fight all night to save his crops from succumbing to a northeasterly storm heading across the country, he would do that also; whatever it took. Which was why he was so well respected amongst those in his community. As an adult, Sebastian had adopted the same attitude: if the factory floor needed sweeping, he would get the broom and sweep it. If a machine needed mending, he would get his tools and crawl beneath it. If it was time for a cup of tea, he would do the rounds. He and his father were as strong-willed as each other.

'I think your dad would be upset if he knew you were contemplating putting off going because of him,' Matilda said, interrupting Sebastian's thoughts.

'I'm sure he would be, but it doesn't make it any easier,' he replied, zipping his case before noticing his wash bag still sat on the bed. '*Fuck*!' he snapped, making Matilda look at him. He stared at her... 'Fuck it, it can stay there!' he said waving a dismissive arm in the air. Matilda sighed, watching him pick up his bag and leave the room, hotly pursued by Panda and the large moth.

Having found a small space for his discarded wash bag in her suitcase, Matilda looked back into the bedroom to check everything had been packed. Unless things changed, she and Sebastian were getting the first flight out to New York in the morning.

~

It was 3 p.m. when Henry arrived in the village, on the outskirts of which lay Taligth and her two hundred or so acres. White knuckled from driving the final few miles around blind bends, his back had stiffened, and getting out of the car to fill up with fuel, he stretched and yawned, forcing his body to straighten. He was five minutes away.

With two antiquated pumps, McGregor's Garage was more than a petrol station; it was something of an institution that sold everything anyone could possibly want. In fact, if it didn't sell it then people couldn't need or want it. The small, dilapidated stone building was overflowing with all manner of goods for sale from sewing threads and knitting patterns to bike wheels and gardening tools.

At the front of the building, there was an array of colourful local produce sourced from nearby farms: fruit and vegetables freshly picked that morning. Alongside it, there was a noticeboard attached to the wall informing the villagers of all that was going on: the mothers and toddlers group held in the village hall on Tuesdays and Thursdays; the ballet class on Monday evening open to anyone of any age or ability; the monthly dance held up at Dallonay's farm and the variety of services on offer to the villagers, from home hairdressing to William Campbell's offer of farm vehicle maintenance in exchange for a pint at the community pub which operated out of Jim McCann's old cow barn. The noticeboard was a good meeting place and a source of local gossip.

'Awright Henry, how ur daein'?' the tall, brawny man behind the counter asked. Henry had known Dougie McGregor all his life. They had both grown up in the village and Dougie, having not moved away, had married a local girl, taking over the garage from his father when he retired. The McGregor's still lived in the houses in which they had been born.

'I'm good, thank you, Dougie, how are you? How's the family?'

'Aye, we're all well ta. How aboot yers? How are yer parents? I've not seen them for a few days,' he asked, running his fingers through his thinning hair.

'My dad had a fall...'

'Och no!' Dougie exclaimed, concern spreading across his face.

'Yes, a couple of days ago,' Henry replied, knowing how fond Dougie was of William and Elspeth. 'So I'm up here visiting them. I'm going to be staying at Seb's and helping out at Taligth whilst Dad gets back on his feet.'

'Is he a'right?'

'He's broken a couple of bones but other than that, he's fine, thanks.'

'Weel, if there's anythin' I can dae just shout. Send him mah best, and all th' best tae Sebastian as weel.'

'Will do, and the same to your lot. I'll see you over the week no doubt,' Henry said, heading to the door with a cauliflower, some green beans, a pint of milk and a pair of socks knitted from the wool of the alpacas on the Donaldson's farm south of the village. It was impossible to leave McGregor's empty-handed.

'Hey, Henry!' Dougie called after him, 'I see ye'v still got th' old red banger.'

'Long may she last Dougie,' Henry called back, laughing as he left the shop.

Henry's 'old red banger' was indeed just that. Every time it passed its MOT Henry decided to keep it for another year. Virtually nothing on the car was original.

Henry headed to Taligth, driving cautiously. With numerous longstanding farms and a scattering of stone houses, the village was a hive of tractors and farm vehicles that flew around the single-track lanes. A person had to have their wits about them if they intended on getting through it without either being planted into a hedge or upside down in a field. Henry had had one near-death encounter when confronted, at speed, by a vicious looking hay baling machine whose thoughtless driver had neither tilted back the spikes nor lifted the front loader before taking it onto the road. Since that time, he had crawled around the village's blind bends.

It was a pretty village that had seen many changes over the years and Elspeth liked to tell stories of what had come and gone. 'When I was wee,' she would say, 'there wur a water pump alongside McGregor's. Lik' th' notice boord today, t'was a great meetin' place to catch up with th' gossip. I'd stand for hours aside my mother and listen to th' stories they'd tell, great long stories they wur. My mother used to blether to Mrs McNaughton for hours. She scared me cos she had no teeth.' The pump had been gone sixty years or more.

She would also tell of the blacksmith's shop that closed when they swapped the shire horses for tractors and as small children Nancy, Sebastian and Henry marvelled at the idea that their mother had once worked the fields with such majestic, hardworking animals. 'We wur one o' th' last farms aroond 'ere to get rid o' th' horses,' she would tell them, and she would repeat the stories of Gertie and Nobleman over and over again.

'There used to be one horse, usually Gertie, on th' tip cart going atween th' rows of cut fodder beet as they wur forked into th' cart. Gertie was a bonnie lassie 'n' she would donder at her own pace. I much preferred usin' th' horses to th' tractor but th' horses went when yer grandad got a Fergie reversible which changed his life,' she'd say. Then she used to tell a well-versed story about the time the cart, being pulled by Gertie and Nobleman, got stuck in the mud and fell over, throwing the farmhand beneath its wheels, nearly severing one of his legs. 'Th' bones wur completely shattered 'n' th' blood spurted from his veins. T'was hard to tell what wur mud and what wur flesh. He had to have it amputated in th' end,' she would say.

The pictures Elspeth painted of the village before mechanisation were fascinating, and the children and grandchildren loved to hear her stories. Henry thought she had more than likely made a lot of them up, and if she hadn't then she certainly embellished them; she was a good storyteller.

The track up to Taligth was almost a mile long. Arriving at the bottom of the drive, Henry pressed the combination of numbers to start the slow opening of the solid, wooden gates, one side juddering to move, followed by the other, gradually exposing the beautiful old farmhouse and its gardens, hidden beyond. It was a sight to behold, and he would never tire of it. Henry rumbled over the cattle grid and watched in his rearview mirror as the gates closed behind him. He slowly made his way up the heavily gravelled drive, which split the lusciously green, immaculately maintained front lawns. The three-story Georgian farmhouse rose in front of him as he pulled the car around to park by the hedge to the left of the steps leading up to the main door. His mother did not like to see cars from the house, insisting on visitors parking out of sight.

Letting himself into the large square hall, Henry gasped as Elspeth appeared suddenly to his right, screeching at the top of her voice, brandishing an old, round-bladed butter knife above her head.

'My god, Mum! What the hell are you doing?'

'I thought ye wur a burglar! I didnae expect ye for another half hour,' she panted.

'Luckily for you I'm not a burglar. What were you intending to do with that thing? Butter me to death?'

'I wouldn't hesitate to use it, so I wouldn't.'

'I don't doubt it for one minute, Mum. I'll be sure to look to my right next time I come in.'

'It'll learn ye for creeping up on fowk,' Elspeth said, leading him into the large farmhouse kitchen where the divine smell of baking greeted them.

'Where are the dogs?' Henry asked, looking out of the back door into the yard.

'Up in the fields with Ade, I have nae time for 'em today,' Elspeth replied.

Since dawn, Elspeth had cleaned out the pigpen, swept the yard, made two loaves of bread, some flat, salty butteries ready for lunch, and a batch of delicious looking apple scones, the fruit for which she had picked from the orchard that morning. She was an exceptional baker. She had been taught well by her mother who had been taught by her mother before her and the old family recipes had been passed down and were now being baked by the children and grandchildren.

At the centre of Campbell life, Taligth had been the family home for generations. It was steeped in history and if its walls could talk, they would have plenty to say. Although it never ceased to be an impressive sight, it was a lofty old place with four bedrooms and two airy bathrooms, each sporting showers over original cast iron roll-top baths. In the eaves, there were three small rooms, once home to the servants but now used as storage for the clutter passed down by bygone relatives. Downstairs, there was a cosy living room and a small snug, an old fashioned dining room that was largely unused, and the kitchen, the heart of the house. It was homely and warm and light flooded in through its tall sash windows. Though well built, the farmhouse was seldom touched in terms of maintenance and was crying out for modernisation.

The front garden was its main beauty. Gardeners tended the well-stocked borders that were awash with colour all-year-round, from ancient roses and well-established plants to ornamental cherry trees and a couple of great oaks which made the front of the house come to life with vibrancy and texture. The lawns were immaculate and woe betide any mole that should venture within a mile of the place, for Elspeth was a dab hand with the spade.

The majority of Taligth's land was laid to pasture. There were some regularly grazed fields closer to the farm with easy access along purpose laid tracks. Beyond these, and as far as the eye could see, the fields lay spread in all their colourful glory from bright green to golden brown, enclosed by ancient hedgerows that had stood in line, guarding them for generations. On the horizon at the top of the hill was dense woodland explored only by native animals and lost trekkers. Out to the west and across the lane in front of the farmhouse were acres of rough grazing fields, the perfect location for their small herd of Highlands.

'Help yersel' to a drink of tea and a butterie, th' scones are a wee taps for the butter to have just as yet. Tis crackin' to see ya, son,' Elspeth said, wiping her butter knife on her apron.

'It's good to see you too, Mum. Would you like a cup of tea?' Henry asked, filling the kettle and putting it on the aga. It was a beast of a kettle and even when only partly full it took five minutes before it started to whistle.

'Aye, please,' she said, sitting down. 'How was yer journey?'

'It was okay thanks,' Henry replied, reaching across to help himself to one of the butteries and carefully slicing it in two before smothering it in thick butter. Henry knew better than to refuse the offerings his mother put before him.

With the kettle whistling, Henry prepared the teapot the way his mother liked, filling it with scorching hot water from the sink tap. There were two temperatures of water at Taligth, boiling hot or freezing cold and little in between. In the shower, one would either burn or freeze; it was a simple choice and a shower was best taken with caution. Elspeth and William preferred to have a bath.

Swilling the water around the fat belly of the old yellow teapot once belonging to his great grandmother, Henry looked out of the window, across the yard to the pigpen. Betsy was lying in her usual spot, flat on her stomach on the other side of the small, green, metal gate with her pink, inquisitive snout protruding beneath it, sniffing out the bits of waste that had slopped from Elspeth's over flowing bucket.

'I expect Betsy's missing Dad. She doesn't look very happy.'

'She's certainly been miserable these bygane few days. Ye da is stupid over her.'

Spooning the tea into the pot, Henry smiled at the thought of his father loving the pig the way he did. William would happily spend time sitting in the yard, mug of coffee in hand, talking to her over the gate. Even though she was old, she was still lively and would come trotting out of her bed at dawn when she heard William pulling back the heavy bolts on the door. Before doing anything else, he would give her a good scratch and an apple from the scrumping bucket. It was no wonder she was missing him as Elspeth gave her little more than a boot in the side to shift her great hulk out of the way.

Pouring the tea into two stained mugs, Henry joined his mother at the table. 'So how are things?' he asked. 'Have you heard from Dad?'

'He'll phone in a bit to say if he's comin' home th' night or not.'

'And how are you feeling?'

His mother sighed. 'I'm fine in masell, just a wee bit tired is all.'

'Sebastian says you were sick at the hospital?'

'Och, th' story he tells! It was only a wee bit. Look at this bonnie weather, let's tak' our tea outside.'

Henry and Elspeth took advantage of the waning warmth of the late summer sunshine. It was lovely sitting in the yard watching the swifts and swallows flit about in search of dinner, fattening up, ready to leave their summer nests. Although the fields were still green, they could sense the coming autumn. It would take six weeks for the swallows to journey back across the Sahara to their winter home. In her sty, Betsy had flopped over on her side taking advantage of the heat streaming across her tummy. She ignored the fat, grey farm rats tentatively skirting the edges of her pen in search of rich pickings.

'Back to school for ye soon then Henry?' Elspeth asked, before the sound of the telephone ringing interrupted her. Spritely to her feet, far quicker than Henry, Elspeth walked through to the hall where she took the phone from its holster, pressing the speaker button to share hers and William's conversation with Henry.

'Hello!' William's voice boomed down the line.

'Hello love,' Elspeth responded, smiling. 'I've got Henry aside me, how ye doin'?'

'Hello there, son,' William replied. 'I'm good other than not being able to sleep on this shoulder. They want to keep me in so I could do with you bringing some things over, if you wouldn't mind.'

'Och no!' Elspeth said, disappointed. 'How come they want to keep ya in?'

'They want to make sure my shoulder's staying in place. That's all.'

'Weel, that's good I s'pose. Do yer want to speak with Henry?'

'No,' William said emphatically, 'I'll see him later won't I?'

Henry laughed and wandered back into the kitchen whilst Elspeth finished up her conversation. Sitting at the table, he picked up his mother's book and looked at the blurb on the back. It was a monstrous read of over fourteen hundred pages of miniscule print. It was all Henry could do to understand the story outline, let alone get to grips with the words on the inside.

An avid reader all her life, Elspeth spent any spare time she had with her nose in a book. Although education had seemed of little importance where she came from, she had attended the small school in the village and later gone on to high school in Edinburgh. She had done well in her exams but was always destined to work on the farm, although her love for books had meant she could explore places she might only ever dream of visiting and meet fascinating characters who led such different lives from her own. As well as reading, she loved writing articles and short stories. In her younger years, she would submit them to the local paper and, to her delight, she was regularly published. As she grew older, she wrote for the local and national farming magazines and became a respected authority. Given the opportunity, she would have liked to travel and write professionally, but the farm called upon her at an early age.

'Och dear!' Elspeth sighed, coming into the kitchen. 'What a thing!'

'You look worn out, Mum.'

'Aye, that I am, 'tis a big place to run alone, and with yer faither havin' a jolly time of it in th' hospital, I'm needin to do everythin' mysel'.'

'Listen,' Henry said, putting Elspeth's book down. 'You don't need to come to the hospital. You're tired and you've got to keep your strength up if you're going to look after this place.'

Elspeth looked at him blankly. ''Tis nothin' I haven't done afore! No, I'm comin' with ye if ye dinnae mind,' she said sternly.

'To be honest, Seb wants to see Dad before he goes to New York. It might be too much for the other patients in the ward with all three of us there.'

'Aye, yer might be right,' Elspeth sighed, conceding all too quickly. She was feeling tired but did not like to acknowledge it. Without speaking, she walked into the hall and went up the stairs. Henry followed. 'I will get th' bits yer faither wants, ye can tak' them with ye,' she called behind her.

Elspeth and William's bedroom was light and spacious and, unlike much of the rest of the house, beautifully decorated and furnished. They had an old wooden bed, which had belonged to Elspeth's great grandparents. It had a very high raised base on which the mattress lay so they had to clamber into it making it enveloping and cosy. For the three children, it was like climbing onto a magic carpet ready to fly them off to faraway lands.

The soft furnishings were expensive and luxurious. Elspeth had an eye for quality and chose beautiful country fabrics to frame the tall windows. Henry remembered, with some pain, the hours he spent, leaning by his mother's side as she visited *every* haberdasher in Edinburgh, searching for the right curtain or upholstery fabric. Her tenacity was well rewarded and she did not hold back on spending, so some of the fabrics in the farmhouse were as old as he was and still going strong.

'I like this room,' Henry said, looking around at the familiar objects. He had not been in his parents' room for some years and everything was as he remembered. 'I'd forgotten how big it is.'

'Big enough to have th' three of ye charging aroond it when ye were wee.'

'I remember that,' Henry laughed. 'You used to get so cross with us. Your slipper hit me on more than one occasion.'

'Aye, well, ye'll have been annoying me. Ye should have learnt not to come atween a farmer and her kip. Anyway, that slipper will have been meant for Nancy. I will have missed her 'tis all,' she said, winking.

'Have you thought anymore about getting in some more help to work the farm?'

'We are fine as we are. Sam and Ade are good enough. Here, these are for yer faither. I've put his book in as weel. It might stop him peepin' at th' cricket all day,' she said, handing Henry a bag with the things William had requested.

'I doubt it,' Henry replied, heading back down the stairs.

'Mak' sure ye phone me as soon as ye leave th' hospital,' Elspeth instructed, opening the front door and giving Henry a reassuring pat on the back. Elspeth stood on the top step watching him walk away.

Getting into his car, Henry took a deep breath. He did not like leaving his mother alone in the farmhouse. It seemed too big for her, even though she had the farm dogs to keep her company if she wanted. Waiting for the gates to open, he called Sebastian.

'I'm just leaving Taligth. Sorry I'm late.'

'There's no rush.'

'I'm conscious of visiting hours. If you walk down to the end of your drive it'll save time. You can jump in my car and we can head straight to the hospital.'

'We'll have plenty of time, and if it's all right with you, I'll drive!' Sebastian said. No one liked being a passenger in Henry's knackered car.

Henry crunched the gears into first and rumbled over the cattle grid, looking in his rearview mirror at his mother, who was still standing on the top step, arms folded, watching him leave. The gates slowly closed, cutting her from his view.

~

After a short exchange with Matilda, Sebastian and Henry finally left for the hospital in Matilda's new Range Rover. She had only had it for a day and was feeling protective over it but Sebastian's car, locked away in the garage, was awkward to get out and, more importantly, Matilda's had a full tank.

'We could go in mine,' Henry had interjected, his voice resonating around Sebastian and Matilda's hall as the discussion about whose car they would use had escalated into an argument, 'it's full to the brim.'

'Exactly!' Matilda agreed, irritated that Sebastian was insisting on using hers. 'I wouldn't mind but I've not even driven it yet! Why can't you go in Henry's?'

'Have you ever been driven in Henry's car?' Sebastian replied.

'Um, hello, Henry is in the room,' Henry said, putting his hand in the air to identify himself.

'Even *you* would agree with me on that one, Henry,' Sebastian said.

'Fair comment - carry on,' Henry conceded, lowering his hand.

Silence fell as Matilda took the keys out of her handbag and threw them at Sebastian. 'Be careful with it,' she said with an air of resignation. Sebastian held the keys flat in his hand and looked at her. 'It's a car Matilda!' he said quietly, making her flush with embarrassment as she glanced across to Henry to see if he was looking. Henry pretended not to notice.

'I do like this car,' Henry commented, looking around at the myriad of buttons and displays and the cream leather interior as they pulled off Sebastian's drive, 'it's very smart.'

Henry had popped into McGregor's on his way to Sebastian's to pick up some chocolate for their father, plus a toy for Panda, a jar of potted shrimps and a rather nice bottle of red wine, resulting in them getting to the hospital later than they had intended. The one advantage was an overwhelming choice of parking spaces right outside the main entrance doors which meant it was not long before they were in the maze of clinical corridors, peering into every bay in ward eleven. They finally found their father sitting in the chair next to his bed in bay nine.

'Hello!' William said smiling, delighted to see his sons as they appeared around the side of the curtain. 'Where's your mother?'

'She's at home,' Henry replied, 'she was tired.'

'Is she okay?'

'She's fine,' Henry said, reassuringly.

'That's good.' William smiled, appearing rather excited for a man laid up in hospital with his arm plastered up to the elbow and strapped across his chest. 'Come, sit down,'

'So, how are you doing?' Sebastian asked, gesturing to his father's sling.

'It's keeping my shoulder in place, so they tell me.'

'We brought the bits you asked for,' Henry said, peering into the bag his mother had given him.

'Marvellous. Thank you. Would you mind putting them in the cupboard for me please, Henry?'

'Mum put your book in. She wants you to read rather than watch the cricket all day,' Henry said, holding William's book in the air as evidence before putting it away. They all knew his book would remain unopened whilst the test match was in progress.

'So, other than your shoulder, how are you?' Sebastian asked.

'I'm very well,' William replied, smiling.

'Good, and what have they said about your shoulder?'

'That it's unstable and they'll not let me go home until it's stopped moving.'

'I don't suppose driving yourself here in the Land Rover helped!'

'I don't suppose it did,' William replied not rising to his elder son's scolding. 'Did you manage to get it back to Taligth?'

'She's back in her usual space.'

'Excellent, and how's Betsy?'

'Missing you,' Henry answered.

'So she will be. Your mother doesn't pay her any attention.'

'Yes she does, when you're not looking,' Henry said, laughing to himself, recalling his mother shouting at her to 'get her big fat pink arse out o' th' way' so that she could get to her trough.

'You seem excited,' Sebastian commented, recognising the signs in his father.

'Well, I'm all the better for seeing you two,' William said, his voice animated, 'but I've also got something very important to tell you,' he grinned. Sitting like an enthusiastic child desperate to be picked to be book monitor, William puffed out his chest.

'England haven't gone and won the test match have they, Dad?' Henry laughed.

'Don't be daft. They still have every opportunity to snatch defeat from the jaws of victory,' William said, leaning forward, beckoning Sebastian and Henry into his confidence. Believing he was whispering, William spoke loudly enough so everyone in the ward could hear, including the man in the bed opposite. 'I thought the man over there was a bit sour,' he whispered. 'When I tried to engage him in conversation yesterday, he didn't want to speak but I've managed to get around him with the cricket. I've found out he grew up in Leeds, Headingley...'

'That's where Lilith's moving to,' Henry interrupted.

'So it is... anyway, he loves the cricket. He came alive when I started talking to him about it and he's been giving me a full run down ever since.'

'Is that what you wanted to tell us?' Henry asked.

'Nope,' William replied, grinning once more.

'Well, you've got your iPad now so you can watch the cricket as much as you like,' Sebastian commented, 'and you've got your newspaper on it as well. Do you want me to set it up for you?'

'Yes please, but before you do that, let me tell you what's happened today.'

'Go on then,' Sebastian encouraged.

'I had a check-up as part of this 'Well-Man' project thing the health service are doing at the moment, and part of the check-up is a chest x-ray, and guess what they found.'

Sebastian and Henry looked at one another vacantly.

'They found out that my heart points to the right!' William announced as Sebastian and Henry looked at him blank-faced. 'Most people's hearts point to the left!' he clarified, rolling his eyes. 'It's called dextrocardia.'

'Well!' Sebastian exclaimed knowing this would be his father's main topic of conversation outside McGregor's for years to come.

'There's more,' William carried on, thrilled to be in the club of one in ten thousand with the same congenital defect. 'I don't just have dextrocardia, I have dextrocardia with situs inversus totalis, which means everything inside me, like my liver and my stomach and spleen are all the mirror-image of their normal positions.'

'Does it affect you in any way?' Sebastian asked.

'It would appear not.'

'And you've only just found out? Haven't you had a chest x-ray before?'

'I've never needed one,' William replied, smiling.

It was lovely for Sebastian and Henry to spend time with their father without the call of the farm to contend with. True to type, he had made friends with the other men in the ward and had already shared his news with them. They spent a further hour chatting about internal organs, cars, cricket and Sebastian's trip to the States.

'I hope you're still intending to go, Sebastian. Your mother told me you were considering putting it off?'

'I'm concerned about leaving Mum to manage the farm...'

'We can manage the farm perfectly well without you,' William interrupted, 'you must go. You seem to be getting on well with this Patrick chap. What's he like?'

'He's nice, I like him.'

'And how are you feeling about letting go of the company?'

'Surprisingly okay,' Sebastian nodded. 'Once I've sold it, the new people can do what they want with it. It's this interim part I don't like, the uncertainty. I'm hoping, if things go well this week, we'll be looking at some time in

October for completion. Patrick's heading over in a few weeks to see us in operation.'

'It's all sounding very positive, Seb,' William said. 'And you, Henry, able to give up teaching yet?'

'Wouldn't that be nice,' Henry huffed.

'But you had a good run in Paris?'

'Fantastic, so you never know.'

'And how's our Lilith doing?'

'Lilith is Lilith,' Henry replied, smiling.

Lilith had been born deaf, and, at twenty-one, was as much a topic of conversation as she had been the day they had found out the life-changing news.

They had watched her grow up, a deaf child in a hearing world, fascinated by how well she coped. Her speech, though poor, was helped by a cochlear implant giving her a modified sense of sound, which allowed her to explore her love for music.

Fearing her deafness would be isolating, Henry and Lorna had chosen to treat Lilith no differently than they might have done had she been able to hear. They put her into a mainstream school and sent her to dance classes and gymnastics with the other girls in her class and she coped well. But as she got older, they came to realise it was important for her to be part of the deaf community as well, so they introduced her to different groups and clubs. Already a proficient lip-reader, Lilith learned to sign, and with that, a whole new group of friends opened up to her.

'She's moving in ten days.'

'Is it nice, the place she's going to?' William asked.

'It's cheap so I doubt it, but she'll love it. She's living with her friends. That's all she's bothered about.'

'Is she still with Matthew?'

'She is, though I don't know for how much longer.'

'Woe betide any boy who takes on our Lilith,' William said, winking.

'Yes, and I'm not sure this one's up to it,' Henry laughed.

Conversation slowed as William started to tire. 'Right you two, off you go,' he said suddenly, 'you've an early start in the morning, Seb. Look after yourselves and have a good trip. I'm looking forward to hearing all about it when you get back.'

'You too, Dad. Be good and I'll see you in a week or so,' Sebastian sighed, hating leaving his father in the hospital.

'And I'll see you tomorrow with Mum,' Henry said.

'That'll be nice, see you then,' William smiled, raising his good arm in the air, waving them off.

Retracing their steps, Sebastian and Henry made their way out of the ward and into the wide corridor leading back to the lift. The corridor had a run of large windows on either side, letting the last of the August daylight flood across the shiny floor. Looking out to the right, there was an internal courtyard across which could be seen wards and offices on different levels of the building. To the left, the windows looked out to the front of the hospital where people could be seen coming in and out of the main doors and where Matilda's car was parked, a ticket stuck to its windscreen.

'Justified?' Henry asked, looking out at the Range Rover shamefully wearing its yellow badge. 'Perhaps you should have bought a ticket.'

'Perhaps not,' Sebastian answered sullenly, pressing the lift button. 'I pay my taxes and employ over a hundred people in this city. The least they can do is let me visit my Dad without fining me.'

'Fair enough,' Henry agreed, nodding. 'Changing the subject, you know we'll never hear the end of this thing about Dad's heart, don't you?'

'I know,' Sebastian said, irritated after seeing the ticket. 'God that ticket's pissed me off!' He snapped. As soon as they got to the Range Rover, he pulled the plastic bag from the windscreen and walked to the bin by the door. Another ticket would go unpaid.

On their way home, as promised, Henry called their mother.

'Did he tell ye aboot his heart?' she asked.

'He did. He was very excited; we'll never hear the end of it.'

'I know!' Elspeth tutted. 'So are ye on yer way to Sebastian's now?'

'We are.'

'Weel, yer have fun together tonight. Tell Sebastian to have a good trip and not to forget to tak' th' vitamins I gave him. He's been looking very pasty recently. I'll see yer tomorrow,' she said, abruptly ending the call.

'What did Mum say?' Sebastian asked.

'Not a lot, just wishing you a good trip.'

'Did she mention the vitamins?'

'She did. How did you know?'

'Because she's mentioned them every time I've spoken to her since she gave them to me last week.'

'And have you been taking them?'

'Of course not.'

It was late by the time they turned into Sebastian's drive and they were both ravenous. Waiting for the huge metal gates to swing open, Henry looked up and thought how he was the only member of the family not to have electric gates. Not that his house needed them - and they wouldn't fit on the drive anyway; it could only squeeze one car on it and even then they had to park an inch off the garage door to stop its back end sticking out onto the pavement. Sebastian could fit a hundred cars on his drive, which meandered up to the house through beautiful tree-lined gardens. At the top it opened up in front of a huge, modern, riverside mansion. It was a beautiful house.

Heading through the long hall and into the kitchen, Henry and Sebastian made straight for the bread bin. Panda went crazy when she saw who had come to dog-sit for the week and leapt around, running in and out of Henry's legs as he chased her, almost tripping him up until she finally secured herself, hanging onto his left leg as he playfully slid her along the shiny tiled floor.

'Hey Panda, I've got something for you,' Henry said, making her sit. Expectantly, she obeyed, her little white booted front paws turned out like a ballet dancer, her short, white-tipped tail sweeping the floor in excitement. Producing a rubbery green sprout from his pocket, Henry threw it across the floor. 'Happy Christmas,' he said.

Unsure, Panda gave it a wide berth, circling one way, and then the other, before deciding it was not going to attack her. She cautiously went over, sniffed it and tapped it with her paw. Then, picking it up in her mouth, she discovered its squeak and she was off, running up and down the room, batting and chasing it, until it disappeared under the sofa, which was where she spent the next ten minutes, backside in the air, sniffing it out.

Matilda joined Sebastian and Henry at the table and together they ate marmite toast washed down with the bottle of wine Henry had bought from McGregor's. Exhausted, Panda settled at Henry's feet whilst he and Sebastian updated Matilda on their father, before their conversation turned to the new cinema suite they had just had built beneath the house. It was a feat of engineering, had taken months to complete and cost an unbelievable amount of money. Henry was keen to be given a tour.

With Panda in front, they went back into the hall and ventured down a wide, glass-walled, stone, spiral staircase. Henry was blown away as he found himself walking up the dark, red carpeted ramp, illuminated by atmospheric wall washers and entering what looked like Screen 5 of the Odeon in Newcastle. To his right, was an immense screen, and to his left was the seating. He stood at the bottom, gazing up at the raised levels towards fifteen black leather reclining seats with individual snack tables and drink holders. The steps were lit by strips of recessed LED lights and at the side of the room was a popcorn machine, help-yourself pick 'n' mix and a hot drinks dispenser which would give any self-respecting cinema a run for its money. Henry stood staring, taking it all in. 'My mind is blown,' he said. 'I thought the gym was impressive but this is something else. How big is that screen?'

'I think it's about thirty feet. Feel free to use it while we're away,' Sebastian offered.

'I will, if I can remember how to find it,' Henry laughed.

'I'll give you a map,' Sebastian said, heading back up the steps.

'Talking of maps,' Matilda cut in, 'let me show you around, so that you know how things work.'

Hotly pursued by Panda, Matilda wasted no time in pointing out all the smart home gadgets that Henry would need to get to grips with during his stay. She had set out the operating manuals on the desk in the study, should he need them. It was a substantial pile. Every appliance had one, from the door communication system, to the intelligent electronics that operated the curtains and blinds. She showed him how to open and close the driveway gates, lock and unlock the windows, the doors, the garages and the boat room down by the river. She showed him how to use the fridges and freezers, switch on the ovens and the hobs, run the dishwashers and use the microwaves and boiling water tap.

Upstairs, in one of the nine en-suite bedrooms, she showed him which buttons to press for the shower with its light show and surround sound system.

'I'll probably just hang around the kitchen,' Henry grimaced, feeling overwhelmed as they walked back downstairs.

'You'll soon get the hang of it,' Matilda said, showing him how to use the smart lock/unlock device to get into the gym, which led from the house through a glass walkway into another building. The 'gym', as they called it, housed a large exercise room, a fully equipped gym and the swimming pool complex with sauna and steam room. Above it was a games room with snooker, pool and air hockey tables, plus a one-armed bandit and an original 1950s American jukebox.

Back in the kitchen, the final thing Matilda showed Henry was the process of putting on and taking off Panda's harness, which was a master-class in distraction, agility and speed.

Luckily for Henry, Matilda had everything written down so that he had something to refer to when he couldn't remember which button to press. He imagined the situation where, on trying to open a window, he unlocked the garage doors and exposed the gardeners to Sebastian's small collection of classic and modern racing cars, which were most definitely out of bounds to Henry.

The three of them talked until they gave in to tiredness. It was late, and a 9 a.m. flight meant the taxi was booked for 5 a.m. Sebastian and Matilda needed to get to bed. The room Henry was staying in was a walk from Sebastian and Matilda's suite and was bigger than his and Lorna's house. Exhausted, he flopped into bed and slept.

Minus Nine

Henry was woken at 4 a.m. by what sounded like a large animal caught in a trap. It was a cross between the final death cry of a creature that had gnawed its own leg off to release itself and Snow White's rendition of 'Someday My Prince Will Come,' and it cut through Henry like a sharp blade. 'What the hell is that noise?' he asked, emerging, half naked and bleary-eyed out of his room to be met by Matilda on the landing, dressed and ready to go.

'Ah!' she said apologetically. 'I may not have mentioned Panda's wake-up call.'

'No,' Henry said, slowly trying to come to terms with the hideous noise resonating around the clean white walls of the house, 'you may have missed that minor detail.'

'Yes,' Matilda laughed. 'Unfortunately, Panda thinks 4 a.m. is her time. If you can bear the noise you might be able to push her back an hour but by that time her bladder will have probably got the better of her. So unless you want to be cleaning out her crate, I'd not recommend it. Come and see what I do.'

Together, they ventured towards the noise that grew more intense the closer they got to Panda's room. Anticipating their entrance, by the time Matilda opened the door, Panda was jumping up and down on her back legs, desperate to be released from her confinement. As Matilda opened the crate, Panda flew out and, like a wild animal, ran around both her and Henry before shooting out of the room and straight to the back door ready to be released into her section of the garden. Well-practiced, Matilda had the remote control to hand, the correct code input and the back door open within seconds. Henry was impressed by Matilda's dexterity and knew the remote was the first thing he needed to master.

Panda was a sweet dog. With jet-black curly puppy fur, which bounced when she walked, she had a permanent grin spread across her little black and white face and a mischievous look in her large dark eyes. By 5.05 a.m. Panda and Henry were watching Sebastian and Matilda's taxi head off down the drive on their journey to the airport.

Henry looked down at his little companion. 'Well my furry friend,' he said, as Panda looked up at him, tilting her head to listen, 'you'd better brace yourself, because you and I are going to have some fun.'

Deciding to take a day off from writing, the first thing Henry and Panda did was head for the swimming pool.

~

'You've slept for five hours,' Matilda commented, as Sebastian opened his eyes and looked up at her.

'I was tired.'

'That's the longest you've slept in years.'

'I've been thinking,' he said, sitting up. 'When the sale goes through, I'm going to help out on the farm again.'

'What's brought this on?' Matilda asked, noticing the familiar signs in Sebastian, which told her he had been having nightmares.

Looking at her with intensely sad dark eyes, he spoke softly. 'Am I a nice person, Til?' he asked.

Having been cradled to sleep by the motion of the aircraft, Sebastian had awoken troubled, his dreams full of doubt and his thoughts filled with panic. In his mind a huge black hole had opened up and he had toppled in and, in the fragment of time between sleep and wakefulness, he had been afraid. He was a complex, sugar-coated mix of self-doubt and ruthlessness, his fragility hidden by defence. As his company had grown so had his confidence, but there were times, like today, when he would wake up feeling very small in a world far too big for him, and his vulnerability enabled an old inner torment to take over. He was seventeen when these feelings had first appeared.

By the time the plane landed on the hot New York tarmac, Matilda had listened for two hours to Sebastian unravel. He had not done it for a long time, but she was well versed in untangling his thoughts and dispelling his fears – like a mother who scares the shadows of monsters away when it's time for bed. But there was still so much unsaid and parts of himself he protected so deeply she could not reach, not even after having been together for thirty years.

Making their way out of the busy airport and into the welcome, tranquil New York sunshine, Sebastian was feeling better. In the car heading to their hotel, Matilda turned to him. 'And if you want to know,' she said, tucking her hand into his, 'I think you are a very nice person... most of the time,' she smiled cheekily.

The temperature in central New York soared to over thirty degrees, and the heat of the midday sun flooded them as they stepped out of the air-conditioned car and looked up at the skyscraper. They were staying in the best hotel New York had to offer and, after being greeted by the manager at the doors, they were escorted into a private lift and taken to their corner suite which overlooked the Hudson River to one side and the vibrant borough of Manhattan to the other.

Ranked one of the best in the world, the hotel was described as 'The most exquisite place to sleep on the New York skyline,' and, as he stood on the seventieth floor looking out of the enormous picture window at the view below, Sebastian could see why.

'Happy?' Matilda asked, wrapping her arms around his waist.

'Yes.'

'It's beautiful isn't it?'

'It's more than beautiful.'

The suite they were staying in had been built on top of New York's most exclusive hotel. It was a clever use of limited Manhattan space, seamlessly fitting into the neck-craning skyline. It was a mastery of craftsmanship, wanting for nothing and, even for a couple who had everything, the luxury of the hotel offered more.

When Colin, their butler, had first opened the door, Matilda had naturally slipped her feet out of her shoes. Made of pure silk, she had never felt carpet like it before and, much to the butler's surprise, she insisted they all took off their shoes. He obliged, trying to act as if it were the most natural request for a guest to make. He tried not to show how much he enjoyed the sumptuousness, or how much he felt the awkwardness.

Each suite had its own private butler who was available around the clock to provide guests with whatever they required. He would unpack for them, bring tea and coffee to their bedside, organise excursions and exclusive boutique appointments and book tables at the best restaurants. He would even iron the morning newspaper or squeeze toothpaste onto their toothbrushes should they wish. Luckily for Colin, Sebastian and Matilda were not the sort of people to want such attention, so he would enjoy a relatively quiet week. They laughed at what they thought he might say to his colleagues when he went downstairs –

'You will never guess what I have just seen!' he might say, his softly accented voice flamboyant, disdain written all over his thin face. 'The occupants of the Flight Suite, not one piece of Louis Vuitton between them! Not one! Can you believe it? In fact *he* had an Adidas hold-all, and not a new one either, a tatty old one with frayed straps! I dared not touch it. And *she* dragged some *hideous* unnamed thing in behind her. Heaven only knows what that was. Luckily, she refused to let me carry it. I asked them if their luggage was to follow and they told me this was all they had! For a whole week! Unbelievable! Who comes to New York for a week with practically no luggage? I hung his *one*, yes, *one* shirt in the wardrobe and pressed his *one* tie and his *one* suit. I mean, who do they think I am?'

They laughed after seeing the shock on his face when he asked them whether they would like Matilda's jewellery and Sebastian's watch to be put in the hotel safe. Sebastian had proceeded to pull back his cuff to reveal an old Sekonda of his father's that he'd had for over 20 years. Although it had seen better days, it kept perfect time.

Exploring their three-storey suite, they started on the lower floor. With light, silk carpet flooding the room and over-sized pink leather sofas carefully positioned in front of the floor-to-ceiling window, the eye was naturally drawn to the world outside, and, on its own, in the corner, enjoying the panoramic Manhattan view, was a gym; perfect for Sebastian who liked to exercise alone each morning.

From the centre of the room, they looked up through the curl of the atrium to the glass roof above from which hung a magnificent chandelier. Cascading down the centre to the lobby, it gently swayed with the movement of the air like a mass of shimmering ice feathers.

A spiral of sparkling glass steps took them up to the middle floor and the three decadent bedrooms, and a further spiral took them to the very top, where, across the beautifully decorated lounge, glass doors opened out onto a large, wooden terrace area with soft inviting furniture and an infinity swimming pool. Not saying a word, Sebastian and Matilda walked outside and stood, looking out over the glass balcony as the sun flooded their skin. For a moment Sebastian felt free, like he was holding on to that briefest of moments in time, when one thing ends, and another has yet to begin.

'Is this what it's all been for?' he asked, 'the thousands of hours slogging our guts out, so that we can stand here? All the time missed with the children, with my parents, your parents. Not going to sports day or the last night of the school play. Missing Isla's prom and Ewan's engagement party. All of it. Is this the dream or the nightmare?'

'Don't make it sound sad,' Matilda said softly, looking at him. She went to speak again but took his hand instead, holding it gently in her own.

'This is the end, Til. Has it been worth it?' he asked searching the sky for answers. 'I missed out on so much. If only the money could buy back lost time.'

'I think you're being hard on yourself. You're only feeling this way because life is about to change. This is a good thing you're doing. Don't regret what you can do nothing about. Look at where you've come from. Would you have done anything differently?'

'I don't know,' Sebastian said, remembering the angry promise he made to himself when he was seventeen. A promise he had made as he walked, shell-shocked and injured out of the woods, across the fields back towards the farmhouse. A promise he had lived by since that day.

'You reap what you sow,' Matilda said profoundly. 'This is the harvest. When you started out you didn't know where you were going to end up, but you were determined. You had a brilliant idea and you were brave enough to run with it. You have been a generous, caring employer and you should be proud of that, but it's been about so much more than the money. Yes, you missed out on stuff, we all have; people have to make choices in life, but think what you can do for the children and *their* children when Tatch-A has gone. You'll have time to spend with them and your parents,' she paused, 'think about the legacy you'll leave.'

Sebastian did not speak. Releasing Matilda's hand, he turned and faced the doors. Looking at his distorted reflection in the glass, he wondered what life would be like after Tatch-A UK was gone. He hoped he would recognise himself.

Walking back into the lounge, adjusting to the change of light, they explored the top floor. There was a dining table set for two and a surround-sound cinema screen accompanied by comfy sofas from which no human, once sucked in, would ever be able to claw their way out. There was also a fully stocked floor-to-ceiling wine cellar. Pouring two large glasses of white wine, they went back out and silently, together, they soaked up the early afternoon sun.

For Sebastian and Matilda, New York was one of the best cities in the world. They had first visited before they were married, before the New York skyline changed after the tragic events of 2001. They had fallen in love with its vibrancy and wakefulness, its smell, and the endless hustle and bustle of the New Yorker way of life.

The first time they had travelled the short taxi ride from JFK and seen the buildings towering in front of them, they felt overwhelmed with excitement. They booked into a cheap, brown carpeted, midtown hotel at the bottom of which was a lively, traditional American diner. They got a visitors' map, sat with a huge plate of pancakes to share and diligently went through it, organising their three-day visit minute-by-minute in the vain hope of seeing everything. They missed most of it, of course, and barely skimmed the surface of what they did see, so they had returned many times over the years. Now they looked back at when they were doing New York on a shoestring with great affection.

Stirring himself before the wine went to his head, Sebastian looked over the balcony at the tiny world below. 'I'm going to check in with Henry and see how Panda's doing,' he said, yawning and stretching. 'Hopefully he's not locked himself out, or Panda in.'

'What do you reckon he will have done first, the pool or the cinema?'

'Knowing Henry, the pool... with Panda.'

'Talking of the pool, I think I might take a dip.'

'I'll join you in a bit – careful not to fall over the edge,' Sebastian said, heading inside.

Suspended off the side of the building, like a skyscraper waterfall, the transparent bottom of the infinity pool deformed the view of the world below. It was not for the faint-hearted and Sebastian was not sure he would be able to swim to the edge; he wasn't good with heights.

~

The phone rang for a long time before Henry located the sound. Running into Sebastian's study, he picked the receiver up just before the answering machine took the call, sending a pot with pens and pencils flying across the desk.

'Is everything okay?' Sebastian asked, hearing the commotion.

'Absolutely fine,' Henry panted. 'Panda and I have just come in from the park and now I'm grabbing a quick tea before I head to Taligth. How was your flight?'

'Good thanks.'

'What's your hotel like?'

'You'd hate it. It's floor to ceiling glass.'

'Sounds awful,' Henry laughed.

'How are things?'

'You've been gone less than a day, Seb.'

'I know. Have you spoken with Dad? Is he coming out today?'

'He's fine. Stop worrying. He's staying in another night, so Mum and I are going over to see him. I'll call you later. Now piss off and relax.' And with that, Henry disconnected from Sebastian.

Three thousand miles struggled to separate the brothers. Despite very leading different lives, they were exceptionally close. Henry neither envied nor resented Sebastian's success and wealth; he admired him for his determination and his relentless pursuit of perfection.

Popping Panda into her sleeping quarters, Henry dimmed the lights and made sure she was settled before leaving. She was tired from her walk, so she curled into a ball and was asleep before he crept out of the room.

It had not taken him long to get used to the house, but getting out without lowering the drawbridge and letting the enemy in was a challenge. Having closed the windows, locked the doors and instructed the house lighting to go into 'night mode', Henry set the alarm, blipped the front door open and made his way to his car, making sure the front door locked shut as he left.

At the bottom of the drive, the gates opened, and he dropped out onto the road, looking in his rear-view mirror to make sure they closed securely behind him. He would get used to it, but he was nervous about leaving the house and Panda on their own. It was a responsibility; not that Sebastian and Matilda were precious about the house, but

Henry's life would not be worth living should anything happen to Panda.

Elspeth was already waiting for him down by the gates when Henry arrived. 'Am I late?' he asked, anxiously looking at his watch. After many years of excellent service, his car clock had finally given up working. 'I hadn't taken into account the time it would take to lock up Seb's house. Are you okay?'

'Tis lik' Fort Knox that place, tis a wonder they ever get anywhere on time,' Elspeth said battling with her seatbelt while Henry slowly navigated the winding road away from the farm. 'Och! I cannae be doin' wi' this thing!' she exclaimed. 'Ye need a new motor Henry!'

'I can't afford a new car, Mum,' Henry said, pulling over into a layby. 'Here, let me do it for you.'

'No! Ye carry on, and watch th' road as ye go. I will get there, tis fiddly that's all. There tis in now,' she said, Henry hearing the familiar sound of the seatbelt clicking into position. 'I do hate seatbelts, they're not designed for short fowk,' she said, fidgeting.

Out onto the open road, Elspeth relaxed and chatted away about her day as they travelled the thirty-minute journey to the hospital. She enjoyed spending time with Henry and was insistent on being kept up to date with everything that was going on in his life.

'So, have ye managed to get much writing done th'day?' she asked.

'I haven't done a jot,' Henry confessed happily.

'Nae a jot? Och! Ye could have come and helped me oot.'

'Did you need me to? I thought Sam and Ade were with you all day today?'

'Aye, they were.'

'Then you didn't need me today, did you? Which is why I decided to give myself the day off and enjoy some of the facilities.'

'Has ye brother shown ye that picter-hoose he's had built? A waste o' dosh if ye ask me, they'll never use it!'

Henry laughed at his mother's bluntness.

'Panda and I will. In fact, we're booked in to watch 'One Hundred and One Dalmatians' later.'

'Ye never are?'

'We are, although Panda doesn't like Dalmatians. We met one in the park today and she was petrified.'

'They're silly lookin' animals, all those plooks!'

Smiling as they drove in comfortable silence, Henry articulated the word 'plooks' in his head. Once in the flow, the Scottish dialect was generally intuitive, but there were some words like 'plooks' that bore little, or no resemblance to their English counterpart.

'When does yer play open?' Elspeth asked.

'In a few weeks, at half term.'

'How are ye feeling aboot this one?'

'The same way I feel about all of them.'

'Och Henry, ye need more confidence in yersel'. Yer dad and I think yer plays are brilliant.'

William and Elspeth had always encouraged Henry's writing. As a child, he had been slow to learn to read, and for a short time had been put in the remedial class at school, with the ones who could not spell. It was a humiliating experience and he worked hard to prove he did not belong there, earning his way out by writing short stories far beyond the comprehension of the other pupils. The feeling of being put in that class had remained with him into adulthood and even now, close to fifty, he doubted himself; he doubted his writing and creative ability because a teacher, ignorant of the effect it would have, had once put him in the wrong class. No amount of success was likely to change that.

Driving onto the hospital site with its maze of roads, Henry found a car park close to the main entrance. He bought a ticket. Walking the short distance towards the building, Elspeth hung back, asking him not to hurry. Although she was still up with the lark and able to trudge across the fields and feed the animals, Henry had noticed how much slower she had become in recent years.

Navigating the multitude of corridors, they found William sitting happily in his chair, plugged into the cricket. According to him, it looked to be one of the tightest and best test matches in Ashes history and England stood a very good chance of winning.

'Interrupting?' Henry asked, popping his head around the curtain.

'It's very exciting!' William exclaimed, delighted to see Henry and Elspeth, and clearly enjoying the excuse to sit all afternoon and watch television. 'Hello love, how are you feeling?' he asked Elspeth as she leant across to give him a kiss.

'Yer prickly!' she commented, stroking his cheek.

'Ah yes,' he said, rubbing his chin. 'Tomorrow's job... for when I come home.'

'They're letting you oot?' Elspeth asked, smiling.

'They certainly are.'

'So your shoulder's settled?' Henry asked.

'Not fully, but they're happier with it, so I can go home. I just need to keep it still.'

'I dinnae suppose getting excited over th' cricket will help. Ye'r always flinging yer arms in th' air,' Elspeth said, resenting the game for having made William take too long to decide he needed to go to the hospital in the first place. William chose not to respond.

'So,' Henry said, 'what's happened today?'

'Other than an x-ray and a walk up and down the ward, not a great deal. The bloke opposite,' William whispered, 'loves cricket, so it's been quite fun.'

'Yes, you told us that yesterday.'

'Did I? Did I also tell you he's from Headingley?'

'You did.'

'Then you know about my heart.'

'We do.'

'I'll shut up then,' he laughed.

'How are you getting on with the iPad?' Henry asked.

'Very well. I've been playing with the calendar. Do you know what date's coming up love?' he asked, turning to look at Elspeth, sadness suddenly in his eyes.

'Date?' Henry asked.

'Och!' Yer faither's gettin' confused, 'tis all,' Elspeth cut in sharply, scowling at William.

'About what?' Henry pushed.

She hesitated. 'He always thinks our anniversary's this month,' she replied, thinking quickly, desperate to get Henry off the scent. ''Tis not, William. You should know that!' she said, shooting him a stern look.

Suddenly realising his mistake, William changed the subject. 'Let me show you what I've found today,' he said, showing Henry one of the twenty pages he had open.

'Are you thinking of changing your car? Surely not!'

'I'm just looking,' he said, catching Elspeth's eye and smiling. 'I rather fancy the new Aston Martin your brother's just bought. Have you seen it?'

'I have. He's locked it in the bottom garage.'

'I wonder why!' Elspeth piped up from the end of the bed.

'I'd be quiet if I were you or you'll be walking home,' Henry teased.

William laughed. Under his seventy-seven-year-old skin, he was still the young man who, having moved to Edinburgh and with a little help from his father, had gone out and bought his first car, a Land Rover Series 2a. It had been perfect for driving from farm to farm and was the one he still insisted on rattling around in fifty-five years later. Despite his love of modern cars, there would never come a time when he would sell his beloved old vehicle.

Henry and Elspeth only stayed a short while before William encouraged them to leave. 'It's time you were off,' he said. 'I'll be home tomorrow so we can catch up then,' and they left, leaving William to chat 'scores' with the man in the bed opposite, who had terminal cancer and might not survive long enough to witness the end of the series.

It was very dark by the time they arrived back at Taligth. Henry pulled up outside the gates and together they walked up the drive to the house. 'Will you be okay?' Henry asked, leaving Elspeth at the top of the steps.

'I'll be fine. I'm going to mak' masell something to eat, would ye lik' to have something wi' me?'

'I'd love to, but I've got a cinema date, remember?'

'Och aye, o' coorse ye have. Enjoy yersel'. Hang on a wee while, let me fetch ye something,' Elspeth said, unlocking the front door and walking into the house. She returned a minute later with a plate of shortbread she had made that afternoon. 'I meant to tak' them to yer dad but I forgot and left them on th' kitchen table. Hopefully th' dogs haven't licked them. Here, ye tak' them, and mak' sure ye bring me back my plate,' she said, handing the uncovered biscuits to Henry. Even with the prospect of them having been salivated on, Elspeth's shortbread was impossible to resist.

Smiling, Henry walked carefully down the steps and along the well-lit driveway. He looked back to see his mother still standing outside the front door. 'Go in,' he shouted, knowing she would remain there until his lights had disappeared out of sight.

Back at Sebastian's, Henry released Panda and she bounced around him, jumping at him, trying to reach the sweet-smelling shortbread in his hand. 'You can have a little bit if you're good,' he said as she chased him down the hall towards the kitchen. 'But first, we need to call your dad,' which Henry did, whilst Panda helped herself to the biggest shortbread on the plate.

~

With dinner brought to their suite, Sebastian and Matilda enjoyed their first evening in New York on the terrace, watching the dancing light show of the city as the sky went dark and the reflection of the lights shimmered across the Hudson. As dusk fell and the sun's orange and red hue sank behind the river, the windows of the skyscrapers sparkled against the backdrop of the star-filled sky.

After his agitation on the flight across the Atlantic, it had taken Sebastian some time to unwind. But an evening meal and a bottle of wine in the cooling warmth of a hot day relaxed him, and he and Matilda talked about life after Tatch-A UK.

Up until now, the sale of the company had been somewhere off in the distance and it was hard for Sebastian to believe that they were actually on the cusp. It was the right decision to sell, but it hadn't stopped him feeling scared. It had been all he had known for twenty-three years and now, just a few hours away, he felt like a child again, sitting on the edge of the table, waiting anxiously for his mother to rip the plaster off a wound it had been protecting. It was hard to tell how the 'new skin' was going to look underneath and whether the wound would have healed properly. Tatch-A UK was Sebastian's plaster. He had hidden beneath it, healing, and wondered what he would be like without its protection. It unnerved him.

'Now we're here, it feels very real,' Sebastian answered in response to a question Matilda had asked over dinner.

'What are you afraid of?'

'That I've been able to hide behind Tatch-A.'

'What from?'

Afraid to go back that far, Sebastian did not answer.

'What do you dream about in your nightmares, like the one you had on the plane?' Matilda asked bravely.

Sebastian took his time to answer. 'That I'm not who I think I am.'

'Isn't that common amongst successful people?'

'Is it?'

'Can I ask you something?' Matilda said, hoping now was the right time. Sebastian looked at her. 'Years ago, when you went through counselling...' Sebastian nodded, his body language changing as he started to lower the shutters. 'I know some of it was to do with what I did,' she said

70

uncomfortably, 'but was it also to do with this, being afraid you're not who you think you are, the things you dream about?'

'As you know, I lost my way, that was all. I just needed a little help,' he said.

'Why won't you tell me what happened, Seb?' she asked, and not for the first time.

'Let's not, shall we Til!' he said sharply. 'I was seventeen. A lot happens when you're seventeen,' and the shutters closed. Matilda knew not to probe any further.

It was a subject she had tried to talk about on numerous occasions, especially after episodes like the one they had gone through on the plane, but she had never got to the bottom of what it was that frightened him so much. He would always clam up and she conceded years ago that there was a part of his life she was never to be privy to. Everyone has a past and is entitled to keep it there, but she was convinced something in Sebastian's had affected him profoundly.

'Are you ready for the meeting?' she asked after a while.

'Almost. I want to go over the papers again tonight, make sure it's fresh in my mind.'

'Have you checked in with Richard?'

'He got in about an hour ago; I'll call him after dinner,' Sebastian paused, thinking. 'Can I ask a favour? Will you come into the meeting tomorrow?'

'I didn't think you needed me?'

'I don't, but I'd like you to be there.'

'Okay,' Matilda said, looking at him as they continued to eat in uneasy silence.

It was late when Matilda headed to bed, leaving Sebastian sitting at the desk in the office on the top floor, working into the night. It was 3 a.m. when he contacted Richard, the company lawyer, who was still awake, reading through some documents to make sure everything was in place for the morning.

Having been in discussions with PMaC over several months, the purpose of their meeting was to confirm everything that had already been agreed in principle including the indicative offer, which had been made a few weeks previously. Patrick McCarthy knew exactly what he was proposing to buy and Sebastian was pinning his hopes on him. The morning's meeting, which was to be held in the sister hotel to the one in which they were staying, was pivotal; if it went well there was no reason the sale should not go ahead.

Minus Eight

Colin delivered breakfast to their dining room.

'Nervous?' Matilda asked, as Sebastian pushed away his untouched food.

'Yes, are you?'

'A little, although I'm not intending to say anything unless you want me to,' Matilda replied. 'I read in the hotel brochure that the room we're going to be in today has witnessed some famous handshakes, so hopefully that's a good omen.'

'Who?'

'It didn't say, but I imagine perhaps someone like Marilyn Monroe or The Carpenters?'

'But you don't know.'

'No, I don't know,' Matilda sighed.

~

Henry had made good progress on his script that morning. The characters were starting to come alive and the story, told from the perspectives of heaven and hell, was developing well in Henry's mind. But he needed a break. So, after lunch, he took Panda and headed over to Taligth to help his mother clean out Betsy's sty. Mother and son both knew it would be the first place William would go when he got home from the hospital. Panda loved the farm and soon disappeared off in search of new smells whilst Henry swept.

'Have ye heard from Sebastian? I'm wondering how his meeting's gone,' Elspeth asked, swilling out Betsy's trough with huge buckets of water.

'It'll have only just started Mum. They're five hours behind remember.'

'Och aye, so they are. I dinnae envy him all that talkin' and paper shufflin'. They just need to get th' thing over wi' and get on. They've bin talking aboot it for months.'

'I've no doubts Sebastian would agree with you,' Henry said, smothering Panda in hay as she dived headfirst into Betsy's freshly made bed.

Standing straight, her back aching, Elspeth looked into the pigsty. Betsy sniffed her clean surroundings in search of the apples that had lured her back in from the yard. 'Tis a good job well done there, Henry. Thank ye for yer help. Shall we have a cupper and a wee slice of cake afore we go fetch yer faither?'

'What do you think, Panda? Fancy some cake?' Henry asked, as Panda emerged, blinking, from beneath the hay.

'Ye can brush her doon out in th' yard afore she comes in 'ere if ye dinnae mind,' Elspeth said sternly. Not one for cute animals unless they had a job to do, Elspeth considered Panda and Betsy a nuisance and just got under her feet.

~

The location for the meeting had been Patrick McCarthy's choice. He was in New York on other business and it seemed senseless dragging everyone out to his offices in California, although having never been to the west coast Sebastian would have quite happily made the trip.

Three hours in, the meeting was intense, the air conditioning keeping the searing heat at bay. However nice, Patrick McCarthy was a businessman and knew what he expected those around him to do. Sebastian was under no illusion that it was a done deal, but he was delighted with his younger self for being so diligent in Tatch-A UK's early days, and Patrick McCarthy was smiling.

Always with the intention to sell, Sebastian had known how critical it was to the business to make sure they kept their finger on the pulse from the day it was conceived to the day they handed the keys over to a new owner. He was integral to the running the company and what he needed to prove today was that it was able to carry on without him at the helm.

Although Patrick McCarthy knew the information from the pre-offer documents, he had requested that Sebastian and Richard present the PMaC team with a clear explanation of the company's structure. Tatch-A UK had a good set up of financial, commercial and technical teams within the office, and structures within the business were all in place with clear reporting lines headed up by trusted employees. Patrick sat and listened, smiling as they talked honestly about their competitors and what they could see on the horizon.

Keeping their competitors at bay, Sebastian had made sure every intricate part of his product design and production had been patented, but the concept was simple and other forms of attachment products were starting to appear on the market. Patrick McCarthy was more than aware of what the market was doing and he was happy with Tatch-A UK's position within it.

In the fourth hour of the meeting, just before lunch, they talked about the potential growth of the company. Having more or less saturated the hair accessory and fashion clothing sectors, Tatch-A UK was now expanding into footwear and bags with 'Tatch-A-Strap' and 'Tatch-A-Popper', each with their own unique attachment. Entering new markets and designing new tooling was challenging and very expensive. By lunch Patrick McCarthy was still smiling.

'So, did Sebastian tell me you've got yourselves a pup?' he asked Matilda, his voice quiet, his Irish/American accent gentle, as they enjoyed a light smoked salmon salad accompanied by iced water.

'We have,' Matilda answered politely, delicately cutting up the leaves on her plate. 'A spaniel called Panda.'

'Panda! I like that name. I have five dogs, all of varying breeds and colour, I'm guessing he is black and white.'

'*She*,' Matilda said.

'She, I stand corrected,' Patrick laughed.

Matilda looked at him and smiled. Although in his seventies, Patrick was a very handsome man. Tall and slim, with lightly tanned skin, he had blonde hair that had taken on a natural silver/grey and framed his strong, expressive face. He did not look his age. 'Yes, she's black and white with little white patches around her eyes,' she said.

'She sounds cute.' Patrick paused, forking a large piece of uncut smoked salmon into his mouth. 'So, how are you feeling about selling?' It was a big question and not one Matilda was sure she could answer, but she liked Patrick's candidness and trusted that he liked what he had heard so far.

'Funnily enough, I asked Sebastian something similar last night. If I'm honest, I feel a mix of excitement and fear.'

'Explain.'

'I'm excited for the company, because you appear to be exactly what it needs,' she said putting knife and fork down, 'and I'm excited for me because after twenty-three years I will get my husband back. But I'm also afraid. Afraid that there won't be enough for him without Tatch-A in his life,' she paused. 'Sorry, that probably wasn't what you wanted to hear.'

'Well, that's where you're wrong. That is absolutely what I want to hear because it tells me a lot about you. Which is very important to me when I'm investing.'

'So, you will understand when I say I have got my fingers crossed that when Tatch-A 'leaves home' we will still be in one piece.'

Patrick put his fork down and wiped his mouth with his napkin. 'I think if my first wife had been as supportive of me as you are of Sebastian, I would still be married to her,' he smiled, 'and my second wife, she wasn't much better,' he said picking up his fork again, chasing his salad. 'It's a difficult job you have when you are married to someone as ambitious and as successful as Sebastian. Just keep an eye on him and keep up with the support when the doubting starts, as it will. He will need to find himself again and work out what he wants to do with the rest of his life. It'll take time.'

'He's talking about working on his parents' farm.'

'I think that's a great thing to do. I have a ranch in Arizona I go visit when I'm looking for time out. There's little phone signal in the desert and I can ride for days without seeing another human. It's good for the soul.'

'Well, it's not quite a ranch, but there's plenty of work to do so I'm hoping it will keep him occupied.'

'Not as occupied as he will be over the next few weeks! Come on let's eat up and get back to it so you guys can start your vacation.'

~

After a cup of tea and a slice of Dundee cake, Henry and Elspeth were ready to go to the hospital to pick up William. Panda was happily settled in an old wooden playpen that Elspeth had dug out of the back room.

By the time they found a parking space, William had made his way to the entrance doors and was waiting for them on a bench in the sunshine enjoying the fresh air, surprised by how warm it had turned. When Henry and Elspeth finally reached him, Henry left Elspeth to catch her breath whilst he ran back to collect the car.

'When we get 'ere later tis practically empty, ye can park right ootdoors so ye can, but not at half past five,' Elspeth panted, tired out by the walk.

'You're puffing away my old girl,' William observed, as Elspeth took time to speak.

'Och! Away wi' ye, just catching my breath 'tis all. Henry walks at a pace, so he does.'

'Do you remember when he was little, how fast he used to run up into the top field to try to reach the sheep before the dogs?'

'He never won that race.'

'No, but he was close a few times.'

'That's because there's nothin' to 'im. He's skin 'n' bone.'

'You'll have to fatten him up with some of your lardy cake whilst he's here.'

'I'm doin' my best.'

Pulling up in front of the hospital, Henry picked up his parents and drove them back to the farm. Whilst searching the dashboard for the non-existent air conditioning button, William regaled them both with an update on the cricket. Sadly, the man in the bed opposite him had taken a turn for the worse during the night and had passed away, so William had had no one to share it with until now.

'It's right next to you, Dad.'

'Where?'

'To your left.'

'My left?' William asked, confused.

'Yes, on the door. That handle thing. Turn it anti-clockwise and the air conditioning comes on.'

'Well I never!' William laughed.

~

In the hour after lunch, Sebastian and Richard went through some of the less glamorous aspects of the company that were not in the public domain. Patrick McCarthy was especially interested in the finer detail of the company's growth forecast and how efficient the operating processes were.

Twenty-three years ago, Tatch-A UK had found a gap in the market and Sebastian was able to prove there was still plenty of room for expansion. The company had a healthy cash flow and profit levels had grown year on year; what was embryonic now had the potential to become profitable later. It was worth a lot of money and Patrick McCarthy knew it.

As the light began to fade, PMaC confirmed the indicative offer of £24 million, requesting they agree to a swift due diligence and to complete within six weeks. They shook hands, sharing a drink to the success of their very long, hot day and the start of what they hoped would be a rewarding and happy relationship. When the meeting finished and they left the conference room, Patrick McCarthy was still smiling.

After an exquisite dinner in their suite, relaxing in the infinity pool, Sebastian and Matilda swam to the edge and stared out towards the city lights. The sky was clear and the water was warm. It felt, tonight, as though they owned the world and were suspended above it in some obscure time machine. They did not speak as much about the day as they might have; there was little to say and perhaps if they did speak, their excitement would be coupled with fear for what the future held. The enormity of what lay ahead was clear; they knew this was just the beginning.

Minus Seven

Late August had decided to spring a last-minute heat wave, meaning Henry didn't object to Panda's shrill early morning call forcing him out of bed. He was able to have a swim and do some good work before lunch, giving him the excuse for a guilt free afternoon. Turning left out of the gates, he and Panda walked down the steep hill to the park with Panda leading the way, her fur bouncing as she trotted along in the warm breeze.

They liked the park that stretched lengthways across the hillside. The last few times they had visited, it had been busy, and today was no exception. There were families playing games, groups of children kicking balls, couples lying on the grass sleeping whilst others were sitting on rugs reading, or leaning against the trees, watching. There was a small group of women doing some kind of yoga class and there were dogs running amok, chasing each other. Henry felt comfortable letting Panda join in the games and he let her run free whilst he appreciated the delights of a strawberry ice cream.

Panda played until she was tired and then came and sat in the shade behind Henry's legs. Once she had caught her breath and eaten the end of Henry's ice cream cone, her new friends soon enticed her out to play once more and, copying them, she decided it would be fun to take a flying leap into the pond that had not seen rain water for some weeks. Sending the ducks waddling along the shallow, watery runway frantically flapping their wings to take flight, the dogs swam amongst the sludge and algae before scrambling out, covered in pondweed, smelling of rotting vegetation.

Disgraced, head down, Panda walked alongside Henry as they made their way slowly back up the hill towards home. It was hot and the hill, alive with a line of small shops and places to eat, was steep. They ambled past, looking in the windows until they came to a little café that caught Henry's eye. Stopping to admire the vast array of cakes and pastries, Henry looked down at his rancid friend. 'We can but ask,' he said, as Panda sat in the shade of the narrow, blue and white awning, which protected the fresh cream from souring in the sun.

Keeping Panda behind him, Henry gingerly stepped in through the open door. He caught the eye of the waitress who smiled invitingly at him as she cleared a vacated table.

'Am I okay to bring my dog in?' Henry asked, looking around the busy café.

'Of course. Dogs are welcome.'

'You might not say that when you see the state this one's in,' Henry said, grimacing and looking down at Panda. The spaniel, fur matted to her face, smiled and looked up at him before popping her head around the door to see who he was talking to.

'Ah,' the waitress said looking at Panda, 'have you been having fun?' she asked, bending down to talk to her. 'What's his... her name?'

'She's called Panda,' Henry replied, smiling down at the waitress, delighted they were not going to be turned away.

'Panda! Well, that's a very cute name for such a smelly pup,' the waitress said as Panda hid behind Henry's legs. 'Well, Panda, come inside and tell me what I can get you.'

Slowly easing into the room, Henry and Panda sat at the table closest to the doorway, allowing the air to waft away the stench exuding from Panda's damp fur. The small, tastefully decorated café, with paintings adorning every wall, was homely and welcoming. Henry watched the waitress walk away as she left him to look at the menu. She was petite, with a fair complexion and freckles, and hair that was tucked into a loose bun at the nape of her neck. A similar age to himself, she reminded him a little of Lorna.

Henry loved cafés. He often went to the one in the village in which he and Lorna lived where he would sit for hours nursing a cold coffee, writing. It was warm in the café and the constant hubbub fed his imagination more easily than the silence of either home or the library.

The slice of cake delivered to his table was enormous and abundant with cherries and walnuts and it smelt delicious, as did the large mug of milky coffee. 'And something for my little friend,' the waitress said as Panda's black nose twitched towards the dog biscuit in her hand.

'Gently,' Henry instructed Panda, who softly took the offering from the waitress' hand. 'This place is lovely,' Henry said, as the waitress cleared the table next to his, 'and this cake is delicious.'

'Thank you. Haven't you been in before?' she asked, sounding surprised.

'No, this the first time.'

'Oh, I thought I recognised you,' she said, looking at him.

Henry wondered whether he knew her from his school days, but was too unsure to ask.

'I love the artwork,' he said.

'Thank you, they're my daughter's. This place is hers.'

'It's amazing. Does she sell it?'

'She does. All the artwork in here's for sale.'

'I can't see any prices. How much does it sell for?'

'She doesn't put prices on. She prefers people to offer what they believe the paintings to be worth.'

'I like that idea. Does she get good offers?'

'Mostly, but she soon puts people in their place if they're insulting,' the waitress said, smiling at Henry. 'Are you from around here?'

'I grew up about fifteen miles away, but I've not spent any time in this part of the city for years. By the sound of it, you're not a local.'

'No, I'm from England, the south coast originally. I'm just here to help out for a bit,' she replied, moving to another table. 'Do you go to the park down the road?'

'We do. We like that park don't we, Panda?'

'That'll be where I'll have seen you then,' the waitress said, taking a pile of crockery back to the counter.

Devouring his cherry and walnut cake and finishing his coffee, Henry left all the change he had in his pocket on the table and, promising to return, waved to the waitress who was busy with a customer. He and Panda walked back into the sun-drenched street. By now, Panda had turned crusty and bits of dried sludge dropped from her fur as she trotted along the pavement in front of Henry.

Trudging back up the hill, which was lined with million-pound properties, Henry got a glimpse into Sebastian's world. A lot of the houses that had once been large, individual, Victorian family homes had been tastefully converted into apartments, whilst others had been made into luxurious, boutique hotels with brass plaques and gold awnings. It was a very nice part of the city.

Out of breath, Henry reached the house, aware of his phone ringing in his pocket. Fumbling with his keys and remote control, he scrambled to answer it.

'Henry, is that ye?'

'Oh, hi Mum,' he said breathlessly.

'Are ye a'right?'

'Yes, sorry, I've been out with Panda. Is everything okay?'

'Och aye, it is.'

'Excellent. Did you and Dad sleep well?'

'We did, lik' babies in baskets,' Elspeth said, 'weel, I did at least; yer dad were a wee bit fidgety. He finds it hard to settle wi' his shoulder. Have ye managed to get some work done th'day, with this heat 'n' all?'

'Seb has air conditioning.'

'Och aye, of coorse he does. I was wondering whether you'd lik' to come over and have a wee bit of supper wi' us?'

'Yes, that would be good. What time shall I come over?'

'Whenever yer lik'.'

'Okay, is seven all right with you? I need to wash Panda.'

'I was thinking mibbie a wee bit earlier, if ye wouldn't mind. Only yer dad could do wi' some help.'

'No problem, that's fine. I'll wash her and then head over.'

'As soon as yer can if ye wouldn't mind.'

'Panda's filthy.'

'Na worries aboot that. I'll give her a hose doon when ye get 'ere.'

'Okay, I'm on my way.'

'Och! That is good o' ye. See ye in a min my sweet laddie.'

Henry laughed. 'Come on Panda, we've been summoned! Brace yourself, that hose at Taligth is freezing.'

~

Sebastian and Matilda woke on the first day of their 'vacation' to the distant hum of the streets below. Sitting in bed, they looked out as the sun rose above the skyscrapers. They could not see the streets, but the sense of life and the smell of the city excited them. Today they were going to explore.

After a phone call to Taligth, and a quick conversation with Paul, updating him on the success of the meeting with PMaC, they chose to have breakfast in one of New York's thousands of old-world diners. Surrounded by locals from all corners of the globe, they sat in the small, curved window watching the world go by. Outside, the air was sultry, and as there was no air conditioning, the door was propped open by a large glass jar half-filled with black olives swimming around in an oily bath. Amidst the smell of exhaust fumes and the blaring sound of taxi drivers' horns, street vendors calling their early morning cry and commuters pounding the streets heading for the cool of their offices, Sebastian and Matilda were in the veins of the city.

After breakfast, they strolled along the river before heading to the Museum at Eldridge Street on Lower East

Side. They both loved history and, with Matilda's ancestry, found the American-Jewish culture particularly fascinating. For a few hours they lost themselves in a world known by thousands who had gone before them, before heading back into the real one, and onto the street in search of the nearest dumpling shop.

~

It was hot work, but Henry enjoyed buzzing about the fields on the quad bike, moving the animals closer to the sheds. The forecast warned of a storm and William was keen for the cows and sheep to be sheltered. By the time they got back to the house, the sky had darkened, and Henry and William had earned their steak and kidney pie supper. They sat at the long, scrubbed, oak table, as Elspeth sweated, busying about the kitchen, bringing dishes of steaming vegetables and buttered mashed potato across from the aga.

'Can I help, Mum?'

'Yer can fetch a jug o' water for th' table, good laddie.'

Henry filled a large, purple jug with iced water. The air outside had become thick, the sky heavy with expectant rain, and the wind had started to pull at the trees. A thunderstorm was heading their way.

'You've mastered the art of eating with one hand then?' Henry said, watching his father deftly cut his pie into small pieces with an upturned fork.

'Aye, not a lot keeps yer faither from his food,' Elspeth commented, pinching her lips in tightly. Carrying on eating, William rolled his eyes at Henry.

'Feels like we might be in for a bit of a storm tonight,' Henry said.

'Anything to break this heat,' William complained, wiping his brow as he chewed.

'S'pose I shuid have done a salad.'

'Not for me you shouldn't,' William replied, pulling away at another piece of meat and shovelling it into his mouth, gravy spilling down his chin. 'I'm enjoying this very much, thank you love.' He smiled at Elspeth.

'Och William!' she scolded, 'ye'r worse than th' bairns when they were babies! 'Ere let me wipe yer chin.'

'I'll come over again tomorrow, shall I?' Henry asked, whilst Elspeth rummaged in the drawer for a napkin.

'I can wipe my own chin thank you very much,' William said, swiping her advancing hand away.

'That would be braw o' ye if ye wouldn't mind Henry. This darned heat is sapping my energy, so it is, and yer dad is useless with his shoulder.'

'Less of the useless,' William said, perfectly aware of how his incapacitation had landed the heavy work on Elspeth. 'I do what I can.'

'I know ye do love,' Elspeth said, smiling warmly at him, 'but wi'out yer brawn, tis hard work for my old bones alone.'

'Then that's settled, I'll come over and help,' Henry said as they finished the evening off with homemade apple pie and fresh cream.

After dinner, they sat drinking tea, watching from the kitchen window as the storm-winds played with the trees, thrashing and bending the branches. Henry decided it was time to head back before the rain came.

'Now, don't go bothering yourself with supper again Mum,' Henry said, leaving Taligth armed with a plate of lardy cake. 'Matilda ordered so much food in before they went. I've set myself a challenge to get through it before they get back,'

'Weel, ye need to get yersel' fattened up. Tis three plates ye owe me now if ye dinnae mind returning them,' Elspeth called, watching Henry go to his car. He buckled Panda into the back seat, making sure to keep the cake out of reach of her twitching nose. 'Not for you,' he said to her, driving away, 'or me either,' for the one cake Henry was not partial to was lardy cake.

As the forecast predicted, a magnificent thunderstorm swept across Edinburgh's sky that night. A squally wind chased the lashing rain and sheets of lightning cracked for hours, bringing energy to the darkness. Every time the lightning struck, the reverberation shook the house sending Panda cowering beneath the covers as she and Henry snuggled up together. It was the first time she had witnessed a storm and she whimpered quietly as it slowly passed overhead before calming to a rainy night, allowing them to sleep.

Minus Six

As the weather settled, beautiful orange and red sunrises were mirrored across the miles separating Edinburgh and New York.

Enjoying their holiday, relaxing, Sebastian and Matilda ventured out early each morning, walking the streets, visiting art galleries, frequenting artisan bakeries, coffee shops and bars and enjoying the daytime festival atmosphere of the vibrant city, whilst Henry spent his last few days in Edinburgh writing, swimming, playing in the park with Panda, going to the café and helping out at Taligth.

Knowing how much helping out over the past days had impacted his time, Elspeth was keen for Henry to know just how much she and William appreciated him. She had been busy baking. 'I have made ye a batch of butteries and scones and a wee Dundee cake to take back to Newcastle wi' ye when ye go home,' she said as he sat around the table one evening, enjoying tea after fetching in hay bales all afternoon.

'Much appreciated, thank you.'

'She's trying to fatten you up,' William muttered.

''Tis th' only way. Look at him. Skin 'n' bone so he is.'

'I'll have you know it's taken me forty-eight years to become the fine figure of the man I am today, so please don't go trying to change me now.'

'Funny how yer al' so different,' she said. 'Nancy were prone to fat, while Sebastian...'

'Yes, I know,' Henry said, flashing his mother a playful scowl. 'We're like the three bears; one fat, one thin and one just right.'

'Nah! I dinnae care much for muscle! Though dinnae go telling yer brother that,' Elspeth whispered, winking. Always a soft spot for her skinny boy.

In silence, they all wondered whether Nancy was still prone to fat.

~

On Sunday afternoon, the day before they were due to fly home, Sebastian received a phone-call from Patrick McCarthy.

'Your beautiful wife told me you love to go out onto your folks' farm,' he said, much to Sebastian's surprise. 'I know this is a little unconventional, but I was wondering whether you might like to extend your vacation by a few days and join me on my ranch in Phoenix? I'm heading out tonight. It appears things are moving quickly for us and there are a number of items I'd like to go over with you, if you need to justify it. What do you think?'

'I think we would like that very much,' Sebastian replied, 'though would you mind if I get a few things sorted at home before I commit? I'll need to reschedule a couple of meetings. I'll get back to you within the hour.'

'Take your time, I'm going there anyhow. Let me know when you land and I'll meet you at the airport. Oh, and Sebastian, it's mighty hot out there in the desert by day, so make sure you and Matilda have sensible clothes and a little something to keep yourselves warm for when the sun goes down. The west offers up scorching days followed by cool nights.'

After talking it over with Matilda, Sebastian called the office. It was early Sunday evening in the UK and Niamh, the company's managing director, was sitting at her desk, exactly where Sebastian knew she would be.

Prior to leaving for New York, Sebastian had instructed external accountants, Ribeck & Ribeck, to go into the office and start the process of pre-due diligence. They knew that should the meeting with PMaC go well, Patrick was looking to move quickly, and they wanted to be prepared. Whilst they were away, Graham Ribeck, whom they had worked with for many years, had kept them up to date with progress. So far everything appeared to be going much as they would have expected. Sebastian had delegated responsibility to Niamh and Paul. To his surprise, it was Paul who answered the phone.

'Paul!' Sebastian exclaimed, hearing his friend's voice, 'what are you doing in the office on a Sunday? Is Niamh in?'

'Yep, she's here as well. Both of us dedicated to the end.'

'And it's much appreciated. How are things going?'

'Absolutely fine. You can leave us to it you know, the place won't fall apart without you.'

'Which is why I'm calling to let you know we're staying out a few days longer.'

'You are? Okay, what are you up to?'

'We're going to Arizona to ride horses on Patrick's McCarthy's ranch!'

'Fuck off, you're not?' Paul scoffed. 'Have you ever ridden a horse?'

'Never.'

'Bloody hell mate,' Paul said laughing at his friend. 'You'll come back with gonads the size of your head.' Sebastian laughed. 'You lucky bastard,' Paul added.

'Someone's got to live the dream,' Sebastian teased. 'How's Graham getting on?'

'All right I think, as weird as ever,' Paul said, having spent time with the ex-military man.

'He's eccentric, that's all,' Sebastian replied. 'How are you getting on with his questions?'

'He's not really asked any,' Paul replied. 'I've tried to get ahead of the game and pre-empt what he needs.'

'That's great. Thanks.'

'When are you back?'

'At the end of the week. Probably Friday, but call me if there's anything urgent...'

'We will. Now, fuck off and enjoy yourself.'

'...or non urgent...'

'Seb!'

'...or just because you want to.'

'See you in a few days,' Paul laughed, ending the call.

Sebastian phoned Henry. 'How are you fixed after Tuesday?' he asked, hoping that Henry didn't have anything pressing to get back home for.

'Other than helping Lilith move house on Wednesday, I've not got anything on before I go back to school. Why?'

'Brilliant! How would you feel about staying at our place a little longer?'

'That's a tough call, Seb, let me think about it...' Henry replied sarcastically.

'We'll organise a food delivery for you...'

'Um... I'm really not sure...'

'From Ballimoreloch's...'

'Done!' Henry accepted quickly, delighted. Ballimoreloch's was his favourite delicatessen and it was way out of his price range. 'How come anyway? What are you up to?'

'Patrick has invited us to his ranch in Arizona... to go riding.' Henry laughed. 'I know!' Sebastian said, 'Paul's just done the same.'

'When are you back?'

'Friday. Would that be all right?'

'My only commitment is Wednesday, so if you don't mind me taking Panda, I'll pop home for a night and she can slum it with Lorna and Mabel whilst I'm in Leeds. Then I'll come back up Thursday. Are you okay with that?'

'Of course. Thanks so much, Hal. Sleep well. Night'

'Night,' Henry said, looking down at Panda who was sitting by his side. She sprung to her feet, wagging her tail in anticipation. 'Sleep?' Henry scowled incredulously. 'Who has time for sleep? The night is young and you and I are off for a dip. Go grab your bikini and I'll meet you by the pool.'

~

With no time to lose, making full use of Colin, Sebastian set him the task of sorting out and rearranging flights. He and Colin had got used to each other's ways. Colin had even started to understand British humour as Sebastian enjoyed some funny moments teasing the butler. Ever respectful, Colin nodded and bowed and did what was asked of him with utter professionalism, but would leave the suite confused by Sebastian's request for him to source items called Marmite and Cadbury's chocolate buttons rather than peanut butter and Hershey's kisses.

Making it appear effortless, Colin organised Sebastian and Matilda's onward journey. Once more they imagined what he might have said about them downstairs –

'Okay, so you know the guys in The Flight Suite, the ones who arrived with those hideous cases,' he might say, gesticulating his excitement. 'Soooooo, as you know, they haven't got Louis Vuitton or Prada or Rolex or anything like that, but I have just booked them one of the 'World Class' private jets to fly them to Patrick McCarthy's ranch in Phoenix, Arizona. Just goes to show, they're quality people underneath it all. I think there is a lot to be said for Adidas.'

Asking Colin to send the clothes they had brought with them back home to Scotland, Sebastian and Matilda took advantage of the relaxed Sunday trading laws and went out shopping for more appropriate attire for the unexpected second part of their trip. Looking at the forecast, the temperature in Arizona was in the forties. In his message following Sebastian's returned phone call, Patrick mentioned riding through the desert and into the mountains and advised them to be prepared for all terrains and some spectacular scenery; they would need riding boots and hats, long lightweight trousers and long-sleeved shirts to keep the flies from biting, and they would need plenty of sunscreen.

Minus Three

The early morning flight to Phoenix took them five and a half hours. It had been hard to leave their New York hideaway, but as they did, shaking his hand firmly, Sebastian tucked $500 into Colin's palm. 'Go buy yourself some Adidas,' he whispered into the ear of the butler who had made their stay all the more comfortable.

'Thank you, Sir. I will do just that,' Colin smiled, nodding knowingly. 'It's been a pleasure.'

~

From his armchair, William was engrossed in the cricket, witnessing what he could only describe as the best day of test cricket ever, better even than Botham in 1981. Hearing William cheer, Elspeth and Henry had been drawn into the front room, and all three were sat forward in their chairs, wracked with nerves. William was having a brilliant day with Elspeth and Henry beside him to share the highs and lows. Elspeth admittedly knew little of the game, but was caught up in the excitement as it went down to the last over.

'Yi'll need to keep yer seat on th' chair else ye'll be risking breaking yer other shoulder if yer not careful, William!' she scolded, watching the old man teeter on the edge as the climatic end saw him jumping to his feet in glory. Elspeth was cross with him for tiring himself out, threatening the healing of his shoulder, and cross with herself for being distracted enough not to have prepared the evening meal.

'Weel, ye'll have to have tatties wi' beans and cheese,' she said, throwing her hands in the air.

'No worries, love,' William smiled.

'Aye, but I do,' Elspeth replied, for it was his stomach she fretted over most. She headed for the kitchen muttering, leaving Henry and William to relive the final ball.

'What time is it in Arizona?' William asked, once they calmed down and the subject had turned to Sebastian's Wild West trip.

'I think they're about eight hours behind. Did he tell you they hired a private jet?'

'He did,' William said, raising his eyebrows.

Having seen the company grow off a scribbled note torn from the back of a box of baby formula he and Elspeth had bought for them when they could hardly afford to eat, William spoke little of Sebastian's wealth other than to raise an eyebrow at what he perceived as unnecessary extravagance.

'It's a different world, Dad,' Henry said, reading his father's thoughts.

'Yes it is, one to which neither you nor I belong,' William replied, ending the conversation.

~

Touching down, the shimmering tarmac welcomed Sebastian and Matilda to the western state. Patrick McCarthy was waiting for them, standing alongside a light aircraft he had flown into the airport. They chatted comfortably as they flew the fifty minutes south to his ranch nestled in Sabino Canyon, just outside Tucson. The scenery was breathtaking. Landing on a dusty field next to the sprawling ranch house, it was like stepping onto the set of a 1950s American western, and the house, surrounded by the Baboquivari mountain range, spanning thousands of acres of dry grazing land, was traditional and homely and about as far away as they could get from the electrifying vibes of inner-city New York.

Following a late lunch of freshly baked bread and ranch-reared beef accompanied by crisp salads, relishes and pickles, Patrick gave Sebastian and Matilda a tour of the homestead before heading into the wooden ranch house in which they were staying.

'I would like to claim this was all my own doing,' Patrick said, showing them into the various rooms, all beautifully decorated in natural, muted tones, 'but unfortunately I have little eye for what goes with what, so we have the second Mrs. McCarthy to thank for all this.'

'She had good taste,' Matilda said.

'She certainly did, that's for sure. She got a little practice on a smaller place we had before this one, so she managed to do this quite easily before she lost interest.'

'In the ranch?'

'In me,' Patrick smiled. 'Come, let me take you out to the paddock,' he said, leading them onto the veranda; the Baboquivari mountains and the open Sonoran desert their panorama.

'How often do you come out here?' Sebastian asked as they paced across the yard.

'As often as I can. I find it recharges the batteries. Here, meet your trusty steeds for the next couple of days.'

Out across the field, a small group of horses, heads to the ground, stood calmly grazing. Becoming aware of Patrick and his friends standing at the fence, they shook the dust from their manes and trotted over to greet their guests. Sebastian took a step back from the fence. The strong, majestic animals bowed their heads, nudging Patrick and Matilda with their soft, warm muzzles, hoping to find a carrot or two secreted in Patrick's pockets.

'This one is called Stalwart; he's my boy, if you didn't already guess. He's the strongest horse I have ever ridden and totally unwavering. I would trust him with my life. Do you ride, Sebastian?' Patrick asked, holding pieces of carrot on the flat of his hand for the horses to fight over.

'I'm afraid not, and if I'm honest, I'm a touch wary of horses.'

'And you, the son of a farmer?'

'Give me a cow any day.'

'That can be arranged if you would prefer,' Patrick laughed. 'How about you, Matilda? You look pretty comfortable there. Her name is Carnival. Isn't she beautiful?'

Leaning into the chestnut mare's strong neck, Matilda could feel the horse's pulse and smell the dust deep within her hair. 'It's a long time since I've ridden,' she said, rubbing her hand along the length of Carnival's nose. 'I'm looking forward to getting back in the saddle.'

'Then hopefully you and Carnival will enjoy riding together. She is as gentle as the breeze and easy to speak to. Just point her in the right direction and tell her where you want to go and she will take you there.'

'I rather like the sound of Carnival,' Sebastian said, nervous he might be seated on a free-willed, galloping stallion.

'No, Carnival is too small for you. Come over here and meet Sangfroid.'

'Sangfroid?' Sebastian questioned, walking a little way along the fence to a large lone horse quietly grazing the edge of the field.

'Sangfroid is named because of her composure and calmness. Take the time to get to know her and she will make you feel like you never want to get off.'

'Okay, I like the sound of Sangfroid,' Sebastian nodded, looking across to the animal who caught his eye and bowed her head before continuing grazing.

With their first trek organised for dawn, they watched the beautiful sunset and spent the evening drinking beer in front of a huge fire pit over which they griddled their meal before the cool night air drove them to their beds. They had expected Patrick to have a team of people buzzing around the ranch providing them with whatever they wanted but that was not his way. He preferred to be there alone, accompanied only by the dogs and animals who shared his land, Bill, the ranch manager, and Grace, the house keeper, who, in the morning would arrive, prepare the house for the day whilst Patrick and his guests were out trekking, and then leave, with the meals prepped, house cleaned and beds made.

The cosy wooden room, in which Sebastian and Matilda were staying, had a sumptuous bed with fur blankets and large, feather-filled pillows. In the wet room, thick towels and bathrobes hung on hooks by folding doors, which opened out onto a balcony, exposing a wooden hot tub and a view that took their breath away. Listening to the sounds of the nocturnal creatures hidden in the darkness, they relaxed in the warm water. It was a lovely way to end a perfect day.

Minus Two

Both with a slight spring in their step, Henry and Panda left the house early, before the cleaners started work. Turning right at the bottom of the drive, they walked down the hill to the park.

Relieved, Henry had finally finished the first draft of his play and had spent an hour on the phone talking to Lorna excitedly about his ideas for the set. Having stood in the garden, distracted by his conversation, he had aimlessly thrown a ball for Panda, who, after many failed attempts, had learned to catch.

So now, as a reward, Henry was taking her to the park to show off her newly acquired skill. Panda could hardly contain herself as she smelt the felted rubber in Henry's hand and she pulled and twizzled on the lead as they walked along the pavement.

With the Scottish children back in school and the office workers at their desks, the park was quiet. Letting Panda off her lead, Henry threw the ball as far as he could, sending her pelting after it at full speed across the newly mown grass. Within seconds, she had retrieved it and she charged back, placing the ball at Henry's feet expectantly. *Again! Again!* she panted, her eyes wide, mouth open, tongue lolling.

Henry picked up the ball and threw it high into the air above Panda, who sat beneath it, open-mouthed. She caught it with a 'thwack' as it landed firmly between her teeth. Delighted with herself, she returned the ball to Henry's feet, smiling. *Again!* she demanded. And so the game went on long enough for Henry to walk to the ice cream seller and, after wiping dog slobber from his hands, buy himself a peanut butter and toffee double scoop as his way of enjoying what was likely to be his last ice cream of the season before heading back to school the following week.

Sitting on a bench with the sun in front of him, throwing the ball time and time again, Henry did not see the lady who said, 'hi there,' as she walked quickly past. It wasn't until she had moved into the shadow of the trees and turned to wave, that he recognised the waitress from the café. 'Are you guys not coming in for your breakfast this morning?' she asked, walking backwards, slowly.

'Not this morning,' Henry replied, waving his ice cream in the air. 'We have a new game we need to perfect before we head home tomorrow.'

'You're going?' she asked. Henry nodded. 'I'll miss seeing my little friend,' she said. 'Say goodbye to her for me and have a safe trip,' she called, turning away.

'Will do,' Henry called back as Panda dropped the ball at his feet.

'You need a drink,' he said, getting Panda's bottle out of his rucksack. 'Do you think the cleaners will have finished by now?' he asked, watching her lap the water before jumping onto the bench next to him, panting heavily and drooling over the last of his ice cream. 'What time do they usually go, do you know? There were a lot of them weren't there? But I suppose that's a good way of doing it. Better to have five cleaners for two hours than one cleaner for ten,' he said, looking at Panda who had licked her moustache clean and stuck it to either side of her mouth. Henry laughed as she smiled at him. 'You don't care about cleaners do you? Come on, let's go home and pack. You're going to see Mabel tomorrow.'

By the time they got back, the cleaners had gone and the house was spotless. Henry, with Panda at his heel, set about packing. He had enjoyed his week of luxury and spending time at Taligth with his parents, but he was looking forward to going home and getting stuck into rehearsals, and a little bit of him was even looking forward to going back to school, but only a little bit. Organised for an early start the following morning, he left their bags by the

99

door, locked up the house, and with Panda, headed to Taligth.

~

It was six in the morning and the purple, silhouetted mountains flickered as the orange and red play of light rose behind them. The sun, making golden the saguaro cactus, was already beating thirty degrees and by late afternoon it would be touching forty-five, so they needed to be back by lunchtime to shelter from its intensity.

With saddles on their shoulders, Patrick led Sebastian and Matilda out to the paddock. Bill, stocky and weather beaten, was standing, waiting to help them prepare and mount their horses. Sebastian felt nervous as Sangfroid was led around and her reins handed to him. Shaking her head, her rear feet stepping out, Sangfroid could sense Sebastian's unease, but he was determined not to show his fear as he 'shushed' her calmly and gently stroked her soft twitching nose. Standing at sixteen hands, with a beautiful grey roan coat, fourteen-year-old Sangfroid was in her prime.

Watching the way Patrick talked to Stalwart like an old friend as he saddled and mounted him, Sebastian marvelled at the old man's connection with the land and the animals on his ranch. Although the terrain, the livestock and the weather were different, farming and ranching were much the same and a welcome contrast to their professional lives. Looking around, as far as the eye could see, this what was what Sebastian was looking for: peace, space and the opportunity to breathe.

Trying to remain calm, but with distinct memories of getting on a pushbike for the first time, helped by Bill, Sebastian mounted Sangfroid. Matilda and Patrick looked on, laughing at his strange posture as he searched for the stirrups with his feet whilst holding onto Bill's head.

After straightening his Stetson, Bill tightened the saddle whilst Sebastian sat with a stiffened back, arms fixed, knuckles white, afraid to move.

'Are you okay?' Matilda asked, bringing Carnival alongside Sangfroid, the two horses greeting each other with soft neighing and friendly bows of the head, making Sebastian grab hold of the reins and lock his elbows into his waist, pulling his hands up to his chest. Matilda laughed. 'Relax,' she said, reaching out and lowering his hands to the saddle. 'These horses have beautiful temperaments. They know exactly what they're doing and will just follow each other. Breathe Seb,' she laughed, as he smiled at her, teeth locked.

They moved off and, after covering a bit of ground with Patrick giving snippets of information about the local flora and fauna, Sebastian started to relax and eventually looked up to enjoy the magnificent scenery around him. Patrick and Matilda rode ahead, sharing stories of life on the ranch in comparison to life on the farm, talking about the first Mrs. McCarthy, and the second, about the dogs, Scotland and inevitably, the weather.

'I have never felt heat like this before,' Matilda said, taking a drink from her canteen.

'This is mild. I've seen the mercury hit almost fifty degrees before now. Where were you born, Matilda?'

'On the south coast of England, near Brighton.'

'Which is why you're not as pasty pale as your old man. I always think of the Scots as pale folk.'

'He's not as pale as his brother.'

'Really? His brother must be almost translucent,' Patrick laughed. 'Let's pull up here a while and give Sebastian's backside a rest from the leather. I had Grace make us something light to eat.'

'Perhaps I'll have mine up here,' Sebastian suggested, struggling to move his legs as Matilda and Patrick helped him dismount. He was amazed that anything as beautiful and as smooth as the broad leather saddle could be quite so harsh on his posterior.

Sitting for an hour in the shade of a large rock, Sebastian and Patrick talked over some business. It was obvious there was more than enough common ground between them and clear that the two men liked and trusted each other. Sebastian was hopeful for the future of Tatch-A UK and pleased that he would still have a part to play whilst it was in transition. He believed he could work alongside Patrick and was looking forward to getting back to it, now he'd had some time away.

'Right,' Patrick said, helping Sebastian stand up. 'Now we have put the business world to rights, how are you feeling about getting back on?'

'Ask me tomorrow,' Sebastian laughed, accepting a helping hand.

~

William and Elspeth were enjoying a late lunch of soup and homemade bread topped with thick butter straight from the fridge, when Henry arrived, ready to roll up his sleeves and help Sam out in the shed with the milking. Mealtimes on the farm were seldom regular and today was no exception, as some sheep, heading for freedom, had escaped from the top field. Gone unnoticed, it had taken Sam, Ade and William most of the morning to find them and bring them back.

'Stupid bloody animals!' William grumbled, clearly worn out and hurting after trudging across the fields trying to round them up.

'You should have called me; you need a four-pronged attack when they go wandering.'

'It was as if they had suddenly won gold medals for sprinting, the speed they disappeared.'

'How did they get out?'

'There's a hole in the fence. They'll squeeze through a gap as small as your thumb given half a chance; they've an amazing ability to stretch!' William chuntered.

'I'll fix the fence before I leave. I'm popping home tomorrow morning, remember?' Henry said, dipping his finger into the soup pan keeping warm on the aga.

'Och, o' course, I forgot,' Elspeth said, raising her eyebrows and smiling at Henry as he cut himself a slice of bread and mopped up the last of the soup. 'Ye'll be glad to see Lorna and Lilith.'

'I will, but I've had a great week and it's been really good to be back here with you two.'

'And we've loved having you around, haven't we love?' William said, turning to Elspeth.

'That we have, ye can come and bide back 'ere any time ye lik',' Elspeth said, putting her hand out to Henry as he squeezed past her to fill the kettle.

'Have you heard from Sebastian today?' William asked, dunking a hunk of bread into his soup and dribbling it across the table and down his front before devouring it.

'Och! William!'

'He sent a message when they arrived. It's forty-five degrees out there, apparently.'

'Rather him than me,' William said. 'It's hot enough here as it is.'

'It is,' Henry agreed. 'So, what's for you now the cricket's over?'

'It's the rugby world cup, next.'

'Bloody sport!' Elspeth piped up. 'He'd spend all day sat in th' chair if he could.'

'Not a great deal else I can do with this arm,' William said, smiling knowingly at Henry.

Leaving Panda in her playpen, and his parents to finish their lunch, Henry took a quad bike up to the sheep field and found the gap in the fence through which the sheep had escaped that morning. He mended it before any more of them smelt freedom and ran amok around the village. Returning, he helped Sam in the milking shed. It was hot, smelly work but the cows, used to the routine, steadily clopped through the stalls in turn before being let out into the fresh field. Henry liked to watch them skip and buck as they were released from the confines of the path, into the long pasture, and he liked listening to the sound of them ripping and chomping the new grass. It was rewarding work.

Henry came back into the house, cleaned himself up and changed out of his father's overalls. After a quick cup of tea, with his arms full of scones and cake, and Panda at his heel, he got ready to leave. At the front door Elspeth gave him an unexpected kiss goodbye.

'What was that for?' he asked.

'To take wi' ye.'

'I'll be back in a day or two.'

'Ah know, but it doesn't mean I'll miss ye any less.'

'Softie,' Henry said, smiling. 'Stay there a minute.' Putting the scones and cake carefully on the step, guarding them from Panda's quizzical nose, Henry retrieved his phone from his pocket and took a photograph of his mother standing in the doorway. 'Beautiful,' he said, smiling at her.

'Get away wi' ye!' Elspeth exclaimed, laughing. 'I'll see ye in a day or two.'

Back at Sebastian's, the cinema room beckoned Henry and Panda in and, sitting in the best seats in the house, they ate popcorn and fell asleep in front of 'Lady and the Tramp' before crawling into bed for a few hours. Having promised Lilith he would be with her by midday, they had an early start in the morning.

Minus One

Arriving in Newcastle in time for breakfast, Henry was greeted by an excited Mabel, so excited that she weed over the hall floor, much to Panda's delight, who promptly weed as well sending both dogs skidding as they splashed their way through the house to get to the back garden.

'We've arrived!' Henry called out, careful not to tread dog wee through the house. Lorna appeared from the garden where she had been in her workshop since dawn.

'So you have,' she said, laughing at the chaos before wrapping her arms around Henry's neck and giving him a long kiss. 'It's good to see you,' she whispered in his ear, holding him tightly before pulling away and looking at the hall floor. 'Right, you can mop, whilst I put the kettle on. What time are you due at Lilith's?' she asked, walking into the kitchen.

'Around 12, is that okay?' Henry said, getting the mop out of the hall cupboard.

'Of course. Do you have time for a walk before you go?'

'Definitely. You need to fill me in with your ideas for the set,' he said, rinsing the mop out in the utility sink as he looked out of the back door at the dogs chasing around the small garden, Mabel refusing to let Panda have her favourite squeaky toy.

Walking the dogs, Henry and Lorna talked excitedly about Henry's script and Lorna's innovative ideas for the set design, which was to be the most challenging yet. She and Henry discussed them intensely during the few rushed minutes they had together before Henry needed to leave.

With Lorna's ideas floating around his head, Henry drove into the heart of Leeds where he met Lilith outside her old flat. With help from her flatmates, she had packed up the hired van and was just about to set off to the house she was renting north of the city.

'You're late!' she said, emphasising the words with rounded articulation and soft enunciation.

'By twenty minutes, you ungrateful child!' Henry replied, making sure she was reading his lips. 'I've come from Edinburgh this morning just to help you out.'

'You're still late!'

'And you're still ungrateful!' Henry said smiling, drawing her in for a hug. Like her mother, Lilith was tiny and Henry wrapped his arms around her like he did when she was a child.

'Right, follow me,' she said, wriggling out of his grip.

Lilith had much the same driving style as Henry, and it was all he could do to keep up with her as she ran orange lights and changed lanes without indication. Just about keeping her in his sights, in his half hour dash across the city, Henry thought about Lilith and how he and Lorna would turn the world upside down for her. In spite of his rather unconventional lifestyle, Henry's family were his constant, and no matter what, the happiness of the person he and Lorna had chosen to bring onto this mad planet was paramount. They encouraged her independence and supported her choices, and they paid her way when she could not afford to. Working as a team, they supported her without smothering her, but in her silent world, Lilith was complicated.

Having studied as a classical cellist, she had left the conservatoire that summer and was stepping out into the professional field of music with all the uncertainly it entailed. Determined to remain in Leeds, she was prepared to do whatever she needed in order to pursue her passion. She had a number of concerts in her diary but the pay was poor and she needed to supplement the work so had got herself a few hours cleaning a local office block. It fitted in well; she was finished by 9 a.m. giving her the rest of the day to practice, which she did without fail.

Pulling up behind the parked van on the opposite side of the road to the back-to-back house Lilith had rented, Henry looked up to see his daughter hanging out of the roof window, waving down at him, her long, blonde hair flying around in the wind.

'Helloooo, this is my bedroom,' she cawed.

'Bloody Hell Lil, how did you get here so fast?' But Lilith had disappeared back into the room and, within a flash, she flung open the front door.

'So, this is the new pad?' Henry said slowly as she showed him in and he looked around. 'It looks a nice road,' he added, trying to find something positive to say, 'and you're not far from the shops and the pub.'

'It's cheap, Dad!'

'Good.' He smiled, thinking of his father as he looked out of Lilith's bedroom window at the roof-topped skyline and the Headingley cricket ground floodlights. 'I don't know about you, but I could do with a cup of tea. Are your flatmates in?'

'No, they've gone into town, we need a new toaster and a bin.'

They headed down the narrow staircase that led into the small kitchen in the basement, and talked whilst Lilith put the kettle on and got the cups ready. Sitting waiting for the kettle to boil, Henry could hear voices. The house shared walls with three other properties so it was never quiet, which reminded him of his university days when he went out with a girl who was studying in Edinburgh and lived in similar accommodation. The feeling from all those years ago momentarily filled his thoughts; what a different life he now led. With his short stature, skinny physique and mass of uncontrolled blonde hair, at university Henry had been a free spirit. He never imagined himself being married and settled with a child.

Finishing their tea and having unpacked the van, Henry and Lilith took the short walk onto the high street where they sat in the window of an Italian restaurant eating cheap pizza. As they ate and quietly looked at the people walking along the street, Henry broke the silence.

'So, what's going on?' he asked, tapping Lilith's hand to make her look at him.

With her head down, examining the pizza in front of her and her foot tapping anxiously beneath the table, Lilith raised her eyes to her father's, and having done so well to keep control until then, tears welled up and seeped out, falling helplessly down her cheeks.

'I thought as much,' he said, hating to see her cry, 'what's the matter?'

'I don't know,' she said, shaking her head.

'Is everything okay with Matthew?'

'Yes.'

'Then what is it?' Henry persisted.

'I don't know!' she said again, getting agitated, 'I'm just feeling wobbly. I keep crying all the time.'

'So, is it life that's bothering you?'

'I guess,' she nodded dolefully.

'I know how tough it is Lil. I remember leaving university and being scared shitless. I remember saying 'come on then world, you owe me a living,' until I realised it owed me nothing and I didn't know what I was doing and it was scary. You're going through a lot of change at the moment and it's unsettling,' he said, watching her push her pizza around her plate. 'You'll be fine once you've found your feet.'

'I want to come home.'

'Do you?'

'No.'

'Thank god for that,' Henry said, smiling cheekily at her. 'Although, as you know, there's always a home for you with us no matter what happens, okay?' This was something William and Elspeth had said to Henry when he left home and he had never forgotten the feeling of security it gave him.

Recovered, Lilith carried on eating as Henry told her about his week and how he had managed to lock himself and

Panda in the garage when he was having a sneaky peak at Sebastian's cars. He'd had visions of Sebastian and Matilda returning home from New York to find him and Panda starved to death on the garage floor! Lilith soon found her smile again, and Henry was pleased he had seen her.

By the time he had helped her unpack her cases and had drunk a last cup of tea, the house sparkled with fairy lights and Lilith's room looked cosy and welcoming. It was important to have somewhere familiar to come back to if Lilith was going to cope over the next couple of months. Henry pressed £20 into her hand and hugged her, telling her to enjoy a taxi to work a couple of times in the week. 'Love you, my spirited little creature,' he said, kissing her goodbye before getting into the car.

~

His phone ringing brought Sebastian out of his daydream. He had woken early and worked before Scotland had gone home for the evening. The previous night they all agreed to have a relaxed morning and Sebastian was sitting alone on the veranda with a coffee, gazing out at the horses in the paddock, trying to see if he could spot Sangfroid. He was looking forward to going out on her later to witness the famous Arizona sunset. Matilda was enjoying a swim before she and Sebastian met with Patrick for lunch.

'Hi Niamh, everything okay?' he asked, surprised to see her number.

'I'm sorry to call you, Seb, but I'm wondering when you're back?'

'I'll be back in the office on Friday, why?'

'I think we have a problem.'

'What sort of a problem?' Sebastian asked, suddenly panicking, sitting forward in his seat.

'Graham's asking me questions about the accounts I can't answer.'

'What about the accounts? Why can't he ask Paul?'

Hesitating, Niamh took a deep breath, 'because the questions are *about* Paul,' she replied seriously. 'You need to speak with Graham. I'm really sorry, Seb, I think you need to come back.'

With his stress level immediately raised, Sebastian sat staring at his phone, searching for answers, wondering what had happened in the office to make Niamh call him; she would have done anything to avoid it. There was nothing she did not know about the business, so for her not to be able to answer Graham's questions, he must have found something that had been hidden well before she joined the company, something that appeared to involve Paul, his oldest and closest friend.

Sebastian and Paul had been friends since their first day at grammar school. Both knowing no one else, they had found each other and clung together as they got to grips with the enormity of the place in comparison to the primary schools they had come from. Academically matched, they had been in most of the same classes and joined the same clubs and played in the same football and rugby teams. Outside of school they spent countless hours together at Taligth, playing on their bikes or kicking a ball or getting up to no good in the woods. Their strong friendship extended through their university years when they seldom saw each other, catching up during holidays and snatched weekends and, as they moved into adulthood, they supported each other throughout their changing lives and growing families. Paul had been by Sebastian's side during some difficult times. Sebastian found it hard to comprehend what questions Graham might have asked Niamh that he could not ask Paul. For a moment he considered calling Paul, but something stopped him.

Instead, he telephone Graham to see whether there was an easy answer that might sort the problem quickly before it escalated in his mind. Walking back into the room, he dialled Graham's number. The phone rang out before clicking to the answer machine. '*Fuck*!' he snapped, hurling the phone against the wall, smashing its screen.

'My god, Seb, what on earth..?' Matilda cried, returning from her swim, opening the door and ducking for cover. 'What's that all about?' she asked, picking up the phone and examining it, turning to Sebastian who was sitting on the bed, wracked with tension. 'Are you all right?' she asked.

'Something's happened at the office. We need to get back,' Sebastian panicked.

'What's happened?'

'I don't know, Til!' he snapped.

'Okay, calm down!'

'Don't tell me to *fucking* calm down!'

'Then tell me what's happened!' Matilda said, matching Sebastian's tone. 'You don't just chuck your phone at the wall for no reason.'

'For *fuck's* sake, Til! Niamh has called okay, and I'm trying to think. That's all.'

Matilda stood silently as Sebastian sat on the bed, sifting through his mental filing cabinet, trying to work out what could have happened. The early days of the company were tough for all of them, and they had been stretched. Perhaps there had been some poorly recorded accounts, perhaps some over or under calculation of tax, but nothing he could think of which might concern the likes of Graham.

'Are you calm enough now to tell me what's happened?' Matilda asked coldly.

'Graham has been asking Niamh questions about Paul.'

'Paul? I don't' understand.'

'She didn't say much. She just said I need to speak with Graham, but I've tried to call him, and his *fucking* answer machine picked up.'

'And that's why you threw your phone?'

'Stop it, Matilda!' Sebastian spat in hushed tones, not wanting their conversation shared outside the room.

'Then don't over react!'

Allowing the silence to settle, knowing better than to push, Matilda spoke calmly. 'Would you like me to see if we can get a flight this afternoon?' she asked.

'Yes please,' Sebastian replied, his breathing shallow. 'Sorry, Til, you know what I'm like,' he said, his head in his hands.

'Yes, I do!' Not smiling, Matilda took her phone into the bathroom and out onto the balcony. As she left the room, the smashed screen on Sebastian's phone lit up with Panda's cheeky smile distorted by the fragmented glass. Without thinking, Sebastian grabbed it, cutting his finger as he swiped it open.

'Graham!' he said, his heart pounding.

~

Henry left Lilith's later than expected. The sky was heavy with rain and, mirroring the past few nights in Edinburgh, a thunderstorm followed him home. The torrential rain, sparkling in the headlights, jumped about the motorway like tiny transparent beads, beating on the car in percussive waves, bringing the traffic to a crawl as the lightning flashed in the darkness.

It was 10 p.m. by the time he pulled onto the drive, wide-eyed from concentration. Walking through the door he was immediately greeted by Panda and Mabel and he chased the excited dogs around the kitchen noisily, their whippy tails beating the cupboard doors and Henry's hot pursuit knocking pictures on the walls askew. Lorna restored calm by opening a bottle of wine and insisting he sat down and updated her on Lilith.

Lorna was grateful to him for spending the day with their daughter. Busy working on the set design for Henry's production and, having had a long day juggling doggy day care, she was tired. However, Henry was awake and wanted to talk more about her ideas and insisted she stayed up with him so she could give him something to dream about. In return, she listened to his animated stories about his parents, Taligth, Panda and the little café on the hill near the park and about Lilith's new house.

It was past midnight when Lorna went to bed. Saying he would be right up, Henry got distracted by his script once more, tweaking lines as he added in Lorna's set changes. When he finally crawled into bed, Lorna was fast asleep. Looking across as he carefully slid in beside her, he smiled, watching her fidget in her dreams. Looking at her back, he took one of her long plaits containing her loose, natural curls, in his hand, and felt the softness between his fingers. Lorna had the most beautiful hair. During the day, freed from its bedtime constraints, it was released and pinned into a loose bun. By evening it tumbled down in feathery strands with individual curls around her neck, which was the way Henry liked it most.

When she was concentrating, Lorna was a hair twiddler, which drove Henry to distraction. 'Don't look at me then, it's my hair. I can do what I want with it,' she would protest when he expressed his irritation at her twisting and turning a tortured strand. She struck a deal with him once, that she would stop twiddling if he would stop swearing. The deal didn't last the day.

Relaxing body and mind, thinking about Lorna, Henry drifted off when suddenly the phone at his bedside startled him awake again and it took him a few seconds to realise what was going on. Grabbing the receiver he looked at the clock before looking across at Lorna, who had not stirred.

~

Slowly trekking across the grassland, Sebastian was preoccupied. Having spoken with Graham earlier, he had been left with a lot to think about and although he had calmed down and was now thinking more rationally, he was ruminating. He had been quiet over lunch, and eaten very little and although Matilda had tried to cover up his distraction, it must have been obvious something was troubling him.

He and Graham had spoken at length and arranged to meet as soon as they could, but in the meantime, he felt unnerved by the little information Graham had given him and the enormity of what he was implying.

Graham had a tendency to go around the houses to get to the point. Having taken over Ribeck & Ribeck Ltd from his deceased father ten years earlier, a wealth of experience passed down by generations of Ribecks had taught him that one should put people in the picture before delivering the news. Today had been no exception and Sebastian knew he had to be ready to listen.

Clearing his throat, speaking articulately and deliberately, Graham started. 'I have a query,' he said. 'In fact, I have a number of queries, but we will start with just one. The others can wait until your return.'

'Right,' Sebastian said, perturbed.

'As you are well aware, my primary function is to provide you with a robust, balanced and independent financial report.'

'Yes, Graham, I know.'

'The report I write needs to give you the information you will require in order to be confident that formal due diligence will enable you to proceed with the sale of Tatch-A UK.'

'Right.'

'Part of the process...'

'For god's sake, Graham,' Sebastian interrupted.

'Part of the process,' Graham repeated, 'is that should any issues arise, you and I must be able to have open and frank conversations and jointly decide how to proceed.'

'What's this all about, Graham?'

'My job is to tell Tatch-A UK's story from a financial perspective; from the beginning of the business, including historical trading, management and forecasts, to the present day. No stone should be left unturned, should it, Sebastian?'

'No, no it shouldn't,' Sebastian agreed, feeling they were about to hit an iceberg.

'Whilst you've been away,' Graham continued, 'I've spent the majority of my time with Paul.' Graham's tone alerted Sebastian to danger. 'Paul and I have been going through a number of things, some of which I know you have already looked at yourself because I can see your hallmark all over them; your work is top quality, Sebastian, but...' Graham paused. Sebastian panicked. This was it. The Titanic was going down. '*Without* Paul, I have been looking into Tatch-A UK's historical accounts, and a number of anomalies have come to my attention, and...' just get on with it, Sebastian silently pleaded, '...I am unable to find anything about one of your employees, and it's perplexing me. Do you know someone called Patricia Martin?' Graham asked.

Not expecting the question, Sebastian hesitated. 'No,' he replied quickly, 'I mean, yes, but she's not an employee.'

'Does she not work for you?'

'No, why?'

'Has she *ever* worked for you?'

'No! What's this about, Graham?' Sebastian asked, getting agitated.

'Hopefully, you will be able to settle my concerns by telling me you know about this and will be able to explain it to me. Why, if Patricia Martin does not, and never has worked for you, does she appear on your payroll?'

Shocked, Sebastian's mind went blank. Paul's wife, Trish, had been as much a friend to him as had Paul over the years, and to hear her name out of context threw him. 'I have absolutely no idea,' he confirmed.

'I feared that might be the case.'

'You know who Trish Martin is?' Sebastian asked.

'I had an idea, but one cannot presume these things.'

'Have you spoken with Paul?'

'No. That would not have been appropriate. After speaking with Niamh, I knew I needed to speak with you directly. I will explain in greater detail when I see you but for now, I have all I need to continue.'

Graham had not wanted to get into a lengthy discussion over the telephone, but had now got enough information without the need for Sebastian to rush back early, which was just as well as there were no available flights.

'Is everything all right?' Patrick asked, dropping Stalwart back to walk alongside Sangfroid, leaving Matilda and Carnival to take the lead. 'You don't seem quite yourself. Is there anything I can help with?'

Despite not knowing fully what was going on, Sebastian felt compelled to tell Patrick he was concerned. He had promised himself he would be transparent, and it was better to say something now than for Patrick to find out later.

'I had a call from Graham Ribeck this morning.'

'Has he come across a problem?'

'It looks like he might have. He wouldn't elaborate over the telephone, he's rather old school and prefers to talk face to face, so I'll have a better idea when I get back.'

'I like the sound of Graham, I admire old school, it's thorough. Are you concerned about what he might have discovered?'

'A little, yes.'

'Isn't that why you've brought him in, to check for and sort out any discrepancies?'

'Of course, but I suppose I was hoping there wouldn't be any.'

'I have bought and sold a number of companies in my time and not one sale or purchase has gone according to plan. Every business has idiosyncrasies, Sebastian. It wouldn't be normal if it didn't. Now stop worrying. There is nothing you can do until you are back in the office. I have every confidence you will be able to sort out whatever it is, and I won't need to know about it, though I might want to if it's interesting,' he said continuing to smile. 'Now, let's enjoy this beautiful day and the amazing picture show you are about to witness.'

Day One

Newcastle – Early hours Thursday.
Arizona – Late afternoon Wednesday.

'Hello?' Henry said, answering the phone.

'Is that ye Henry?' the familiar voice asked.

'Yes, who is this?' Henry asked, swinging his legs out of bed, unable to place who was on the other end of the line in the middle of the night.

'It's Dougie McGregor, Henry. I'm sorry to wake ye but I'm at Taligth.'

Henry's heart quickened. Standing, he fumbled in the darkness for his dressing gown. 'Taligth?' he questioned, trying to get his eyes to focus, 'what's happened?' The silence on the line screamed out. 'Dougie?'

'I'm really sorry, Henry, there's no easy way to say this; yer ma's collapsed this evening.'

'Mum?' Henry asked, panic flooding his senses as he walked out of the bedroom, closing the door behind him. Holding his breath, Henry feared what he was about to hear.

'I'm really sorry...' The phone stopped breathing as Dougie tried to speak. 'She died, Henry,' he whispered, his voice breaking.

Unable to catch his breath, Henry felt the walls close in around him. 'Died?' he said, his throat constricting. 'What happened?' he asked, sitting at the top of the stairs with Panda and Mabel quietly behind the gate at the bottom, looking up with furrowed brows, at their stunned human.

'Ah dinnae know much. I'm so sorry, Henry,' Dougie said sorrowfully.

'She was all right yesterday; I spoke to her. I don't understand.'

'Would ye lik' to speak wi' yer da?'

117

He could hear Dougie take a deep breath as he passed the phone to William.

'Henry.'

'Dad.'

'I'm so sorry, son,' William said pitifully.

'What are you sorry for, Dad?'

'I should have known she wasn't right.'

'How could you have known?'

'Because she's my girl,' William said, his voice weak.

'Can you tell me what happened?' Henry asked.

~

Glad that he had spoken with Patrick, Sebastian enjoyed the rest of the trek without going over his conversation with Graham again. Now that he was more used to it, he found trekking on the back of Sangfroid liberating. He liked being on his own with the controlled, steady movement of the horse beneath him, her body dipping and rising with the uneven terrain. Looking around at the land from on high, he could see the heat quivering above the dusty plain and the waves of grasses swaying in the late afternoon wind.

In Tucson, at this time of year, the temperature across the desert went from hot to hotter and back again, and there was little respite from its intensity even when riding towards the mountains. After the first day, they had adjusted to it a little, though it had not stopped a pool of sweat sitting at the base of Sebastian's spine. Looking ahead at Matilda, he could see her skin glistening and tight curls of hair sitting in the nape of her neck.

Heading the horses up the saguaro-dotted hills, they came upon a view of the vast sprawling landscape and of the mountain ranges in the distance.

'We'll stop here,' Patrick said. 'This is where the magic happens.'

Dismounting, and walking the horses a few steps towards a huge rock, they sat on the best seats in the house in anticipation of that moment between day and night which initiated a heart-stopping lightshow of golden fire and deep red embers sweeping across the mountain tops where the earth and sky meet.

The land had taken on an unearthly hue and the wind had died down to a soft, gentle breeze, and for a few minutes they were transported into the spirit of a perfect place, suspended in their own silence, savouring the tranquility as the plethora of small desert creatures and nightjars began their sunset calls.

Unaware of his phone vibrating silently in his pocket, Sebastian was somewhere far away. In his imagination, he was close to paradise. But his phone persisted until it brought him back to earth and got his attention and, trying not to break the magic, he took it from his pocket and looked at the screen. It was Henry. For a second he considered not answering.

'Henry!' he whispered into the phone, 'we're watching the most amazing sunset on the planet; such incredible colours I can't begin to...'

'Seb!' The emotionless sound of Henry's voice made Sebastian stop.

'Are you okay?' he asked, looking at his watch, suddenly realising the time back home.

'No,' Henry said trying hard to stay composed. 'I'm sorry, Seb... it's bad news.'

Standing up, walking away from the rock and from Patrick and Matilda who were wondering why Henry would be calling in the middle of the night, Sebastian listened as Henry told him.

Letting out a harrowing, primeval cry, Sebastian's wretchedness filled the darkening sky.

Matilda stood to go to him, but Patrick reached out and touched her arm and she stopped for a moment as Sebastian curled into a ball listening to the night crickets and to Henry telling him what had happened...

It had been a good day on the farm, and other than his shoulder playing up, William had spent the afternoon watching the rugby and Elspeth had done some baking. At teatime, they'd enjoyed a hearty meal of roast chicken and vegetables, and Elspeth had cleared away whilst William went out to check on Betsy. It had been another warm day and Elspeth had been feeling tired, much as she had over the past few months; the heat taking it out of her.

At 9.30 p.m. William decided to turn in early. His shoulder was sore and he wanted to rest it in a more comfortable position. Elspeth still had a few chores to do and chose to stay up for a while and read a few pages of her book. William kissed her goodnight before heading up.

Then, at around 11.30 p.m. William was woken by the pain in his shoulder. He couldn't get comfortable so he got up to get some painkillers from the kitchen. When he saw that Elspeth had not yet come to bed, he assumed she had slept in one of the other bedrooms, which she occasionally did.

Coming downstairs, noticing the light was still on in the living room, William thought Elspeth must have forgotten to turn it off, so he went in and noticed her asleep on the sofa with her book across her chest. She looked so peaceful, he did not want to disturb her and so he took a blanket from the box and, with care, placed it over her. Taking her book gently out of her hands, his hand brushed against hers. It was cold...

Sebastian could not speak.

Henry struggled on. 'Dad called Dougie, and Dougie called 999 and the paramedics came very quickly, apparently. They did everything they could, Seb, but it was too late.'

The phone line went quiet as the news travelled the five thousand miles that gulfed between the brothers.

'Where is she now?' Sebastian whispered as Matilda went to him.

'She's still at Taligth. Dougie's called the undertaker.'

'Angus Stewart?'

'Yes.'

'What time is it?'

'2 a.m. I'm in Newcastle. I'm going to head off in a minute.'

'I feel a million miles away.'

'I know. Dad told me not to set off until it was light, but I want to get back.'

'I'll get home as soon as I can. Go carefully, Hal.'

~

Back at Taligth, William did not speak as Dougie encouraged him to leave the room where he had shared so many happy times with Elspeth. William did not like the idea of her being on her own, but did not want to stay and watch her spirit leave, if it had not already done so. He had known she was dead as soon as he had touched her skin, and one look at her face told him she was no longer with him. It was as if she had been spirited away by fairies. The paramedics had been very kind and had done everything they could, but everyone in the room that night knew it would be to no avail.

~

Slowly, Sebastian stood up. Matilda held him in her arms, listening to his heartbreaking news. Patrick tightened the saddles on the horses waiting to guide them back.

~

Walking downstairs, Henry was greeted by Mabel and Panda who leapt to their feet in excitement. Mabel, unable to hold back, barked loudly, filling the house with her deep voice and, as Henry sat hunched on the bottom step holding the two dogs close, burying his face into their soft fur, the bedroom door opened and Lorna looked out. 'Henry?' she said quietly. She didn't get a response.

Sensing something was wrong, she pulled on her dressing gown and, tying it around her tiny frame, cautiously crept down towards him. Panda was curled on his lap and Mabel was sitting dutifully by his leg. 'Henry?' she said again, inching closer. Not noticing her, Henry did not move even when she squeezed past and Lorna could see something was terribly wrong. 'Henry, what's the matter?' she asked again, now standing on the hall floor in front of him. 'What's happened?' With her blood running cold, she took his face gently in her hands and forced him to look up at her. 'What's happened, Hal? You're frightening me,' she said, looking into his eyes, searching his sadness. 'Is it Lilith?' she asked, trying to guess what could have drawn Henry out of their bed so early in the morning. What could be so bad?

More or less inaudible, he told Lorna that a few hours earlier his mother had died.

Stunned, it took a moment for her to take in what he had said. Without saying anything she crouched down in front of her husband and took him into her arms. As she held him, she was transported back to the time her father turned up at her college flat to tell her of her own mother's death. Lorna could still remember the crushing pain she felt as he stood on the doorstep, looking at her, telling her without compassion or care. He had left her mother years before so that he could live a single life with whomever he chose. Lorna had loved her mother and, as an adult, she acknowledged the gaps in her parents' relationship, promising herself she would not follow the same path. The pain of losing her mother was made all the worse by her father's indifference. As an only child, Lorna had had no one with whom to share her sorrow.

Lorna coaxed Henry back upstairs.

'We need to tell Lilith,' Henry said, gathering his clothes, 'we can't just message her.'

'I'll go to Leeds first thing,' Lorna said softly, watching Henry get dressed. Having not unpacked, he was ready to head back to Scotland within minutes.

After kissing Lorna goodbye, Henry got into the car and secured Panda into the seat next to him.

'Drive carefully,' Lorna whispered before giving Henry a final kiss and retreating to the doorstep.

Unaware of Henry's sadness, Panda looked across, 'smiling' at him as he reversed off the drive. Lorna and Mabel stood, watching them go. After the earlier storm, it was a cloudless night.

~

The ride back to the ranch was quiet, the sombre mood amplifying the sounds of the evening chorus as all living things prepared for night.

Numb, Sebastian relied on Sangfroid to sense the feel of the earth beneath her feet as darkness descended. He was glad no one could see the turmoil in his head.

~

With little traffic, the A1 led Henry back to Taligth. It was 4.45 a.m. when he arrived. The gates were open and the undertaker's van was parked outside the front door. It felt so out of place and Henry's first thought as he rattled across the cattle grid was that his mother would not be happy about it being there. For a few minutes, he sat looking at the house in which he had grown up. It looked the same on the outside as it had when he'd left it last, but on the inside he knew everything had changed. He put his head in his hands not noticing Dougie who had come down the steps and approached the car, opening the door. Dougie crouched down to his friend.

'What on earth's happened Dougie?'

'T'was her heart, Hal. She went peacefully, one minute there, th' next gone. No struggle 'n' no pain.'

'Can you be sure?'

'Th' paramedics told me 'n' yer da. They said it looked lik' her heart just stopped beating 'n' she fell asleep.'

'I hope so.'

'C'moan, yer da will be glad ye'r 'ere,' Dougie said.

Followed by Panda, the two friends walked towards the heavy oak front door, the door that had witnessed so many happy family events. It was the door before which they had stood together to have their photographs taken on the first days of school, and graduation days; it was where they had smiled for a camera on their wedding days, it was here they had celebrated the arrival of a grandchild or a puppy, and it was outside this door that Henry had taken the last photograph of his mother, a couple of days before.

Stopping, Henry looked at the door. It had gone silver over time. The strong frame, now scarred by deep splits, had warped as it swelled and shrunk with the seasons, releasing some of its strength with each year that passed. Roses that his mother had planted, now past their best and preparing for winter's sleep, surrounded it.

'How's Dad doing?' Henry asked, walking slowly up the steps.

'He's not saying much; he's in shock.'

A little before Henry's arrival, the undertakers had come to take Elspeth's body to the mortuary. Dougie had made some tea and the kitchen was silent when Henry entered. William acknowledged his presence but did not say anything as Henry went to him. The undertaker and his colleague left the kitchen silently and went into the front room where Elspeth lay in order to prepare her for the journey.

Watching his mother go was the saddest thing Henry had ever witnessed. He could not believe this wonderful woman he had loved all his life was leaving them and the house she had grown up in, never to walk back through its door again.

As the sun rose, Dougie said his goodbyes, leaving Henry and William to go back into the house alone.

William would be forever grateful to Dougie.

~

Arriving back at the ranch, Sebastian and Matilda packed their bags in silence while Patrick prepared his plane, waiting to take them to Phoenix airport. Without hesitation, he had called ahead and organised a private jet to take them back to New York, where, by luck, there was already an aircraft preparing to make an empty-leg flight back to the UK. Pulling some strings, Patrick arranged for it to return to Edinburgh. It could take them overnight across the Atlantic, getting them home by mid-morning.

Before leaving, Sebastian had gone to the paddock and given Sangfroid an apple, thanking her for her sweet nature, patience and understanding. She had cured his fear of horses.

'I can't thank you enough, Patrick,' Sebastian said flatly as they prepared to leave Arizona.

'There's no need for thanks, just get yourselves home. I know what you are going through. If you need me, please call,' Patrick said as the two men shook hands. Sebastian and Matilda boarded the plane and waved as they taxied along the runway. Patrick had said very little but shown a great deal of kindness and compassion, consciously leaving Sebastian and Matilda to themselves. He had known how Sebastian was feeling as he, himself, had been embroiled in the biggest business deal of his career when he had received the devastating news of his parents' deaths. They had been in New York on the morning of September 11th 2001.

Both flights were long and tiring and they were relieved to arrive in Edinburgh. While Matilda returned home in a taxi, Sebastian hired a car at the airport and drove straight to Taligth. With Henry meeting him at the door, they walked through the kitchen into the yard where William, with his back to them, was sitting looking out into their small back garden towards the secret hiding places of childish games and Easter egg hunts. The bushes had been their hideout when the children were small. Wrapped in blankets, they had sat there with Elspeth as she made up stories about the magical creatures that lived in the roots of the trees. Other than Nancy, they had all believed in fairies.

Hearing Sebastian's voice, William turned. He looked shattered and pale. 'Hello son,' he said weakly as Sebastian hugged him and the three men sat in the yard, in silence, knowing there was nothing any of them could say. William continued to stare out.

'Would you like a cup of tea?' Henry asked.

'Yes please,' Sebastian said, following him into the kitchen. 'How's he doing?' he asked quietly.

'He's knackered, he's not slept,' Henry said, filling the kettle and putting it on the aga whilst Sebastian warmed the teapot. 'How are *you* doing?'

'I don't know. What about you?'

'I just feel numb,' Henry replied sadly. 'I've started on a list of things we need to do. Angus talked me through some of it last night, but I wasn't listening properly.'

On the flights home, unable to sleep, Sebastian had also made a list: a list of people who needed contacting. The one name that came sharply into focus was Nancy's and it was playing on his mind.

They took the tea out to William. They talked, between long silences, about what happened, trying to piece together the clues, trying to understand, and they talked about what was to come, although William did not want to think about that. He wanted the world to stop turning so that he could steady himself and make sense of the pool of space that had appeared in his mind. He was quiet but occasionally allowed his thoughts to surface. 'Why didn't I check on her?' he asked, looking blankly out towards the garden. He was not looking for answers. He was doing as both his sons were, checking himself against the power of hindsight.

Eventually the quiet, sporadic conversation turned to Elspeth's funeral and, inevitably, to Nancy. 'We should find her,' William stated. 'Your mother has an address somewhere, though it'll be years out of date I expect.' He paused, looking at Sebastian and Henry's expressions. 'She has a right to know.'

'Does she?' Sebastian asked brusquely. 'Does she Dad, really, after what she did to you and Mum?' he said, pausing for a moment, thinking. 'I didn't know you had an address for her. Since when?'

William sighed heavily. He was not prepared for a fight.

'Seb!' Henry interjected, looking at his brother. He was used to Sebastian's reaction upon hearing Nancy's name but today it was harsh and unnecessary.

Henry was sixteen when Nancy left and the events of that day were etched on his memory. Despite asking at the time, no one had ever given him a reason for her sudden departure. They had all shrugged their shoulders and looked away, and said 'she'll be back', but she never did come back. Not as far as Henry knew. He and Nancy cared little for each other.

Over the years, she had come up in conversation, but when Sebastian was around none of them dared utter her name, yet he was the one Nancy had loved the most, until one day she had stopped, packed her bags and left. She had left him, her parents and Taligth, and until now, Sebastian believed none of them had heard from her since. For his mother to have an address for her made him wonder whether she had been in touch.

'What do you think, Henry?' William asked.

Sebastian shot his brother a look.

What do I think? Henry thought, looking from one to another. You want to know what I think? I'll tell you what I think. I think our world has just fallen apart and even when we are in pain Nancy manages to chisel her way in. That can't be right. How can someone who caused such enormous damage thirty-two years ago still have a hold on this family? Why do we continue to let her control us? I wish I had her power, I'd *fucking* bottle it and sell it, that's what I think! But he remained silent choosing not to say the words aloud; instead, knotted by grief, he sat looking at his father and shrugged, unhelpfully.

Unknown to Sebastian and Henry, for a brief time, William and Elspeth had been in contact with Nancy through someone they once trusted and loved. But for the past twenty-three years there had been nothing.

~

Nancy was difficult from the day she was born, prematurely in the front room of William's grandparents' house. She was tiny and not expected to survive but she defied the odds and became known as the 'little one'. She was born small and stayed small until she hit puberty, then she grew, but was not much taller than Elspeth.

At the age of eight, she was the height of a five year old and hated it. She hated being referred to as the 'little one'; she hated people's surprise when told her age. 'Oh, goodness,' they would say, 'isn't she tiny? We thought she must be a lot younger than that,' as if Elspeth were lying. 'She'll grow,' they would say and Nancy would think, 'as if you would know!'

She was an unusual looking child with dark hair that would go darker when she was older and which she would come to despise. Her sparse, dark, auburn tipped eyelashes framed her vivid amber eyes. She was the only one in the family to have eyes that colour and they were oddly compelling to look at.

Elspeth preferred to keep Nancy's hair long, so at five, as soon as had mastered scissors, Nancy cut it all off, so short Elspeth was unable to enjoy the pleasure of ribbons and bows. When she was old enough and had a little money, she bleached and dyed it a myriad of colours, though by this time William and Elspeth had come to expect such things and did not react the way Nancy might have hoped they would. When she was older, she upped her game with numerous piercings and two large tattoos. William and Elspeth declined to comment but were saddened she should mutilate herself in such a permanent way.

When Nancy was four years old, Sebastian was born and from the moment she saw him, she *adored* him. He was the first human she had known who was smaller than her and she bonded with him well before Elspeth did. Elspeth was especially tired after Sebastian's birth and, along with working on the farm, lent heavily on Nancy. Seeing the positive impact Sebastian had, Elspeth eagerly involved her, and Nancy enjoyed her elevated position. She was tasked with fetching and carrying and, when allowed, feeding. She would choose his clothes and brush his soft hair and pretend he was her own baby and talk and coo like a mother would. She had never been one for dolls; they were too static and did not respond other than to get bunged up with pretend food and to wee all over the carpet. To Nancy, Sebastian was her doll; he did everything she wanted her plastic dolls to do and more. He was perfect.

When he was strong enough to sit up, she sat at the plug end of the bath so the hot tap didn't scold his back. She shared her toys and her books and fed him ice cream on a plastic spoon when the weather was warm. When he was ill with croup, she was so scared he was going to die, she sat with Elspeth all night, watching him, her hand resting gently on his chest, feeling him breathe. She loved her little brother more than anyone. He was her baby and when, on his first birthday he let go of the sofa and toddled across to her, rather than her heavily pregnant mother, her heart skipped a beat and she clutched hold of him, determined never to let him go. She had bought him a little red car for his first birthday. She and her father had gone to the shops together and she had taken ages searching the shelves for just the right one, a red car with rubber wheels and doors that opened. Sebastian loved the little car and played with it every day. It had been his best present that birthday.

Six weeks after Sebastian's first birthday, Henry was born. With a few days more than thirteen months between them, Nancy found the collective attention the boys received from Elspeth difficult, and she felt a thread snap between her and Sebastian. Over time, like in quicksand, the more she tried to claw back what had been between her and Sebastian before Henry was born, the more it got further away until eventually it was out of sight and the damage was irreparable. Once Henry arrived, the little red car was abandoned, lost amongst all the other toys as they were gathered into the basket after a day's play.

Nancy's feeling of rejection came to a head a week after Henry arrived home from the hospital. As they had for the days proceeding, the brothers lay together in Sebastian's cot. Nancy stood behind her parents' legs as they showed the boys off to friends who cooed and marvelled at their two tiny creations. Nancy was small and could not see the babies. Nobody lifted her up to join in. She stood, all five years of her, and held onto Elspeth's leg and was ignored. It was minutes, but to her it felt like forever; enough time to cement the feeling of despair and misery that would plague her childhood.

As she stood holding Elspeth's bare leg, Nancy dug a jagged edge of one of her nails into the soft, smooth flesh on the inside of her thigh, dragging it quickly down. Elspeth shrieked in pain and pushed Nancy away from her. In shock, she stood and stared at the child, trying to fathom why she would do such a thing. Elspeth, followed by William and their friends, went into the kitchen to examine the wound, leaving Nancy alone in the front room with the now crying babies. Nancy went up to the cot, now able to see her brothers lying side by side for the first time. Reaching in, she drew the jagged edge of her nail across Henry's face from top left of forehead to bottom right of jowl, narrowly missing his right eye. There was a moment, as the baby, red faced and angry, holding his breath, drew in his legs before flinging them out with an ear piercing cry indicating pain of such intensity it brought his parents running back to the cot.

For a second, in horror, they stood looking. Nancy remained perfectly still avoiding eye contact, rounding the sharp nail with her teeth. It was from that moment Elspeth felt disconnected from Nancy and, for the first time, she and William argued about Nancy's strange behaviour. Elspeth had seen it many times already, but William had failed to notice or chosen not to acknowledge that the little girl they had brought into their lives did not behave like a normal five year old. Although it would fade, the scar would be carried by Henry for life and, from that day on, Elspeth vowed to protect him. She never relied on Nancy again, longing for the August day when she would start school.

The detachment anxiety Nancy felt leaving the house for school was not from her mother; for she had grown to resent her mother, but from her 'baby'. She became difficult to control both at home and in the classroom, refusing to engage with the other children and becoming indifferent. She could not understand why they wouldn't listen to her when she talked about Sebastian and how she felt when she was parted from him. She would be purposefully obstreperous in the classroom resulting in her being kept in at playtime, which enabled her to spill her heart out to the teacher, or anyone else who would listen.

When she was collected in the afternoon, her teachers would speak with Elspeth about what Nancy had been up to. Exhausted by her behaviour, all Elspeth could do was shrug and say, 'what tae do? We've tried everythin'.' She would look to the teachers for guidance, and although the promise of help was made, it never materialised and as Nancy progressed up the school years, her behaviour worsened.

Elspeth struggled with her feelings towards Nancy so much so that she had to make a conscious effort to spend time with her. She would organise for William to look after the boys while she and Nancy went to the toyshop. But Nancy did not want to go to the toyshop with her mother and choose a dress for her doll, her unresponsive doll that weed down its own legs and got so bunged up with food that one day the only way to cure it was to drown it in the bath before decapitating it. Nancy had found the act of pulling off its head, arms and legs unnervingly pleasurable. She did not cry when it couldn't be mended and was glad when her mother unceremoniously placed the mutilated corpse in the bin.

Nancy was not like other children. She did not want to go to ballet lessons or Brownies when her brother was at home playing with Henry. She resented Henry and her mother, and blamed them for everything that had changed in her life since Henry arrived. Whenever anything bad happened, Nancy would point the finger of blame squarely in Henry's direction. For a quiet life, he would capitulate, and even though Elspeth knew the truth, neither of them wanted to experience the consequences of disagreeing with Nancy. This only served to fuel Nancy's intolerable behaviour further and, as she got older, the disdain she felt towards Henry and her mother grew. If either of them came into the room, she would leave. If they sat at the dinner table, she would turn away. To Nancy, Henry and her mother were the cause of her despair.

During her childhood she had been presented in front of many clinicians, all trying to explain why it was she behaved the way she did. Why she refused to eat for days on end and then, after so much abstinence, gorge herself on Henry's dinner. Snatching his plate and stuffing the food into her mouth, chewing it before opening up and showing him the contents, then regurgitating it onto his plate and giving it back to him.

They had no explanation for why she pulled the rubber wheels off the little red car she had given to Sebastian, which Henry loved to play with the most. She ruined it by snapping the doors off and cutting its wheels up into tiny pieces so that he could no longer enjoy it. He had cried for days for that little car. Sebastian had given it to him, it was his favourite, and now it was gone. He did not understand.

The clinicians could not explain why she had scratched the passenger side of her mother's car from boot to bonnet, with the end of her coat zip, as she left for school one day and, returning, do the same to the driver's side. No one could understand why she took the family photographs and cut Henry and Elspeth out of every one of them, or why, when she was older, she stole Elspeth's jewellery, the little there was of it, and sold it. She had plenty of money given to her by William, but she stole from Elspeth's purse.

As she grew up, the gap between them became more noticeable and Nancy became harder to connect with. Unlike Sebastian and Henry, who, although reasonably bright, had to work hard at school, Nancy was naturally gifted. She seemingly only had to brush past a book and the knowledge was soaked up, but she refused to apply herself to her schoolwork and so, when the time came, she did not progress to the girls' high school, where she would have thrived. Instead, she went to the local school where she could easily outsmart the majority of her peers, making her geekish and unfashionable. She would watch the high school bus pass the end of her road and she learned to feel contempt for those poor girls forced through the exam system like sausages forced into their skins, one after the other, after the other; a production line of intelligent but stupid sausages.

Convinced she did not wish to become a product of the education system and firm in the belief that she would not fit in with the sort of girls who passed their entrance exams, she decided not to apply herself, which gave her a sense of freedom from the constraints of societal expectation. Having not turned up for most of her exams, she left school with few qualifications. She enjoyed art so had applied herself and got the predicted 'A'. She also got an 'A' in English literature, books having been her comfort after Henry was born, and an 'A' in biology, her doll experience providing her with a fascination for the human body. But she saw little point in knowing about the kings and queens of England, or the geography of the Scottish moorlands, or how to say 'this is my dog' in German, so she didn't bother turning up for any other exams.

Desperate to get away from Taligth, Nancy took a place at the local college on a child psychology course. She hated every minute of it, but Sebastian was at the grammar school and, as she was in the middle of town, she would meet him at the end of the day and go home with him and his friend, Paul, on the bus. Sebastian was happy enough, as was Paul who grew infatuated by his best friend's older sister, fantasising about what it would be like to kiss her. Paul loved hearing her stories of rebellion and listening to her going on about how she felt misunderstood and marginalised. In her second year, much to Paul's disappointment, Nancy no longer joined them on the bus home. She stayed in town until late and got an evening job in one of the less reputable public houses, making friends with an undesirable group of people. She blamed her mother for pushing her away and Elspeth did little to persuade her to stay around. Although terribly sad, Elspeth conceded that, despite trying, she had done her best but she just wasn't a good enough mother.

The one good thing to come out of the torment William and Elspeth went through with Nancy was their relationship with Sebastian and Henry. They were desperate to make sure the poison Nancy dripped onto the family did not harm the boys and Henry in particular, for he seemed the major target of Nancy's venom.

The day Nancy packed her bags and left was the day she vowed she would never return to Taligth or set eyes on any of them again, especially Sebastian, whom she had loved more than anything in the world.

~

Elbows on his knees, burying his head in his hands, Sebastian ran his fingers through his hair. Then, lowering his hands and looking out onto the garden, towards his father's distant gaze, he spoke. 'Do you really want Nancy at Mum's funeral, Dad?' he asked calmly, *'really* want her there? Think about it. We've not seen her for years; we don't even know where she is. Although the address you say you have could be a start.'

William did not turn to look at Sebastian but answered as if drained of the ability to think. 'I suppose not,' he sighed.

Sebastian paused for a long time, thinking hard about what he was going to say next. 'I will not go to Mum's funeral if there is any chance of Nancy being there,' he announced.

So that was it. Sebastian's words were final; the decision had been made. Neither William nor Henry could countenance the idea that Sebastian would not be at his mother's funeral so had no choice other than to agree with him. Nancy would not be found, not now at least. How William was going to live with that decision, he would not know. He was already living with over fifty years' worth of decisions, some good, some bad and some for a quiet life — those were the ones he would regret the most.

Eventually, after a long, awkward silence, it was Henry who broke Sebastian's introspection. 'I think we need to start letting people know,' he said, clearing his throat.

'Your mum told me she wanted to be buried,' William interrupted sharply, 'or do you have a different opinion on that too, Sebastian?'

'Dad!' Henry said softly, trying to calm his father. Sebastian stood up and walked over to Panda, picking her up, plucking strands of straw from her black curls.

'I don't want to go,' William said quietly.

'No one wants to go,' Henry said, as the image of his mother, lying in the mortuary waiting for them, seized his misery. He felt so unbearably sad.

Unable to comfort him, William looked at his younger son. He loved him - he loved them both. 'Sorry,' he said catching Sebastian's eye. He was thankful to have them there.

'We're all tired,' Sebastian said. 'Perhaps we should talk about it tomorrow; there's nothing we can do today. I'll contact Angus in the morning.'

'You'll need her papers,' William mumbled, remembering the aftermath of his own parents' passing. 'Everything you'll need is in your grandfather's leather document case on top of our wardrobe.'

Relieving himself of the tension in the yard, Sebastian located the document case and sat in the kitchen looking through it as Henry made yet more tea.

Thanks to William and Elspeth's fastidiousness, everything they needed was in the case, plus things Sebastian and Henry had not seen for years. Pulling out a delicate piece of paper, and carefully unfolding it, Sebastian read the telegram sent to his grandmother when his grandfather had gone missing in action somewhere over France. There were cuttings from the local paper dating back to when they were children. There were countless reviews and shocking pictures of productions in which Henry had appeared and, poignantly, the most recent, carefully put in its rightful place, from his Paris production.

Following the events of the past weeks, Sebastian had not had time to properly catch up with Henry and find out how Paris had gone but, reading the reviews, he learned that Henry's 'dexterous, obscure drama' had made a good impression and Paris looked forward to watching what this 'insightful, young writer would next bring to the stage'. Sebastian laughed and looked at Henry.

'What?' Henry asked.

'Insightful' I'd agree with, but 'young'? They didn't actually meet you then, the reviewer?'

'No,' Henry said contritely, 'and I may have been a little evasive when asked my age. They want fresh blood.'

As Sebastian got to the bottom of the case, he came across an envelope labelled 'Nancy's birth certificate - duplicate'. As he held it, he felt the umbilicus pull towards his mother. No matter how much he had blocked his sister out of his own life, for his parents she was still a part of theirs, and if ever in doubt, the paper between his fingers was proof. 'You do understand why I don't want Nancy at Mum's funeral don't you, Dad?' he asked, going out into the yard.

'I would like to know whether things worked out for her,' William replied, 'but perhaps your mother's funeral is not the best place to find out. So, God forgive me for saying this, but it's probably best she doesn't know, yet. Perhaps after the funeral you can try to get a message to her.'

'Of course,' Sebastian said as he turned to go back into the kitchen.

Returning the envelope into the bottom of the case where he had found it, Sebastian confirmed silently to himself that he had no intention of contacting Nancy.

By now the September sun had dipped and the chill of autumn tiptoed in. It was time to go back into the house, leaving the farm in Sam and Ade's safe hands. Going into the kitchen Elspeth was everywhere, in every corner, papered into every wall, and on the table was her book, accompanied by her last bake, scones that sat, untouched.

Taking the document case with him, Sebastian left for the night. It had been a long day and he and Panda needed to go home. He would be back tomorrow and every day after.

Having spoken with Graham as they flew back into the country, he had explained his situation. It was important for them to get together as soon as possible so they agreed to meet early the next morning, allowing Sebastian time to get back to Taligth for the rest of the day.

As he walked down the drive, he turned and looked back at Henry and his father who were standing on the doorstep watching him leave. He was grateful they had each other. Once in the car, out of their view, he wept.

Following their supper of soup and bread, William went to bed early. He had not slept the night before, and with his shoulder giving him little respite, he was exhausted. As he passed, he patted Henry's arm. No words were needed.

Henry cleared the kitchen and set the dishwasher running. Before going to his room, he telephoned Lorna to find out how she had got on with Lilith. Lilith was sad and had cried but she didn't want to come home, which gave Henry one less thing to worry about.

Heading to his childhood bedroom, Henry checked in on William and was pleased to see he was asleep. Hopefully, dreams would not wake him.

~

Sebastian took Panda into the garden for a late walk along the river. Looking out into the darkness he thought of his mother and the enormity of his loss. 'My mum's dead,' he whispered to himself, trying to believe what he knew to be true. He was drained and stayed sitting in the long, riverside grass, until the night mist settled on his hair. Dragging himself to his feet, he and Panda trudged back to the house. Matilda met him at the door and took him into her arms. He looked dreadful. He needed to sleep.

Day Two

Daylight filtered into the room and Henry awoke, for a second forgetting what had happened. Peace did not last long before the pain of grief gripped him once more.

He forced himself out of bed and looked out of the window across to the fields where the cows were grazing; the long grass beaded with early morning dew. Heads down, they would not know they were never to see Elspeth again or feel her hand upon their backs; they would accept the change and carry on regardless. Oh, to be a cow, Henry thought.

A footpath ran between the woods and the far end of the fields, and as he got dressed, Henry could just make out one or two stoical, early-morning dog walkers. In the summer months, his parents often had to guide ramblers out of their fields as they strayed off the footpath. Occasionally in the winter, they would bring lost souls into the farmhouse to dry out or warm against the aga before sending them back on their journey, laden with homemade scones and a refill of their flasks. It was one of the things his parents loved about farm life, the feeling of remoteness without being remote. Taligth was surrounded by life and they enjoyed the comings and goings. Unseen, they often idled over breakfast, simply watching.

It was 6 a.m. and Henry could hear his father's radio downstairs. It was going to be a long day.

Making his way into the kitchen, Henry could see his father outside, busy in the yard. Betsy's pen looked spotless with new bedding and she was already snuffling after her breakfast, pushing it around with her snout, chasing it into the fresh straw whilst William was attempting to sweep.

'Morning,' Henry called, standing in the doorway.

'Morning,' William replied, looking up miserably, struggling with the broom.

'Why don't you let me do that?'

'Would you mind?' William asked, giving in all too quickly.

'Here, give it to me. Go and put the kettle on and sit yourself down,' Henry said, taking the broom from his father. William and Elspeth had always kept a clean yard so it didn't take long to sweep up what little mess there was.

Finished, Henry leant the broom against the wall and went back into the kitchen. 'How did you sleep?' he asked as he took his shoes off and left them on the doormat.

'Dreadfully,' William replied.

'Me too,' Henry added, sadly.

The mournful mood did not lift and the two men spent the morning sitting at the kitchen table, talking in subdued voices about Elspeth and the weather and the coming of autumn, with the inevitable drop of leaves being a particular bugbear for William, who was very proud of his front lawn. They talked about the migration of the birds and how it must be nice to be able to fly away for the winter. And they sat in silence. A lot of silence.

~

7 a.m. was not unusually early for Tatch-A UK employees to arrive at the office and, as promised, Graham was waiting for Sebastian outside the main doors. A small, quietly spoken man, Graham had resisted going into the family firm for as long as he could. Preferring to experience something other than accounting, he had chosen the military. His army background oozed out of him. He was always immaculately attired and turned up each day in a three-piece suit with freshly pressed white shirt, military tie, black socks and very expensive, exceptionally clean, shoes with steel heel protectors that tapped rhythmically as he walked. He had thinning, grey, slicked-back hair and a neatly trimmed moustache. Now in his early sixties, he was close to

retirement and, luckily for him, had two children who were happy to carry on the Ribeck name into the next generation of accountants.

'May I pass on my sincere condolences, Sebastian,' he said kindly, his etiquette and intense politeness awkward. Sebastian nodded as they walked slowly up the steps. Graham had recently had a hip replacement and it had taken longer than expected to settle, leaving him with an uneven gait. Now, looking after his wife who was in poor health herself, he was tired and ready to finish, but he knew his business, and his services were greatly sought after. Sebastian was relieved when he agreed to do pre-due diligence for Tatch-A UK as he knew Graham was one of the best and he trusted him. Graham was sharp and could smell a rat at a hundred paces, but, as was his way, he remained exceptionally professional and calm and was more than able to guide his client through a minefield without either of them getting a leg blown off.

Sebastian showed Graham into his office, leaving him for a moment as he, followed loyally by Panda who had insisted she went into work with him, headed into the kitchen to make himself and Graham a drink. As the kettle boiled, Sebastian picked Panda up and held her in his arms as his eyes wondered around the exposed brick walls of the small room. The offices and factory had once been a large, thriving woollen mill and still retained many original features. Expertly converted, it was a positive environment in which to work.

Having made the drinks and put a few biscuits onto a plate, Sebastian went back into his office where Graham appeared not to have moved a muscle. Sebastian handed him his milkless tea, and offered him a biscuit, which Graham politely declined. Sebastian sat at his desk pensively waiting to hear what Graham had to say.

'Right, Graham. Tell me what's going on, and if you can do it succinctly, that would be really helpful,' Sebastian said, trying not to offend.

Graham lifted the cup to his lips, took a tentative sip of the scorching tea and put it back down carefully, clearing his throat. He was a precise man. He did not have a biscuit for he did not consume anything that contained refined sugar.

Graham did not refer to notes. 'I have discovered salary payments made to Patricia Martin over a period of eleven months in your third year of trading. I have also come across names of two further individuals receiving salary payments during the same period for whom I am unable to find employment details,' he said.

Much to Sebastian's surprise, Graham had gone straight to the point, stopping as quickly as he had started. Sebastian was encouraged to fill the silence as the two men looked at each other.

'Right,' Sebastian said. 'So... you're telling me we've paid people who have not worked for the company.'

'That appears to be the case.'

'Why would we do that?'

'Would you like me to tell you the names of the other individuals before I explain further?'

'If it helps, yes please.'

'They are John Stevenson and Isabel Parish. Do you remember these individuals, Sebastian?'

'No, but then I wouldn't necessarily know all the names. We've always had a number of temporary workers in the factory. I've relied on Paul to keep track of employee details.'

'Yes, that's quite obvious,' Graham stated.

Sebastian suddenly felt a finger of blame pointing at him and he rose quickly to defend himself.

'You know as well as I do, Graham, that when you're running a business, you have to trust the people you employ. I learned that early on when I was trying to do everything myself. Ironically it was Paul who told me I had to let people get on with their jobs and trust that they were working in the best interests of the company.'

Graham looked earnestly at him. 'Your level of staffing was modest and your order book was growing rapidly,' he continued, unaffected by Sebastian's outburst. 'This was a significant period of growth for Tatch-A UK and easy for an individual to overlook or bypass traditional accounting procedures, especially as some of the more secure systems and financial regulatory controls that the company has today, did not exist at that time.' Sebastian got the point. 'I have been able to account for all employees during that period other than Patricia Martin and the two individuals I have mentioned,' Graham said, taking a sip from his tea before continuing. 'Over that eleven-month period, John Stevenson was paid £4,421, Isabel Parish was paid £6,400 and Patricia Martin was paid £26,787, which is an interesting figure.'

'They're all bloody interesting figures,' Sebastian said, getting agitated.

'The last figure,' Graham continued, 'was precisely fifty percent of Paul Martin's salary over the same period.'

Sebastian looked at him. 'Before you carry on, let me make sure I get this right,' he said, deciphering the information. 'If you're saying Paul has made salary payments to employees who never existed, are you suggesting he's paid the money to himself instead? Because there's absolutely no way he'd do that. No way. I've known him nearly all my life. It'll be an accounting error, Graham. It was a long time ago.'

'Although I understand, I do not agree, but we have no evidence and are unable to find any form of paper or electronic trail, so I cannot be definitive in my assumptions.'

Sebastian sighed, heavily. 'Okay,' he said, 'so, going back to this money that was paid to Trish Martin, which you say was half Paul's salary. Did Paul pay himself the other half or did he pay himself his full salary as well?'

'He paid himself the other half.'

'He divided his salary between them? Why would he do that?' Sebastian asked before answering his own question: 'to avoid higher rate tax. But why? Surely that's pennies.'

'Yes, that is my conclusion also, but one that only Paul can confirm.'

'Right, well, I think it's time for him to do that. Do you agree?'

'Yes. I do.'

Sebastian was sure Paul would have an explanation for the anomalies in the accounts. They had always been honest with each other, even when they had made mistakes that might affect their friendship, like the time, as a pubescent teenager, Paul had made a pass at Nancy and had received short shrift from her. Risking a beating from his sister, Sebastian had stood up for his friend, saying she led him on. When Sebastian floated his idea for Tatch-A UK over a beer one afternoon, Paul had been the first to set about researching the market for potential competitors, negotiating prices with contractors and letting agencies to help begin building Sebastian's dream, all while holding down a low-paid accounting job. It wasn't until the company was up and running that Paul had become Tatch-A UK's Financial Director. Sebastian would trust him with his life.

Assuming Paul was already in, Sebastian called the office directly above his own.

'Hey Seb! It's great to have you back. How was your trip?' Paul's familiar voice danced down the receiver.

'It was good thanks,' Sebastian answered a little stiffly. 'Paul, would you mind coming to my office for a minute, please?'

'Of course,' Paul replied.

Standing up, Graham took the opportunity to stretch his legs. Sebastian put the phone down and looked towards the ceiling, listening to the muffled sounds of Paul moving in the office above. Searching for answers, he hoped there was a logical explanation.

Graham sat back down, carefully straightening his trousers and positioning his tie to lie perfectly, covering the first four buttons of his shirt before disappearing into his waistcoat. Smoothing down his moustache and crossing his legs, he took up his cup and sipped his now, cold tea. 'Are you okay?' he asked Sebastian as they waited. Sebastian nodded.

Knocking on the door and blustering into the room, Paul stopped suddenly, not expecting to see Graham sitting in front of Sebastian's desk, and Sebastian looking as if someone had a gun pointing at his head. He hesitated, trying to read the situation; the half-finished drinks, the uneaten biscuits implying that a meeting between Graham and Sebastian had already taken place, the result of which was to summon him down. His blood running cold, he pulled a chair forward.

Sebastian felt nervous and got straight to the point. 'Right, Paul, I'll cut to the chase as I'm sure you'll be able to explain this to us, and then we will all be able to get on...'

'Oh! Shit!' Paul cut in with a nervous laugh, his heart speeding up. 'Why don't I like the sound of this?'

'Don't panic,' Sebastian replied. 'It's just that Graham has brought something to my attention. Actually, I'll hand over to you Graham. You'll be able to explain it far better than I can, if you don't mind.'

As was Graham's way, it took him some time to recount everything he had communicated to Sebastian earlier. He spoke with little punctuation while Sebastian sat watching Paul intently, looking for clues in his friend's reaction and changes in his body language. Paul remained motionless, giving no sign of either agreement or denial. When Graham stopped talking, the room went quiet. In such an old building the walls were solid and the doors heavy. In this sound proofed space, the air hung thick with anticipation as Sebastian prayed Graham was wrong.

Paul, his face devoid of emotion, but his head spinning, considered his situation.

'I'm presuming there's a simple explanation?' Sebastian asked, confused by Paul's silence. Full of dread, he had promised himself he would not rise to anger. But looking at Paul's blank face, the face of a man he loved and trusted, he was holding back the urge to scramble across his desk and shake him.

They waited until Paul broke the silence. He tried to speak with conviction, but struggled to hold his nerve. 'I can see how it might look,' he started, 'and I'll be honest with you, in the early days with the things the way they were and the rate at which we were growing, perhaps I wasn't as... as accurate in my record keeping as I should have been.' He stuttered to a stop, but the faces of his inquisitors allowed him no respite and he had to continue. 'If I can address the two individuals you mentioned, um...' he looked down at the note of the names he had made on his pad. 'I do remember them. They were temporary staff, along with many other people we brought in to help with the Saunterton order, do you remember?' Saunterton's was Tatch-A UK's first key customer. Tatch-A UK had struggled to fulfil the over-promised first order and nearly came to a grinding halt under the pressure. It was quite feasible that things got missed as they rushed to meet the client's tight timescale.

'As you know, Seb, it was a crazy time. We were all working flat out - god knows how many hours - every one of us working each other's jobs. You were on the factory floor, remember?' Sebastian did remember. 'I'll admit perhaps I cut corners, perhaps I didn't fill in the proper paperwork for everyone we recruited at that time, but it was manic.' He took a breath and sighed it out quickly. 'These will have been two people I'll have missed out of... of... I don't know, a hundred people we employed, I'm really sorry for that, Seb, but you know what it was like. We were up against an unreasonable deadline,' he protested nervously. What he was saying was plausible and Sebastian looked towards Graham for guidance. Graham raised an eyebrow and tilted his head, communicating understanding but not necessarily acceptance of Paul's explanation.

'Okay, I get that. It was a busy time,' Sebastian said, 'but how do you explain Trish? Who to my knowledge has never worked for us.'

Paul shuffled uneasily in his seat. 'Well, that's where I might have fucked up,' he said, sweat darkening his blue collar. 'Like I've just been saying, we were working around the clock weren't we? In the midst of it I got excited. I could see how well we were doing and where the company was going and I overstretched myself, committing not only to buying the house, but also to getting married, which was costing a fortune. I can see how bad it must look now but...'

He was interrupted by Graham who was unable to listen any longer and provided instant clarity. 'Let me tell you how I see it, Paul,' he said dispassionately. 'You didn't want to pay higher rate tax on your earnings and, in order to avoid it, you fraudulently split your salary between yourself and your wife. Am I correct?'

'I don't like your use of the word 'fraudulently', Graham,' Paul faltered, rubbing his neck.

'How else would you describe what you did?' Graham replied, looking at Paul in disbelief.

'I was in a corner. I was naive.'

'Oh! Come on!' Sebastian interjected, raising his voice.

'I was, Seb! I was stupid and I got it wrong and yes, in the eyes of the law, I suppose it was fraudulent, but that wasn't the way I saw it. I wasn't stealing from the company, Seb, I wouldn't. You know that. I just saw it as a way of... I had a lot going on at the time,' he said quickly, staring at Sebastian.

'How much tax do you think you saved?' Sebastian asked.

'I've no idea. I only did it a couple of times.'

'Eleven times,' Graham interjected.

'Eleven times?' Sebastian said, his exasperation obvious. 'I don't get it Paul. Why would you compromise yourself and Trish and the company for a few pounds?'

'I was stupid. Trish doesn't know.'

146

'Well, she's in for a shock,' Sebastian said.

Listening to Paul's heavy breathing, Sebastian watched him nervously rearrange his shirtsleeves as the fabric twisted beneath his trembling fingers. What a cheap shirt, Sebastian thought, raising his eyes to look at the face of his friend who looked away, evading capture.

'Is there anything else Graham's going to find out, Paul?' Sebastian asked, 'because now is your opportunity to say, and I'd suggest you take it.'

'There's nothing, Seb, I promise,' Paul said quickly, raising his hands in surrender. 'What are you going to do?' he asked.

'I don't know. I need time to think. But for now, I want you to go home and tell Trish what you've done... *everything*... and work out how much money we're talking about and we'll take it from there. Let's give it the weekend and I'll see you on Monday morning,' Sebastian said, trying to remain calm.

'If I can...'

'GET OUT!' Sebastian suddenly shouted, his erupting voice sending Panda scurrying for cover under the desk. The windows reverberated against the bellowing sound as time froze and no one moved, until, without speaking, Paul slowly pushed his chair back and walked out of Sebastian's office. Graham dared not breathe until Sebastian spoke; it seemed an inordinate amount of time to hold his breath.

'Sorry, Graham.'

'I understand.'

'What do you think?'

'Unfortunately, Sebastian, I think we are only scratching the surface,' Graham replied.

~

At just after 10 a.m. William and Henry were about to have their third cup of tea of the morning when Sebastian and Panda arrived. Panda was so excited to see Henry she weed all over the kitchen floor and Sebastian shouted her out of the kitchen into the yard where she found a butterfly to chase.

At the kitchen table, William and Sebastian sat quietly with their thoughts whilst Henry started to make arrangements. He made an appointment for them all to see the undertaker on Monday afternoon, and one for William and Sebastian to go to the registrars later in the week. He cancelled Elspeth's pre-arranged optician and dentist appointments and contacted friends and relatives to tell them the sad news. It was draining work. After lunch, conversation turned to Elspeth's funeral, a burial in the village graveyard to be held the week after next. Sebastian and Henry felt it best for William not to wait too long to say goodbye.

For the rest of the afternoon they moved from tea to talk, to silence and back again before Sebastian left for the night.

Driving home, he telephoned Patrick McCarthy.

'Sebastian!' Patrick greeted him. 'I've been thinking about you. How are you doing?'

'I'm getting there, thank you, Patrick. I know I said it before but I wanted to say again, thank you so much for everything you did to get us back so quickly.'

'It was my pleasure. Tell me, how are your father and brother?'

'Shattered, but they're keeping going.'

'Yes, I know that feeling well.'

'I wanted to keep you in the loop regards the meeting I had with Graham today.'

'Although I appreciate that, there really is no need, unless of course you think there is something I ought to know before I see you again. This is your business, not mine, not yet anyway.'

'Okay, I hear what you're saying, thank you.'

'You take care of yourself and let's speak again soon. Goodnight.'

Putting the phone down, Sebastian felt all the richer for knowing someone like Patrick McCarthy.

Sebastian spent the next two days between home and Taligth, whilst, with his permission, Graham spent the weekend working in Tatch-A UK's offices.

With a thin crescent moon high in the sky, the nights were especially dark and the small desk lamp shone brightly. Graham was determined to prove himself right.

His suspicions confirmed, at 6 o'clock Monday morning, he telephoned Sebastian.

Day Five

At 8 a.m. Paul arrived at work, harrowed and dishevelled. Sebastian had told him to go upstairs to his office and not come down unless asked to do so. He walked in to find his computer had been removed, filing cabinets locked, shelves cleared, and by the door, a box, which had once housed reams of photocopy paper, now packed with his few personal belongings.

On Friday he had done as Sebastian asked. He had gone home and told Trish what had happened in the office that morning, and what he had been accused of. The email he sent to Sebastian said, amongst other things, that Trish had gone to her parents for a few days. Sebastian couldn't help but wonder what Paul had told her to make her leave their home. If he had only told her about the tax evasion, then her reaction was not what Sebastian would have expected. There was more to come for sure, and, having spent the weekend going over it again and again, and then speaking with Graham, Sebastian was filled with foreboding.

Armed with a tray carrying one black tea, a black coffee and a plate of biscuits, Graham knocked on Sebastian's office door and waited to be let in. Having been in the office all weekend, he had placed a copy of his report on Sebastian's desk in readiness.

'Morning Graham,' Sebastian sighed, having read the report in depth. 'You look tired. Are you all right?'

'Once I get the bit between my teeth, there is little that stops me until I have satisfied myself I have done a thorough job. I believe I have done that,' Graham replied. 'I understand you need to be elsewhere this afternoon so perhaps it's best if I just get on with it,' he said, sitting down as Sebastian watched him go through his trouser and tie routine. He was a strange man, Sebastian thought; old fashioned and set in his ways, trustworthy and honourable. There were not many like him anymore.

'I'm afraid, as you have seen, it is not good news,' Graham said.

Struggling with the gravity of Graham's words and the feeling of betrayal by his best friend, Sebastian took a moment to compose himself. Looking at his desk, he focused his attention on a globular, glass paperweight proudly puffing out its engraved chest, telling anyone, who cared to look at the words, 'Entrepreneur of the Year', that he had achieved something. Casting a wry smile, he remembered the day it had been awarded, a day when, unlike today, he had been proud. Breathing deeply to settle his growing agitation, he swallowed hard before looking up and nodding for Graham to continue.

Without interruption, Graham condensed almost a decade's worth of misappropriation into twenty-seven minutes.

Sitting still, his pen poised as he heard the 'summing up', Sebastian stared intently at the blank cover of the report which sat squarely on the desk in front of him, each page lying heavily on top of those beneath it.

Without reacting, he listened to Graham's summary of how Paul had cheated the company and how he had lied to cover up his actions and how, with each lie, there had been another lie and another after that, a thick web of deceit. It had gone on undetected until a time when the installation of sophisticated software and regulatory accountancy practices made it too dangerous for him to carry on without being caught.

'He will have started modestly,' Graham suggested, 'his fingers in the petty cash tin perhaps.' Then he went on to tell Sebastian how Paul had moved onto tax evasion and then, when he got away with that and his confidence grew, greed had emboldened him, so he had falsified invoices sent from companies whose names and addresses no longer existed, and how he had channelled the self-authorised payments into accounts only he had access to, this embezzlement totalling over £100,000.

Sebastian listened to how Paul had stolen £80,000 by fabricating casual workers; their jobs short lived during busy periods when the order book was strong and the factory floor too busy to notice. He had paid their salaries into his own greedy pocket. And Sebastian heard how his best friend had claimed expenses he had not incurred to the sum of almost £40,000, how he had paid for £20,621 of personal items on the company credit card and how he had transferred small, but regular sums of money, unnoticed, to the value of £155,720 into false creditor accounts, accounts only he knew about.

By the time Graham had finished, on the blank front cover of the report was a scrawl of numbers each written over again, heavier, before being captured within deep, dark circles. Sebastian had scored the paper, forcing the nib through to the pages beneath where the evidence lay. When Graham stopped talking, Sebastian did not look up. He remained unnaturally still, watching the dust, caught by the light of the morning sun, floating in the air.

'I suspect there may be more,' Graham said, quietly, watching Sebastian's pen revolve, 'but we are unlikely to find out the true extent of his breach of trust. I am so sorry.'

Devastated, Sebastian raised his eyes to Graham. If Paul could do this to him, this warm, funny man who had been his friend since childhood, then who else, in the office or working in the factory, had done the same? When does someone move on from pinching envelopes and teabags to stealing thousands of pounds, and what's the difference? It was a sobering thought, and one which Graham could see written all over Sebastian's face, choosing this moment to give him a break from his torment.

'You know, Sebastian,' he said, pulling his waistcoat down, 'there are a lot of despicable people out there who think it is okay to steal from their employer. Some go unnoticed, getting away with it for years, but others, the greedy ones, off guard, get caught. We can never know how many people there are out there, but be assured Tatch-A UK is not alone. Every, and I repeat, *every* company has them.' Looking at the emptiness in Sebastian's eyes, Graham contemplated the consequences of one man's greed and betrayal.

'How much do you think he's stolen?' Sebastian asked flatly.

'In the region of £500,000.'

The atmosphere in the room teetered as if it were on the edge of a precipice. The silence waited for Sebastian to speak.

'Half a million pounds,' he said slowly, the muscles tensing in his jaw. 'Half a million pounds!' he repeated. 'Do you think we should call the police?'

'If you want to make this a legal matter then yes, go ahead and call, and no one will question your reasoning for doing so. I'd certainly be tempted. But equally, I'd want to rip him apart limb from limb and make him eat his own body parts in the street and show everyone what a contemptible person he is, but that's just me,' Graham said, smiling wryly as he caught Sebastian's eye. 'You need to look at the bigger picture, Sebastian. You are selling your company. You are not obliged to call the police and it would be a protracted process bringing him to justice, and even then, you may not be satisfied with the result. If you want my advice, and it is my personal advice, you have a good business. It is a sound investment and Patrick McCarthy has seen that. I think you would be ill advised to involve the police.'

Sebastian appreciated Graham's insightfulness and candour. He smiled weakly, seeing the human in this wonderfully stoical man, who straightened his trousers and neatened his tie and didn't eat biscuits. It was clear he had Sebastian's best interests at heart and he obviously cared for Tatch-A UK. It wasn't about money for Graham; it was about loyalty, trust and integrity.

'What do I do?' Sebastian asked.

'You get him by the balls, squeeze so hard his eyes pop out of his head and his ears burst and the truth rolls off his swollen, bleeding tongue and you don't let go until he has paid the money back. Only then, when he is writhing in pain, do you kick him out of your life. That way he will be gone and you can get on with selling your company. Involve the police and it may damage the business. This way, you will have ruined his life without ruining your own.'

'Once a military man, always a military man,' Sebastian said with a despondent laugh, acknowledging the inconceivable reality that Paul's life, and their once inseparable friendship, was over.

It was time to call Paul into his office.

~

Waiting for the kettle to boil, Henry lent against the worn wooden work surface and looked out of the window. One of Taligth's three pigmy goats was looking hopefully in his direction. 'You'll have been fed already you greedy thing,' he said, returning to his tea making. 'I wonder if goats eat used tea bags?' he asked himself, resisting the urge to open the door and fling the one he was squeezing into their enclosure. He laughed.

'What's funny?' William asked, walking into the kitchen with his good arm full of Elspeth's magazines, which he put into recycling.

'I was asking myself whether goats eat teabags.'

'They do,' William said bluntly. 'I don't want to go this afternoon. I think just you and Sebastian should go.'

'No Dad, you need to be there as well. I'm not even sure Seb will make it, he's got a meeting.'

'He's always got a meeting. What is it this time?'

'I don't know,' Henry replied. Treading on eggshells, Henry found silence the safest place to be. Sitting for hours, watching his father mourn was draining and, although he did not want to go either, the distraction of the undertakers that afternoon would be welcome.

~

Placing the phone back on the receiver, Paul knew this was his time of reckoning. What kind of a man had he become to think he would get away with what he had done? Where once he had been the spider and the company his prey, he was now the fly trapped by his own insatiable greed and arrogance.

He knew that Sebastian would not believe that Trish had no knowledge of the money he had stolen. But had Sebastian been in the room when he had sat her down and told her *everything*, he would have seen the horror in her eyes. Trish was one of life's innocents, naive and forgetful. She wore no makeup, dressed like her mother and cut her own hair. She was an eternal optimist and quick-witted. Easy to like, she was a nice person and she had loved Paul from the moment she met him.

After asking him to leave her alone, Trish, in shock, and feeling sick, had sat in the kitchen crying, trying to digest the details and implications of what Paul had told her and how, whilst he spoke, she had looked at him and had seen the face of her husband change from being one she loved to one she could no longer recognise.

If someone else had told her what he had done she would have laughed. She would have accused them of getting the wrong person, telling them they had made a mistake. 'Not Paul,' she would have said, 'not my Paul, no way! He's as honest as the day is long, is my Paul. There's no way he would risk losing everything he has.' But her Paul had. Her Paul had been stealing and lying and cheating all of their married life.

Others would tell her, 'there was no way you'd have known what he was up to.' They would say, 'he was very clever, he hid it well.' But how could she tell them that she had been suspicious once? That she had had a feeling something was going on, but had never questioned him? She would never have guessed he was stealing. She did, however, suspect there might have been another woman. A woman she could not compete with, and, like a fool, she had buried her head in the sand. She felt terribly ashamed.

Angry with herself, she packed her bags and went to her parents'. Too embarrassed to tell them why she was asking to stay, she lied and told them Paul was away on business and she didn't want to be alone. They were very fond of their son-in-law and she didn't want to upset them until she had decided what she was going to do.

~

Slowly descending the stairs that led down from his office, Paul felt like a traitor walking his final steps towards the gallows. He imagined the hush of the baying crowd as he was brought into the town square, the creak of the gnarled wood as he walked up the steps and out onto the platform and the feel of the noose being slipped over his sacked head, the knot tightening around his neck. He imagined how it might feel when the trapdoor opened beneath his feet and he dropped – hoping his neck would be broken and death would come quickly. But, in reality, walking into Sebastian's office that morning, he had known he faced a slow death, the worst kind. There was nothing he could say and he had resigned himself to his fate.

Before Paul arrived, Niamh joined Sebastian and Graham in the office. She had been with the company for five years and was a perfect successor to Sebastian; everything the company could have asked for, bottled into one person. She had worked for a large manufacturing company for the previous seventeen years and arrived with in-depth knowledge and experience. She was commercially astute, reliable and innovative, so was quick to identify gaps in a market ripe for exploitation. In her late forties, having never married, she had dedicated her life to her work and she was loyal and expected loyalty in return, so today she was angry, *very* angry.

In order to make sure things didn't get out of hand during the meeting, Sebastian had arranged for the three colleagues to speak together before Paul was allowed into the room. Sebastian felt a mixture of sadness and adrenaline and the room was energized. Any one of them could explode at any time but Sebastian wanted them to remain calm.

The objective of the meeting was to get Paul to explain why he had done what he had done and to confirm the amount he had stolen. Sebastian had searched for the answers but was dumbfounded. He had made sure that the people who worked for him were well rewarded. Directors had good salaries, company cars, private health and dental care and performance related bonuses. Employees were given long holidays, could work flexible hours and were never denied time off if they needed it. He was a generous employer.

'Right,' he said, 'you've read the report haven't you, Niamh?' Niamh nodded. 'So, our objective this morning is to get Paul to explain himself, nothing more, nothing less. Are we all right with that?' he asked. 'What happens after today I've yet to decide, but for now I just want to know why and how much he stole. I've no intention of telling him we're not going to call the police at this stage. I want him to think we are and I should think he probably does. I would if I were him. Any questions before we let him in?' No one spoke. 'I know how tough this is for you because we're a team, so please, let's keep our cool, okay? I don't want this to become a brawl. Let's get it over and done with. Is everyone ready?'

Waiting, the small team felt a collective anticipation and each of them jumped slightly when Paul knocked on the door. Sebastian stood up, preferring to be face to face with the condemned man as he entered the room.

'Come in, Paul,' he said, not looking at him as he turned and walked back to his desk. 'Take a seat.' A chair had been placed at the end of the room, where Paul would be facing his judge and jury. 'Before we start,' Sebastian said seriously, 'if you have a friend or colleague in the building you think you might like to have with you during this meeting, now is the time to ask them to join us.'

Unshaven and devoid of expression, knowing he was damned, Paul did not move. Crimes committed years ago had been uncovered. The 'body' had been found and he had been exposed. With his dignity in tatters, he deserved everything coming to him. He knew he had lost his job and his best friend; he suspected he would lose his wife and devastate his parents who were so proud of all he had achieved. He wanted today to be over.

Before Sebastian spoke, Graham gave Paul an overview of the report. Paul sat listening, his eyes, unblinking, fixed on Graham.

'The facts and figures in the report speak for themselves. I see no benefit in going over them any further,' Sebastian said, 'so let me put you in the picture before I ask you to speak. By the time you leave this room, everyone in the office will know what you've done. So when you walk out of here and no one looks at you or speaks to you, that is why,' Sebastian said, feeling his heartbeat quickening. 'You have no friends in this building...' he paused... 'not one,' he said, staring at Paul. 'Where we go from here will be determined by what you say this morning. So, the purpose of this meeting is for you to explain the findings in this report.'

Staying silent, Paul stared blankly.

'I presume you *can* explain?' Sebastian added, the tension between them tightening, 'I presume you had your reasons... to buy a yacht, perhaps?'

Still Paul did not speak. Although sweat was forming on his brow, he showed nothing in his expression to indicate how he might be feeling or whether he was going to try to defend or justify his actions. Sebastian continued to stare at him and, as the atmosphere in the room strained, Paul looked Sebastian in the eye.

Eventually he spoke, his voice unmodulated.

'I can't...' he stopped; thinking what to say, searching the room, hoping it would swallow him up. 'I can't tell you,' he said, hating himself for being so weak.

'You *can't* tell us?' Sebastian questioned, shocked by Paul's answer. Paul neither moved nor spoke. 'You *can't* tell us? Or you *won't* tell us?' Sebastian asked, spitting the words.

Again, Paul showed no expression. 'How did it start, Paul? Can you tell me *that*? Was it ten pounds out of my wallet? Or was it twenty pounds out of petty cash?' Paul suddenly looked at Sebastian about to protest but decided not to speak. 'Was that not exciting enough for you? Is that why you *ramped* it up? Let's make it a thousand pounds next. Is that what you thought? How about *ten* thousand? *Fifty* thousand... now that's a nice round number - how can you not *tell* us?'

Paul remained silent.

Everyone in the room could feel the tension squeezing against the walls. Any one of them could have launched themselves at him, but it was Sebastian who threw the first punch.

'I don't understand,' he exclaimed, exasperated. 'When you're sitting in my office in *deep shit*, you *can't* tell us why you stole hundreds of thousands of pounds? Who the *hell* are you? You *fucking* piece of *fucking* worthless *shit*! Get out...!' Frozen to his seat Paul did not move. '*GET OUT*!' Sebastian bellowed.

Avoiding eye contact with anyone in the room, Paul stood up. As he reached the door, holding the handle, he stopped for a moment as if to turn back.

'*GET OUT*!' Sebastian shouted.

Paul left the office, the door slamming closed behind him.

Dust played with the sunlight as it fell from the walls. All sitting motionless, no one dared breathe. Sebastian sat looking at the thunderstruck faces of his colleagues.

'I think that went very well, don't you?' he said.

~

By one o'clock, still smarting, Sebastian made it just in time to join Henry and his father at the undertakers.

Although they had known each other's families all their of lives, Angus Stewart remained exceptionally professional, as well as compassionate, guiding them

159

through what needed to happen immediately, and over the next few days.

They agreed a date for Elspeth's burial and talked about the type of service she might have liked. They chose her coffin, decided on the cars and talked about flowers and then they added up the prices, like a list of groceries. It seemed a lucrative business working amongst the deceased who could not speak for themselves, William thought, though the expense was a small price to pay for the joy Elspeth had brought into his life.

Before leaving, Angus asked them one final question. It did not need to be decided there and then but could be considered over the next few days leading up to Elspeth's funeral.

Driving back to Taligth with Sebastian behind them, Henry and William did not talk; they did not mull over the hour they had spent with Angus Stewart or dissect the price of every item on the list of costs and, after Angus' question, William did not articulate his feelings about whether he wished to see Elspeth one last time before she was laid to rest.

By the time they arrived back at Taligth, William was tired and he sat in the front room watching the television while Henry and Sebastian prepared some food.

Over dinner Henry broached the subject of him needing to get back to Newcastle and back to work. He did not want to leave, but he did not particularly want to stay either. He was struggling with his own grief while trying to manage his father's. William and Sebastian understood.

~

Sebastian left Taligth for the night when Henry and William went to bed. He had decided not to go into the office the following day, but to spend it at the farm, out in the fields with the animals. He needed time with them, time to come to terms with the loss of his mother, and Paul, his best friend, who had sent him countless messages since leaving the office, but none which answered the question Sebastian desperately wanted answering.

It had been a long and draining day and Sebastian's tank was empty. Panda charged around his feet as soon as he opened the front door and jumped up to gain his attention. She was impossible to resist and Sebastian chased his crazy pup who, with a flurry of fur, playfully ducked and dived to avoid capture. 'It's good to see you my lovely dog,' he said as they stopped to take a breath, 'have you been a good girl?'

'She's been a very good girl,' Matilda called from the kitchen.

'Well that's good to hear,' he said holding Panda's head in his hands and burying his face into her silky curls, 'and has mummy been a good girl?' he asked Panda, who looked at him, quizzically. 'She has?' Sebastian replied, 'well that's also good to hear.' He stood up as Panda grabbed hold of his leg and he dragged her, hanging on, into the kitchen.

'Are you okay?' Matilda asked. 'What a day!'

'Yes, what a day!' Sebastian sighed. 'That *fucking* bastard!'

'Any closer to knowing why he did it?'

'No,' Sebastian answered, going to the fridge and getting a bottle of wine out, 'but there'll have been a reason. I know Paul.'

'What do you think?'

'God knows,' he said, shaking his head. He poured the wine. 'It was good to get out this afternoon,' he added, changing the subject, 'even if it was only to the undertakers. Mum's funeral's booked for next Friday.'

'How's your dad doing?'

'Not good. He's so sad, Til. I can see him searching for Mum all over the place.'

'Poor man.'

'How was it in the office after I left? Was everyone gossiping?' Sebastian asked. Kicking his shoes off, he sunk into the sofa.

About to speak, Matilda hesitated before deciding it would be better to wait for morning before telling him the news. It was a difficult enough time without something else creeping under the door and she wanted to pick her moment.

Day Six

In his fretful dreams, Sebastian was visited by ghosts; a friend from school who at seventeen went home one Friday afternoon feeling unwell and never returned; his maternal grandfather who had taught him how to play cards and roll tobacco; and his mother, who came to him when the night was at its darkest to tell him she had found her 'place' and was safe. By breakfast he had spent an hour in the gym running off his visions.

Matilda was dressed and ready for work by the time he emerged into the kitchen, dripping with sweat.

'Another bad night?' she asked.

Sebastian didn't answer, opening the fridge in search of something to quench his thirst. Emptying the last of the orange juice into a glass, he leant against the work surface, wiping the sweat from his face with the tea towel. Taking a fresh one out of the drawer, Matilda chose not to say anything.

'I'm unfit,' he said bending over, trying to regulate his breathing.

'What time are you going to Taligth?'

'I don't know.'

'Are you going into the office at all today?'

'I wasn't planning to, but I might do, for an hour or so. Why?'

'There's something I want to tell you.'

'Sounds ominous.'

Putting toast on the table and then filling the cafetiere, Matilda told Sebastian that Patricia Martin had turned up at the office the previous afternoon, after he had left.

Trish was distraught. She had only been to the office a handful of times and always under much happier circumstances: a Christmas party, a product launch, a contract celebration. She despised what Paul had done, all of it, and she felt foolish and embarrassed that she had not been aware. She needed Sebastian and Matilda to know how sorry she was. Certain that Sebastian would not believe her, she had hoped he might come around if he saw her and listened to what she had to say.

When she had arrived, the receptionist, not knowing who she was, told her Sebastian had left the office for the day and it was at that point Matilda had walked through the reception area.

Matilda had shown her into her office where Trish proceeded to breakdown in great gulfs of tears and despair, not only for what Paul had done, but for the loss of everything: her marriage, her friends, her pride. Matilda believed her when she told her she'd had no idea about the money.

'I don't see why she came into the office, I don't *want* her in the office,' Sebastian said irritably, scraping his toast with hard butter. 'For *fuck's* sake, this bloody butter!'

'Perhaps it was good you weren't in because at least I could talk to her calmly.'

'Without me flying off the handle you mean? Why didn't you say something last night?' he sniped at her, ripping his toast. 'I give up!' he sparked, pushing the plate away. 'They were our best friends, Til!'

'I know they were, and I didn't tell you last night because I knew this would happen!' Matilda snapped back. 'Did you know he'd had an affair?' she asked.

Shocked, Sebastian looked at her. 'For *fuck's* sake! When?'

'Around the time that they were getting married, apparently.'

'Shit! Who was it with?' Sebastian asked, unable to believe he did not know.

'I don't know.'

164

'You must have asked.'

'Of course I asked. Trish didn't know. Paul wouldn't tell her.'

'Why wouldn't he tell her?' Sebastian pushed.

'I don't know. The only thing I can think of is that perhaps it was someone she knew.'

'Who?'

'I don't know, Seb!' Matilda repeated.

'Has she only just found out?'

'I think so.'

Sebastian sat thinking. 'What else did she say?' he asked.

'Not a lot, she was in a terrible state. She could hardly speak.'

'Did she say why he stole the money?'

'No. She didn't know. She said she didn't know anything about the money.'

'Oh my god! How could she not know?' Sebastian asked, getting increasingly agitated with Matilda.

'I have absolutely no idea! Don't get cross with me, Seb. I'm just telling you what she told me.'

'I don't understand why I didn't know about his affair. Paul tells me everything.'

'Well, obviously not everything!' Matilda commented.

'Thanks for that!' Sebastian snapped, looking at her. He stood up. 'I'm going for a shower,' he said, leaving her sitting at the table to continue breakfast alone.

Appearing back in the kitchen ten minutes later, Sebastian got ready to take Panda for a walk. 'I need to clear my head,' he said, not looking at Matilda. Crouching down, he wrestled Panda into her harness. 'I'm guessing Trish didn't just want to tell you about Paul's affair?' he asked bitterly.

'No,' Matilda replied, coldly. 'She asked me to ask you not to go to the police.'

'Bloody cheek! She can piss off!' Sebastian snapped. 'I want them to think that any day they could get a knock at the door. I want them to be looking over their shoulders for the rest of their *fucking* lives.'

'And she offered to pay back the money.'

Sebastian laughed. 'Does she know how much it is?' he asked, looking at Matilda. Matilda did not react. 'Well, as per Graham's advice, tomorrow, I'm going to get that bastard by the balls and squeeze so hard he tells the truth. Then she'll find out just how much he's stolen and she might change her mind,' he said, standing up to leave.

~

Henry looked out of his bedroom window, across the fields. The scene was much the same as on the preceding days: the animals were grazing, the birds were flitting back and forth and the day ahead looked the same as the last.

William had been up for hours, already busying himself downstairs where he had emptied the bins and set a load of washing going in the machine. He had opened the curtains in the living room and the snug, which was where Henry found him rifling through one of the chest of drawers.

'What are you looking for?' he asked.

'A list your mother made of her favourite songs,' William replied sharply.

'Of course,' Henry said matching his father's abrupt tone. He was not about to become target practice for his father's frustration. 'I'm making tea, do you want some?'

'Yes please,' William said, stopping and smiling at Henry. For a second, before resuming his frantic search, Henry's lovely dad was back in the room. Henry stood still, looking around. The room was a mess. There were pieces of their lives crammed on every surface, each one a reminder of time that had passed. On a shelf, there was a small cup that Henry had made at infant school, painted sludge-brown as the colours had merged together beneath his brush. There was a framed photograph of him, Sebastian and Nancy on a beach somewhere; despite the brilliant sunshine the weather must have been cold judging by the heavy coats and winter boots being worn by people in the background. In their swimming costumes, the three children were oblivious to the chill. There were games and puzzles and books no one had looked at for years, ornaments and knick-knacks. There were pictures on every wall and, suspended from the curtain rail, a bobbin-knitted mouse hanging from a tiny knitted ladder which Nancy had made for William one birthday. Henry hadn't looked at the room properly for years.

Leaving, Henry went into the kitchen and, even though the washing machine was running and the dishwasher had been emptied, looking out of the window, into the yard, Betsy and the goats appeared not to have been fed. It was normally the first thing William would do in the morning before he and Betsy shared breakfast together but there was no sign of William, nor the animals having had anything to eat. Henry's first job of the day was to slop out.

~

Sebastian's choice of walk was either around their garden and down to the river, or, if he wanted to go a bit further and see some life, he could go to the park by turning right out of their gate and down towards the greenhouse and the manicured lawns. But today, still agitated, he decided to mix things up. He and Panda headed left out of the gate and down the hill. In all the time he had lived there, he had never once stopped to look at the collection of small shops halfway down. Panda pulled on the lead as they walked, eager to get to the park, the luring rancid smell of the pond already in her nostrils. As they walked past the shops, some open but most closed, they came to the café Panda knew so well. Spotting her favourite waitress through the open door, she dragged Sebastian in; taking herself to the small table she had shared with Henry a few days earlier. Enticed by the smell of coffee and the bustling atmosphere of the café, Sebastian did not resist. The waitress soon appeared and Panda shot out from beneath the tablecloth, wagging her tail. The waitress bent down to make a fuss of her little friend.

'Well hello my beautiful girl. How are you?' she asked, delighted to see her. 'I wasn't expecting to see you again so soon,' she said fluffing Panda's fur as she stood up. Only then did she look at Sebastian. 'Oh!' she said in surprise, expecting Henry to be at the end of Panda's lead.

She and Sebastian froze, staring at one another.

'Sebastian!'

'Meggie!'

Dumbfounded, Sebastian searched the waitress' familiar face. He had not seen her for almost thirty years, but she was instantly recognisable and instinctively he hugged her.

'What are you doing here?' she asked, confused as she extricated herself, looking down at Panda. 'Was that Henry? It is Panda isn't it?'

'Yes, it's Panda. It's been a long time, Meg.'

'It has,' Meggie replied. 'How are you?'

'I'm... I'm... fuck!' Sebastian said, running his fingers through his hair, 'I don't know to be honest. I'm in shock! You look amazing.'

Age had been kind to Meggie. Her face had softened and her mass of blonde hair had taken on a lovely soft silver-grey between the colours, which suited her. It was still as she had always worn it, held loosely at the back with fine wisps falling around her face. Her face was still pretty and her freckles had spread over the years to cover a high proportion of her pale skin. She was as slim as she had always been when they had known each other and, standing close to him, her smell took him back to a different time.

'Is this place yours?' Sebastian asked, looking around the busy café.

'No,' Meggie replied, 'it's my daughter's. I'm just holding the fort for a while.'

'I can't believe it's you,' he said again. 'Are you able to sit with us?'

'I'd love to, but you can see how I'm fixed. Another time though? Can I get you something?'

'I'll have a coffee please,' Sebastian said, sitting down without taking his eyes off her.

Coming close, Meggie crouched down to ruffle Panda's ears. Sebastian looked at the curve of her neck and was transported back to the day they met. It's so good to see you, he thought as she turned away.

Meggie was the first girl he had fallen in love with and she had managed to keep a bit of herself inside Sebastian's heart. Before he met her, in the summer before his eighteenth birthday, he had been in a dark place. He had struggled with anxiety, and, through his exams, had lost himself to the fear of the enormity of the world. He had questioned everything he once believed and did not know who he was and he was scared. Then he had met Meggie, and she had grounded him. Settling his thoughts, she had helped him understand himself, reassuring him there was nothing to fear. He had always been grateful to her for that.

They met on a campsite in the south of France during the summer before university. Sebastian had made the mammoth journey from Edinburgh onboard a coach with Paul and two other school friends; it was a long way to go squished in with no air conditioning. Meggie, with her three friends, had flown.

Arriving at the same time, their tents pitched next to each other, the two groups had made an instant connection and from the first night, the eight of them joined forces and spent a crazy week together venturing little further than the campsite which spilled onto the beach. For a group of teens experiencing their first taste of freedom, they went completely wild. Too much drink, too much food and too much sex was a great way to break into adulthood, and they all promised that they would keep in touch.

None of them did, except Sebastian and Meggie who embarked on an intense long-distance relationship. It was ten years crammed into ten months and they thought it would never end. Until one day it did.

They took their first tumble when they went their separate ways to university, which was where Sebastian met Matilda. He had the two relationships running side by side for a while before Meggie suspected something was wrong.

The usual indicators that the romance had run its course flagged up: her letters went unanswered, the phone stopped ringing and Sebastian became too busy to meet. All of a sudden, the connection between them had gone, so Meggie ended it in a series of letters without hearing an objection back from him. Until this day, they had not seen or spoken to each other since.

Seeing her today made Sebastian desperate to feel that sense of perspective she had given him once before; here he was, middle-aged and fearful again.

He watched her as she moved around the café. Occasionally she caught his eye and smiled. With a promise to return the next day, he and Panda left, each with a spring in their step. Seeing Meggie had lifted his spirits and Panda was excited to be continuing down the hill rather than back home. As they walked towards the park, casting an eye into the basement kitchens of the houses as they passed, Sebastian looked at the scrap of paper on which Meggie had written her number. Her handwriting had not changed, it was still soft and round; he had always loved her writing.

By the time they got home, Matilda was just about to leave for the office. Adrenaline was flowing through Sebastian's veins and he was smiling. With everything he was going through, breathing the same air as Meggie had made him light-headed.

Matilda looked at him as he leapt up the stairs two at a time. His demeanour had changed. He had returned home buoyant. 'Okay Panda, what have you done with your dad? Where did you bury him? I don't recognise this one you've brought home,' she said as she thought how strangely he was acting. She was worried about him. One minute he was mourning his mother, the next he was thumping tables and kicking walls and now he was skipping home after a walk in the park before heading to the office to humiliate the man who had once been his closest friend. She knew he had previously benefitted from counselling and wondered whether he might be open to a revisit, just to even himself out. It had worked once before, apparently. He was a closed book but he might open up to a stranger. She finished getting ready for work but not before she contacted an acquaintance.

~

Before heading to Taligth, Sebastian went into the office. Sitting at his desk with his phone in his hand, he thumbed the piece of paper holding Meggie's number, suddenly desperate to reconnect. With his finger poised, his peripheral vision alerted him to a figure standing in the open doorway to his office. Quickly looking up, thinking it might be Matilda or Niamh, he was surprised to see Paul standing in front of him.

Earlier, Sebastian had sent Paul a message. Initially he was going to tell him to stay away from the office, but regrettably there were things about the company's accounting processes that only Paul knew and he would be needed if Graham required answers. He was advised not to talk to anyone, but to go straight to his office and sit and wait. Other than for a chair and desk, his office had been emptied.

'I wanted to say how sorry I am to hear about your mum,' Paul said, solemnly. 'She was a...' Instinctively, and without letting him finish his sentence, Sebastian grabbed hold of the glass globe paperweight, which was sitting proudly on his desk, and flung it in Paul's direction.

'FUCK OFF!' he shouted, as Paul yelled and ducked, the missile skimming past his head and hurtling towards the desks outside the office. Screams from their occupants could be heard as they dived out of the way. The glass ball bounced across the desk like a skimming stone on a millpond before smashing into the face of an iMac. A small price to pay for nearly braining the jerk, Sebastian thought.

Recovering from the shock, everyone returned to their desks and examined the damage as Sebastian waved an apology of 'momentary madness'. Knowing what had happened and having seen who was in his office at the time, they would have understood.

Seething, Sebastian spoke quietly. 'I suggest, unless you want to be hung from the window by your dick, you go upstairs and don't come down until one of us asks you to do so. And if you *dare* mention my mum ever, *ever*, I will rip you to *fucking* shreds! Do I make myself clear?'

Leaving Sebastian's office, Paul did not speak again.

Sebastian grabbed his keys and jacket and headed for the fields.

As he got to his car, a message lit up on his phone, Panda's smiling face fractured behind the smashed glass making him smile. The message was from Patrick McCarthy. He was arriving in Edinburgh on Friday. He had a number of meetings arranged and wished to meet with Sebastian later in the day to see how he was. Nothing else, no business agenda unless their meeting went that way. Patrick was a good man.

~

The afternoon spent working on the farm with Sebastian gave Henry some respite from the sombreness that had shrouded Taligth. He was going back to Newcastle the following day and, getting outside into the fresh air, catching up on news other than funeral arrangements did him good, although Sebastian's shocking revelation was hard to digest. He could see how much it hurt his brother to admit how beaten he felt and how he was now constantly looking over his shoulder, suspicious of everyone.

Although Sebastian usually told Henry everything, for some reason he did not want to tell him about his chance encounter with Meggie in the café on the hill; he wanted to keep her a secret for a while, having already decided to return to the café in the morning before work.

172

Day Seven

After an hour in the gym and a quick shower, Sebastian took Panda for her early morning walk. Still half an hour before the café opened, they headed to the park where, much to Sebastian's horror, Panda took off across the grass and launched herself into the pond, emerging a few minutes later covered in black, slimy pond weed and reeking of the stagnant water. She ran around as he tried desperately to wash her beneath the cold tap near the children's sandpit, but nothing was shifting the stench and, like walking a skunk, he led her back up the hill.

'It's good to have the old Panda back,' Meggie commented, the pungent bog smell wafting into the café.

'Sorry,' Sebastian frowned.

'It's fine, I'm used to it aren't I, Panda?' Meggie said, bending down and talking to the soggy pup.

'You're not on your own today?'

'No, I have my niece helping out this morning.'

'Your niece, who's...?'

'Jo's.'

'So she is, I can see,' he said, taking a considered look at the young waitress grappling with the overzealous steam pipe on the coffee machine, remembering Meggie's sister. 'How is Jo?'

'We lost her to cancer three years ago.'

'I'm sorry to hear that,' Sebastian said. Unsure as to whether there was anything profound he could say after hearing such news, Sebastian was fearful of taking the lid off his own grief so did not dwell. 'Do you think your niece could cope if you stopped for five minutes? It looks like she might be winning the battle with the coffee machine.'

'She hates that thing. Do you want a drink?'

'Coffee please,' Sebastian said, sitting at the same table as the day before, with Panda exuding a miasma of damp fur, steaming beneath it.

Watching Meggie walk away, Sebastian suddenly became aware of himself in this strange little café looking at a woman he no longer knew, with his dog, innocent and oblivious sitting at his feet. What am I doing here? He asked himself. What do I want? And for a split second he contemplated getting up and leaving, but something compelled him to stay. Knowing he was playing with fire, he stayed rooted to his seat. Remembering location services were enabled, he switched his phone off.

'So,' Meggie said, bringing drinks and joining Sebastian to the table, 'from what I've read, things have worked out well for you.'

'I've done okay,' Sebastian said, looking at her.

'More than okay,' Meggie replied, raising her eyebrows.

'I suppose,' he said coyly, not wanting to talk about himself. He wanted to talk about Meggie, reminisce about France, hear that she had never stopped loving him and find out she was happy but unsatisfied. He wanted her to put her arms around him and tell him everything was going to be all right as she had done when he was seventeen.

The conversation between them was comfortable and natural and the years peeled away as they laughed about their hedonistic week in France and about their time on fruit farms and their countless, ridiculous journeys across the country to spend a day together, both agreeing life had been much simpler when they'd only had themselves to think about. They did not talk about the Easter of their first year at university.

'So, this is your daughter's place,' Sebastian remarked after Meggie told him she lived in Hexham on an alpaca farm with her second husband and only visited Edinburgh to help out in the café when her daughter needed her. 'She's a long way from Hexham.'

'She is, but she likes it up here.'

'It looks to be a good business.'

'It's hard work for little reward, but it makes a living and she's happy.' Without pausing, Meggie asked Sebastian about what life had brought him, beyond riches. He told her a little about Matilda and the children until she asked after his parents. He wasn't prepared, and in an instant, with an overwhelming sense of loss, his face dropped. Meggie gasped but did not speak as she looked at him, observing the same pain in his eyes she had seen when they had first met.

'We lost Mum a week ago,' Sebastian said, trying to control his voice. 'Out of the blue.' Looking at his past sitting in front of him, he felt an overwhelming urge to cry. Conscious of a café full of people, he tried to control himself. He buried his head in his hands. Understanding his suffering, for Meggie had been through much sadness in her life, she reached across to him, resting her hand gently on his arm. Sebastian put his hand over hers and held onto it until he had composed himself. 'I'm sorry Meg,' he said. 'I shouldn't have come. I need to go.' Embarrassed, he hurriedly gathered Panda's lead, his wallet and phone, and apologised again. Unable to look at Meggie, and desperate not to catch anyone's eye, he and a ruffled Panda rushed to the door.

'Don't be sorry,' Meggie said, trying hard to ignore the feelings she'd felt while touching the man she had once loved.

Holding onto the door handle, taking a breath to speak, he turned back to her. He hesitated. A long moment dragged slowly by as they looked, wide-eyed at each other, but he could not find the words. At last he drew his eyes away from Meggie's. 'Come on Panda,' he said, closing the café door softly behind him. Meggie watched him walk away until he turned to look back, and she waved. He smiled whilst savouring the memory of the feeling of her hand within his own. He had needed that.

So, Elspeth had died, Meggie thought to herself as she went back to serving tables. She had often thought about

William and Elspeth and wondered whether they were still alive. They had been very kind to her after she and Sebastian had split up. She had wanted to keep in touch but it had become too difficult and she had not seen them since her life became complicated, after she was befriended by Nancy.

~

'You were gone a long time,' Matilda said as Sebastian arrived home with a pungent Panda.

'Panda jumped into the pond so I walked around for a bit to let her dry off,' Sebastian lied.

'She stinks! Are you all right?' Matilda asked, concerned.

'Not really,' Sebastian replied.

'Has something happened?' Matilda asked, sensing Sebastian's unease.

Looking at her, Sebastian hesitated. How could he tell her that he had sat in a café and had held the hand of the woman who had once saved him? How could he tell his wife that even now Meggie could reach a part of him that she had never been able to, no matter how hard she tried? How could he tell her he cried with Meggie when he could not cry with her?

'No,' he said. 'I was just walking.'

'It will get easier, Seb, I promise.'

'I know,' he replied, nodding. 'Right! Panda and I are going for a shower.'

'Brace yourself Panda, not a pretty sight,' Matilda said, smiling.

'Some people would walk over hot coals for a bit of this you know,' he mocked.

'Only the ones who are too stupid to realise their feet are on fire.' Laughing, Sebastian swiped at Matilda with the dog lead, and missed. He and Panda trudged upstairs.

'Two showers in one morning? Who is she?' Matilda called after him.

His heart suddenly pounding, Sebastian stopped, before continuing a touch slower than he had been, his eyes searching the stair-treads. People who play with fire, get burnt, he thought.

After loading the dishwasher, Matilda went upstairs to get ready. Listening in, she could hear Sebastian talking to Panda in the shower and she was reminded of when she used to eavesdrop on him telling the children bedtime stories. His stories were nonsense, but he put great effort into the voices of the characters and the children loved them.

Sitting at her dressing table, she turned to her mirror. Looking at her reflection, she wondered what Sebastian had seen in her when they first met. He was so handsome and could have had his pick, but instead he settled for her. Why? What was it he saw? She wondered whether he still saw it or whether they had become so thoroughly entwined as a couple that he didn't need to anymore. She could no longer see her own beauty.

Coming out of the bathroom, noticing her staring, Sebastian put his face alongside hers. 'My god, it's your mother!' he teased, a wicked smile on his face. He kissed her cheek and walked into the dressing room. Panda was running around the bedroom drying her fur on any surface that availed itself; wall, bed, carpet and back again.

Sebastian came back into the bedroom buttoning up his shirt. In her mirror, he caught Matilda's eye. 'I was only teasing,' he smiled. 'I didn't mean it.'

'I know.' Matilda hesitated, uncertain whether now was a good time to broach the subject. 'I hope you don't mind,' she said, picking up her moisturiser, 'but I called an acquaintance of mine yesterday, Juliet Ellsworth. Her daughter's a counsellor...'

Taken by surprise, Sebastian stopped and looked at Matilda. 'What are you suggesting?' he asked defensively.

'You're dealing with so much at the moment...' she replied, dabbing lotion onto her cheeks.

'What's that supposed to mean?'

'The paperweight?' she said, raising her eyebrows into the mirror.

'He deserved it,' Sebastian spat, going back into the dressing room.

'No one says he didn't, but you nearly killed Ava.'

'I apologised,' he replied, indignantly.

'Listen to yourself. Listen to the way you're speaking. It's like living with Jekyll and Hyde, and since your mum died...'

'Am I not allowed to grieve now?' he snapped, coming back into the bedroom, tucking his shirt into his trousers.

'Stop being so defensive, that's not what I'm saying and you know it. I'm trying to help.'

'Since when have I asked for help?'

'Exactly!' Matilda exclaimed. 'You try to do everything yourself. You don't let anyone else help. Henry is desperate to help. I'm desperate to help, but you won't let us in.'

'When did you speak to Henry?' Sebastian asked, threading his belt.

'He called while you were out. Why?'

'What did he want?'

'To speak with you.'

'What about?'

'I don't know! I don't think it was anything urgent. Stop it, Seb! He would have said if it was urgent or he'd have called you on your mobile. He said he'd catch up with you when he sees you later. He's worried about you, Seb, we're both worried about you.'

'Well stop it, because it's not fair. If I say I'm fine, I'm fine. Let me deal with it my way,' he said. 'Henry shouldn't talk to you.'

'What?' Matilda exclaimed, putting her moisturiser down and turning to look at Sebastian.

'He should talk to me,' Sebastian replied, sitting on the bed to put his socks on, his back turned to Matilda.

'So that you can keep control, is that it?' she asked. 'It is, isn't it? You want to control everyone and everything around you! Isn't this *exactly* what I'm saying? You cannot do it all yourself. You cannot organise your mum's funeral, support your dad, be there for Henry, for me, the kids, the bloody dog, sell the company all at the same time. No one human can do all those things and hope to function properly. You were all over the place yesterday.' Sebastian stopped what he was doing. 'I'm not having a go at you,' she said, 'it's only been a few days since you lost your mum and I expect you to be all over the place, but...' she took a breath, '...even before that, before we went to New York you were spending night after night lying on the factory floor picking tiny bits of dust out of machines which were working perfectly. You were painting the office walls at three in the morning, laying carpets only replaced a year ago, filling the already full coffee machines, emptying the bins... need I go on?' she said softly. 'There are people who can do these things for you, people we *pay* to do these things, but you're obsessed, Seb. When will you learn you cannot do it all?' she sighed. 'I just thought speaking to someone might help you get through the next few weeks unscathed because you sure as hell won't let me help you!' she said, turning back to her dressing table.

Sebastian continued to get dressed in silence, mulling over Matilda's words. He had never been good at admitting weakness; far easier for him to walk away, which was what he did, leaving Panda running around and Matilda at her dressing table. Not in the mood for breakfast, he retrieved his phone from the pocket of his coat and switched it back on. Along with several work messages, there was a missed call from Henry followed by a message about one of the tractors. There was nothing from Meggie. Matilda did not come downstairs. Before he left the house, he drafted Meggie a text.

It was good to see you this morning. Sorry I lost it, how embarrassing. I promise I've not gone soft. I'll try to contain myself next time... hoping there is a next time. Seb x

Pausing before sending it, he looked back up the stairs towards his and Matilda's bedroom and then again at the screen, re-reading what he had written. Did he want this? There had been other occasions when he had held his phone in much the same way over the years. He had always resisted temptation, but this time the compulsion was too great. He pressed 'send' and, picking up his overnight bag, he left without saying goodbye.

With a busy day of meetings, followed by dinner with their biggest client in the evening, it was after midnight by the time he arrived at Taligth. He let himself into the house to find Henry sitting in the kitchen pouring over his script.

'I'm sorry Hal, you should have gone,' he said,

'I don't mind a midnight drive. Do you want a coffee?'

'No, no, you need to get off. You'll be knackered.'

'I'm fine. How did your meetings go?' Henry asked, packing away his things.

'They were okay. There's still a lot to do, and we're dealing with Paul of course but, otherwise... how's Dad?'

'He went to bed an hour ago, he had a bit of a headache.'

'That's hardly surprising. How's his shoulder been today?' Sebastian asked, looking through the cupboards to find something sweet to eat.

'Much the same.'

'It's been tough for you staying here hasn't it?' Sebastian said, discovering his mother's last batch of scones and deciding to leave them where he had found them.

'At times,' Henry replied, picking up his bags. 'Right, I'd better hit the road.'

Henry found it difficult to walk away from Taligth. At the farm, he felt connected to his mother and leaving he could feel her apron strings tugging at him to stay. He dared not look back as his car clattered over the cattle grid.

Sebastian waited on the top step until Henry had disappeared. Back in the house, he checked on William, watching his father's troubled sleep; he was clearly uncomfortable and called out in his dreams. Sebastian could not determine the words, but understood that sleep did not bring relief.

Back downstairs in the pantry, Sebastian looked through his father's wine selection. The small room was cool and dark with a narrow staircase scaling one wall leading to an empty loft space. During daylight, the sun barely touched it, making it colder than the rest of the house. Sebastian remembered how, as children, they had been told the room was haunted, making them afraid of being shut in. He knew, in reality, it was to stop them stealing biscuits, but the feeling had stayed. From the outside, it was hard to see in through the small, dusty window. Anyone could be lurking in the shadows. It was a difficult room for Sebastian to be in and, pained by memories, he retreated quickly, clutching a bottle that was hidden at the back. Elspeth had never shown an interest in William's wine collection, but much to Sebastian's delight, his father had developed an expensive palette.

It had been an intense few days and Sebastian was not ready to go to bed. In spite of the late hour and autumn chill, he lit the outdoor wood burner and, with his father's winter coat across his back, sat on the bench looking across the garden and into the quivering blackness. It was good to feel the cold air in his lungs and look out into a clear night. All that could be seen were the stars illuminated by a thin orange crescent of the new moon.

Checking his phone for messages, Sebastian was disappointed to see his screen empty. Perhaps he had misread Meggie; perhaps she had given him the wrong number; perhaps it would be a good thing if she didn't message back. He lay down on the cool wood and looked to see which star shone brightest.

Day Eight

Thursday

The wine allowed Sebastian better sleep on the hard wooden bench than he'd had over the past week. He awoke to dewy cobwebs strung across openings, occupied by resplendent autumn spiders waiting patiently for breakfast to become ensnared.

Opening the back door, William was startled by Sebastian's slow emergence from beneath his heavy coat, which had protected him from the cold.

'Sebastian!' William exclaimed, catching his breath. 'What are you doing out here?'

'It was too nice a night,' Sebastian replied, as William noted the empty wine bottle beside the bench. Not questioning him, he absently threw Betsy and the goats some food and shuffled back into the kitchen, putting the kettle on the aga on his way back upstairs to the bathroom.

'Morning Mum,' Sebastian whispered, looking up towards the sky. 'You didn't come to me last night. What does that mean?' he asked, for in his dreams she had visited him every one of the previous nights.

Stiffly making his way into the house, he looked around the kitchen at the things his parents had gathered over the years. Nothing matched, yet everything looked right. The kettle whistled as he checked his phone. Although the damp had got behind the shattered glass, he could just make out two messages. Disappointingly, both were from Henry. The first said that he had arrived home just after 3 a.m. an hour added to his journey by motorway closures and that despite feeling a complete wreck, he had to be in school by 8.30 a.m. to meet some disgruntled parents before registration. Remembering his own school days, Sebastian did not envy him.

The second message was a PS. *Let me know how today goes*. Glancing around at the kitchen, which looked the same as it did a week ago, Sebastian knew today at Taligth would be much like every other had been since their mother had left them.

Still no word from Meggie. He wondered whether to message again.

Coming slowly back into the kitchen and sitting in Elspeth's favourite chair, William joined Sebastian at the kitchen table. It was strange for Sebastian to see his father sitting in his mother's space, leaving his own vacant. William looked drained, and the tea Sebastian had made for him went unacknowledged.

'You're still not sleeping well are you, Dad?

'Well enough, considering.'

'Do you want some breakfast?'

'I don't think I do.'

'You should eat something,' Sebastian said as William shook his head. Sebastian sighed. 'We've a few things we need to do today,' Sebastian added, getting the last of the bread out and cutting himself and his father a slice, hoping the smell of toast might whet his appetite. 'Our appointment at the registrar's is at half past ten. Are you okay with that?' William nodded his response. For fear of looking foolish he did not say he wasn't. The truth was that he was frightened of leaving Taligth, and Elspeth there on her own. 'I've got some calls to make,' Sebastian continued, 'which I'll do before we go.' Again, William nodded. 'I think we should come home via the shop. You need some food. This is the last of the bread.' Another vacant nod and Sebastian sighed, wondering whether his father was listening at all.

William did not eat the toast Sebastian had made for him. He sat at the kitchen table nursing a cold cup of tea, nervously waiting until it was time to leave. He found driving away from Taligth difficult. He looked at the oak trees that lined the single-track lane leading to the road. Some of them were centuries old with thick trunks that twisted and turned their way up to gnarled branches. In their younger days, he and Elspeth had liked to climb them and watch the farm from on high; William found it impossible not to dwell.

After picking up Elspeth's death certificate from the doctors' surgery on the outskirts of the village, they headed into town. The registrar's office was housed inside an old school building. In a drably painted anteroom, William and Sebastian sat upright on uncomfortable wooden chairs, waiting for the registrar.

William, feeling uneasy and nervous in the daunting and unfamiliar surroundings, talked in hushed tones about the strangeness he felt finding himself in this unwelcoming place. Of course, one of them was bound to have visited it at some point, but it was not something they had prepared for. No matter how quietly they spoke, the walls of the soulless room echoed their voices back to them, and eventually they fell into an awkward silence. Minutes passed.

'At least she's not a vegetable,' William suddenly said, mumbling his thoughts, breaking the tension.

Unable to help himself, Sebastian laughed. 'What, like a parsnip or a sprout?'

'You know what I mean,' William said, half smiling at his son who was trying hard not to laugh. But William was a terrible giggler, and the sight of Sebastian coupled with the silent tension held captive in the room was not helpful. Before he could control himself, he started. He spluttered out little chuckles at first, his shoulders shaking. His chuckles grew, becoming silent, speechless, tear-spilling laughter, and the two of them fell about whilst mouthing incoherently what sounded vaguely like a vegetable shopping list. What the registrar must have thought when he respectfully opened his door to ask them into his office, they would never know. He must have been expecting to see two mournful souls twisting tear sodden hankies between their fingers, whereas he was greeted by William and

Sebastian acting like two badly behaved schoolboys waiting to be beckoned into the headmaster's office.

'Mr. Campbell?' the registrar asked sombrely.

'Um, yes,' Sebastian said, 'yes, sorry, yes, that's us... sorry,' he said, trying to ignore a final splutter from William.

The registrar's meeting was a formality. It took less than thirty minutes to provide the details requested: the date and place of the death, the address of the deceased, their full names, including the maiden name or other names by which the deceased had been known, where and when they were born. It was at the mention of Taligth that made William want to leave.

On their way home they agreed that their behaviour before their appointment was inexcusable and they laughed, knowing how Elspeth would have chastised them when they got home. 'Och! Ye naughty wee jimmies!' she would have said with a wink.

Sebastian enjoyed seeing his father laugh.

~

Having arrived home in the early hours, rather than going straight to bed, Henry had lain on the sofa with Mabel, listening to sad music. Lorna had got up to go to the bathroom and crept to the top of the stairs to see whether he might come to bed, but she could hear him talking to Mabel, telling her how he was feeling. Knowing the pain he was in, Lorna decided to leave him; grief being the price a person pays for loving someone.

Henry did not make it to bed, but slept the few hours on the sofa, waking in a rush for work. He and Lorna exchanged a quick kiss 'hello' and 'goodbye' as he frantically ran out of the door with a piece of toast in his mouth and the promise of catching up later.

After his meeting with Mr. and Mrs. Cox, Henry was not in the best of moods. They had insisted on seeing him first thing to discuss their son's apparent lack of progress under his tutelage, their precious son who was not very bright and was incredibly lazy. However tempted he felt to offload both barrels and tell them exactly what he thought of their 'darling boy', he skirted positively around the truth as best he could, which for Henry, and his current mood, did not come easily. It was not good for business to upset the fee payers, not in this uncertain economic climate, no matter how much he wanted to tell them they were wasting their money.

His day did not improve. He muddled through, hoping for the opportunity to catch forty winks in his classroom during lunchtime, but was denied it by a sixth former who wanted help with differential equations – not a five-minute job. He did manage a brief catch-up with Sebastian though, who confessed his and their father's antics at the registrar's. Henry wished desperately he had been there.

After school, he drove straight to the rehearsal rooms. He had not seen the team since returning from France and it was good to be back with everyone again. However, as he walked in, he was confused by the setup of the stage area, which appeared not to be laid out to the theatre's floor plan. Before Lorna had chance to speak with him, it was Eve who clumsily alerted Henry to the problem. 'What do you think to the new theatre, Henry?' she asked, innocently, assuming he knew.

'What do you mean, 'new theatre?' he asked, looking straight at Lorna, who immediately put down her paintbrush and went over to him.

'The Sheep Shed,' Eve continued, looking at Henry's perplexed expression, 'we lost the Morrilox didn't we? Or have I got it wrong?'

'You haven't got it wrong, Eve,' Lorna said, approaching.

'Sorry, I assumed you'd told him,' Eve said, grimacing to Lorna as she backed away.

'Told me what? Would someone care to explain?' he asked, irritably, opening his voice to the room, causing everyone to stop what they were doing and look at him.

'Don't worry, everyone,' Lorna called. 'Carry on,' she said, taking Henry to one side.

'I'm really sorry, Lorna, I thought he knew,' Eve said as they passed her, feeling terrible for blurting it out so carelessly.

'It's not a problem, Eve, it's not your fault. Carry on whilst I explain to Henry what's happened.' They went back to rehearsal whilst Lorna flicked the switch on the kettle.

'What's going on?' Henry asked impatiently.

'I'm sorry I haven't told you but you were home so late last night and then to work so early this morning I...'

'Okay, I get it, but what's happened to the Morrilox?' Henry asked.

Lorna let out a deep breath. 'They've gone bust, Hal. They went into administration a few days ago.'

'You what? SHIT!' Henry shouted bringing the room to a hush as rehearsal stopped and everyone looked his way, then at each other before resuming.

Handing him his mug, Lorna continued. 'It was really sudden and I was desperate to sort it before you came home, which I have, I think, thank goodness!'

'How come we didn't know?'

'Because they didn't tell us until it happened.'

'This play is doomed, isn't it? First of all Dad has his fall which pushes the script back by weeks, then Mum bloody dies...'

'Henry!'

'... and now this! Why the *fuck* do I bother? Perhaps someone is trying to tell me something. Maybe someone out there is saying, 'hey Henry, you *prick*, you've been unsuccessful all your life! Well, here you are, let's to put you in your place. Just when you think you're about to get your big break after all these years of working *every* hour God sends, sinking your life savings into some black abyss, doing a *hundred* jobs you *fucking hate* because you need to put food on the table whilst you're trying to 'live the dream', well, you knob, have we got news for you! It's... it's like the last scene of the bloody Truman Show when the producers are throwing everything at...whatever his name is...trying to stop him getting to the back of the set...! For crying out loud! *Fuck!*' he expleted, spilling his tea.

Lorna stood, arms folded, waiting. 'When you've quite finished,' she said calmly.

'I guess we've lost the deposit?'

'I expect we'll be at the back of a long list of creditors. I can't see we'll get that back.'

'*Shit!* We might as well pack up and go home. PACK UP AND GO HOME EVERYONE,' he shouted into the room as Lorna shook her head behind him.

'Stop it, Henry! If you want to carry on like this than go ahead, but if you stop shouting for a minute and *listen* I will tell you what I have sorted,' she said sternly, waiting for him to calm down. 'Are you ready to listen?'

'Yes,' he replied sullenly, as if being told off by a formidable, but lovely, school dinner lady. 'Sorry, yes, I'm calm. *Shit!* Sorry,' he said, looking at her, smiling weakly.

'Right,' she said, smiling back. She reached her hand out to his. 'Okay, so it's taken some work and a million phone calls, but I've found somewhere else. I think it's absolutely perfect, Hal, much better than The Morrilox.'

'Okay...' he said, his sad expression reflecting the multitude of emotions he was feeling.

'It's called The Sheep Shed, and it's in Scotland.'

'Scotland?'

'Listen! It's close to Taligth, on the other side of Edinburgh, and I've checked with everyone here and they're all up for it. It's a newish venue, so just starting to get going which is why we've managed to get in. It's a brilliant space, Hal. You'll love it.'

'But if it's new, how do we get an audience? The Morrilox had such a good reputation.'

'The production that's in next week has sold out, as has the one after that. It's only small; it'll be like Paris.'

'Paris was different.'

'I don't see how. Give people some credit. Those who go to a place like The Sheep Shed love the sort of stuff we put on. If we advertise it well, I think it'll be great, I really do. The venue is so up for doing anything to help. We did it in Edinburgh, and then Paris, and if we can do it there, we can do it here. It also means you can be close to your dad,' she said, squeezing his hand. 'There's a production in before us, which only gives us a two or three-day window to turn around, but I think it's doable. Have a look at their website and let me know what you think. But to be honest, we've not really got much choice. There's very little out there that isn't already booked and virtually nothing that's suitable. We either do the production in four weeks at The Sheep Shed or we cancel it. That's our choice.'

Looking at Lorna, Henry could tell she had been running on adrenaline for days. She was excited and he was shattered.

'By the way,' she added, as she turned to put the kettle on again, 'it's Truman.'

'What?' Henry asked, confused.

'The character who was trying to get to the back of the set; the clue's in the title,' she said cheekily.

Shaking his head, Henry laughed.

With a refill of his mug, he clicked onto the theatre's website, examining every detail. It certainly looked like the sort of place they could do well in and, reading the technical specifications and understanding the layout of the performance space, he could see why the rehearsal room was set out the way it was. Lorna and the team were already way ahead of him.

Having spoken with both his and The Sheep Shed's production team, Henry confirmed their provisional booking by paying a hefty deposit. With fingers crossed for good publicity and a fair wind, Henry went back into rehearsal. Four weeks was a tall order but the challenge ignited his excitement once more and for a few short hours he was able to put his 'real' life to one side.

~

Not knowing quite how the rest of the day was going to pan out, Sebastian set William on a mission of deciding the music he wanted played at Elspeth's funeral. William had found the list Elspeth had made of her favourite songs tucked neatly between the pages of a book called 'The Power of Words' about how lyrics of songs reflect human emotion. All very profound and a load of rubbish William thought.

With intermittent signal, Sebastian kept checking his phone for messages. There was a lovely one from Matilda, which he did not reply to, and a load of work ones that needed dealing with urgently, but there was nothing from Meggie. He looked at the phone as if it held the answer; maybe he would call her tonight if he had not heard from her. As he held it in his hand it suddenly rang, and with shocked excitement, he answered quickly.

'Meggie?'

'Hi,' she said, the weak signal making her voice distorted and difficult to hear.

Walking out of the kitchen into the yard, with his heart pounding, Sebastian melted into a burble of vocal stupidity; 'Hi... Meggie...! I was just thinking about you... not in a creepy way, just thinking... you know...' he stuttered. 'It's good to hear your voice.'

'Are you okay?' she asked.

'Yes, fine, sorry, I'm at Taligth... it's... the signal here... it's... oh, I don't know what it is, it's just...'

'I thought you might have come into the café this morning,' she said.

'Did you want me to?' he asked, smiling. The pause pulsated. 'Did you get my message?' he continued, trying to fill the void he had opened.

'I did.'

'So...' he said, picking at the straw caught in Betsy's hair.

'So?'

'So, what now?' he asked, excitement in his voice.

Since meeting Sebastian again, Meggie had been unsettled. The surprise of seeing him and being reminded of what it was about him that she had loved, and loathed, had prayed on her mind. She hadn't been able to shift the thoughts.

She had often wondered what it might be like to bump into him again, imagining what she would say, what *he* would say, what he would be like. Seeing him again was nothing like she had thought it would be and she was no longer as brave as she had been in her daydreams.

Before calling him, she had given herself time to get things straight in her head and to plan what she wanted to say. In spite of her heart quickening when she first saw him in the café, she had no desire to pick up with him again and was hoping he would not be so foolhardy as to think she might. There was so much she wanted to say, and she never believed she would ever have the opportunity. But here it was.

Even though their relationship had been short, Sebastian had changed her life and she had grown wary and distrustful. Distrust had ruined her first marriage, destroying the man who had tried to help her recover and she vowed she would never let herself become emotionally dependent again. Married for a second time, she and her husband were friends more than lovers, but at least she had finally let someone new into her life. However much her heart skipped beats, she was not about to risk her recovery by getting involved with Sebastian again. Yet something compelled her to call him. Why? What was it she wanted? To have her say? To tell him everything? To explain? She did not know.

'When are you home?' she asked.

'At the weekend. Will you be in the café if Panda and I come by Saturday morning? I've missed seeing you today...' he said, his brain not quite knowing what his tongue was playing at. His sentence tangled awkwardly, making him feel like some kind of lovesick schoolboy trying to look cool in front of his jeering mates after tripping on the school field in front of a group of girls. Meggie listened carefully, trying to hear the seventeen-year-old. She didn't recognise him anymore.

'I'll be here,' she said. 'Perhaps we could have breakfast, if you've got time?'

'I would like that,' he said, smiling down at Betsy who was rearranging her bedding with her snout. 'I'll see you Saturday.'

Putting his phone in his pocket, Sebastian felt excited but also nervous as he thought back to a time when he had not behaved well. He was ashamed of his younger self and welcomed the opportunity to make amends, maybe even offer up some kind of explanation.

Back then, when they returned from France, he and Meggie had spent as much of the summer together as they could, before the start of a new term. They had crammed in camping in Wales, climbing in Scotland, trekking in the Peaks and strawberry picking on southern fruit farms.

In October, they went off to their chosen universities. Bright and interested, Meggie was on the south coast studying Politics and Economics while Sebastian was in the North East studying Engineering. As often as they could, they met up and they wrote to each other every day without fail, repeating what they had said on the phone the night before, telling each other over and over again how much in love they were.

At the end of their first term they spent a magical Christmas together, but returning to university for their second term was difficult. The winter months were tough and the Friday night journey up and down the country began to take its toll. Sensibly, they talked and agreed to meet up less often, but they kept up the nightly phone calls and letters, for a while at least.

As time went by, the letters became increasingly unsatisfying until, one day, a letter did not land on Meggie's doormat and in her heart she knew their seemingly impenetrable bond was breaking.

A few weeks before the end of the second term, with desperation to salvage their dwindling relationship, they talked again, agreeing to take the pressure off and allowing each other a little freedom. They arranged to talk again during the Easter holidays.

In Meggie's eyes they were still together. Sebastian however, like a dog with its tongue lolling out as it runs towards the sea, saw this as a green light, and embarked on a rampage of debauched drunken fumblings and one-night stands until the week before Easter. It was then that he met Matilda at a college gig.

The atmospheric college venue was beneath the old building and perfect for a band whose mantra was 'If you go home able to hear - you've not been listening hard enough.'

The students attending the gig were true 'rockers', and Matilda was right at the front. The room was packed and sweltering when Sebastian and his friends walked in, and Sebastian spotted Matilda straight away. Her long hair stuck to her face with sweat. She wore no makeup other than mascara, which was making its way down her cheeks. Free spirited, she had cleared a space and, engrossed in the music, she had completely lost herself, unaware of the attention she drew. Sebastian was captivated.

Despite his unwillingness to embarrass himself on the dance floor, Sebastian did not lack the courage to approach Matilda at the bar and spent the rest of the evening talking to her. Before the band had finished playing, they moved their conversation back to Matilda's flat and spent that, and every night after, together. Matilda was different from level-headed Meggie, and excitingly wild. Sebastian had never met a girl quite as unpredictable, and she understood him in a way Meggie no longer did.

To keep his conscience clear, over their first sleepless night, they sat up chatting and Sebastian told Matilda about his split from Meggie. He had convinced himself it was permanent, but knew, in his heart, that that was not the way he and Meggie had left it. Once he met Matilda, he no longer wanted to be with Meggie, but found it impossible to be without her. She had been his first love and he had told her things he would never speak of again, but that was not enough to make him stop what he was doing.

He was weak, and did not tell Meggie about Matilda, so that when Easter came and he and Meggie met up as agreed, they talked about a future he knew would not exist. Away from university, with Matilda back at her parents' house, Easter felt like the summer before and Sebastian picked up with Meggie once more. Meggie was the happiest she had ever been. They talked about everything they had done whilst away from each other; Sebastian even braving to tell her he had been unfaithful. Meggie was hurt but accepted it. When they returned to embark on the third term, Sebastian knew it was over.

The end of the relationship became evident in the first few weeks back. Meggie waited desperately, night after night, for the promised phone calls that never came, and the messages she left for Sebastian received no reply. When her birthday came and went without contact, she knew it had run its course and she was devastated, scarcely believing that Sebastian no longer shared the feelings she had for him.

On the way to her final first year exam, she posted a letter. The letter was punctuated with hurt and betrayal and steeped in sadness, but it did not convey everything she wanted to say. She would save unwritten words for when they next met, as she assumed they would... but they never did meet again, and Meggie never had the chance to say what she wanted. Not until now.

~

Listening to the long list of music choices for Elspeth's funeral had exhausted William, so he went into the front room to rest.

After helping Ade and Sam with the milking, Sebastian was in charge of dinner. He and William shared a bottle of wine as they ate the burnt offerings Sebastian laid before them.

194

'Mum never did teach me how to cook,' he said, pushing his plate away and bringing his glass of wine forward.

'I can tell,' William replied.

'So, we've got the music then?'

'I think so, though it's probably more what I like rather than what your mother liked,' William said glumly.

Sebastian sighed.

After dinner, William moved into the front room. Once settled, he appeared comforted, as if the day had stopped making demands on him. The repeated programmes on the television held his attention for the most part, only interrupted by long periods of sleep. When he finally gave in to fatigue and went to bed, Sebastian was able to pour himself another glass of wine and respond to the messages he had received during the day. Tomorrow night, Henry would return to Taligth and Sebastian could go home.

He could go back to the café.

Day Nine

Leaving his father alone at Taligth for the first time was difficult. In a few hours Henry would return, but still, Sebastian felt like he was abandoning William.

Other than venturing into the yard each morning to check on Betsy, William appeared to have lost interest in life. He no longer wanted to go out to section the fields or move the livestock. He no longer seemed interested in the milk yield or the condition of the calves born during the summer months and, despite his shoulder, he would normally have found a way of tinkering with the tractors, but even that was not happening. Over the past ten days, he had not once pottered down to McGregor's or the pub to catch up with the gossip.

It had been a long morning and, after persuading William to have some lunch, Sebastian left him settled in the front room. Heading down the drive, he looked back at the house in his rear-view mirror. The roses, having succumbed to the first chill of autumn, had dropped their petals; carpeting the borders beneath. The colours, which lit up the face of Taligth during the summer months, had started to turn and fade, the leaves dangling from their stems ready to fall. It was the first time he had looked back and felt the gaping absence of his mother, no longer standing on the top step. He missed seeing her there, watching him go. As he rumbled over the cattle grid, the gates closed behind him and the house went out of sight.

Even though it had only been ten days since they last met, Sebastian was looking forward to seeing Patrick. A frequent visitor to Edinburgh, Patrick knew the city well and was at home within its walls. The hotel was nothing fancy, but Patrick had a personal connection to it and it was warm and welcoming. It was the first time Sebastian had been in or even noticed it. After they had parted in such a hurry, today's meeting needed to be face to face. There was only so much that could be done via video conferencing and email, and it was good to talk without risk of poor internet connection. Patrick was in the country for a couple of business meetings and to spend time with an old friend, someone who connected him to the wonderful city. Sebastian walked into the bar where Patrick was waiting for him.

'It's good to see you Patrick. How are you?' Sebastian said, smiling, and shaking Patrick's hand.

'I am remarkably well, thank you, but more importantly, how are you? It's good to see you smiling,' Patrick replied, gesturing for Sebastian to join him at a table near the window which looked out to an amazing view of the city, with the castle in the distance.

'I'll be honest, it's floored me,' Sebastian said to the man who had seen him at his lowest.

'I would have expected nothing else. Do you want coffee or is it too early for a little scotch?'

'It's never too early for scotch, thank you,' Sebastian said as Patrick nodded their order to the barman.

'Tell me about your mother, I'd like to know what sort of a woman she was,' Patrick asked, settling at the table, 'unless of course you don't want to talk about her, which I would understand.'

'No, I'd like to. I talk about her a lot.'

'I remember doing that,' Patrick said, reflecting on the loss of his parents and remembering how people stopped talking about them for fear of upsetting him. But he wanted to be upset because, whilst it still hurt, they were still a part of his life.

'Other than my dad, she was the only person who really understood me...' Sebastian said, pausing, 'well, one of the only people,' he mumbled, for an instant thinking of Meggie. 'Don't get me wrong, she was a formidable Scottish woman who called a spade a spade and people who didn't know her found her a little intimidating, but she wasn't, she was quite the opposite in fact. That's what I loved about her. She was well read, intelligent, funny, and she had the biggest heart. There was room for everyone in Mum's world.'

'She sounds a lovely lady. I know you have a brother, are there any more of you?'

'I have a sister.'

'Oh, I don't believe I've heard you mention her,' Patrick said as the waiter placed their drinks on the table.

'She's estranged from the family,' Sebastian said. Taking a sip from his drink, Patrick sat back. Sebastian took a moment to work out how much he wanted to divulge, if anything. He decided to give Patrick a brief movie-poster style summary. 'She didn't make life easy for us, and on her twenty-first birthday, something happened and she left. We haven't seen her since.' Again, Patrick remained silent. 'My parents were devastated and things were never quite the same afterwards.'

'It must have been very hard.'

'It was.'

Sensing the end of the subject, Patrick changed it. 'I have a message from your favourite mare. She sends her love.'

Without warning, Sebastian could feel himself getting upset. He took a breath and focused. How easily he could have opened up to Patrick, a man he hardly knew. How he wanted to tell him everything. Why? He could not even open up to those nearest to him. Perhaps Matilda was right, perhaps he did need a stranger to talk to.

'I often think about her. She's a beautiful horse.'

'She's a very loyal girl and she will be waiting for you, whenever you need a break.'

Quietness fell and the two men sat looking out at the darkening Edinburgh skyline. The lights of the city were effervescent against the walls of the old buildings and the ancient castle sat majestically, looking over into its narrow streets and steep stairwells.

'Can I ask you a question?' Sebastian said, staring out towards the lights. 'Are you this kind to everyone whose company you buy?' he asked.

Throwing his head back and laughing raucously, Patrick's voice filled the small room and the bartender stopped what he was doing and glanced across, smiling. 'You make it sound like I buy companies like I buy lunch,' Patrick said, laughter bouncing along his words. 'Actually, I suppose in some ways I do. Lunch is very important. I like to know exactly what I'm getting and, knowing it is the best quality, I like to enjoy it. So, if you're not offended that I liken your question to lunch, then yes, it's important to me that I get to know who I'm dealing with, and more importantly that I like them. I'm not being kind; I'm being honest. Come, talking of food, I'm hungry, let's order something.'

Over plates of fresh bread with cheese and meats, pickles and salad, they talked about the horses and the weather in Arizona and what brought Patrick to Edinburgh so frequently.

'The lure of an old friend I have known forever.'

'A third Mrs. McCarthy?'

'No, that would spoil things. I come over here pretty often for business and she and I meet here regularly. It works for us,' Patrick said, smiling at Sebastian's suggestion. 'So, tell me, how's your father doing?' he added, quickly changing the subject. Sebastian laughed.

'Did I tell you he had a fall just before my mother died?' Sebastian said, answering Patrick's question.

'You mentioned it. It was his shoulder wasn't it? Is it mending?'

'It seems to be taking its time.'

'Shoulders are awkward things. I have broken both of mine! It comes with riding tetchy horses over rocky ground. I still get twinges and discomfort even now. Give it time, but don't be afraid to get it checked out. You don't want it setting wrong else he'll be forever plagued by it.'

'He's got an appointment after my mother's funeral.'

'Which is when?'

'A week today.'

'It's early days, Sebastian. It'll get easier over time, but there's no quick fix. You're starting down a long road I'm afraid. You'll need to take care of yourself as well as your father. You've got a lot on your plate.'

'You haven't been speaking with Matilda have you?'

'No, should I have been?'

'She said something similar to me a couple of days ago.'

'Then you should listen to her; she's an astute girl. And, talking of a lot on your plate, along comes Paul.'

'Yes,' Sebastian sighed. 'How the hell did I not see that one?'

'It was a long time ago and you trusted him. I don't think that's unreasonable. These things happen to the best of us,' Patrick said, catching Sebastian's eye as he bit into a hunk of bread. 'I'd have got rid of him anyway. He's been in the business too long. He's become complacent.'

Alerted, Sebastian wanted to make sure his company wasn't going to be picked apart. 'Are you planning on getting rid of many of the team?' he asked, trying to sound casual.

'Not at all. Niamh is a diamond, is she not? I like her no-nonsense approach and her vision. She is the perfect MD for the UK arm of the business and I'll put my trust in her to retain or employ whoever she needs. You've got some good people working for you, Seb. There's nothing they need worry about, I give you my word on that, and when the time comes I will assure them as well. I am excited for the future of Tatch-A. We have big plans.'

'Don't tell me too much or I might not want to sell.'

'Well, assuming you still do, we need to talk about how you're going to fit into the business.'

Sebastian had agreed to stay with the company for a year following completion, as had Matilda. Patrick was encouraging of them to remain; their experience was invaluable and he felt they would play a crucial role in the transition. He needed Sebastian as much as Sebastian needed him.

~

After a long day at school and a busy, early evening rehearsal, Henry made his way back up the A1, filling the car up at McGregor's as he arrived in the village.

'How's yer da daein?' Dougie asked, 'A've nae seen him since ye lost yer ma.'

'He's bearing up thank you, Dougie.'

'If there's anythin' ah kin dae please dinnae hesitate to shout me,' Dougie replied. 'Those ainlie cam in this mornin,' he added, referring to the pot of pens for sale on the counter. 'They'll sell oot quickly.'

Henry smiled. After paying, he left the garage with a light-up pink pen, that he knew Lilith would love and two packets of biscuits made by Mrs McCrae who ran the local WI.

It was dark on the drive as the gates opened at Taligth. Unusually, the outside lights had not been switched on and Henry had to pick his way carefully across the gravel and up to the house using the torch on his phone. Letting himself in, he found William dozing in front of the television. 'Sorry, Dad, I didn't mean to wake you,' he said as William stirred when he opened the door.

A little startled, William awoke and sat up straight. 'Did you have a good journey?' he asked sleepily.

'I did thanks. The roads were empty. How are you doing?'

From his chair, William smiled up at his younger son. Since losing Elspeth the boys had taken over her caring role and William was perfectly happy to let them. He was thankful for the joy they brought into his life. He loved all the children, but Nancy had brought such unhappiness and he felt he had made so many mistakes with her. If only he could go back and repair the damage, he thought. 'Yep,' he said, getting up unsteadily and patting Henry on the arm, 'I'm okay... you know,' he sighed.

Henry did know. 'Would you like a cup of tea?' he asked.

William followed Henry into the kitchen and sat in Elspeth's chair, watching him make the tea. 'You look smart,' he said, commenting on Henry's mix of suit trousers, sweatshirt and trainers. Henry laughed.

'I bought some biscuits from McGregor's.'

'Just biscuits? You got off lightly.'

'And a pen that lights up, for Lilith.'

'It's good to see Dougie hasn't lost his touch,' William laughed. 'I'm very grateful to you and Seb, Hal,' he said as Henry put a mug of tea in front of him.

'You're not going to get all soppy are you?' Henry asked, seeing the look in his father's eyes.

'No, but it needs saying.'

'It's what families are for, isn't it? Would you like a biscuit?'

'No thank you.'

'Mrs McCrea's...'

'Go on then, although they'll not be a patch on your mother's.'

Elspeth's biscuits had a reputation for being the best in the local WI and her fierce competitiveness meant she had won numerous prizes during her time as a member.

Sitting opposite his father, Henry watched him take bird-like sips of tea; he had aged ten years in ten days and grown visibly frail, hunched and protective of himself.

'Your brother had me looking through music yesterday; it tired me out,' William said dolefully. 'I think we've decided what we're having, although I'm sure Sebastian will want to go through it with you tomorrow to make sure you're happy with what we've chosen. I said to him, I don't know whether I've chosen music your mum liked or music I like.'

'I would expect they are pretty much the same, aren't they? Anyway, you'll have saved us a job for when it's your turn,' Henry said smiling.

'The way I'm feeling right now, I'd keep the list handy,' William replied.

'We could do without another week like this one, so if you wouldn't mind hanging on, just for a bit, that would be much appreciated,' Henry said, and they shared a warming laugh over tea and biscuits, talking about Elspeth's choice in music and how neither of them could understand her love for Lonnie Donegan. Finishing up, having taken a sleeping pill, William went to bed leaving Henry to settle Betsy for the night. Tomorrow they were going to the village pub, with Sebastian and the family, for lunch. It would be the first time William had seen his grandchildren, Ewan and Isla, since he lost Elspeth. He felt uncharacteristically nervous.

~

Getting home late and, joined by Panda, Sebastian sank into the sofa in the kitchen with her on his knee, reading a message from Henry. He had asked him for some information about their mother's service and Henry had replied with a message which could almost have been cloned from the conversation Sebastian had had with Matilda a day or so before. This, added to Patrick's earlier comment, made him feel self-conscious. He wondered why they were all so concerned. Was he really being unreasonable or difficult? Was he behaving irrationally, he questioned, struggling to see what they all appeared to be pointing out?

He did not reply to Henry's message and, with Matilda out, he went for a swim. With the pool lights dimmed and the music on low, he was able to regulate his breathing, relax his mind and think about Meggie.

Day Ten

A shower before walking Panda was not Sebastian's usual routine and he was conscious of Matilda's 'who is she?' comment the other morning, his two showers having been noted. To deflect attention, he went for a swim after he had been in the gym, which gave him the excuse to shower before going out.

It was early and the café was empty other than for Meggie and a woman who was dressed in heavier clothes than the September weather required. On sight and smell of Panda as she bounded in, post pond, the woman made it clear the dog's arrival was unwelcome and, putting the money on the table, promptly left.

'Sorry about that,' Sebastian said, referring to the loss of custom.

'It's okay, she'd finished anyway.'

'Is your niece not in today?' he asked, looking around while Meggie busied herself making tea and toast.

'She'll be in later. This part of town takes longer to wake up on Saturday mornings, so we tend to have a later rush. How are you? How's your dad?' she asked, filling the teapot with boiling water.

'He's okay,' Sebastian said, sitting down. 'It's a strange time.'

'When's your mum's funeral?' Meggie asked, bringing over the tea and toast and joining Sebastian at the table.

'Friday.'

'I imagine there'll be a lot of people there. Your mum was popular. Is it at the church?'

'It is.'

'A burial then?'

'It's what she wanted.'

'Will *everyone* be there?' Meggie asked, pouring the tea.

Sebastian knew exactly who she was referring to. When they were together he had told her everything, so Nancy was bound to come up in conversation.

As his mother's death threatened to expose painful history, he considered lying, saying 'of course she'll be there, everything's fine between us now,' but he couldn't bring himself to. Feeling he had deprived his parents of their daughter, he wished he had told them what happened at the time. But if they had known, they may have been deprived of their son as well, and their daughter would still have left. Nancy was never going to be as loyal a daughter as he had been a son. He consoled himself that her contempt for the family had been clear well before the day she left.

Hesitating long enough, Meggie answered the question herself. 'She doesn't know, does she?'

'No,' Sebastian replied, shaking his head.

'Why not?'

'Because we've not seen her for thirty years.'

'But she's your sister.'

'Please don't say that, Meg. Even if we did want to tell her, we don't know where she is.'

Meggie sat quietly, thinking, trying to find the right words. 'How do you feel about what happened now, after all this time?'

'I don't want to talk about it, Meg.'

'Why? Does it still affect you?'

Sebastian looked at Meggie surprised, struggling to understand why she would ask such a question when his whole life had been shaped by the events of that day. 'I find it difficult to hear you ask that. You of all people.'

'Have you ever spoken to anyone about it?'

'Christ!' Sebastian suddenly snapped, 'not you as well! What the *fuck's* going on? Is this some kind of conspiracy?' he said angrily. 'It serves me right, I should have dealt with it at the time, what a fool! But as usual I stuck my head in the sand, hoping it would all go away... which it did, for years,' he said, 'and then my wonderful mother dies, and it all rears its ugly head again. You know what, Meg? It's how I would imagine it feels to have murdered someone and buried the body under the patio. You know it's there and you have to live with the knowledge, knowing that one day the house could get sold and the patio might get dug up and 'boom', the truth would be out. The thing is, you also know there's a chance that no one will ever find out. It's like playing Russian roulette with time...'

'You're over-reacting!'

'Am I? The trouble with a secret is that it has to stay a secret. If I had told my parents what had happened at the time perhaps they'd have accepted it and forgiven me...'

'More that they might have been able to help you. There was nothing to forgive,' Meggie argued back, 'you didn't do anything wrong.'

'Yes I did! I was an arrogant seventeen-year-old who thought he knew best. I enabled it to happen and it drove Nancy away!' he argued.

'It wasn't your fault Nancy left!' Meggie persisted.

'You don't know that!' Sebastian snapped.

'Yes I do!'

Silence flooded the room.

'What?' Sebastian asked.

The arrival of new customers broke the atmosphere and brought Panda, commando-crawling, from beneath the table. Meggie stood up.

'Please,' she said quietly to Sebastian. 'Give me a minute.' Making excuses to the customers at the door, she rotated the 'open' sign and closed the café. It was time she told him about Nancy.

~

William woke up not feeling well. He was stiff after a restless night and the chill from his open window had made him cough which had jarred his shoulder. He and Elspeth had always slept with the window open, even on the coldest nights. Henry was concerned about him but, as ever, William shrugged it off, refusing to make an appointment to see the doctor. Henry offered to go to the chemist, to get something to ease his chest or soothe his discomfort but, on opening a cupboard in the kitchen, William showed Henry Elspeth's array of medicines. Henry was satisfied there was enough in it to cover any potential illness or outbreak of tropical disease for years to come. Henry's amazement made William giggle.

'Don't start all that again,' Henry said, 'I heard what happened at the registrar's; that'll be why your shoulder's playing up.'

'Most of them are your mother's,' William said. 'She couldn't go to McGregor's without coming back with a medicine to cure whatever ailment she thought one of us might get one day, bless her. I'm sure there's something to cure the Black Death at the back,' William said going back to Elspeth's chair and sitting down at the table.

'McGregor's has a lot to answer for,' Henry said, closing the cupboard.

'It does indeed.'

'Are you up to trawling through a million photos before we go out for lunch?' Henry asked. 'I was thinking it would be nice to have some pictures of Mum at the church.'

'You can trawl, I'll sit here and watch.'

'It'll be nice to see everyone later, won't it?'

'I suppose,' William replied, thinking he would much rather stay behind and watch television.

Sitting quietly having his breakfast, William listened to the radio and to the news of what was going on in the world outside his own for his had shrunk and it unnerved him to venture out. He would have a rest, hoping he might feel a little brighter later. He could not bring himself to look at photographs.

~

'If you can stay,' Meggie said, 'I'll explain about Nancy.'

Sebastian needed to know what Meggie had to say. Much to Panda's disappointment, he stayed sitting as Meggie retreated to the counter. Waiting, he switched his phone on and sent Matilda a message. They had not spoken much and he wanted to smooth the waters before heading out with the family later; he could do without tension between him and Matilda spilling over into lunch.

'I'm confused, Meg,' he said as she came back to the table with fresh tea. 'Do you know Nancy?'

Meggie sighed. 'Do you remember the letters I sent to you, at the end..?'

Sebastian looked into his cup. 'Yes, I do. I feel ashamed I never replied. Sorry.'

Meggie looked at him long enough for him to know she was not accepting his apology. 'I feel a bit stupid saying this now, after so many years, but when our relationship finished, I thought my life was over,' she said. She paused, taking her time, considering what to say next. 'You'll not have been aware, because I hid it well, but from my early teens I was a pretty heavy drinker, and I'm not just talking about getting legless on a Friday night. I mean drinking before breakfast,' she said, looking at Sebastian's shocked expression. 'I thought the answer to my problems was at the bottom of a bottle. That was how I met Nancy, in a bar where she was working on the south coast,' Meggie said, remembering the state she was in at the time. Sebastian did not speak.

'Unlike my flatmates, I didn't go home that first summer and, because I was on my own, I became a regular and Nancy was nice to me. We got talking as girls do, and eventually we realised our connection. It was one of those coincidences in life, like walking along a beach in Australia and bumping into your old physics teacher,' Meggie said, smiling. 'Anyway, we became quite good friends for a while. At least that's what it felt like to me,' she said, her expression changing. 'We talked about you, obviously, but neither of us ever talked about what happened to you. I never broke your confidence, Seb. I promised you I wouldn't.'

'So she didn't tell you why she left?'

'All I know is that it wasn't to do with you. It was to do with your parents, something she found out that day. I've no idea what, she never said. But then I was off of my head most of the time.'

'What did she find out?' Sebastian asked. 'Why didn't my parents ever say?'

'I've no idea. Shall I carry on?'

Momentarily absent, Sebastian nodded.

'When I started second year, things had changed and I didn't go back into the pub,' Meggie continued. 'Nancy moved away and we lost contact. Then, eight years later, our paths crossed again.' She paused. 'I'm going to tell you this because I think you should know, but it might not be easy to listen to.'

'Why do I suddenly feel nervous?'

Meggie chose her words carefully. She was not about to reveal the full extent of her relationship with Nancy; she was saving that for another time, or perhaps never. For now she wanted Sebastian to know that Nancy was alive, so he could tell William. It was too late for Elspeth, but William still had time.

'We came into contact again twenty-two years ago. I was still living down south, as was Nancy. Nancy had been involved in a terrible car accident leaving her with severe leg injuries. The medics worked hard to save her legs but eventually she had to have her left one amputated.'

'Oh my god!'

'As you can imagine, Nancy was determined, so it didn't take her long to recover, physically at least, and as soon as she could ditch the wheel chair and get up on a prosthetic, she tried to get back to normal. However, despite her eagerness, she struggled, because life wasn't normal anymore and it took her a long time to come to terms with that. She grew thick skinned and intolerant, shunning anybody who offered help. She even stood up to her husband,' she said, thinking about who Nancy had become.

'Who did she marry?' Sebastian asked pensively.

'I'll come to that. Anyway, she's struggled with depression over the years; deep depression. I think she's probably suffered with it from a very young age, which might explain some of her earlier behaviour. Who knows? The accident definitely made it worse... especially as she was pregnant and had a still birth at thirty-six weeks.'

Sebastian looked shocked.

'Following that, she took an overdose, which is how I came into contact with her again.'

Sebastian ran his hands through his hair and sat back in his seat. Panda popped her head out to see if it was time to go home. 'What happened?' he asked. Letting out a long sigh, Panda settled back down.

'I run a self-help group for people affected by suicide, either by attempting it themselves or having a friend or family member take their own life.' His heart beating quickly, Sebastian looked at Meggie. 'My first husband killed himself,' she said, answering his unspoken question. 'Which is why I set up the group.'

'Oh Meggie, I'm so sorry.'

'It's okay, it's not your fault,' she hesitated. 'Not really. It was a long time ago and I've come to terms with it... less so with the blame he laid at my feet. Anyway, Nancy...'

'No, no, no, no, no, hold on, you can't say something like that and then just move on. What do you mean by 'not really'? Are you implying your husband's suicide had something to do with me?'

'No, Seb,' Meggie retorted, 'my husband's suicide was to do with *him* and with *me*, not *you*. What I meant by that comment was the person I was when I met *him* was the shell of the person *you* left behind.'

Sebastian winced.

'I'm sorry, but it's true. Among other things, by that time I was an alcoholic. I *am* an alcoholic. He tried to save me.'

Shocked, Sebastian looked at the floor, his eyes scanning the pattern of the tiles, searching for clarification. 'You're an alcoholic?'

'I am. I have no intention of sharing details of my marriage with you, but let's just say that I could not give him what he wanted. For every problem we had, I drank. When I could not love him the way he craved, I drank. I found it difficult to be kind to him because I would not allow anyone to be kind to me, in case they found out what sort of a person I was, so I drank. I did not like myself so how could I accept anyone loving me? So, I drank to make it all go away. I lost the ability to be affectionate and all the normal things you find in a happy and fulfilled marriage. When we met, he thought he could fix me, and he did so much good, but it wasn't enough for him. He took his own life because he believed he had failed us both.'

The strength of Meggie's words choked Sebastian. 'What did I do to you that was so bad?' he whispered.

Meggie continued. 'Not knowing it was me who ran it, Nancy joined my group on the advice of a midwife after the loss of her baby. The day she had the accident she had been feeling so low, she'd taken a handful of anti-depressants, not with the intention of killing herself but out of desperation to outrun her feelings.' Sebastian went to ask a question but Meggie stopped him. 'No, let me carry on,' she said. 'Shortly after the accident, Nancy's husband left her...' Meggie paused, looking at Sebastian empathetically. 'It was Jacob, Seb.' Again, Sebastian went to speak, but Meggie carried on. 'I know what you're thinking and I don't know why she married him. Out of fear perhaps... maybe spite...' she added, 'who knows, but it was a very unhappy marriage.'

A chill ran down Sebastian's spine and he straightened in his chair.

'After Jacob left, she met a nice man at my group. He's Swiss. He was working and living in the UK at the time and was struggling with some demons, so he joined us for a few sessions. He was a multiple amputee having had meningitis

211

in his twenties. They used to say between them they had one fully functioning body.'

Sebastian smiled weakly. 'Do you know where she is now?'

'She's in Switzerland. She's lived there for eighteen years.'

'Switzerland,' Sebastian repeated, relieved to know she was in a different country. 'When did you last see her?'

'A year ago.'

'Why?'

Meggie did not answer Sebastian's question.

'I have her contact details if you want to tell her about your mum,' she said. 'I understand why you might not want her at the funeral, but I think she should know.'

'Really?'

'I've tried to understand her over the years. I'm not saying she's changed, but she's been through a lot. I think if you told her but asked her not to attend, she might respect your wishes. Or I could tell her for you if that would be easier.'

'No!' Suddenly feeling trapped, Sebastian pushed his chair back and Panda immediately joined him at his feet in anticipation of leaving. 'No way! You *know* what she was like, how manipulative she could be. Why the hell would I trust her? After all the things she did when we were young? Do you think she would have any compassion at all for anyone else's feelings, and not come? She hates Henry and she was downright cruel to Mum and Dad.'

'I know.'

'No! You don't know, Meggie,' Sebastian said, raising his voice, sending Panda cowering back under the table once more. 'She was evil and she didn't give a shit. A leopard does *not* change its spots,' he continued, his rage growing, 'and even if it does, a leopard is still a leopard! And as for Dad... my poor, shattered Dad, if you could see him... Please,' he said, leaning forward, taking Meggie's hands in his own, 'I'm *begging* you, Nancy must not know about Mum.' He held on tight as Meggie tried to pull her hands away. 'Promise me you will not tell her, Meggie. Please! Nancy is not a part of our lives anymore. I feel sorry for her and all she's been through and, had she had the decency to stick around, Mum and Dad would have done anything they could for her, you know that, you know what they were like,' he said desperately, taking a breath, trying to calm down. 'I don't want to get melodramatic about this, but genuinely I think it would kill Dad if he thought Nancy might just turn up at the funeral. It's going to be difficult enough for him when I tell him what you've told me; he's only just holding it together. I beg you, Meggie, please do not tell her!'

Taken aback by the strength of Sebastian's pleading, Meggie could see he was terrified. Looking at the lost soul in front of her, she pitied him. He had no idea the secrets his father kept, and Meggie was not about to tell him.

Meggie pulled her hands away and cradled them safely in her lap. 'She won't hear it from me,' she said, 'but don't burden yourself with this along with everything else. It's a heavy load to bear, Seb.'

'I've done okay so far.'

'It doesn't do well to keep things locked inside. That's what I did when I married my first husband and look what it did to him. You've lost your mum. How sad it is to think she never knew what happened to Nancy. Your dad now has a chance of catching up with his daughter. Just think about it.'

It was a lot to take in and Meggie wanted to give Sebastian time to digest everything she had told him. Making the excuse that she needed to open the café, she encouraged him to leave. Sebastian was glad to be released, his walk home with Panda filled with visions of Nancy, her legs crushed and of a baby suddenly stopping kicking. He thought about her overdose and Meggie's husband and the alcohol, and Jacob…

It was a slow, troubled walk home. Sebastian couldn't decide whether to tell his father and Henry what he had discovered or whether to keep it to himself, at least for now, until he could work out what they should do.

Matilda was still frosty when he got in, but he was too distracted to be bothered by petty squabbles. Aware they needed to leave soon for Taligth, he and Panda ran upstairs and jumped into the shower, emerging ten minutes later, smelling fresh again. Bounding into the car, Panda joined Sebastian and Matilda. Had someone been able to read her little doggie mind, they might have been wondering how a man could have breakfast with one woman and then be heading out for lunch with another!

The ten days since Elspeth's death had passed slowly for the family. With everyone, other than Lorna and Lilith, gathered at Taligth, they were grateful for the warm, dry weather, and were able to walk to the pub, which was less than a mile down the hill. Although slow, it was nice to get out.

'I thought Panda would be shattered, you were out so long this morning,' Matilda said, watching the spaniel bound in front of them.

'You know what she's like,' Sebastian answered, not looking at Matilda. 'She'll have recharged her battery in the car.'

Typical of a small village pub, The Old Forge was popular with the locals and everyone knew everyone. William did not wish for the kind attention of others, but he smiled, accepting their condolences.

Aware of their collective pain, the family focused on getting through lunch without succumbing to tears. Henry was convinced he would be the first, but he managed to hold on. Sebastian sat quietly, thinking, eyes downcast, not engaging in the conversation going on around the table, and Matilda watched him, wondering what was going on in his head. In his own world, William felt the pressure; he was the barometer, the gauge by which everyone acted; if he smiled, they smiled; if he laughed, they laughed, but all he really wanted to do was go home. He sat patiently, listening to the conversations, longing for it to be over. Everyone was aware the next time they were to meet would be on the day of the funeral.

214

Back at Taligth, after a cup of tea, accompanied by one of Mrs McCrea's biscuits, everyone went their separate ways, leaving the house quiet once more. Sebastian, wanting to stay a little longer with Henry and his father, asked Ewan to take Matilda and Panda home. Ewan, every bit of him a younger version of his father, was happy to help.

Whilst William went into the yard to talk to Betsy, Sebastian and Henry sat in the kitchen making final decisions about their mother's funeral. Henry did not ask Sebastian how his morning had been, and by this time, Sebastian had decided not tell him.

Pandora's box had been opened.

Day Eleven

Sunday

Henry spent the morning at the table, Trawling through photographs. William pottered aimlessly around the kitchen and the yard. Betsy's pen had not been cleaned for days and her bedding was in desperate need of fresh straw, but William could not seem to find the energy to do it. It was on Henry's list of jobs before he left that evening. As William shuffled, Henry filled him in on the situation with the theatre.

'... Which was why I was up virtually half the night trying to find accommodation,' he said.

'I'm sure I read something in the paper about the Sheep Shed. It got good reviews as far as I remember,' William said, getting a large meat cleaver out of the drawer.

'That's encouraging,' Henry replied. 'One of the good things to come out of this is that Lorna and I will only be half an hour up the road from here. We'll be able to come over. I can still help out and you can come and see the production,' Henry said, his pile of 'to use' photographs getting taller.

'That will be great, Henry. Do you want to stay here?'

'We might have to if I can't find somewhere. There are eleven of us. How are you at mass catering?' Henry asked, smiling at his father who was struggling to cut an enormous beet. 'Here, let me do that for you,' he said, quickly getting up and taking the cleaver out of his father's hand. 'You'll take a finger off if you're not careful and Betsy is none too fussy about what she eats.'

Sitting down in Henry's vacated chair, William picked up a photograph and studied it; a faded print of Elspeth, standing in a field in front of a tractor with her father, his hand on her shoulder, and a couple of farm hands five paces

216

to the side. She could only have been nine or ten years old and William found it hard to imagine there was a time before they met, a time when he did not know her. 'Eleven of you...' he muttered, picking up another photograph, a more recent one taken at Henry and Lorna's wedding. 'These photographs are all muddled. Why are you looking through them?'

'Like I said yesterday, we thought it would be nice to have some pictures of Mum at the church. What do you think?'

'That's a nice idea.'

'Good,' Henry said, his hand aching from chopping. 'These things are massive!'

'Fodder beet are always tough buggers. You need a machete to do it properly. It's much easier out in the field. You can hold them by the stalk.'

'Like decapitation.'

'If you say so,' William said earnestly, picking up several more photographs. 'So, where might you stay?'

'We'll find somewhere, but if we get stuck we'll pitch tents in your garden,' Henry said, looking over to his father who was now sifting through the pile of photographs Henry had put to one side.

'I like this one,' William said, holding up a lovely photograph of Elspeth sitting in a large deck chair with her skirt hitched up and a beaming smile. They rarely got away from the farm, but when they did, Elspeth's favourite place was the beach. 'I remember that day,' William said softly, 'it was so blowy it was all your mother could do to keep her skirt down and her hat on her head. It became a battle of wills, which your mother lost in the end, hence the skirt around her midriff in this picture.'

Coming over to the table, Henry looked at the photograph again. 'How about we use that one on the front of the order of service?'

'Not with her underskirt showing...' William said, starting another pile.

Henry sensed it was going to be a very long day.

~

Taking Panda out for her morning walk, Sebastian avoided going down the hill towards the café by turning right at the bottom of the drive. Although he was desperate to see Meggie, he did not think it a good idea until his mother's funeral was over. He wanted to avoid her questions.

As he walked, with Panda trotting excitedly in front of him, he thought about what Meggie had told him the day before; the way she had described Nancy's life, how she had justified her behaviour. The Nancy she talked of bore no resemblance to the Nancy he had known, the one who had vanished and never once looked back to see the trail of destruction or the damaged lives she left behind. Why Meggie felt Nancy should know about their mother's death baffled him, and why she thought she had the right to give her opinion irked him. Mulling it over, he felt angrier with Nancy now than he had at any other time. Had it been fate that he had bumped into Meggie? Nancy had not been a part of their lives for more than half his life and suddenly here she was, yet again, wreaking havoc. The more he walked and churned it over, the angrier he became. The cruelty of the situation weighed heavily on his mind and by the time he and Panda reached the park he was furious with Nancy, annoyed with Meggie and angry with himself. And he had made the decision he was not going to say anything to anyone.

Much to Panda's delight, Sebastian took her across the well-kept lawns to her favourite bit of the park. The working cocker picked up the scent of the stagnant pond as soon as they went through the gates and before Sebastian could grab her, she sped off across the green. Hurdling benches, nimbly negotiating legs of joggers and early morning strollers, she ran at full pelt before impressively launching herself over the pond reed and disappearing into the black pool beyond. After swimming her way back to the bank, she emerged smiling, with boots of thick pond sludge and her mouth full of a tennis ball, which must have been lost by some poor unfortunate.

A pungent stench accompanied them home.

'If you didn't take her to the park, she wouldn't jump in the pond,' Matilda pointed out when, once again, Sebastian and Panda returned from their walk bringing with them the toe curling cesspit smell of decaying pondweed.

'We're in trouble again, Panda,' Sebastian said as Panda looked up at him, the ball clamped between her jaws. 'She found another ball,' he informed Matilda.

'No, Panda is not in trouble, because Panda is a dog and she doesn't know any better, whereas you... Not only do you both absolutely stink, but I'll assume Panda drinks some of the lovely water she dives into,' Matilda scolded, light heartedly. 'You need to go for a shower.' Panda and Sebastian looked at each other. 'By the way,' Matilda added, 'what time's your meeting with Paul tomorrow?'

Sebastian's mood changed in an instant. 'Half nine, why?' he asked, irritably.

'Because, hopefully, afterwards, you'll be able to move on and stop all these mega walks with Panda. The poor thing is a foot shorter than she was,' Matilda said. 'I've baked some scones. Will you want one after your shower?'

'Yes please. I'll be five minutes,' Sebastian said, running out of the kitchen.

'Take Panda in with you,' Matilda called after him.

Busy in the kitchen, Matilda's attention was drawn to the effluvious aroma emanating from beneath the kitchen table. 'Excuse me young lady,' she said, bending down and peeking at Panda who was sitting, smiling, the ball still gripped firmly between her teeth, 'you should be upstairs having a shower. Go on, off you go.' Not moving, Panda continued to smile at Matilda.

'Sebastian!' Matilda shouted, 'call your dog. She's not followed you and she stinks!' Waiting for him to shout back, Matilda shooed Panda up the stairs, following her onto the landing and towards the bedroom. As they approached the bedroom door, Matilda could hear Sebastian talking on the phone. Curious, she 'shushed' Panda and tiptoed closer, pressing her ear to the wood, trying to hear what he was saying. Holding her breath, it was difficult to make out the muffled sounds and his tone was hushed. Unable to decipher the words, Matilda gave up and, opening the door, walked into the bedroom. Sebastian frantically put his phone into his trouser pocket and started to unbuckle his belt whilst kicking off his shoes. 'Panda needs a shower,' Matilda said, looking at him suspiciously. 'Who was that on the phone?'

'No one,' Sebastian answered too quickly.

'There must have been someone. You were talking.'

'Well, when I say 'no one', I mean, there was no one there, I was leaving a message.'

'Who for?'

'What is it with the inquisition?' Sebastian asked, taking his sweatshirt off.

'I was wondering that's all.'

'Well, if you must know, I've done as you asked. I've booked your counsellor friend,' Sebastian lied.

'On a Sunday?'

'Well, not 'booked', I mean I've left a message saying I want to book,' Sebastian said, feeling flustered.

'How did you get her number?' Matilda asked, sure she had not given it to him.

'You said her name was Ellsworth, I looked her up.'

'Right,' Matilda said, unsure she believed him. 'So, when are you planning to go?' she asked.

'I don't know, Til!' he replied sharply. 'Not before Friday.'

'No, of course not, but I'm glad you made the call. So, you think it's a good idea then?'

'I think it'll get you off my back.'

'Seb!'

Sebastian carried on getting undressed. He had lost weight, Matilda thought.

'I'm really pleased,' she said. 'I think it will do you good and if it doesn't, then there's nothing lost.'

'Other than a few hundred pounds.'

'It's not about the money though, is it?' she said, going to the door and then turning to look back at him. 'I'll leave you to it,' she added, closing the door behind her.

Making sure she wasn't about to come back, Sebastian sat on the bed, his heart racing. 'Fuck,' he whispered, looking at Panda, as he tried to steady his breathing, 'that was close!' He consoled himself with the fact that he had not completely lied to Matilda. He had left a message, although it was not on the counsellor's answering machine, it was on Meggie's.

'Only stupid people play with fire', came into his head as he went into the bathroom. He had no idea why he was behaving the way he was. He felt compelled by Meggie, as if an invisible force were dragging him down the wrong road and he was powerless to fight against it, his tangle of half-truths convincing him he was doing nothing wrong.

As he lathered Panda, he reflected on his and Meggie's conversation and came to the conclusion that, despite everything she had said, Meggie had given little away. He struggled to see the alcoholic in her or the damaged eighteen-year-old girl. In fact, his memory of the end of their relationship was that it had been a breakup much like any other; messy, which he had handled badly, and for that he was sorry. But the relationship had run its course and they had both known it. So why had Meggie been so adversely affected? His mind began to play games and he started to think that there had to be more to it. Something Meggie wasn't telling him. The woman he met in the café looked like Meggie, but she had changed, and it scared him to think that she might dig up the patio, when he had once been certain she would not.

After a quick rub with the towel, hurtling down the stairs, Panda charged around the kitchen rubbing herself along the surfaces before skidding her cheeks across the rug, first left, then right, then left again.

Having made another phone call, Sebastian followed the crazy pooch into the room where Matilda had prepared the sweet-smelling scones and a pot of coffee.

'I've just spoken with Verity Ellsworth's secretary. She called back. Seemingly they do work on Sunday,' he said, sliding his knife into softened butter. 'No doubt they charge double for the pleasure as well. I've got an appointment in a couple of weeks.'

'Good,' Matilda replied, coolly.

'How do you know her?'

'I don't, she's the daughter of someone from book club.'

'Oh,' he said, studying his wife, trying to fathom why he was playing such a dangerous game.

He had been tempted to stray a number of times during their marriage, but Matilda had always been enough for him and far too precious to risk losing. Why it should feel different this time, Sebastian did not know. Was it his state of mind skewing his judgment? Were he and Meggie too familiar? Did Meggie feel safe because she knew his history? After all, he wasn't doing anything with Meggie he had not done before. He'd had coffee with Meggie before. He'd had breakfast with Meggie before. He had talked for hours with Meggie before, but what he hadn't done before was to imagine what it would be like to have an affair with Meggie. Today though, in his mind, that was exactly what he was doing – or was he? Was thinking about it as bad as doing it? Is a person a murderer if they imagine killing someone but don't act on it? Of course not...

~

With decisions on photographs made and Betsy's pen cleaned, the goats fed, the milking done and the cows seen back out to the field, Henry prepared dinner before he left Taligth.

'Have you thought about going in the morning?' William asked over Henry's shepherd's pie. 'It's late.'

'I've got school tomorrow, Dad.'

'You were always keen to miss school when you were younger, especially on Mondays.'

'That's because I didn't get paid to go... and I hated PE.'

'They're very good, letting you take time off when you need it.'

'They are, I can't complain.'

'There's so much going on for you and Sebastian at the moment. You could have done without all this as well.'

'Yes, perhaps next time you could tell Mum to get her timing a little better if she wouldn't mind - the summer holidays usually work best for me,' Henry said, knowing his father would smile, which he did.

By the time Henry left Taligth, William was sitting comfortably in the front room, watching television. Henry would be back on Wednesday night after rehearsal. On Thursday he, Sebastian and William were due to say their final 'goodbye' to Elspeth – it was going to be a tough week.

Day Twelve

Before assembly, Henry telephoned William. He liked to make sure his father was awake before his day at school began. He had left him exhausted the previous evening and was worried about how he was going to manage when he and Sebastian were no longer staying over. William answered the phone, incoherently mumbling that he was fine and was just about to get up. 8 a.m. was a late rise for the old farmer.

For once, Henry was grateful for the distraction of school. The students, although perfectly understanding in the beginning, had soon forgotten what he was going through and had started pushing their luck. Not ten minutes into a full school assembly, Henry had confiscated two mobile phones, expensive ones far better than his own, a pair of diamond earrings, which, knowing the student, were probably real, a compass being used for anything other than its intended purpose, and a vibrator one of the Year 7 students had found in his mother's bedside cabinet. He marvelled at what they brought into school. The usual things like make-up, jewellery and mobile phones were a daily occurrence but he remembered one student bringing in his pet rat and letting it loose in the girls' changing rooms just before a PE lesson. The screams could be heard for miles, the rodent bringing the girls running out onto the hockey field far quicker than any teacher had ever achieved.

One of the most unnerving things he confiscated once was during a Year 10 maths lesson. It was a very good drawing of himself lying slumped over his desk with knives sticking out of his back. The picture had the student, easily identifiable, standing over him, grinning. It was obvious it was his classroom and, that paired with the oath the boy had written about 'stabbing Mr. Campbell to death', was a little disconcerting.

~

Niamh was already hard at work when Sebastian arrived in the office. Usually the first in and the last to leave, she was almost as committed to the company as he was.

'Morning,' Sebastian said, putting a mug of tea on her desk as he made his way to his office. 'How are things?'

'Morning. Good thanks,' Niamh replied, her eyes fixed to her computer screen.

'What time did you get in?'

'Normal,' she said, not looking up, engrossed. 'How are *you* doing?' she asked.

'I'm wearing my wife's knickers.'

'Excellent.'

'Not listening then?'

'I'm listening, just not surprised,' she laughed, looking up for the first time, catching Sebastian's eye. He smiled at her. Getting up with her mug and wandering over to his office door, Niamh leant against the frame watching Sebastian organise his desk. 'Seriously, how are you?' she asked.

'I'll feel better when today's over.'

'How much do you think he'll admit to?'

'God knows. I'm not sure I'll be able to look at him without wanting to punch him in the face.'

'Don't give him the satisfaction.'

'I'll do my best.'

'I know you will,' she said quietly, understanding how worn down he must feel. 'You've got a lot of friends here, Seb,' she said, looking at him for a moment before returning to her desk.

Sebastian had first encountered Niamh when she was the Managing Director of a potential customer with enormous buying power. They were trying to squeeze Tatch-A UK's margins so tightly Sebastian could only meet them by moving to overseas production, which did not sit comfortably with him. Having not reached a satisfactory agreement, he had walked away from the deal but made it his mission to recruit Niamh. He had needed someone like her, and once she was on board, Tatch-A UK had not looked back.

Sitting at his desk, thinking back to the time before Niamh had arrived, Sebastian looked around his office. With high ceilings, thick metal pillars and exposed brick walls, it had retained most of its original features. It had witnessed many extraordinary events in the time they had occupied the building and Sebastian wondered what life would feel like the day he cleared his desk. Times were uncertain. With the death of his mother, meeting Meggie, the sale of the company, Nancy, Paul, Matilda, Henry, his father and the children, Sebastian felt as though he had the weight of the world on his shoulders and so finding Graham standing in his doorway holding a tray, was a very welcome surprise.

'Graham!' Sebastian smiled. 'I thought your work here was finished?'

'I'm not one to leave a performance before the finalé. I thought you might like some moral support.'

'I would be very grateful for that,' Sebastian replied, feeling comforted by Graham's arrival. 'I read your report. Thank you.'

'My pleasure,' Graham said, straightening his trousers as he sat down. 'You've created an exceptional company; you should be very proud.'

'No more skeletons?'

'Let's hope not. Everyone has been very thorough, so, as far as I am concerned, nothing should get in the way now. PMaC Inc. have all the information they need. How are you feeling about the sale?'

'I'm not sure. A mixture of excited and scared shitless.'

'That's hardly surprising. When I left the army, I felt much the same. It was like stepping off a secure flat rock into the dark turbulent waters of the sea; it looks enticing and exciting but you don't know what's beneath the water or whether your feet can touch the bottom,' Graham smiled, 'but you have to take that leap to know that you can do it. Don't rush into anything, Sebastian, however tempted. Stay at home for six months, don't make firm decisions, travel, and see a few places. You don't need the money, although I expect, as the dust settles, it'll be the challenges that you might crave. That's the dangerous time, the time where men like us dive onto the sharp coral because we weren't concentrating. Give yourself time. Especially now, when in all honesty, you should be with your father and brother, not here.'

'Wise words.'

'I speak from experience,' Graham said, as Niamh joined them in the office.

'Morning, Graham,' Niamh said, as he got up to shake her hand.

Taking a moment to gather his thoughts, Sebastian turned his attention to the reason for the morning's meeting and waited in the office with Niamh and Graham for the 9.30 a.m. knock on the door indicating Paul's arrival. When it came, Graham let him in, telling him to take a seat next to his own. Showing no emotion, Paul sat, looking straight ahead. From the email he had received, Paul knew exactly what was expected of him. This morning he was to agree a figure and discuss the date by which the money was to be repaid.

Although Sebastian had a figure in his mind, he could not help wondering how close Paul's would be to his own. Would Paul see everything Graham had uncovered as stolen? Or, over time, had he justified some of his actions to himself? What if his figure were higher than the one discussed between Sebastian and Graham? That could alter things. Unlikely, but what if Graham had missed something?

'I am not going to offer you a drink,' Sebastian said, 'because you won't be here long enough to finish it. So, you've spoken with Trish?'

'I have,' Paul replied.

'Is she still at her parents?'

'She is. This has destroyed us.'

227

With a blank expression on his face, Sebastian raised his eyes to meet Paul's. 'If it's sympathy you want, you're looking at the wrong person.'

'I'm not asking for sympathy.'

'Well, that's good,' Sebastian said, 'because this is all of your own making. You've stolen my money. Money that has fed your family and put clothes on their backs, paid for fancy cars, private schools and lavish holidays, and you haven't even got the decency to tell us why you did it. The only conclusion I can come to is that you did it because you could.' Sebastian said, taking a long, thoughtful pause. 'I blame myself for that, Paul. I blame myself for trusting you, someone I thought was my friend. But if my worst crime is to trust people then so be it, because I am not prepared to live my life being suspicious of everyone in it. What I am prepared to do, however, is get rid of people who let me down, like you have.' Sebastian said, staring at Paul. Paul shifted uncomfortably in his seat. 'So, without wishing to turn this into a game of 'Play Your Cards Right', the purpose of today's meeting is for you to tell us exactly how much money you intend to pay this company back.' Sebastian stopped speaking and sat back in his chair waiting, the walls screaming figures at him. He and Graham exchanged glances, indicating to each other to sit tight and wait.

After running his hands over his trousers to remove the sweat, Paul lent forward on his thighs examining the threads of the carpet pattern as it twisted and swirled. 'I went through everything and made a list,' he said.

'The bottom line, Paul, that's all we need. Just give me the figure.'

Paul took a deep breath and a mumbled figure fell from his mouth.

Laughing, Sebastian asked him to repeat it before he said it out loud himself to see whether he had heard it correctly, his laughter having vanished. 'Did I just hear you say £200,000?' He asked. Paul did not speak. 'Did I hear it right? That's a lot of money!' he exclaimed. 'A *huge* amount in fact,' he added. 'Just imagine what we could buy with that amount of money. What would you buy, Graham?'

With the spotlight suddenly on him, Graham looked surprised and took a long time to think. 'I believe I'd buy a beach hut on the south Devon coast,' he said.

Sebastian looked at the kind man and started to laugh. Only Graham would give the question such an unequivocal answer. 'I like the sound of a beach hut, others might have said a Ferrari but I like a beach hut.' He smiled briefly before the expression dropped from his face as he stared at Paul. 'Do you have a lovely beach hut on the south Devon coast, Graham?'

'No, I don't.'

'And why is that?' Sebastian asked, still holding Paul's eye contact.

'Because I can't afford one.'

'Ah, because you can't afford one! But you could afford it if you *stole* the money, couldn't you, Graham?'

'I suppose I could,' Graham replied.

Paul was sweating profusely, mopping his brow with a handkerchief taken from his jacket pocket.

'What did you spend £200,000 on, Paul?' Sebastian asked. Paul did not reply. 'What did you *spend* it on?' Sebastian asked again, getting agitated. 'It's an easy enough question. You clearly have spent it on something, this £200,000 you're offering to pay back, so what have you spent it on?' Paul still did not answer. 'It's a lot of money. Did you save it and buy something big or did you fritter it as it drip-fed into your wallet?' Paul remained silent. '*ANSWER ME*!' Sebastian's voice ricocheted around the room like a bullet. '*WHAT DID YOU SPEND THE FUCKING MONEY ON*?' he shouted, his face ablaze with anger. Breathing hard, but unflinching, Paul stared ahead. '*AND THE OTHER £300,000, WHAT DID YOU SPEND THAT ON*?' Sebastian added. Paul looked at Sebastian, sweat running into his mouth.

Sebastian rose to his feet sharply, flipping his chair off its castors sending it tumbling sideways, smashing against the bookcase. Graham moved to recover it.

'How *dare* you insult my intelligence,' Sebastian snarled, coming around the front of his desk, standing inches away from Paul. 'How *dare* you! £200,000 is a drop in the ocean and you know it! How *dare* you have the effrontery to sit in my office, in the company that has given you *everything* you could ever have hoped for and tell me £200,000! You're having a laugh, Paul, a *fucking* laugh!'

Paul opened his mouth to protest.

'*Don't*! Just *don't*!' Sebastian warned, pointing his finger squarely at Paul. 'Before I completely lose it with you,' he said, trying to calm his breathing down, 'I'm going to ask you one last time. How much money have you stolen? And no *bullshit*,' he spat. Paul did not speak. Sebastian sighed heavily. 'Right, well I think your silence has given me your answer, so I'm going to strike a deal with you.'

Paul's expression changed. He wondered what Sebastian was going to say.

'I'm going to suggest that you pay back twice what you *admit* to having taken. Would you accept that's closer to the figure we should be talking about?' Paul shook his head but did not speak. 'Okay. Let me put it another way,' Sebastian said, 'if you don't agree to pay back £400,000 I'm going to call the police.' Graham and Niamh raised their heads simultaneously. 'What do you think, Paul?'

'You can't do that!' Paul objected, coldly.

'Why can't I?' Sebastian snapped back.

'It's blackmail.'

'Okay, if that's the way you want to play it...' Sebastian said, shrugging as he turned to go back to his desk.

'No,' Paul interrupted sharply. 'Okay, I agree,' he said, praying that the police would not be involved.

With incredulous laughter in his voice, Sebastian turned back. 'So, you'll only be honest when there's something in it for you, you piece of *shit*!' The room went silent as he walked back to his desk and sat down. 'So, we agree £400,000. Well, there we go, we appear to be getting somewhere. Now, tell me how you intend to pay it back. I'm assuming you do not have that sort of money at your disposal and I'm afraid my generosity of spirit appears to have run out so I won't accept ten pounds a week for... however long it would take to pay back £400,000.'

Paul did not speak.

By force of habit, Graham sat calculating.

Exasperated, Sebastian sighed. 'I want the money by Friday,' he announced.

'Friday?' Paul questioned, coldly.

'You heard!' Sebastian snapped. 'Now get out.'

Paul did not move.

'*GET OUT*!' Sebastian screamed picking up the paperweight and hurling it across the room, smashing the ornate glass inset in his office door.

Paul pushed his chair back and left the room, leaving Sebastian, Graham and Niamh shocked, staring at the seat he had vacated. Sebastian put his elbows in his desk and his head in his hands. Graham stood silently and rested his hand gently on the crumpled man's shoulder, holding it there long enough for Sebastian to understand. Closing the office door gently behind them, Graham and Niamh left.

Matilda heard the commotion and rushed to Sebastian's office, with Panda running behind her. She looked at the shattered glass on the floor and through the smashed pane she could see Sebastian. Scooping Panda into her arms, she stepping carefully over the glass.

'Go to him,' Graham said softly, 'allow me to clear this up.'

'Thank you, Graham.'

'Tell him he owes me a drink when all this is over, for scaring the life out of me every time he launches that paperweight across the room. I think perhaps now is the time to confiscate it.'

'You might be right,' Matilda smiled.

'Oh,' he said, turning to leave, 'and can you tell him it would take 769 years, give or take a month or two. He'll know what you're talking about.'

Walking cautiously into Sebastian's office, Matilda put Panda into Sebastian's lap. He held onto her, burying his face deep into her fur.

'I think it's time you concentrated on your mum now,' she said. 'Your dad needs you; you should go to him. We are more than capable of handling everything here. Graham told me to tell you it would take 769 years... I've no idea what he's talking about but he said you'd understand.' Sebastian looked towards the door, watching Graham leave with a dustpan full of broken glass.

'The world needs more Grahams,' he said taking Panda's face in his hands.

~

Knowing Sebastian was on his way, William got dressed. Following Henry's telephone call, he had laid back on his pillow and drifted in and out of sleep. With her side of the bed cold and undisturbed, he had dreamt about Elspeth. Throughout their marriage he had slept only a handful of nights without her and now, when he was between dreams, he had forgotten and had reached out into the void, thinking perhaps she'd had a bad night and slept in another room. Waking, remembering, he felt abandoned. It was strange how still the house had become now that he was the only person in it. He knew he had no choice other than to carry on without her, but it wasn't what he wanted. He didn't much care for spending the rest of his life waking up alone.

Standing in the yard with Betsy staring at him, he looked across to the goats and the small kitchen garden Elspeth had tended since she was a child and at the plants she had bought the week before she died, waiting patiently in their pots. William would ask Sebastian to plant them for him, for the garden would never feel the same, not without Elspeth to nurture it.

William sat on the bench in front of Betsy's pen as she snuffled around her straw. He looked at the view that he and Elspeth had shared every morning. Today he had no reason to speak aloud and did not say 'it looks like it's going to be a lovely day,' or 'there's no wind in the trees,' or 'the crows are flying high this morning.' He missed their first conversation of the day. He missed her telling him what they were having for dinner, what she'd bought at McGregor's and the gossip she'd been party to. He simply missed her.

Fetching himself a fresh cup of tea, he returned to the yard and sat on the bench looking at Betsy. 'Be with you soon,' he whispered sadly into the sky.

~

With his overnight bag in hand, Sebastian let himself into the farmhouse around lunchtime to find William sitting at the kitchen table eating breakfast. 'Afternoon,' he said, looking at the cereal in William's bowl.

'I got up late.'

'That's unlike you. Are you okay?' Sebastian asked. William nodded. 'Is everyone in today or do they need a hand?' Sebastian continued, looking out of the window towards the sheds.

'I've no idea.'

'I'll go check in a bit. Tea?'

'Yes please,' William said, looking at his son as he filled the kettle. 'Did you have a meeting this morning?' he asked, noting Sebastian's suit.

'I did,' Sebastian replied, sighing.

'The sale's still going ahead okay?'

'Seems to be,' Sebastian replied, getting the mugs out and pouring the milk.

'I prefer the tea first,' William pointed out. 'It'll be sold just in time for Henry's play.'

'Will it? When is that?'

'He did tell me, but I've forgotten. He lost the theatre, did you know? The one they'd booked in Newcastle; it went into administration last week, Poor Henry, he's not having much luck. Lorna's found somewhere new though, somewhere near here.'

'How does that work with school?' Sebastian asked, replacing William's mug of cold tea with a fresh one.

'They're giving him the time off again. They're very good, aren't they? Not many schools would do that. He said two of the weeks are during half term. He gets two weeks at half term, I don't think I knew that.'

'Some private schools have two weeks. It would be good if he could make a proper go of it,' Sebastian said, 'not that I know the first thing about the theatre, but it looks to me like he's getting very close to being able to work in it full-time. He's taking so much time off school. I've offered to sponsor them, but he won't have it.'

'He wants to do it on his own. I told him he could do with me popping off.'

'And what did he say to that?' Sebastian asked, sitting down.

'Thankfully, he didn't like the idea else I'd have hidden the knives,' William replied with a weak laugh. 'Will you book a ticket for me?' he asked. 'Just one ticket,' he added, solemnly. 'You go to all his productions, don't you?'

'When I can,' Sebastian said, smiling as he remembered Henry's last production. 'What's this new one about, do you know?'

'I don't know really, something about heaven and hell,' William said, his forehead furrowing. 'That's terrible of me; I should know. Your mother would have known!'

Seeing the panic in his father's face, Sebastian came to his rescue. 'I don't know either, Dad. I'll ask him.'

'I think it might be a comedy,' William said flatly.

Picking up a piece of paper propped against the butter dish, Sebastian read a list of jobs his father had made. He could see the unplanted pot plants sitting in the back border: a job for the afternoon.

'How long are you staying?' William asked.

'A couple of nights, until Henry's back on Wednesday.'

'I'm very grateful to have you here.'

'I know,' Sebastian said, reading down the list. 'We need to add something to this. We need to get some clothes together for Mum, so we can drop them at Angus Stewart's.'

'Is she not dressed?' William asked, looking bemused, imagining Elspeth lying naked in a cold mortuary drawer.

'She'll be in whatever she was wearing when they took her. If you want her to be buried in that, that's fine, but if you'd rather she had something else on then we need to take it over so they can get her ready for us to see her on Thursday.'

'I don't want to go on Thursday.'

'You don't have to go. How about the dress she wore at Christmas?'

'With a cardigan. The weather's changing,' William said, turning his gaze to the window.

Sebastian felt desperately sad for the old man and sorry he was pushing him to face things he would rather not.

'You've written 'paperwork' on this note, what does that mean?'

'I was hoping Paul might take a look at the accounts for this place. I usually send them off to Loftus' but I've not got round to it. There's a pile of paperwork on the side I've not sorted. I'm worried it's a bit muddled.'

'I can take a look. You don't need Paul.'

'He's looked at them before. He was very good and didn't ask to be paid.'

'That's because *I* paid him, Dad! Leave it to me, I'll look at it.'

Picking up on his tone, William looked at Sebastian. 'Has something happened?' he asked.

Hesitating, Sebastian wondered whether burdening his father with his own problems was a good idea, but desperate for his father's approval and confirmation that he had reacted justly, he wanted him to know.

For almost an hour, William sat and listened as Sebastian told him what had happened. Seeing the child in his son, William felt every bit of the betrayal as if it had been against himself. He could see Sebastian searching for clues as to where he had gone wrong. He could see how upset he felt that someone he had loved and respected could behave in such a way. William was powerless, other than to offer a parent's solution by seeing the atrocity from his son's point of view and agreeing with him, which he did most emphatically. 'Dishonesty inevitably leads to distrust and, once discovered, will destroy any relationship no matter how strong it may seem. I'm sorry you've lost a friendship in all this,' William said earnestly. He reflected on the profundity of his own words, always desperate to say and do the right thing. He thought about what he and Elspeth had kept tucked away all these years. Life was full of secrets.

As his father paused, Sebastian's mind switched to Nancy. Looking at his father sitting, old and hunched, at the kitchen table, he imagined what he would say if he knew what Sebastian knew and for a moment he thought to tell him, but the moment passed.

Breaking the mood, Sebastian agreed to look at the paperwork as long as his father did the planting. Although windy, it was a lovely afternoon and the soil was soft and easy to dig. Despite his bad shoulder, with a warm coat and the September sun on his back, William was happy pottering. It was a comical sight watching him battle the wind. To dig the holes and knock the plants out of their pots, William popped his arm out of its sling. 'I can see you,' Sebastian called, opening the back door. 'Put your arm back in that sling!' Laughing, William gave him a two-fingered salute.

Looking through his parents' papers, Sebastian came across their wills. He had wondered where they were, having expected to find them in the document case. They were more or less identical other than for the details of the farm, and looked pretty straightforward. If either of them died, the estate was to go to the surviving spouse and if both of them died the estate was to be divided equally between himself and Henry. To Sebastian's surprise, there was no mention of Nancy.

Attached to the wills was a letter in his father's handwriting, addressed to himself and Henry with the words – 'To be opened after we have both gone,' and signed, 'William and Elspeth Campbell'. Sebastian sat holding the letter for a long time, desperate to know its contents. He put it up to the light and peered into the well-sealed corners but found it impenetrable and knew it would have to remain where it was until such time as they were looking at the wills once more. The letter bewildered him. What could it contain that was not written in the wills? And why was it only addressed to him and Henry and not Nancy? It took Sebastian all of his willpower not to say something to his father when he came in from the garden. Over dinner, he tried to skirt around the subject hoping his father might volunteer some information.

'I've been through your papers. You're fine, just get the accounts to Loftus' when you can,' he said, taking a breath, hesitating awkwardly over his next phrase. 'Yours and Mum's wills were amongst the paperwork. Did you know?'

'Ah, not in the case then?' William replied, looking up from his plate. 'I wondered where they were. Your mother must have moved them.'

'I hope you don't mind, but I took a look at Mum's,' Sebastian said, waiting for a reaction, 'in case she had anything in it we needed to know.'

'Was there anything?'

'Not that I could see.'

'Good, then I wouldn't mind the wills going back in the case. That's where they belong.' With that Sebastian sensed that the opportunity to mention the letter was gone and nothing more was said.

Before bed, he put the wills and the letter back into the case that he had looked through the day after his mother had died, and put the case back on top of the wardrobe in his parents' room.

~

After rehearsing until late, Henry was back, lying on the sofa listening to music. He had become accustomed to doing this over the few days he was home and, with plenty of work to be getting on with, Lorna was happy to leave him to it; it was his time to be alone. She was amazed at how well he was coping. It was his way and she respected him for it, although she wished he would look to her for comfort, but that was not the Campbell way.

Thinking about Sebastian, Henry sent him a midnight message, suggesting he should leave their father to his own devices during some of the following day. He suggested that Sebastian went out and spent time doing something normal, go to the gym, go for a run, get away from the sadness for a few hours. Henry knew how intense it had become within Taligth's walls.

As Sebastian lay in bed reading Henry's message, Meggie sprung into his mind. He was tempted to call her, to see whether he could spend some time with her, but he could smell danger. He decided he would not take Henry's advice, and instead, spend the thirteenth day following his mother's death out in the fields, which is what he did. Come the evening however, the compulsion to contact her was too great and he gave in, leaving a message on her answer machine.

~

For Henry, the following day was full of school and a rehearsal, which, once more, went on late into the evening. Ever conscious of the time the team was giving to the production, Henry had worked out a tight schedule for the coming weeks. Most of them had day jobs, much like his own, with understanding employers, a few were self-employed, taking opportunities of work wherever they could, but for a couple, acting was their profession and Henry had their current performances and rehearsals to consider when devising the schedule. It took an inordinate amount of organising.

Despite being knackered and penniless, Henry was looking forward to being back in the theatre. It was what drove him to get up and go to school. Whilst supervising lunchtime detention, he made a phone call to The Sheep Shed, arranging a visit for Thursday morning where he hoped his father might join him. He also found some accommodation; three perfectly located adjoining properties owned by someone who had been recommended by someone working in the theatre; there appeared to be a strong local community. Henry could already see ticket sales on the computer system even though they had only gone live a couple of days before. He allowed himself to get excited and felt he had used his hour in detention wisely.

Once home, he packed a bag and hung his one good suit in the bathroom with the hope that the steam from the shower would relieve it of its creases. He chose a tie, not a black one, and made sure his shoes were clean. Before retreating to his nightly spot on the sofa, he sat with Lorna to make sure they were organised.

'Are you okay?' he asked, perplexed by his wife's skittish behaviour.

'I'm fine,' she said, smiling weirdly at him.

'If you say so,' Henry replied, not convinced. 'So, when's Lilith coming home?'

'Thursday night. She's got a gig, so she'll be late. We'll head up to Taligth on Friday morning. Is that okay?'

'Of course,' Henry replied.

'And I know it's a lot to do in one day, but we need to come back on Friday night.'

'Why?' Henry asked, a little disappointed Lorna and Lilith would not be staying.

'Lilith has a date first thing Saturday morning,' Lorna said, grinning.

'A date?'

'With the Philharmonic!' she announced, hardly able to contain her excitement.

'An audition date?'

'Yep!'

'London?'

'Liverpool.'

'Bloody hell!' Henry exclaimed, sitting up in his seat. 'Oh my god, Lorna!'

'I know!'

'How come she didn't tell me?'

'She has! She's literally just messaged. It'll be on your phone. It's only an audition, but... it's nice to have some good news.'

'It is,' Henry agreed, seeing the message from Lilith. 'That's the best news. I'll send her a message,' he said, picking up his glass of wine and earphones and kissing Lorna before leaving her sitting in the kitchen playing with a model of the set.

It was good to have something to smile about, he thought.

Day Fourteen

Despite his promise to himself that he would not, Sebastian had arranged to meet Meggie. So close to the funeral, desperately not wanting Nancy to turn up, his lack of contact with Meggie had made him nervous and the more time he was away from her, the less confidence he had in her keeping her word. After all, why would she *not* tell her? He asked himself. Perhaps she still felt loyal to him, he hoped, though surely not, not after she told him how his actions had affected her life. He needed to see her again.

Meggie's reply to Sebastian's message came in after midnight and Sebastian called her first thing.

'Are you in the café today?' he asked, after exchanging awkward pleasantries.

'No. I'm not heading back up to Edinburgh until later,' Meggie replied. 'Why?'

'I was wondering whether you might like to meet for lunch, or a coffee somewhere.'

'Are you okay?' Meggie asked, sensing Sebastian's unease.

'Not really.'

'Okay. Do you know Dungorian Village?'

'I've heard of it.'

'We could meet there, if you like.'

'What time?'

~

William knew how precious Sebastian's time was and he was grateful that Sebastian chose to spend the little he had with him. So, when over breakfast Sebastian said he was going to meet a friend for lunch, William encouraged him.

241

They both needed time on their own and, whilst Sebastian was out, William took a gentle walk with the farm dogs. It seemed a long time since he had seen the land and he wanted to remind himself what the world outside the yard looked like. He had given himself a stern talking to the night before. Unless he wanted to die a miserable old man, he needed to be more positive.

~

Having switched his phone's location services off, Sebastian enjoyed a drive along the east coast. Just north of the English border, was Dungorian Village, a family-run garden and craft centre. Home to wood turners, glass blowers, wool crafters, silversmiths, bakers, potters and artists plus organic food retailers and a market on Fridays, it was a popular place to visit.

Sebastian was surprised by the size of the place. He had expected a few stalls scattered around a lake, but this was clearly a well-organised operation and by 2 p.m. it was packed with 4x4s squeezed into tight parking spaces. It was not the sort of place he would have normally gone to; there were far too many prams.

Walking along the line of huts towards the restaurant where Meggie had suggested they meet, Sebastian looked at the workmanship of the crafters as he passed. He watched them paint or weave or blow or turn and was amazed by their skill and creativity. Their attention to detail did not seem to match the prices they were charging, and he wondered how they made a living.

Meggie was already waiting as he entered the warm room, and he was surprised to see she was not alone. As he cautiously approached the table where they were sitting, Meggie stood up and introduced her companion. 'Sebastian, this is my husband, Aled,' she said, as Aled stood up and reached out to shake Sebastian's hand.

'Hello, Sebastian. It's good to meet you. Did you find this place okay?' he asked, his soft Welsh accent colouring his words.

'I did,' Sebastian replied, smiling at Aled who was at least fifteen if not twenty years Meggie's senior. 'I was marvelling at the skill of the crafters in the huts as I walked by.'

'Amazing aren't they? Meg's daughter, Florence, often shows her work here. She does pretty well too, doesn't she, Meg?'

'She does. Would you like a drink, Seb?' Meggie asked. 'Aled, do you want another one?'

'Only if you don't mind me staying for a minute, but let me get them,' Aled said, heading off to the counter. 'What would you like, Sebastian?'

'Just a black coffee please, if that's all right?' Sebastian said, sitting down.

Meggie rearranged her coat on the back of her chair. 'Are you okay?' she asked, as she sat down, noticing Sebastian's gaze fixed on Aled.

'Yes, sorry, I just wasn't expecting your husband to be here, that was all.'

'Do you mind?'

'No, of course not,' Sebastian replied, unconvincingly.

'He sometimes drives me back to Edinburgh, or to here. It saves me getting the train all the way and means we can have lunch.'

'Don't you drive?'

'Not anymore,' Meggie replied as Aled, having placed his order at the counter, returned to the table.

'Meggie tells me you own Tatch-A UK,' Aled said.

'That's right.'

'It's a big company,' he replied, sitting down. 'I owned a business before I met my lovely Meggie and settled for a less stressful life.'

'What line of business were you in?'

'Sports. I owned... well, part owned... a sportswear company.'

'Not Valley Sport?' Sebastian asked.

'Yes, that's the one.'

'Are you Aled Pritchard?'

'I am,' Aled replied, smiling at the waitress as she brought the drinks to the table.

Sebastian struggled to recognise the man who he had seen dominate the business pages when Valley Sports had gone up for sale. Aled was larger than Sebastian remembered and, with his grey hair and long beard, he looked nothing like his media profile.

'So,' Aled said, picking up his cup, 'if you know Valley Sport, do you know my good friend Patrick McCarthy?'

'I do,' Sebastian replied, surprised to hear Patrick's name mentioned.

'Then the jungle drums were right,' Aled said, taking a long drink of his coffee. Sebastian looked at him. 'And good luck to you. If you're doing what I think you're doing, Patrick is a decent man,' he added downing his coffee and standing, placing his chair tidily under the table. 'A bit of advice though, from one businessman to another. If you sell, make sure you go out there and do something different with your life. It's too short to waste in another boardroom and although Patrick is a good man, he's best left to get on with it. He has his own way of doing things which may not be yours... that's only if you're doing what I think you're doing, mind...' he said winking. 'Right, I'm off. Unfortunately, alpacas do not look after themselves. Sebastian, it's been a pleasure to meet you. Hopefully we will see each other again some time. No doubt you have some catching up to do. Would you be kind enough to drop Meg at the station, it's about ten minutes from here.'

'I can get a taxi,' Meggie protested.

'It's not a problem. I can take you back with me,' Sebastian suggested.

'I prefer to take the train.'

'Well, you two agree it between you, and I'll see you in a couple of days,' Aled said leaning down to give Meggie a kiss. Sebastian stood-up to shake his hand, and Aled left, waving in the air behind him to the grateful waitress into whose hand he had squeezed a twenty-pound note.

'Well, that was a surprise,' Sebastian said sitting back down. 'Why didn't you tell me you were married to Aled Pritchard?'

'I didn't think to.'

'Does he know who I am?'

'Yes, of course.'

'Oh,' Sebastian replied, feeling foolish. It suddenly occurred to him that perhaps Meggie saw this as nothing more than a meeting of old friends.

'Have you told Matilda you're here?' Meggie asked.

'No, I haven't,' Sebastian replied sheepishly.

'Why not?'

'You know what, Meggie, I have no idea,' Sebastian replied, 'but bearing in mind our history, I'm not sure she'd appreciate knowing,' he said, feeling his face redden. 'Your husband wasn't around at the time, so to him I'm just an old friend, whereas to Matilda you are rather more than that.'

'Am I, still?' Meggie pushed.

'Don't be so naïve, Meggie. Of course you are. You always have been,' Sebastian said, confused by his feelings.

Meggie looked at him knowingly, and an embarrassed silence fell between them. She knew how he was feeling.

'I shouldn't have said that,' Sebastian whispered. Meggie remained silent. 'Listen, this is going to come out wrong,' he continued, 'but I'm going to say it anyway.' He hesitated before speaking again. 'Meggie, I need to know you won't tell Nancy about my mum. I seriously can not have her turning up on Friday.'

'Is that why you wanted to meet up with me?'

'Meggie, please!' Sebastian said, looking into her eyes, aching to reach out and touch her hand.

'Have you told your dad?' she asked.

Desperately not wanting to, Sebastian knew he was about to lie. 'Yes, I told him,' he said quickly, 'but it hasn't changed anything,' he said.

'I'm really pleased you've told him,' Meggie replied, 'and, as I said to you the other day, I have no intention of telling Nancy. That's for you to do.'

Thinking about William, whom she had not seen for such a long time, Meggie remembered him with deep fondness. Always laughing, he had been very kind to her when she was most in need of kindness, and it was difficult to imagine him as an old man with no one to talk to. 'It's not easy, is it?' she said.

'What's not easy?'

'Life.'

Sebastian nodded.

Meggie looked across the table, studying him. She could almost see the troubled, seventeen-year-old boy she had known a lifetime ago. With his elbows on the table, his hands were closed in front of his lips as if in prayer. 'Shall we order something to eat, or do you want to head off?' she asked.

'Something to eat would be nice,' he said, lowering his hands as if his prayer to God had been sent. 'How hungry are you?' he asked, taking the menus out of the holder and handing one to Meggie.

'Ravenous,' Meggie replied with a slight laugh, 'you know me.'

Sebastian sat back in his chair, wondering whether he did.

Whilst they had been sitting, the restaurant had filled up around them. There were mainly small groups of young mothers with babies in prams, plus a few older couples out for lunch. Across the table, behind Meggie, Sebastian watched a couple similar in age to himself and Meggie, engaged in deep conversation. He tried to work out whether they were married or not and, if they were, whether they were married to each other. Their body language gave little away. One minute she would speak great long sentences, throwing her arms in the air, shaping the words with her hands, whilst he sat quietly nodding. The next minute, he would take over and do much the same as she sat motionless, her face perplexed. It seemed to Sebastian she was trying to get him to see her point of view.

After the time he'd had, it was nice to see normal life going on around them. He and Meggie talked for an hour over lunch before they needed to leave. As he stood up, he wondered what the gesticulating couple might have thought about him and Meggie, if they had been looking their way.

'How would you feel about meeting up sometime after my mum's funeral?' he asked, helping Meggie with her coat.

'Let's see how things go,' Meggie replied, slipping her bag onto her shoulder. 'Are you okay to drop me at the station?'

'I can drive you back.'

'I prefer the train.'

During the short drive to the station, they spoke little, other than to remark on the stunning landscape as it unveiled itself ahead of them.

'I appreciate you dropping me off,' Meggie said, as Sebastian pulled up in front of the small, run-down station.

'It feels wrong leaving you here,' he said, looking at the unmade car park and the dilapidated looking building.

'It's fine. This is where Aled drops me. There's a direct train. It only takes twenty minutes, which gives me a chance to read the next chapter of my book. I hope it goes okay on Friday,' Meggie said, opening the door. Hesitating, she turned back to look at him. 'I'm really sorry, Seb.'

'What are you sorry for?' he asked, confused.

'Everything,' she said. 'You, me, us, lies, secrets, Nancy, your mum and dad, everything,' she sighed, leaning over and kissing him on the cheek. 'There's my train. I need to go,' she said, jumping out of the car.

Getting out of the car, Sebastian shouted after her. 'Meggie!' he called across the car park. But it was too late; she'd run past the gates and onto the platform, as the train pulled into the station.

Watching her train leave, Sebastian stood taking in deep breaths of fresh air before walking back to his car. Getting in, he sat for a moment, looking at the empty station, wondering what Meggie had meant.

He started the car and pulled slowly out of the car park. As he drove back, he mulled over the lie he had told her and thought that perhaps, when he got back to Taligth, he would tell his father and Henry the truth. He battled with himself, questioning the value of the information, wondering whether it would help them to know that Nancy was somewhere out there with no interest or desire to see her family.

Occasionally, Nancy had come to Sebastian in his dreams and he'd confronted her. Sometimes it was obviously her, other times she materialised as some strange creature, or someone he knew but didn't recognise. But it was her all the same. Dreams were a regular torment for both Sebastian and Henry, but Sebastian, in particular, had suffered horrific night terrors as a child. As an adult he had learned to handle them, either by distraction or avoidance. In recent months, with the sale of the company taking up every waking moment that the death of his mother wasn't, he would go into the factory and find something to do. He would lie on the floor examining the undercarriage of one of the machines into the small hours to avoid sleep and the nightmares it brought. He preferred to be tired than face his enemy.

By the time he got to Taligth, he had answered seven telephone calls, six concerning the company sale and the seventh, a call from Niamh to say that £200,000 had been deposited with a message saying the rest would be with them by Friday. He wondered how Paul had got the money so quickly.

Remembering to switch location services back on, Sebastian waited at Taligth's gates, watching them slowly open. He could see Henry's car parked behind his mother's. One of the hardest things following his mother's death was seeing her car sitting on the drive, patiently waiting for her.

It was inconceivable to imagine that just a few hours before her death she had driven it to McGregor's, bought a loaf of bread, chatted with Dougie, popped to see Mrs Foster to take her some flour and then driven back to make lunch and bake scones. How normal life had seemed two weeks ago.

As he parked behind Henry's car, Sebastian convinced himself it was better to not say anything to his father and Henry about Nancy. However, he decided to tell them that he had met Meggie in order to give him credence for when he might, one day, sit them down and tell them the whole story from the very beginning. He found them in the kitchen.

'Hey there,' Henry said, welcomingly.

'When did you get here?' Sebastian asked.

'About an hour ago.'

'Are you staying for dinner, Sebastian?' William asked, getting up in the vain hope the fridge might offer up suggestions for an evening meal.

'Not tonight, Dad, I can't stay long. I need to go into the office. I'll grab a coffee though before I head off. Does anyone want another drink?' William and Henry both declined, they were already on their second cup of tea within the past hour and there was only so much the human bladder could contain.

'Anything happened while I've been out?' Sebastian enquired, filling the kettle, as William busied himself in the depths of the almost empty fridge. Having already told them about Lilith's audition, Henry looked blank, considering whether he had any more interesting news.

'Gordon phoned,' William said turning to look at the boys, raising his eyebrows. Gordon was William's oldest friend.

'Oh, right. What did he say?' Sebastian asked.

'Nothing. I wasn't in. He left a message,' William said from within the fridge.

'Where were you?'

'I walked up to the back fields with the dogs.'

'That's good, Dad. Did you feel okay?' Sebastian asked.

249

'I felt better for getting some fresh air,' William said, backing out of the fridge empty handed. 'Sorry, Hal.'

'No matter Dad, I'm not all that hungry anyway,' Henry replied.

'There's some bread. We can make a sandwich,' William suggested. 'I wondered whether you might phone Gordon back for me, Sebastian?'

'Sure, I can do that for you...' Sebastian replied, hesitantly, 'or perhaps, Hal? Could you give him a call?'

'Thanks for that you two,' Henry laughed. They all knew Gordon could be rather morose and would talk, moaning about his ailments, low pitched and monotone, and Henry would be lucky to get away with less than an hour on the phone. 'I'll do it later... or tomorrow... or maybe next week,' Henry said smiling at his father.

As they drifted into silence, Sebastian, feeling nervous, decided now was the time to tell William and Henry about Meggie. Bringing his coffee over, he sat at the table next to Henry, the two brothers facing their father. 'Guess who I met for lunch?' he said, his heart in his mouth. As ever Henry came out with something silly: 'Charlize Theron,' he suggested.

'Better than that,' Sebastian replied.

'Who could be better than Charlize Theron?' Henry asked.

'Meggie!' Sebastian announced.

'Meggie?' Henry exclaimed in surprise, 'as in *your* Meggie? I haven't heard you mention her name for years.'

'Meggie,' William repeated slowly.

'You remember Meggie don't you, Dad?'

'Yes, I remember Meggie,' William answered, suddenly nervous; desperately wishing Elspeth was beside him.

'So...?' Henry asked, 'how did you meet her?'

'Well, actually it's your fault,' Sebastian said, looking at Henry. 'She's been running the café down the hill from my place, towards the park... ring any bells?'

'The small one?' Henry asked, 'with the artwork? Of course!' he said, suddenly seeing the face of young Meggie in the waitress he had befriended. 'I can see her now. How could I not have recognised her?'

'She's in Scotland?' William asked.

'Yes,' Sebastian said, 'but not permanently, she lives in Hexham.'

'How is she?' William muttered.

'She's good.'

'And her family?' William asked, and in his empty hand was Elspeth's, squeezing it gently, reassuringly.

'I don't know. We didn't really talk about them.'

'What made you go to the café?' Henry asked, still matching his vague memory of Meggie to the waitress he met.

'Panda dragged me in there!'

'That's my fault. Sorry,' Henry conceded. 'So you met for lunch? Does Matilda know?'

'No, she's funny about Meggie,' Sebastian said, 'not that there's anything going on,' he added looking at Henry's expression. 'Her husband was there.'

'Still...'

'Behave! She's married to Aled Pritchard, Dad.'

'Who's Aled Pritchard?' Henry asked.

'A very successful businessman who must be more my age than hers,' William commented.

'Patrick McCarthy bought his company.'

'Small world,' William mumbled. 'Do they have any children?' he asked.

'No. She has a daughter from her first marriage though.'

'Married twice,' William said, nodding gently. 'Did you tell her about your mother?'

'I did, why?'

'How did she react?'

'As you might expect,' Sebastian said, surprised by his father's questions. 'She said to pass on her condolences.'

251

'Right,' William replied, standing up, 'I'm going for a rest.' With that, he left the brothers in the kitchen to talk.

'Is he okay?' Sebastian asked once their father was out of earshot.

'He seems to be. So, go on. Do you still fancy her?'

'For god's sake, Hal!'

'Ah, you're not denying it. Was it all 'there' still, you know, the...?'

'Pack it in!'

'I'll be honest, I fancied her when you were going out with her.'

'I can't believe you sometimes!'

Looking at his brother as he finished his coffee, Henry sensed there was more to this 'lunch' than Sebastian was letting on. There was little about his brother's behaviour he could not read, and he knew when he was being evasive.

'Right, I'm going to make a move,' Sebastian said. 'Are you still okay for tomorrow?'

'Yes,' Henry said, sighing heavily at the thought.

'And Dad?'

'He'll be there.'

'I've got a couple of meetings in the morning, so I'll meet you there.'

Leaving Henry to tidy the kitchen, Sebastian popped his head around the living room door to say goodbye to his father, who, having exhausted himself walking across the fields, was asleep in his chair. Not wanting to wake him, Sebastian retreated quietly and left instructions with Henry to say 'goodnight' for him.

Driving away, Sebastian was pleased he had told his father and Henry about Meggie. It was one less thing to trip himself up on. But something his father said was praying on his mind. Why did he make a point of asking whether he had told Meggie about his mother?

Day Fifteen

Thursday

Before heading to the theatre, William and Henry had a job to do. One of the sheep had got caught on the barbed wire fence overnight and needed rescuing. With Sam and Ade busy getting the cows in, Henry volunteered to do it, but it was a two-man job and William was keen to help, so trudged slowly behind him as they made their way across the fields. It was good to get out, and with hardly a wind, it felt mild for late September though the threat of autumn hung in the air and the ground was damp and uneven under foot. In their heavy boots they picked their way through the long grass, which hid deep divots and slippery cowpats, making their way to the top field where the sheep were grazing. Looking down the hillside, William commented on how peaceful it was. The children were in school and it was quiet along the roads leading away from Taligth. Even the main road, which could be seen from the top, was deserted, allowing William and Henry to hear the cries of the crows that swooped and glided in and amongst the uppermost branches of the huge oak trees.

By the time they got to the entangled ewe, she had given up her struggle and was dangling from the barbed wire in an attempt to sit down. It took a joint effort to release her and, once they had checked her over for injuries, William was happy to let her go back to the flock which had scattered in all directions as soon as he and Henry had opened the gate, ending up stuffed in the top most corner panicking that they might be next.

'Are you all right?' Henry asked, as they headed back towards the house, noticing William rubbing his shoulder.

'I am,' William said, determined not to give in to the pain. 'Stupid bloody animal,' he complained, 'she was strong.'

'I don't think she took kindly to your manly grip,' Henry said, laughing at the image of his father with his good arm between the sheep's rear legs. 'So, a quick clean up and then we need to go. We'll not come back here before going to see Mum,' Henry said, taking his boots off and going into the kitchen. 'Are you okay with that?'

'Of course,' William replied, trying not to think about what lay ahead.

An hour later they were approaching the theatre. On top of a hill, it loomed into sight. With a river running below, the recently converted old barn, with its huge glass window and enormous doors, looked out onto unspoiled countryside with rolling hills rising and dipping in the distance. Henry was instantly enthralled. Well done Lorna, he thought, what a find.

The young, dynamic theatre manager, Tom, with long, dark hair tied loosely in a bun, took them along narrow corridors with deep red carpets and walls of exposed brick, leading them into the auditorium. Enthusiastically, he talked about the innovative performance space. In the round, it lent itself to the intimate, immersive nature of Henry's work. The lighting rig was vast and packed with lanterns and surrounding it was a circular rail with a walkway for access from which scenery could be suspended. Walking around the auditorium, William and Henry were shown the different ways in which the space could be configured. Nothing was fixed, not the seating, the entrances, the staging or the lights. It seemed, more or less, anything was possible. The place felt vibrant and alive. Tom toured them around the building, giving them a lively, potted history as they went. It was a fascinating place, which had played many roles prior to being converted into a theatre. In more recent years it had been a wedding venue and before that, a second-hand bookshop, a florist and a printers. In the mid-1800s, much to William's fascination, it had belonged to a one-armed sheep farmer. William chatted about his own experience of trying to grapple the sheep earlier that day.

The Sheep Shed had been operating as a theatre for nine months and had welcomed some interesting up and coming companies who had brought innovative and creative ideas to its stage. During quieter times, its versatility meant the space could be used for regular cinema nights, live music and the occasional open mic nights for wannabe comedians. It also ran a number of community initiatives, which Henry liked, and had a thriving youth theatre and dance school, story-telling mornings, a weekly Knit 'n' Natter and a book club, which met every second month. William thought of Elspeth and how she might have liked to join a book club in such a place.

Henry felt good being back in the theatre and William, swept along by Henry's excitement, added valuable insight into the way the space could be best used. It was lovely to see the old man smiling. He reassured Henry that his plan to suspend part of the set from the rail would work and that all that was needed was a simple mechanism to propel it.

'Do you think a bike would work?' Henry asked, as they looked up.

'It might,' William said, craning his neck and walking around the stage in a circle. 'Is it strong enough?' he asked Tom.

'More than strong enough for what Henry wants,' Tom replied, as he tucked a stray piece of hair back into his bun. 'We had a car hanging from it a couple of weeks ago.'

'I saw that on your website. It looked incredible,' Henry commented.

'Are the actors going to be working this cube thing?' William asked.

'That's the idea,' Henry replied.

'Rather them than me.'

'Here, let me show you,' Henry said, opening his folder and taking out a copy of Lorna's sketch.

255

'I see,' William said, taking the drawing from Henry. 'I had visions of it being solid.'

'No, it's just a frame made from scaffolding poles. Imagine that suspended from the rail. What do you think?'

'Well, if they've hung a car from it, I can't see why they can't hang something like this from it.'

'Yes, but I want it to move around the rail so that it can be seen from different angles.'

'Does it need to rotate as well?' William asked, thinking. 'What's going to be in it?'

'I don't want anything complicated; I just want it to move,' Henry replied, looking up. 'There's going to be furniture attached to the structure, a chair, half a table, a picture, that sort of thing. It's meant to be a small room, but the actors need to be able to climb around it, so it has to be strong. We've been rehearsing with the cube, albeit not suspended, so we know that, in the principle, works.'

Sitting in row 'A', now able to visualise what Henry was describing, the engineer in William came up with a simple and workable solution, which delighted Henry and fascinated Tom, who was sure they would be able to accommodate it.

On their way to the funeral directors, Henry and William talked excitedly about The Sheep Shed.

~

It seemed that every day brought with it almost insurmountable hurdles but, one by one, Sebastian was dealing with them. Getting into work early, he'd had a busy morning taken up by a series of meetings as they made the final preparations.

Before he left the office he wrote a letter, a long letter, explaining everything. As he wrote he could feel his mother's hand gently resting on his own and hear her voice saying, 'ye dinnae need to, I understand...' It was the hardest letter he had ever written.

With fifteen minutes to spare, Sebastian flung his car at the side of the road and sprinted into the florist's. He needed to make the final arrangements for the floral display to adorn his mother's coffin before making his way to Angus Stewart's. He was glad to stop for a while and welcomed the solemnity of the funeral directors and the time to reflect. Henry and William arrived a few minutes later, their mood changing as they got out of the car.

After a warm greeting, Angus respectfully showed the three men into the room where Elspeth lay. The room was small, well-lit and decorated with fresh flowers. A sweet-smelling candle filled the air with the scent of jasmine. At one end of the room was a soft chair on which sat a range of cushions and a well-loved teddy bear that smiled at William as they walked in and he smiled back, allowing it to give him something to focus on before his eyes rested on Elspeth.

The room was taken over by a sense of absolute stillness and they stood looking at Elspeth, as if, for them, the world had stopped turning. For Henry, seeing his mother was too much to bear. Sebastian came to his brother's side and rested his hand on Henry's forearm, 'I know,' he whispered, 'I know.'

Henry could only remember once watching his mother lie in such a way. When he was a small child, she had been in bed for weeks, ill with pneumonia, and when her fever was so bad and she was drifting in and out of consciousness, Henry would creep into her bedroom and watch the rise and fall of her chest to make sure she was still breathing. He wished he were that child again and this, her bedroom.

The three men stood looking. Hesitantly, William walked forward and put his hand upon Elspeth's. With a little courage he took it into his own. 'So cold,' he mumbled, rubbing it, trying to share some of his warmth with her. 'That's not like you my lovely old girl, 'Och!' you would say, 'tis tae stuffy in this room,' and you'd have all these windows open,' he said, stroking her hand, looking at her.

She had been tenderly laid out and was clothed in her tartan Christmas dress and matching cardigan. She looked thin and pale and, without life, she was no longer there.

Henry could hear her voice in his head and waited for her to speak but he found the silence unbearable and was the first to leave the room after kissing her goodbye for the last time. Following, Sebastian tucked the letter he had written that morning into his mother's hand. 'Here,' he said, 'to take with you,' and putting his cheek alongside hers he whispered, almost silently, into her ear, 'forgive me.'

Last to leave was William. In the sixteen days since her death he had not shed a tear. He felt too empty and alone to cry. When he saw Henry unable to hold back, he wished he was able to do the same and join him in his grief, but nothing came. He ached to lie alongside her so they could go together. But he could not do that and tomorrow her body would be buried in the cold, dark ground. Giving her one last kiss, feeling her cool skin beneath his lips, he spoke softly. 'Sweet dreams,' he said. 'I'll see you soon.' He left without looking back. 'When it's my turn,' he said, to Sebastian and Henry, outside, 'cremate me, I'm afraid of the dark.'

~

By the time William and Henry got back to Taligth, William was exhausted and went for a rest whilst Henry caught up with Lorna.

'A tough day?' she asked, hearing the weariness in Henry's voice.

'A strange one,' Henry replied, sitting at the kitchen table, idly thumbing the pages of his mother's book.

'How was the theatre?' Lorna asked.

'Amazing! Thank you so much for finding it, and Dad had some good ideas about the cube. I'll fill you in tomorrow.'

'Good, phew! And how was it seeing your mum?'

'Better than I expected,' Henry replied. 'Dad did really well but he's shattered so he's having a sleep before dinner.'

'If you're making it, he might not want to wake up until breakfast.'

'Very funny!' Henry scoffed. 'Is Lilith on her way?'

'Her train gets in at eleven. She's got a gig remember?'

'Of course, I'd forgotten. And how's the other love of my life?'

'She's good. We've not long been back from a walk. What are you going to do tonight?'

'I'm going to get on with the lighting plan. They've got some impressive tech. The new equipment they were talking about went right over my head. I'm hoping Jim will know what it all means.'

'Don't worry, Jim will have it rigged up before lunchtime and then he'll be twiddling his thumbs. Do I hear a little excitement in your voice, Henry Campbell?'

'You do. It's weird. My plays are starting to sell, the productions are turning a profit, we broke even in Edinburgh this time, then Paris, and with what I can see coming up, I think this could be it. I know we're not making enough to live on yet, but we're getting there.'

'Your mum would be very proud of you,' Lorna said as Henry went quiet. 'Listen, I'm going to leave you to it. Go and make something to eat, and get a good night's sleep. Give my love to your dad. I'll see you tomorrow, love you, Hal.'

~

'Tomorrow' dawned, with the morning of the funeral bringing rain for the first time in weeks.

Sebastian and Ewan arrived at the house early, with boxes of plates and cutlery, glasses and mugs and food and drink; more food and drink then anyone could possibly consume.

Leaving Ewan to fill the pantry and put the remaining drinks outside, Sebastian hopped onto one of the quad bikes and headed out to the field behind the cattle shed. He wanted time to himself to gather his thoughts and practice his speech. For as long as he could remember, he had loved being with the cows and often helped his father feed them and move them from field to field. They were calm, affectionate animals and loved to be petted and stroked and scratched behind their ears. And they were forgiving. When

259

Sebastian was alone with them, he felt safe telling them his secrets. He trusted them, for they never told anyone the things they knew.

In the open air, with the cows around him, Sebastian talked to his mother. 'So, this is it, Mum, time to say goodbye,' he said, stroking the muzzle of one of the heifers who, having recognised him, had sidled up for a scratch. 'I'll admit I'm finding it tough. I'm trying to hold it together for Dad and Henry's sakes, but not very well if I'm honest,' he said. 'Dad will be okay, you know. We will look after him and this place...' He looked around at the cows and across to the sheep and the woods beyond, and back towards the farmhouse, where he could see Henry standing in the yard looking out, cup of tea in hand. 'You mustn't worry, Mum,' he said, trying to reassure himself and stay composed, though it was a battle of wills he would not win that day. He lent his head against the soft nose of the inquisitive heifer. 'I'm so sorry, Mum, for not being brave enough to talk to you... and for forcing Nancy to leave...' he said, pausing to breathe. 'The letter I gave you yesterday explains everything.'

After giving the heifer one last stroke, Sebastian made his way back to the house.

~

In the chaos of the morning, William chose to stay in his and Elspeth's bedroom until it was time to leave.

To Henry's delight, Lorna and Lilith arrived earlier than he had expected, followed shortly after by Matilda and Isla: the small family of eight, reunited.

Virtually unnoticed, the funeral cars crept up the drive as Elspeth, her coffin adorned with her favourite autumn flowers, came back to Taligth for the final time.

It was the saddest of days in the village church as friends and relatives gathered to say their farewells. The vicar, who had known Elspeth for most of her adult life, was sensitive and sincere.

In turn, those who wished to speak stood and shared the memories of a life spent with mother and grandmother, and Lilith played a mournful piece of well-known music on her cello, bringing tears to those who had so far managed to hold them back. The music resonated around the beautiful old church; Elspeth would have loved it.

William, eyes cast downwards, remained stoic throughout.

The last to speak, Sebastian walked slowly to the lectern. Until standing in front of them he had not seen the faces of the people who had come to pay their respects. Swallowing hard, waiting until he was fully composed, he kept his head down, scanning the words on the paper in his hands.

Breathing deeply he started, quietly at first, making sure he articulated every word until the flow drew him across the page and he was able to lift his eyes and look out towards family and friends, so many, gathered in unison. Towards the back of the church, the faces became less familiar. People Elspeth had known from the village, or even further back than that, people Sebastian had not met but who had all, at some time, been touched by his wonderful mother. Old school friends, neighbouring farmers, people who had worked at Taligth, a lifetime of acquaintances.

It wasn't until he was fully engaged with everyone that he noticed Meggie, sitting alone at the back. Momentarily distracted, he faltered, stumbling over well-rehearsed words.

~

Outside the church, as Elspeth's body was committed to the ground, with the rain still dancing in the air, Meggie stood with her umbrella up, a little way from the rest of the congregation, looking at the display of beautiful flowers and messages of love which sat waiting to adorn the mounded earth.

As soon as he could, Sebastian approached her. 'Meggie,' he whispered, looking around, gently guiding her out of view. 'What are you doing here?' he asked, his voice hushed.

'I wanted to pay my respects.'

'Why?'

'I knew your mum. Don't make me feel bad for coming.' Sebastian went to speak, but Meggie interrupted him. 'I kept in touch for a while after you and I split up,' she said.

'Did you? Why?'

Looking down at the order of service in her hand and at Elspeth's face smiling back at her, Meggie could almost hear her speak. 'Tell him,' Elspeth would have said, 'tell him one day, but not here, not now.' Hesitating, Meggie looked back up at Sebastian. 'I just did,' she said.

'What's going on, Meg? Please tell me you're not coming back to the house,' he said, looking around, hoping they were not being watched.

'Don't panic. I'll leave in a minute, but I'd like to say hello to Hal and your dad first, if that's okay?' Meggie asked, spotting Henry. 'I'll see you soon,' she said, touching Sebastian's arm as she walked away, leaving him standing alone.

Sebastian hoped Meggie's sensitivities ran deep enough to not mention Nancy and to avoid Matilda. He wished now he had told his wife. The irony being that he had decided to, practicing what he was going to say as he drove home after telling his father and Henry the night before, but, by the time he pulled onto the drive he'd lost his confidence and talked himself out of it. He had not wanted an argument or the inevitable questions that would follow the mention of Meggie's name; he was too tired.

Standing on the wet grass, the rain having stopped, Meggie waited for Henry to finish his conversation with an old friend of his mother's. Saying his goodbyes, he turned to her.

'Hello Henry,' she said, gently touching his arm.

'Meggie!' Henry smiled, 'we meet again.'

'Ah, Seb told you then?' she said. 'You see, I was right. I knew I knew you. How are things?' Meggie asked softly.

'Okay, I guess,' Henry said sighing.

'I'm so sorry for your loss.'

'Thank you,' Henry replied. 'So, Seb told us he'd bumped into you.'

'He did,' Meggie said, turning and glancing at Sebastian. 'It was a bit of a shock.'

'I bet it was. I hear Panda dragged him into the café,' Henry smiled.

'She did! I recognised her before I recognised Seb,' she laughed. 'We met for lunch yesterday, did he tell you?'

'He did.'

Hesitating, Meggie wondered whether now was the right time. She decided there would be no other. 'Is Nancy not here?' she asked, looking around in pretence.

'No,' Henry replied, his autopilot switching on. 'She's estranged from the family. It was her choice and we respect that.' Expecting such questions from people who were less familiar with the family, it was a stock answer they had agreed upon prior to the funeral.

'Her choice not to attend her mother's funeral?' Meggie asked, probing.

'Her choice to have no contact with us. I'm sure Sebastian's told you,' Henry said, a chill entering his tone.

'No contact at all?'

'None,' Henry said, not comfortable with Meggie's questions.

'Do you know where she is?'

'We've no idea. As I say, we've not heard anything of her. Why do you ask, Meggie?'

So that was it. Sebastian had lied. It was time for her to leave.

'I'd better go, let you get on; your family need you,' she said. Looking at Henry, she paused. 'I'm really pleased I came,' she said. 'Look after yourself, Henry,' and turning, she walked down the bank and away towards her waiting taxi. She did not look around to find Sebastian but, as she made her way across the grass, she spotted William. For a moment, the two held eye contact, exchanging the briefest of smiles. William nodded his head in recognition before Meggie walked away. William was not surprised to see her there and he looked around to see if she was alone. When Elspeth died, he had considered contacting her but had thought better of it. He was pleased she had come. It meant a great deal. He and Elspeth were both very fond of Meggie. If only things had been different, William thought to himself, as he watched her leave.

~

Unseen, throughout, Paul had been standing a little way up the hillside above the graveyard, waiting for the funeral party to come out of the church. When they did, he had spotted his parents: his mother dressed in a long black coat, his father in his best suit and black tie. Alongside them he had seen William, Henry, Lorna and Matilda, and then, searching the friends and family who were making their way to the graveside, he had spotted Ewan, Isla and Lilith, walking together, looking so grown up but out of place amongst the aging congregation. Finally, at the back, he had seen Sebastian.

Recognising the uncomfortable body language of his former friend, Paul had watched as Sebastian ushered a woman away from the congregation. It had been over thirty years since he had seen Meggie, but even from a distance, the familiarity between the pair was obvious: Sebastian's hand in the small of her back as he guided her into the shadows, the way they stood close together, the intensity in the way they looked at each other as they exchanged words. Paul had seen Meggie gently touch Sebastian's arm as she moved to speak to Henry, and he had watched Sebastian watch her as she walked away.

Before he was spotted, Paul left, smiling to himself as he walked quickly down the hill towards the road, where his car was parked, hidden, around the corner.

~

Taligth was busy for two hours as everyone who loved Elspeth came back and celebrated her life. By teatime, they had all gone and the house was still once more. It felt good to have the day behind them.

As soon as the last guest left, Lorna and Lilith prepared to make their way home and said goodbye to the family. Before they went, Henry pulled Lilith to one side. 'How are you doing?' he asked, looking at her.

'I'm okay,' Lilith replied.

'Really?' he asked. Lilith hesitated long enough for him to realise she wanted to tell him something. 'What is it? Come on.' She looked at him, her eyes filled with tears. 'Oh Lil,' he said, hugging her close.

'I wanted to tell grandma,' she said through her tears, as Henry looked at her to understand. 'I wanted to tell her I got the audition,' Lilith sobbed.

Henry couldn't breathe; he looked across at Lorna, and desperate for his little girl he held Lilith tightly. He was broken. Holding his sobbing daughter's hands, he made her look at him. 'Grandma would have known the good news before you did. She was your biggest fan, you know that,' he said. 'She loved you and was so proud of you, and she will always be with you. You can tell her anything at any time and she will be listening. And when you are playing in that fantastic orchestra, as you will be, because you are going to blow their minds in that audition tomorrow, she will be tapping her feet just like she always did. I am so, *so* proud of you,' he said looking at Lorna, 'both of you. I am a very lucky man,' and the three of them hugged in an awkward embrace before Henry released them. 'Now, bugger off. It's getting late and I've got three million sandwiches to eat before bedtime,' he said, swallowing hard.

Henry watched from his mother's step as Lorna and Lilith walked to the car and headed off down the drive. He was worried that Lorna might be too tired to drive; she had been working long hours and was exhausted, but she reassured him she would be fine and if she felt weary she would swap with Lilith, which in all fairness worried him more as Lilith had graduated from the Henry Campbell school of driving.

As the gates closed, Henry went back inside. Wishing to speak with Sebastian alone before they left, he checked on William who was asleep in the front room. Leaving him to rest, he went into the kitchen where Sebastian was helping Matilda, Ewan and Isla to clear up. As was Matilda's way, it was being performed in military fashion. Ewan had donned the washing up gloves and Isla, with her long hair tied back with one of her father's Tatch-A Bobbles, was mastering the tea towel whilst Matilda packed everything away. Henry nodded to Sebastian, indicating for him to join him in the yard. He closed the door behind them. 'It went well today,' he said.

'It did,' Sebastian agreed.

'Dad did well.'

'He did brilliantly.' Looking through the kitchen window at the mountain of food left on the kitchen table, Sebastian sighed, 'looks like it's curled up prawn sandwiches for the next two weeks.'

'Who can resist?' Henry laughed. 'So, Meggie! I guess you weren't expecting her to turn up?'

'No, I wasn't.'

'Did you speak to her?'

'Briefly. Did you?' Sebastian asked, pretending he had not watched her every move until she had left.

'I did, but not for long. I'll be honest, I was a bit confused,' Henry said, watching Sebastian's body language alter.

'Right, why?' Sebastian asked nervously.

'Now hear me out on this...' Henry said, 'but she was asking me about Nancy.'

'What about Nancy?' Sebastian asked, his mouth going dry.

'She asked whether we'd heard from her or knew where she was.'

'What did you say?'

'I gave the stock answer. I just thought it was a bit weird, that's all. I don't know why she wanted to know.'

'Me neither,' Sebastian said coolly. 'What did you tell her?'

'The truth.'

'Of course you did,' Sebastian replied sighing, realising that Meggie now knew that he had lied to her.

'Is there something going on, Seb?' Henry asked gently.

Sebastian paused. It was late. If he was going to have this conversation with his brother, it would be best saved for another day; now was not the time. 'Listen,' he replied, 'with Mum's funeral, the company sale, Paul and then meeting Meggie, my head's full of shit. Just let me get myself together.'

'What are you not telling me?'

'Not now Henry!' Sebastian replied abruptly.

'Okay,' Henry conceded, quickly, shocked by Sebastian's reaction. 'Right, well, I'd better go and help in the kitchen,' he said, picking up a box of wine bottles which had been cooling outside the back door. 'We can pack your two off with some of this.'

Sebastian stood in the yard, slowly breathing in the dank autumn air before going back inside.

Eventually, with the house shipshape Sebastian, Matilda, Ewan and Isla left. Leaving William to sleep, Henry stood on the top step waving them off. Exhausted, he felt the weight of the past two weeks seep into his bones as he walked back to the kitchen and sat heavily at the table. Picking up his mother's book, he held it in his hands. He could not believe she was gone. He glanced at the clock. It was getting late and he would have to wake his father soon to go to bed, or he would not sleep, he had such disturbed nights. But for now, he intended to open another bottle of wine and eat some curled-up prawn sandwiches. It was the least he could do, he thought.

~

Back home, Sebastian took Panda into the garden. With the moon hidden behind thick cloud, it was a dark night. Turning on his phone for the first time after laying his mother to rest, Sebastian read a message from Niamh confirming that the second payment of £200,000 had been deposited into their account.

Now it was all over, he wasn't sure how to feel. He had buried his mother and lost his best friend. Under normal circumstances, Paul would have been beside him today. Sebastian thought about Paul's parents and how they had greeted him so warmly that afternoon. He wondered if they knew, and if not, what Paul's excuse had been for not attending.

Day Seventeen

The days following Elspeth's funeral were quiet. If they were not out on the farm or in the garden, William and Henry could be found sitting at the kitchen table drinking tea and looking out of the window in silent contemplation or leaning over a plan that William had drawn of the Sheep Shed's lighting rig, its rail and Henry's metal cube, working out how to get it to move. William was keen to help; it kept his mind from wandering.

Sebastian spent the weekend either at work or walking Panda anywhere other than down the hill towards the park. He wanted to fill the days after burying his mother with happy memories so that in years to come he could look back with fondness. Having neglected Matilda, he also needed to spend time with her.

With the weather forecast promising to stay dry, he and Matilda planned a long walk around some of Edinburgh's less famous landmarks. With Panda alongside them, they started amongst the bustle of people thronging up the Royal Mile. They circled the castle but did not join the tourists who queued for hours and were willing to pay the entrance fee. They walked the streets, ascending and descending the uneven, well-trodden steps. They walked over North Bridge which connected old with new and had lunch in a pub frequented by locals; a lunch of cheese and tomato sandwiches washed down with a Guinness, by way of a nod to Elspeth who had been partial to the drink every now and then.

Taking it slowly, they walked and talked until early evening and then found a restaurant tucked away down a curving path of cascading cobble stones, at the bottom of

Victoria Street, before heading home. It did them good to escape for a few hours. Panda, who had got slower as the day progressed, was shattered and needed to be carried back to the car. When they got home, she slept for the rest of the evening on her side, legs stretched out in front of her. It had been a much needed, but exhausting day. They should all have slept well that night.

But, as ever, although his body was willing, Sebastian's mind was intent on keeping him awake, flitting between his mother, the funeral, his father, and Meggie... and Meggie... Unsure of her next move, he felt uneasy. There was something different in the way she had behaved at his mother's funeral. Her manner had changed and he could sense her determination to weave Nancy back into their lives, but he failed to understand why.

In the early hours of Sunday morning, he gave in to his insomnia and drove to the factory to join the skeleton staff working the late shift. He was back home in time for breakfast, but, unable to clear his head of Meggie, he packed an overnight bag and headed to Taligth. He arrived to find William and Henry at the kitchen table engrossed in what looked like complicated engineering drawings.

'What are you doing?' he asked, making them all a drink.

'Dad's helping me with something for the set,' Henry replied.

'Get you, theatre boy,' Sebastian teased. 'How are you doing, Dad?' he asked, joining them at the table.

'Oh, I'm okay,' William sighed, sitting back in his chair, 'tired after your mum's funeral.'

'But we've kept going, haven't we, Dad?' Henry chipped in encouragingly. 'We've been up to the cows this morning and we've moved the sheep. I've cleaned out Betsy's pen and raked the leaves off the back garden...'

'Of a fashion,' William butted in, rolling his eyes. Henry sighed. 'You look tired Sebastian,' William added.

'I am. I spent the night in the factory.'

'Not again,' William tutted. 'Where will you go when it's gone?'

'Hopefully he will sleep when it's gone,' Henry pointed out.

'You need to let go, Sebastian,' William said, his voice sounding vague, 'of the whole business. It was a long time ago.'

'What?' Sebastian asked, confused.

'Your mother and I tried to put it behind us,' William muttered, his eyes glazing over.

'What are you talking about?' Sebastian asked. William fell silent as Sebastian and Henry looked at each other, trying to make sense of what their father was saying.

William looked at his sons. 'What?' he asked, suddenly aware they were staring at him.

'You just said, you and Mum tried to put something behind you. What do you mean?' Sebastian asked.

'Did I?' William responded, looking confused. 'Ignore me, I don't know what I'm saying,' he said, his face full of panic.

'It's okay,' Sebastian said, seeing his father's fear. 'How about something to eat?' he asked. He stood up and walked over to the fridge to examine its contents. William and Henry looked at each other. 'No more prawn sandwiches, please, no more,' Sebastian could hear them say.

In the afternoon they took a slow walk to thank Dougie for organising the food on Friday, then the family of three spent the early evening sitting with glasses of wine and a box of jumbo caramel Stroop Waffles purchased from McGregor's. Nowhere local sold them and they were a sweet-tooth's delight. Enjoying each other's company, it was a strange situation in which they now found themselves and it would take some getting used to. For once they did not speak about the funeral or even about Elspeth. They talked about other things, less relevant things, such as their next family holiday, the children and the fantastic opportunity that had presented itself to Lilith, whose

271

audition had gone well. They talked about the garden and the silly sheep, Henry's play and the cube with no sides and for the first time in eighteen days they laughed. Properly laughed.

Having enjoyed a dinner of baked potato and beans, and a final cup of tea, Henry left Taligth with bags filled with buffet leftovers, arranging to come back on Friday after rehearsal. It would seem this was going to be the pattern of things for the time being. The road to normality was going to be a long one and they needed to support each other as they ventured down it.

'I've made a list of things we need to do,' Sebastian said to his father as he went back into the kitchen after waving goodbye to Henry from the top step. 'There's no rush but I could do with going through it with you.'

'Thank you, Sebastian. Let me have a rest first and then we can take a look at it. I appreciate you doing all this. I know how busy you are,' William said quietly. Standing up, he started walking slowly towards the front room, resting his hand on Sebastian's shoulder and patting it reassuringly as he passed. Just before reaching the kitchen door he turned and looked back. 'Oh,' he said, 'whilst I think about it, can you put Nancy at the top of that 'to do' list please? If we do nothing else, we need to find her and tell her. There's an address in your mother's book in the cupboard in the snug.'

With his heart quickening, Sebastian nodded slowly. 'Of course,' he said, watching his father shuffle off. Now the funeral was over, there was no reason why Nancy should not be contacted, but Sebastian would not be the one to do it. He was afraid of what he might say. As far as Sebastian was concerned, if his father wanted Nancy to know, then he should speak with her himself. However, for his father's sake he would do as asked and find the book containing her address, but after searching, Sebastian was unable to locate it.

'That's odd,' William sighed, having woken up from his nap. 'I was sure it was in there.'

'I didn't know she'd kept in touch,' Sebastian said.

'She didn't, not really,' William replied, walking into the kitchen and searching through the drawers in the dresser.

'Have you seen her since she left?' Sebastian asked.

'No,' William cut in, his answers short and not forthcoming as he bent down, pulling out a box from beneath the dresser full of scraps of paper with various phone numbers, addresses and business cards. 'Will you help me look for her address please, Sebastian,' he said abruptly, struggling to stand up then walking past him into the hall towards the front room.

Sebastian stayed in the kitchen looking in the drawers whilst William went from room to room rummaging through every cupboard in the house. 'I don't know what your mother's done with it,' he said, irritably, returning to the kitchen where Sebastian was sitting turning his phone over in his hand, deep in thought. 'Sorry,' William said, 'I didn't mean to get cross, my stomach's hurting.'

'Is it?' Sebastian asked, concerned. 'Why didn't you say?'

'Don't make a fuss,' William replied, sharply. 'It'll be those prawn sandwiches, I had a few too many, that's all,' he said, sweat forming on his brow, 'I think I might go to bed.'

'Do you want me to bring you anything? How about a hot water bottle?'

'That would be good,' William said, starting to make his way towards the stairs.

'Okay, I'll be up in a minute, and don't worry about Nancy, I'll find her address,' Sebastian said, knowing it meant he would have to contact Meggie.

~

With heavy Sunday night traffic, it had been a very dark, wet journey back to Newcastle and Henry was shattered by the time he crawled into bed after midnight.

Having thought he might continue his nightly sleep on the sofa, Lorna was glad to have him cuddle up and put

273

his arm around her. 'Hey,' she said sleepily, Henry snuggling into her back.

'Hey,' he whispered as they wrapped themselves in each other's arms and fell asleep. Mabel, seizing the opportunity, jumped onto the bed and curled up behind Henry's knees. She stayed still all night, knowing one wriggle would result in her being ejected from her favourite place.

~

Monday was not Henry's best day. First period was Year 10 maths, and although he only had fifteen students, they all had parents. Longing for the time when he could give it up, he crept into school hoping none were lurking around corners, ready to catch him.

Walking into the old building, the coast clear, he ran up the main oak staircase which twisted its way up the wall from the elegant reception hall. He then leapt up the three flights of narrow stairs to his room in the roof, which, full of awkward beams, was one of the nicest in the building. The old part of the school had changed little since the 1800s when it had been a private house.

Thinking about his day ahead, Henry sighed. Year 10 followed by Year 7, then lunch, Upper Sixth and a free, meaning if he wasn't on cover, he could slope off early.

Emptying his bag in search of his pens which had gravitated towards the bottom, Henry took out three rounds of prawn sandwiches, a pork pie, mini sausages, some prawns wrapped in something that had once been crispy and two cartons of orange juice, plus four fresh cream filled shortbreads and a family packet of crisps. Lunchtime was going to be fun he thought, looking at the picnic. It felt strange but a relief that for the first time in nineteen days, today was going to be normal.

~

Sebastian got up a little later than planned. Before leaving Taligth, he sent a message to Meggie. Knowing that she knew he had been dishonest made it difficult to word but he

274

hoped she might understand why he was now asking for Nancy's address.

Looking into the darkness of his parents' room before leaving, he could see his father sleeping soundly. He chose not to wake him, for William had been up a number of times in the night. Watching him sleep, his dreams had not appeared as tormented as they had on previous nights so Sebastian left him and drove to the office. By the time he got in, Niamh and Matilda were at their desks. Panda wagged her tail in excitement when she saw Sebastian come in through the door.

'Afternoon,' Matilda teased, following him to his office. 'Did you have a lie in?'

'Dad was up in the night. I didn't want to leave too early,' Sebastian said, looking at his desk and the pile of papers which needed his attention.

'Has his tummy not settled?'

'Not really. I'll call him in a bit. Is everything okay here?' he asked, looking around.

'Everything's fine,' Matilda said, as Panda played with an elastic band ball on the carpet. 'Niamh got the glass in your door replaced. Remember to thank her,' she whispered, turning and walking back to her office.

Sebastian looked at the beautifully etched piece of glass matching the one in the panel next to it. On his desk, along with the papers, was a packet of his favourite biscuits and a note saying, 'for when the road ahead looks long'. Picking up the note he smiled knowing exactly what Niamh meant. 'Thank you,' he said, popping his head into Niamh's office, 'for everything.'

'My pleasure,' she said glancing up from her computer. 'How are you, after Friday?'

'I'm fine,' he said nodding. 'Listen, I'm going to work from home this afternoon. I need to start detaching myself from this place.'

'Of course.'

'And I'll take this one with me as well, get her out of your way,' he said, bending down and picking up Panda.

Swinging her into his arms, he cradled her like a baby as she scrambled to right herself.

'She could do with a walk,' Matilda called from her office. 'I didn't get chance this morning, and besides, it was raining.'

'Then that is what we will do, won't we,' Sebastian said, talking to Panda who had given in and was lying on her back in his arms, 'after we have done some work.' As he spoke, Panda dropped a huge woof-filled sigh. 'I know how you feel,' he said, laughing at her as he walked back into his office.

~

Unshaven, dressed in jeans and an old jumper, Paul sat low in the driver's seat of the small grey car his mother had lent him. He had told his parents that he had left Tatch-A UK and, as a result, had surrendered his company car. Ashamed, he could not bring himself to tell them the truth, but had lied, saying that because of the company sale, it had been something he had been thinking about for some time. He told them Sebastian was angry with him, and asked them not mention it at the funeral. It was also his excuse to them for not attending.

Paul had parked in the side-road adjacent to Tatch-A UK's offices almost every day since leaving; watching Sebastian's every move. Today was no different, although his compulsion to know what Sebastian was up to had increased since he had spotted him with Meggie at Elspeth's funeral.

Days before, he had wondered what was drawing Sebastian into the café on the hill near his home. It wasn't until he realised that it had been Meggie he had seen at the café door, and then again at the funeral, did he put two and two together.

Now, like a private detective, hiding up alleys, sitting on park benches, lurking behind trees, he was watching Sebastian intently. Out of sight, he had followed him home from the office, and was now walking a little way behind, as Sebastian ventured down the hill.

~

With the rain having eased, Sebastian and Panda walked quickly. Meggie had not answered his message, so in spite of not wanting to, but having promised his father he would get Nancy's address, he decided to call in at the café. As they approached, noticing the awning had not been lowered and the tables and chairs were not out on the street, the briskness in their step slowed. Confused, Sebastian saw the shutters were down on the door and the 'closed' sign turned outwards. Cupping his hands and straining his eyes to see into the dark room, he could just make out the shapes of the chairs stacked on the tables and the chiller, lights off, empty of cakes and pastries. He looked at the door in hope of reading a note saying 'back soon' but there was no such note. Peering in again, a tap on his shoulder made him jump.

'They're closit,' a woman said, her accent thicker even than his mother's had been when she was anxious or upset.

'So I see,' Sebastian replied, reeling from the fright the woman had given him. 'You made me jump.'

'Och! Sorry aboot thon,' she laughed heartily.

'Do you know when they'll be open?'

'I've nae idea. They closit Friday afternoon. I only know because ah walk up here on a Friday wi mah wee girl to get mah meat for the weekend from the butchers, well...'

'Closed for good, do you think?' Sebastian interrupted.

'I've nae idea aboot that either, but it doesn't look like they're aboot to open any time soon. I said to mah wee girl, 'let's go to the café for a wee something' an' she were so excited, so imagine her disappointment...'

'I can imagine, thank you,' Sebastian said dismissively. 'You didn't see anyone, did you?'

'I didnae, sorry.' And with that the woman walked away up the hill leaving Sebastian staring at the empty café.

Meggie had given him no indication she was closing; in fact, when they had first met she told him she was there for the foreseeable future. It closed on Friday afternoon, the woman said. Was that before his mother's funeral or after?

He checked his phone again. There was still no reply to his message. He sent a second one as he and Panda carried on slowly down the hill, towards the park, with Paul following. Panda was thrilled and, as ever, they returned home a few hours later in a terrible state, but still with no answer from Meggie.

~

Paul returned to his car and left.

Now, back in his empty house, having not deleted Sebastian from his location tracker, he continued his surveillance by following him on his phone; as he had done every day over the past few weeks, intrigued as to why, at times, Sebastian's location appeared to vanish.

Paul did not like being in the house on his own, but the consequence of a marriage built on lies and unfaithfulness had resulted in Trish staying away as she battled with what she now knew, against the desire to forgive a man who she still loved and had once trusted.

~

Before Matilda had time to draw breath, Sebastian threw his hands up in surrender. 'I know,' he informed her. 'Come on Panda, I'm in the doghouse... again,' he said as they trooped upstairs.

'Are you okay?' Matilda asked later, over dinner. 'You've been very quiet since you came in.'

'I'm tired, that's all,' Sebastian replied, irritably.

'Why don't you get an early night?' Matilda asked.

'Because I need to go back into work. I have some reading to do.'

'Can't you do it here?'

'No, because the things I need to read are there, not here.'

'I thought you brought everything home.'

278

'I didn't bring the filing cabinet!'

They finished their meal in silence.

On his way back into the office, Sebastian telephoned Meggie, several times, but each time the call went straight to her answering machine. On his final attempt he left a message.

In the emptiness of the old building, Sebastian sat at his desk beneath the dim lights, enjoying the solitude. He had mountains of legal papers to read which he could only concentrate on in complete silence.

As he sat reading, his phone rang.

~

Finishing just shy of 11 p.m. Henry was delighted with the way the rehearsal had gone. The play was taking shape and the set was nearly finished and the cube was in the process of being mechanised. He felt confident about opening. On their way home, he and Lorna talked about how it was going and what they still had to do before heading to The Sheep Shed in three weeks time.

Just as they got into the house, Henry's phone rang. With his heart in his mouth, he looked at the clock on the kitchen wall as he answered. It was midnight. Lorna sidled up to him and put her arms around his waist, listening in.

'Sorry for the midnight call,' Sebastian said, 'but I'm at the hospital. Dad's had another fall.'

'Shit! What's happened?' Henry asked, as Lorna moved away looking at him.

'I'm not sure to be honest. It was Dougie who found him. He dropped by Taligth on his way home to check Dad was okay and found him collapsed in the yard.'

'Collapsed?' Henry exclaimed, running his hand through his hair.

'Dougie managed to get him into the kitchen and made him a drink, but apparently he wasn't very responsive, so he called me and I told him to call an ambulance. I've just got to the hospital.'

'Have you seen him?' Henry asked as he paced around the kitchen.

'Not yet. He's still being assessed.'

'What was he doing in the yard so late?'

'He'd gone out to see to Betsy.'

'That bloody pig has a lot to answer for! Is Dougie still there?'

'He's gone. I put him in a taxi.'

'Is it his stomach, do you think?'

'Whose stomach?'

'Dad's, you idiot!'

'Sorry. It could be. I'm wondering if he might have an infection. I'll see what they say.'

'Do you want me to come up?' Henry asked, desperate to get in the car and drive.

'There's no need.'

'Let me know if there's anything I can do. I can come any time.'

They ended the call, and Henry sat with the phone in his hand as Lorna made him a drink.

'He'll be okay,' she said softly, bringing it to him at the kitchen table, 'he's as tough as old boots, your dad, they'll sort him out.'

'I think I'll stay up for a bit, if you don't mind,' Henry said, knowing he would find it difficult to sleep.

'Do you want me to stay up with you?' Lorna asked.

'No, you go to bed.'

'Okay, but wake me if you get any news,' she said, kissing Henry on top of his head before she headed up the stairs.

Henry stayed sitting at the kitchen table twisting his mug in his hands. He tried to imagine what was happening at the hospital. He imagined his father sitting on the bed as the doctors and medical staff buzzed about plugging him into machines and inserting needles. He imagined his father wondering what all the fuss was about. It was 2 a.m. when his phone rang again.

'The doctors think he might have an infection,' Sebastian informed him.

'Okay,' Henry replied

'They've checked him over and said his shoulder seems okay, but he's got a high temperature, so he's on IV antibiotics and they're going to keep him in and do an x-ray and some more tests tomorrow.'

'Have you seen him?'

'I have, he seems pretty bright.'

'Has he said what happened?'

'Apparently he went out to see to Betsy but must have collapsed before he got to her because the bucket was still full. After that I don't think he remembers anything until Dougie was there. Hopefully, the antibiotics will bring his temperature down and he'll feel better. I'll stay until he goes up to the ward and then I'll go home and come back in the morning.'

'Okay, but I'm just a call away, remember.'

Reassured, Henry dragged himself to bed and was only woken when the shrill call of the house phone screamed for attention. Waking with a start, he answered in a panic, and it took him a moment to realise it was the school secretary on the other end asking whether he was coming in.

'Shit!' he said, looking at the clock on his bedside, seeing first period had already started. 'I'll be there as soon as I can,' he gabbled before putting the phone down. 'Shit! Lorna!' he said, shaking her awake, 'I've overslept.'

'What?' Lorna murmured, trying to wake herself up as quickly as she could.

'I've overslept. I'm late for school. I hate Tuesdays.'

'You hate every day at school. How's your Dad?' she asked, groggy from sleep.

'He's okay. I'll call Seb when I get in,' Henry replied breathlessly, rushing around the room gathering his clothes.

'Did you hear from him again last night?' Lorna asked, swinging her feet out of bed and using them to search the carpet for her slippers.

'Shit! Shit! Shit!' Henry said, hopping around the room tugging frantically at his socks whilst Lorna sat on the edge of the bed rolling her hands around her eyes and yawning, forcing herself to wake up. Mabel, unsure what music Henry was dancing to, ran around seeking a safe place to hide. 'They think Dad might have an infection. They've put him on IV antibiotics and they'll do some more tests today. Have you seen my belt?' he asked in a panic.

Henry was never late; Henry did not do late. Late had not been a part of Henry's life since he was a child, since the time Miss Hickman had hit him with a heavy book in front of the class for being late when he was in infant school. She had scared and scarred him in equal measure and time had been an issue for him ever since.

'Fuck!' he said buttoning his shirt wrongly. 'Come on, come on,' he muttered, slinging his tie round his neck and pulling the rest of his clothes on, combing his hair and spitting toothpaste all over the tiles above the sink. Shoving the last of the buffet into his bag, he flew out of the door. 'Shit!' he said, the door clicking shut behind him. He grappled for his key to let himself back into the house where Lorna was standing hand outstretched with his wallet and phone.

'Thank you! Love you,' he said, kissing her quickly on the cheek and dashing to the car. Like a madman, he drove down the lanes to school, bumping kerbs and grazing bushes. Apologies all-round, he skidded into his room just in time for morning break, which gave him a few minutes to call Sebastian.

'He's not too good I'm afraid,' Sebastian told him.

'What?' Henry said, his heart dropping.

'I know. Sorry, Hal. He's not feeling well. He's been sick overnight and he's not slept.'

'What have the doctors said?'

'Nothing yet, they've not done their rounds. I'm about to go back in and see him in a minute. I'll call you when there's any news.'

After making another unanswered call to Meggie and putting his phone in his pocket, Sebastian went onto the ward to see William once more.

'Hello you,' William said, smiling weakly as Sebastian peeped around the curtain to see if he was awake. 'I hear I caused a bit of a fuss last night.'

'You did,' Sebastian said, confused by the way William was talking as if they had not spoken just an hour earlier.

'Just as well that nice man popped over, otherwise I could have been there all night.'

'Yes,' Sebastian said cautiously, 'that was Dougie.'

'Dougie, was it? I didn't recognise him,' William said, looking perplexed.

'Do you remember what happened, Dad?' Sebastian asked, repeating a question he has asked earlier.

'I remember going out to see to Betsy, but after that I can't remember anything until that man was with me. It was very good of him to call the ambulance, wasn't it? You must thank him for me.'

'I already have,' Sebastian said, thinking maybe a high temperature could cause confusion. 'How are you feeling now you've had a nap?'

'Sick still, but hopefully this lot will sort me out,' William said, referring to the antibiotics dripping along the tube into his arm.

'Do you know when the doctors might come round?'

'No.'

'How's your shoulder?'

'Much the same,' William said, yawning.

'I'll leave you to sleep, but I'll hang around the hospital until you've seen the doctor. I've got some calls to make so I'll go outside. Do you want a drink before I go?'

'I'm fine with water, thank you, Henry.'

Sebastian hesitated, wondering whether to correct his father, but chose not to. 'Call me if you need me to come back, okay?'

'Okay,' William replied. 'You're a good boy,' he said, smiling up at Sebastian.

'You've not said that since I was a kid.'

Sebastian checked the doctors' ward round times with the nurse at the desk and, buying himself a coffee from the stall outside the hospital, went for a walk around the grounds. It was nice to be outside in the fresh air. It was damp underfoot as he walked along the paths, which wound their way around the vast maze of buildings. There were so many parts of the hospital he had not seen before and he was amazed at the number of departments he had never heard of or knew existed. It was a sprawl of mismatched buildings, built and rebuilt over the decades.

Sitting on a bench in the well-kept gardens, Sebastian made a number of calls, one to the company lawyer, one to Matilda, one to Patrick McCarthy's answering machine in California and yet another to Meggie. Not expecting an answer, this time the phone rang and Sebastian's heart started to pound.

'Hello, Sebastian,' she answered, coldly.

'Meggie,' Sebastian replied, faltering. 'Is everything okay?'

'Everything's fine, why?'

'I've been trying to get hold of you. Did you get my messages?'

'I did.'

'Panda and I went to the café, it was closed.'

'I know.'

'Why?' Sebastian asked. Meggie did not answer. 'Is it closed for good?' Again, Sebastian's question was answered with silence. 'Where are you?'

'We've gone away for a few days, not that it's any of your business, Sebastian.'

Sebastian knew from her curt tone that any further conversation was futile.

'I'm sorry I lied, Meg,' he said eventually, sighing. He looked ahead at the flower border in front of him and at a yellow rose, desperately hanging onto the last of its petals.

'Right,' Meggie replied dispassionately.

'I see,' Sebastian said, dispiritedly nodding to himself after taking in a breath and pausing for a few seconds.

'I've got to go,' Meggie said suddenly.

'Before you go, Meg, could you send me...' but Meggie had disconnected.

'*Fuck*!' he snapped, resisting the urge to aim his phone at the yellow rose. Standing, he started to make his way back towards the main entrance. He sent Meggie one final message asking, again, for Nancy's address. All he could do now was wait. His father had to take priority.

When Sebastian got back to the ward, William was awake and sitting in the chair next to his bed. He seemed in better sprits than he had earlier.

'The doctor came by,' William said.

'Really? They said not before twelve.'

'She was early.'

'And?'

'And what?'

'What did she say?' Sebastian asked irritably.

'Are you okay?'

'I'm fine. What did she say?'

'Well,' William said, looking at the notes he had made for fear of forgetting, 'she examined my shoulder and asked me some questions about the pain I've got in it, so she's ordered an x-ray to see what's going on.'

'And how's your temperature?'

'Ah yes, she took my temperature as well. She was very thorough,' William said, smiling as he looked at his scribbled notes once more. 'It's 38.2, but she said the antibiotics will hopefully bring it down.'

'Okay. Are you still feeling sick?'

'A bit.'

'That could be the temperature.'

'I suppose so,' William said. 'The doctor thinks I'm a little confused. Do I seem it to you?'

'Do you feel confused?'

'Sometimes.'

'Did you tell her about Mum?'

'Of course.'

'And what did she say?'

'She said that might explain it.'

'I'm inclined to agree with her.'

'Yes, so am I,' William said sadly.

Sitting in silence, William closed his eyes. Sebastian sat watching him. He had seen such a change in his father over the past three weeks and he thought about the promise he had made to contact Nancy and about the letter they needed to write.

~

Henry's dislike of Tuesdays was confirmed. The students were being unruly and irritating. The Year 7s, buzzing with excitement, were in their own clothes as they were heading off for a three-day trip to an activity centre somewhere in the middle of the Derbyshire countryside. The Year 9 and 10 students were in school tests all day, so they were tetchy and unpleasant, and the Sixth Formers were just their normal belligerent, know-it-all, selves. During second period, Henry had confiscated a smart watch and was sat playing with it over lunch when Sebastian called with an update.

'How's he doing?' Henry asked, eager to hear better news.

'He's okay,' Sebastian replied. 'Can you believe it, I was with him most of the morning and then, in the twenty minutes I took to go for a walk, the doctor came to see him!' he said. 'They're still thinking it's an infection, maybe in his shoulder.'

'Not his stomach?'

'They don't think so, but they're not sure. So they're going to carry on treating the infection, wherever it is, and then this afternoon they're going to do an x-ray on his shoulder to see what's going on. I'm hanging around for a bit in case the doctor comes back, I wouldn't mind a word.'

'What do you want to ask?'

'I don't know really.'

'Seb, go home. They'll call you if they need to speak with you. Dad has got to be able to be left. We've been with him constantly for almost three weeks. We can't keep that up.'

'Okay,' Sebastian conceded quickly, 'that's what I was thinking, to be honest.'

The brothers chatted for a few minutes before the hospital porter interrupted them to take William for his x-ray.

Sebastian ended the call.

'Do you want me to come with you?' he asked his father as the porter wheeled William past.

'No, you head off,' William answered. 'I have your mother's phone. I'll call you if there's anything to tell you,' he called back. Waving his good arm in the air with the plastic intravenous tube dangling from it like a parasite, he disappeared through the double doors.

Leaving the hospital, Sebastian drove to the office.

The result of William's x-ray was inconclusive. The break was not healing and the doctors wanted to run further tests. Whether or not they saw something that they were not disclosing, William did not know, but he would be staying in hospital a further night.

Day Twenty-One

Wednesday

Sebastian needed to go into the office first thing, so Matilda went to the hospital to see William. She was very close to her father-in-law and enjoyed his company, and although he had not been one for visitors since Elspeth had died, Matilda hoped she would be welcome.

When she arrived, he was out of bed, sitting in the chair with his uneaten breakfast in front of him. Despite feeling sick and uncomfortable, William smiled warmly when Matilda popped her head around the curtain and asked if anyone was 'in'. Leaning over to give him a kiss, Matilda was shocked to see how much frailer he seemed since she had seen him last and, although he had washed, he was unshaven and looked unkempt which was not the way William liked to present himself no matter where he was. However, he welcomed her, grateful for her company and touched that she wanted to visit a sad old man in hospital on a Wednesday morning.

'I can't think of anything I'd rather do,' Matilda said, placing a cup of tea on his table and perching herself on the edge of his bed.

'I can think of a million things you'd rather do,' William stated. 'Thank you for the tea.'

'Seb sends his love. He had to go into the office; he has a couple of meetings he couldn't re-schedule.'

'He should sell that company,' William said flatly, his hands shaking as he picked up his cup. 'He works too hard.'

'You're right, he should,' Matilda said, having been warned by Sebastian that William might seem confused at times. 'So, how are you doing?' she asked.

'I'm fed up with being in this wretched place. They keep trying to feed me.'

'They want you to keep your strength up.'

'I can't see how this is going to keep my strength up,' William said, referring to the congealed breakfast cereal in his bowl. 'I wouldn't feed this to Betsy.'

'That's because you spoil Betsy.'

'She's the only thing I have to spoil,' William said sorrowfully. 'Would you mind checking in on her for me please, Elspeth?'

'Of course,' Matilda replied, not correcting William's mistake.

'She'll be lonely without me. There's food in the fridge she can have.'

'She'll be fine, don't worry,' Matilda said, reaching over and placing her hand on top of William's. He brought his drip-fed hand across and placed it on top of hers, enjoying the human contact.

'So, what's going on in the world?' William asked, 'tell me something interesting.'

Amidst the bustle of the ward, William and Matilda spent an hour talking. They talked about Australia and the terrible bush fires, about the British economy, about television highlights and about how William had met Elspeth, his early days on the farm and the things they'd got up to before children came along. William's storytelling was vivid and Matilda enjoyed listening to him. He talked about Sebastian and Henry and touched on Nancy. Then, as he grew weary, his speech slowed and he became unguarded and muddled. The last thing he told Matilda was that Nancy had a child.

'Sebastian never said,' Matilda reacted, surprised by what William had told her.

'He doesn't know,' William said, fighting sleep. 'She'll be grown up now,' he mumbled, his eyelids getting heavy. Drifting off, his cup of tea tipped, threatening to spill in his lap. Matilda took it carefully out of his hands and put it on the table. Covering him gently with a blanket, she kissed his cheek and leaving him to sleep, she left the hospital and called Sebastian.

'How is he?' Sebastian asked.

'I was really shocked when I saw him. He seems so much frailer than he was on Friday.'

Sebastian sighed. 'I'd hoped I'd imagined it. How was he in himself?'

'You know your dad, chatty and full of stories but he was very tired.'

'Do you think he's really ill?' Sebastian asked.

'I've no idea, Seb, but he's in the best place,' Matilda said, reassuringly.

'Did you see the doctor?'

'No. I think he has some tests today, doesn't he?'

'He does. Thanks for going.'

'I'm glad I went. I wanted to see him,' Matilda said. She hesitated for a moment, 'he talked a lot about Nancy.'

'Did he? What did he say?'

'He was telling me what she was like as a child, mainly...' She paused, 'haven't you got a meeting to go to?'

'In a minute.'

'Then I'll fill you in you later.'

On her way home, Matilda drove to Taligth to check the house and to make sure Sam and Ade were happy getting on with things in William's absence. Dougie had rallied some troops and there were plenty of hands available to keep the farm going should they need them. Letting herself in and picking up the post, Matilda checked around to make sure everything was in place. From the contents of the fridge, she made up a slop bucket for Betsy, who was the only pig in the area to be fed prawn sandwiches and sausage rolls, washed down with fresh cream scones and fruit mousse. On reflection, Matilda wasn't sure pigs should eat pork, it seemed wrong somehow. Sam promised to look after Betsy whilst William was in hospital. 'God forbid should anything happen to that pig,' he said.

'How was everything at Taligth?' Sebastian asked when Matilda got home.

'Absolutely fine,' she said, taking some shortbread out of her bag, which she had brought back with her. 'Dougie's amazing. He's organised a rota with some of the local farm workers and they're taking it in turns to help out. I put the contents of the fridge into Betsy's trough. Do you think that will be okay?'

'Of course. She'll eat anything.'

'I wasn't sure about the sausage rolls and mini pork pies...' she said, getting a plate from the cupboard.

'Don't worry about it,' Sebastian said, laughing.

'How were your meetings?' Matilda asked.

'Fine. Do you want a coffee with those?' Sebastian asked, looking at the shortbread.

'Yes please,' Matilda said, putting the plate on the coffee table and sitting on the sofa. Panda jumped up, demanding Matilda's attention.

'So, you think Dad looked frail?' Sebastian asked as he spooned the coffee into the cafetiere. He was concerned at how quickly his father appeared to have deteriorated since the weekend.

'He's not eating.'

'I suppose if he's got an infection it's going to knock him. Hopefully the antibiotics will work,' Sebastian said, bringing the cafetiere and cups on a tray to the coffee table. 'So, you talked about Nancy. Did Dad say anything interesting?' Sebastian asked, pouring the coffee.

'Not too much, but he did tell me that she has a child. Did you know?'

'No,' Sebastian replied. Confused, he tried to think whether Meggie had mentioned a child other than the one Nancy lost.

'He'd nodded off before I could ask him about it.'

'I didn't know Mum and Dad had been in contact with Nancy until Mum died. I don't understand why they didn't tell us. Why do you think Dad said something today?'

'He was saying all sorts of things, Seb, he even called me Elspeth at one point.'

Sebastian sighed. 'Did he say anything else about Nancy?'

'Not really, other than he thought she'd moved abroad but couldn't remember where. He said they'd lost touch.'

'You know what,' Sebastian said, lifting his cup, 'it would be typical of Nancy to have come back, waved a grandchild under their nose and then pissed off again. That would be just her style,' Sebastian said bitterly.

'You'll have to ask your dad about it when you see him. Do you think Henry knows?'

'If he does, he's never said anything.'

Phoning the hospital early evening, Sebastian was informed that his father had been subjected to numerous tests during the day and was yet to be assessed by the doctor. The nurse on the desk told him that he was comfortable but had not eaten his meal. She suggested it might be best if Sebastian did not visit that evening as his father was finally sleeping.

Sebastian would not sleep well again.

~

The phone ringing at 6.30 a.m. confused Henry. He grappled for the snooze button on the bedside clock.

'It's the phone, Hal,' Lorna murmured, stirring from her sleep.

Instantly awake and looking at the clock, Henry reached over and picked up the receiver. 'Hello?' he said quickly.

'I've had a call from the hospital and I'm driving over there now,' Sebastian said, his voice sounding strained. 'Dad's had a bad night and he's become very agitated. They've asked me to go in. I just thought I'd let you know.'

'What's going on?' Henry panicked.

'I've no idea, Hal. Sorry.'

'Listen, I'm going to chuck a bag together and head up.'

'Why don't you wait and see what today brings and then come up later if you need to.'

'Okay, but call me if you need me. I can leave at a moment's notice.'

Feeling afraid, Henry sat hunched on the edge of the bed, with his head in his hands. Lorna reached out.

'Why don't you go to him?' she said softly.

'I will, tomorrow, unless Seb calls.'

~

On his way to the hospital, Sebastian managed to speak with a doctor on the ward. It was early and the desk was unattended, but luckily the doctor in charge of his father's care picked up the phone. She spoke kindly and quietly and explained that William had deteriorated overnight and wasn't responding to the antibiotics in the way she had hoped. She said she would be sending him for a scan that morning as his stomach had not settled and the pain in his shoulder had worsened, moving down his spine.

William was out of bed and sitting in his chair when Sebastian arrived. The ward was not properly awake, but the nurses allowed Sebastian in, drawing the curtains to give the other patients some privacy.

'How long have you been up?' Sebastian asked quietly, sitting on the bed.

'Most of the night,' William mumbled, fatigued.

'Why are you out of bed?'

'It's more comfortable.'

'Are you warm enough?'

'I am.'

'The nurse said you've been feeling anxious.'

'Which isn't like me is it, Henry?'

'I'm Sebastian, not Henry.'

'Of course. Sorry,' William said, studying Sebastian's face. 'Where's Henry?'

'He's at home in Newcastle. He'll be up to see you tomorrow.'

'Oh yes, silly me. That'll be nice,' William said, shutting his eyes.

Sebastian sat watching him. 'Dig deep, Dad,' he whispered to himself.

By 9 a.m. William had been collected by the porter and taken to a specialist assessment unit within the hospital where he spent the majority of the day. Whilst he was gone, Sebastian called Henry.

'He's stronger than he thinks, but he seems to have given up,' Sebastian said.

'Don't say that,' Henry replied, standing outside his classroom looking in through the glass panel of the door at the backs of the heads of Year 9 who had been threatened with detention should they look up from their books or make a sound. 'We need to be patient and wait for answers, that's all, and then they can treat him.'

'Maybe,' Sebastian said, melancholy in his voice. 'They said the antibiotics aren't working.'

'Perhaps he needs different antibiotics. When will he be back on the ward?'

'It's a whole day of assessments so it'll probably be late afternoon.'

'Okay, then you need to get yourself out of there. There's nothing you can do that waiting around will help. Go home and get into that lovely pool of yours, or take Panda for a walk, or go to the café...'

'It's closed. Meggie's gone.'

'Where's she gone?'

'I've no idea.'

'How do you know she's gone?'

'Because I called her.'

'Then take Panda to the park instead. She loves the park.'

'I might go into the office.'

'Go into the office then. Do whatever you want, just don't hang around the hospital, waiting.'

'I hear what you're saying. You'd better get back to long division or whatever it is you're teaching.'

'It's 'probability' today.'

'Sounds fun. Speak later.'

'Speak later,' Henry said hearing the noise level in the classroom reach fever pitch. He entered, stealth like, from the back and stood patiently leaning against the wall until one of the students noticed him and hushed the rest.

'I think you will find that is six minutes of your lunchtime you have wasted,' he said calmly, walking to the front of the class. He watched as they looked at each other accusingly. 'No one's fault but your own,' he added, setting them an extra-long piece of homework.

~

Sebastian went back to the hospital at 3 p.m. where the consultant took him into a side room. Sebastian felt nervous. The consultant was a compassionate young woman with a gentle approach but no matter how kind she was, bad news was difficult to hear.

Although they were still waiting for some results to be returned, she was honest with Sebastian and said that the first tests had revealed some abnormalities in William's shoulder and spine which needed investigating further, but what she had seen so far did not look encouraging. He questioned her, but she danced around the subject, unable to confirm anything. Sebastian pushed, her downcast expression telling him everything. She suggested William should stay in hospital for one more night and that the following day he should undergo further tests before they made any decisions. It did not sound good.

In the early hours, William awoke sharply from his sleep and, feeling disorientated, cried out in panic. The nurses rushed to his bedside and tried to reassure him but all he could think of was Elspeth and he called her name hoping she was close by. He became agitated when he realised she would not be visiting. Eventually, the doctor was called and William was given a hot water bottle, which soothed his stomach, and a sleeping pill, which allowed him to sleep.

~

Waiting for a call from the hospital, Sebastian spent Friday morning with his nerves on a knife-edge. He could not go to the office and make small talk or pretend to work, and he did not want to stay at home pacing the floor. Instead, he went into Edinburgh with Panda and they walked up and down the streets, looking at the faces of people they did not know. His head was so full of fear that he could not see or hear anything other than the heavy, dark thoughts that were going through his mind. He remembered the look on the consultant's face when he had asked her whether his father was dying. It was a look that haunted him.

~

Sitting, waiting, William accepted what was happening to him. He did not mind the tests, or care what people did, no matter how uncomfortable. He nodded off a couple of times and had to be woken to be moved to a new location, where again, he waited. It was another long day and he was exhausted. By the time Sebastian got to the ward late in the afternoon, William was resting on a bed in a side room, his intravenous antibiotic removed. He was dressed and ready to leave.

'Have you been discharged?' Sebastian asked, smiling at his father.

'I think so,' William said, uncertain of anything.

'That must be good news then. They wouldn't send you home if they were worried.'

'True,' William agreed, and they sat in silence as he drifted in and out of sleep for another hour until the consultant finally came to see them. She closed the door behind her, the atmosphere changing from one of hope to one of apprehension as Sebastian stood up and shook her hand. She pulled up a chair and sat close.

The consultant explained the details of the tests William had undergone and told them her findings directly, without complication or fuss. Like a student hearing results of failed school exams, William sat stoically, listening. The news was not good. Not one test brought hope, and the consultant believed much of what they had found had been going on, undetected, for some time. 'Do I think it's cancer?' she asked rhetorically, 'unfortunately I do, and I think it's advanced,' she said.

'So, this is it,' William said.

With the heaviest of hearts, the consultant agreed and suggested they go home and spend as much time as they could together. They would 'refer it up to specialists,' she said, 'as a matter of urgency,' and 'talk about treatment options but...' But Sebastian knew as well as she did that this was unlikely to help his lovely father, his lovely, wonderful father.

William, as brave as he had been since the day he lost Elspeth, looked up to the ceiling. 'I'm on my way, sweet girl,' he said.

Day Twenty-Three

Friday

The journey to Taligth seemed to take longer than ever. Having pulled over to read a message from Sebastian, deep in thought, processing the words, Henry carried on driving, taking little notice of heavy Friday night traffic, speed restrictions and flashing warning signs. Fines were sure to land on the mat the following week, but he was too preoccupied to care. It must have been punishing for Sebastian to say what he had said in a message, but Henry was grateful. It gave him time to digest the detail of his brother's words, and Sebastian had pulled no punches, reporting everything the consultant had said, verbatim. It was heart-breaking news. Henry tried to focus. How could his amazing father, who had been so brave over the past few weeks, now be so ill? What had they missed?

By the time he arrived at Taligth, Sebastian had left for the night.

'If it's all the same to you,' William had said to Sebastian an hour earlier, 'I think I'd like some time alone before Henry arrives. I'm tired and I wouldn't mind a word with your mother.'

'You know she's not here, don't you, Dad?' Sebastian reminded him gently, settling him in the front room and placing a blanket across his knees. He got him a glass of water and, as requested, a large glass of whisky.

'I know, but it doesn't stop me talking to her and I need to make arrangements.'

'For what?'

'For when I see her,' William said matter-of-factly, as if he were joining her on holiday.

Anguished and desperately not wanting to, Sebastian left.

Quietly letting himself in, Henry found William drifting in and out of sleep in Elspeth's chair. It had only been five days since he had seen him last and the sight of his father, thin and pale, was a shock. He looked gaunt, his hair was lank and lifeless and his movement slow and painful. As warm as ever, William delighted in a tentative hug from Henry although he winced with the pain.

'Can I get you anything?' Henry asked.

'Another one of these,' William said weakly, tapping his empty whisky glass.

'Should you be drinking that?'

'It can't do me any harm now, can it?' William replied, looking Henry in the eye. 'Ask your mother if she wants one, and get one for yourself.'

Henry tried not to react or look too hard at what he saw. He knew deep in his heart he was watching his father die.

If someone had told him a week ago that this would be happening, he would have laughed. 'Not my dad,' he would have said. 'He'll outlive us all! There's just no way!' but now, looking at his father sitting awkwardly in the chair, Henry would not disagree. How could he have not seen the signs? How could this disease creep up so quietly and take someone away so quickly without anyone noticing? How cruel can God be to make them face this when they have been through so much already?

Henry made them both a hot drink with a dash of whisky and they sat together in the front room, in silence. His drink finished, William was exhausted. He'd had a long day and, apologetically, wanted his bed. He struggled out of his chair and cautiously made his way into the hall. For the first time, his weak bones would not carry him up the stairs so Henry helped him, before undressing and settling him. Kissing his father goodnight, Henry looked at the frailty of this wonderful man who had loved him all his life. William had not once questioned his role as protector and provider, and, for forty-eight years, he had been there for Henry. It was now Henry's turn to be there for his father.

Throughout the night, William became increasingly restless, and Henry spent the hours awake, sitting in his room listening out for his father's fretful cries, hearing him call for Elspeth in his sleep. Before light, Henry took two cups of tea into his parents' bedroom where he and his father talked on and off until dawn started to break and the birds filled the sky in search of breakfast. Henry opened the curtains wide so that William could see the front garden and the fields beyond the gates. It was a beautiful morning.

Although he was very weak, William insisted on getting up and going downstairs without help. He ushered Henry out of the room, asking him to go and see to Betsy. Leaving him alone, Henry went out into the yard to clean Betsy's pen and fill her trough. For an old girl, she seemed to look younger each time he saw her. She snuffled up to the gate grateful for his attention. She was a lovely pig who moved very little and asked for nothing more than a bit of company and good food. As Henry refreshed her straw and filled her trough, he talked to her, telling her the sad news. She looked up at him with her sorrowful, button eyes, and he was sure she was weeping when he told her not to be afraid.

'I think Betsy looks younger every time I see her,' Henry said, as William shuffled slowly into the kitchen.

'Who?'

'Betsy.'

'Who?' William asked again.

'Betsy, your pig,' Henry repeated, seeing the confusion on his father's face.

'My pig?' William asked. 'Is there any tea in the pot?'

William managed a spoonful of breakfast but did not drink his tea. Fatigued, he spent the morning resting in the front room while Henry busied himself out in the yard and garden. At lunchtime, Sebastian and Panda arrived. Panda's doggie senses twitched as soon as she spotted Henry's car on the drive and she hurtled through the hall and into the kitchen where Henry was up to his elbows in soapsuds. As if on springs, she bounced up, knocking the pots and pans all over the tiled floor making an almighty din which brought William shuffling slowly out of the front room, his back arched, his arm held awkwardly.

'Hello, Dad,' Sebastian said. 'How did you sleep?'

'Well, thank you,' William replied, not remembering how fretful he had been. Sebastian looked at Henry, who shook his head.

'And how are you feeling?'

'Much the same.'

'Do you want some painkillers?'

'No thank you.'

'How about another cup of tea then?' Henry asked. 'You let the last one go cold.'

'A cup of tea would be nice, thank you, Henry.'

'Do you fancy going for a walk in a bit, Hal?' Sebastian asked, filling the kettle. 'Would you mind, Dad? We could do with checking on the sheep.'

'Go ahead,' William answered, too tired to care.

Settling William in front of the television, Sebastian and Henry headed across the fields.

'Has he been confused much?' Sebastian asked, trudging through the mud and trying to get Panda to avoid the lure of sheep poo.

'He comes and goes. Sometimes he's lucid and then other times he doesn't seem to know who I am.'

'That's how I've found him. The consultant said the fall he had the other week was probably part of it.'

'I thought he'd tripped.'

'We all thought he'd tripped, even Dad,' Sebastian said sadly.

'Can tumours grow that quickly?' Henry asked.

'If they're in the wrong place they can.'

'How come they didn't see it when he was in the hospital before?'

'Because they weren't looking for it.'

They fell silent as Henry opened and closed the heavy metal gate leading into the field where the sheep were grazing. As soon as Panda saw the woolly creatures she stopped, her head held high, sniffing the air. On seeing Panda, the sheep froze and stared at her. Their beady black eyes, set within black and white faces, warning her not to approach. Panda bounced back and forth, uncertain what to make of these strange looking things staring so intently back at her. In the end, she clawed her way up Sebastian's trousers, covering him in mud, demanding to be lifted to safety.

'We need to keep Dad going, as much as we can,' Sebastian said, holding Panda whilst Henry checked the ewes, 'but at the end of the day, he needs to *want* to keep going and if I'm honest, I don't think he does.' Henry stopped, turning to look at Sebastian. 'Sorry, Hal,' Sebastian said.

Continuing to check the sheep, they talked. It was obvious that they were both exhausted. Henry insisted Sebastian should go home, just for a day or so. He had so much going on and Henry could see the effects of the strain on him. Some time away from Taligth would do him good. Sebastian did not disagree. But back in the house, having cleaned himself of mud and after saying goodbye to his father, Sebastian found it difficult to leave.

'Go,' Henry insisted.

'Call me, any time, yes? Any time!' Sebastian said, opening the front door.

'Of course. Now go and do something nice.'

'I can come straight away.'

'I know you can,' Henry said, pushing Sebastian out.

'Other than Monday, late afternoon; though I might cancel that to be honest.'

'Why, what's happening?' Henry asked, opening the car door for Panda to get in.

'I'm seeing the counsellor Matilda insisted I book.'

'Don't you want to go?'

'No.'

'It might do you some good.'

'That's what I'm afraid of,' Sebastian said laughing weakly as he started the car.

Henry went back into the house and checked on William who was asleep in his chair. Unable to help him, Henry felt useless, but there was plenty to do on the farm to keep him occupied and, whilst William rested, he walked down to McGregor's for a few provisions.

Passing the time of day with Dougie, he broke the awful news as gently as he could. Shocked, Dougie listened. 'You've been so kind, Dougie. We really appreciate everything you've done,' Henry said.

'I'm only repaying kindness wi' kindness,' Dougie replied. 'Yer parents hae always bin there fur us. I wanted to dae th' same fur them. If there's anythin' I can dae please let me know, 'n' 'ere, tak' this,' Dougie said, handing Henry a bottle of the best whisky he kept behind the counter, 'if he's allowed.'

'Thank you, Dougie.'

Henry left and, in the fading daylight, walked slowly back up the road, back to Taligth.

By Sunday, William had deteriorated significantly and Henry was becoming increasingly worried. He called the district nurse who came quickly and could see how much William had gone downhill over the past 24 hours. The district nurse arranged for the doctor to visit the following day but by the time Monday dawned, William had been in bed for thirty-six hours and was so weak he was struggling to sit up.

The doctor arrived at the house mid-afternoon, followed shortly after by Sebastian. Having examined William and make him comfortable with morphine, he spoke quietly with Sebastian and Henry outside William's bedroom. He was unable to give the definitive answers they craved, but he was as open and direct with them as he could be.

'From what I can see, we are talking end-of-life,' he said kindly when Henry asked for his honest opinion. When asked 'how long?' he again answered honestly. 'The way I view it, is if you are seeing changes in months, he probably has months. If you are seeing changes in weeks then he probably has weeks and if you are seeing changes in days, then it's probably only days,' he explained.

'Could the same be said for hours?' Henry asked, knowing what he had been witnessing.

'In your dad's case I think he is near the end, but I think you still have some time; a few days perhaps. I'm so sorry.'

Sebastian and Henry were grateful for the doctor's frankness. They could now accept what they had previously suspected.

'What now?' Henry asked Sebastian after the doctor had left.

'We keep going,' Sebastian replied.

'What do we say to Dad?'

'Nothing, unless he asks. He knows what's happening. Do you want me to stay tonight?'

'Yes, but you should go to your appointment first.'

'I can't.'

'Yes you can. There's nothing the two of us can do here that one of us can't, and Dad won't want us sitting watching him. Go, it's a couple of hours. Nothing will happen, you heard the doctor. I'll call if I need you.'

As Sebastian drove away, Henry closed the door to the outside world. He stood leaning against it, looking towards the stairs, listening to the sound of his father's cries in the distance. He felt terribly alone.

~

Early for his appointment, Sebastian sat in the small waiting room outside Verity Ellsworth's office and he was reminded of the moment he and his father had started giggling whilst waiting for the registrar. Having lost a relative, it would have been far nicer to have sat in a room similar to the one he was in now, the pretty wallpaper, the splash of colour, the tasteful lamps, the light ambient music. But sitting, waiting, Sebastian struggled with his thoughts.

He felt as if he was watching someone else about to take a leap of faith. He had spent so many years trying to move on, shielding himself by being Sebastian the businessman, Sebastian the husband, the father, the charity man; that he had lost sight of who he really was, and he was fearful of meeting himself again. He was a very different person to the one he had been when he was seventeen.

Looking at the pictures on the walls, pictures of happy, smiling families, Sebastian found himself thinking back to his childhood and his teenage years. He thought about his early twenties, reflected on his marriage, then back to his teens, into his thirties, his business, his forties, the children and back to his teens again. It was just a matter of time before his thoughts landed on Nancy and her twenty-first birthday.

In the months following the horrific events of that day, the damage Sebastian suffered may have been repairable had he spoken to his parents about what happened. But he was seventeen. All he wanted was for it to go away, which it did when Nancy left. Once she was gone, he became increasingly angry with her until he despised her, and when he was older, he pushed her so far out of his life that he thought there was no coming back. But now, since his mother died, he knew that what he had buried for the past thirty years was about to bubble to the surface like the face of a woman having drowned in mud.

What happened on the day of Nancy's twenty-first was so unforgivable in Sebastian's eyes that he wasn't able to speak about it to the people who could have helped him. The only person he ever told was Meggie, and at the time that was enough, but things were different now. Meggie had been his saviour back then. Now he was beginning to feel she might be the cause of his damnation. Was he about to relive it all? Here? With this woman he did not know?

~

Composing himself, Henry took a cup of tea to his father who, having been helped by the doctor into a more comfortable position, was sitting up in bed. With his mouth open and his head back, he was struggling to breathe and his eyes looked sunken and vacant. He smiled weakly as Henry went in to see him. 'I've brought you a cup of tea,' Henry whispered. William did not speak, though he smiled again. 'I'll put it on your table. Do you want anything to eat?' William shook his head slowly and grimaced. Henry was not going to insist.

Sitting at the end of his parents' bed, Henry talked quietly as William listened. When he could summon up the energy, William smiled and nodded and occasionally opened his eyes slightly to look at his son. He knew his time on this earth was short and he was ready. He had been ready to go the moment Elspeth had died and even more ready when the consultant had confirmed what he had known all along, deep down. He did not find the process of dying frightening. He had loved every minute of being alive, but now it was his time. He was looking forward to seeing Elspeth again. He had been blessed, he thought, closing his eyes. Henry left the room taking his father's un-drunk cup of tea with him.

Downstairs, Henry felt forlorn. The doctor did not believe they would lose their father that night, but Henry was not convinced.

Taking his father's cold cup of tea into the yard, Henry went to look in on Betsy who, like William, was asleep. It was going to be a long night.

~

Sebastian sat in the waiting room, tortured with anxiety, unable to stop himself going back to the awful events of that weekend. He wondered how much of it he would be forced to confront. Some of the detail was difficult to remember, but most of it, impossible to forget, was as vivid as it was the day it happened.

Nancy had always been at the centre of trouble. William and Elspeth did their best, but in the end they more or less gave up. Nancy did what she wanted, when she wanted, with whom she wanted and cared little for the consequences. She would disappear for weeks without a word and then turn up again, out of the blue, asking for money or to stay while she found the next 'no-hoper' to love, before vanishing once more. Then, when she was nineteen, she met Jacob, and things changed for her.

Ten years older than Nancy, tall, blonde, and unconventionally good-looking, with a well-paid job, Jacob was unlike any of the other men she had been with. Well-spoken and exceptionally polite, Jacob was assertive and confident, and when Nancy introduced him to the family it was as if she had brought their saviour into the house. William and Elspeth had welcomed him with open arms. They had never met anyone like him before. Something about him was utterly compelling.

Having grown up in the leafy suburbs of the home counties, Jacob had come from a highly privileged background and had attended one of the top, and toughest, boys' boarding schools in the country. During the holidays he had travelled with his father and often regaled the Campbell family with colourful stories of his trips to South America, Africa, South East Asia and Australia. He was expressive and animated and fascinating, and it didn't take long for William and Elspeth to hope that this relationship might be the one to settle Nancy and give her the future they wanted for her.

Working for a large brewery on the south coast, Jacob appeared to have it all; he even appeared to have tamed Nancy, which no one had been able to do before. Shortly after they met, seemingly happy, Nancy moved south with him and their visits to Scotland stopped.

Almost two years since they had last seen Nancy, just before her twenty-first birthday, William and Elspeth put out a tentative invitation to her and Jacob, inviting them to Taligth, to stay for the weekend, with the intention of having a small, family party in celebration. Not expecting them to accept, for they had declined so many before, William and Elspeth were delighted when Nancy said they would come. The party was to be nothing formal; a few relatives, family friends, drinks, nibbles, a cake.

From the moment Nancy and Jacob arrived, it was obvious something was terribly wrong. The instant William and Elspeth saw her, they could tell Nancy was not the happy girl who had left two years before, and there was something different about Jacob. Towards the family, he had not changed. His warm smile and charming confidence still remained and he was as polite and as helpful as he had been before. He laughed and joked with Elspeth as he helped her prepare the table for the evening meal, and he boyishly jostled Henry in the yard as they fought over the hose. But towards Nancy his behaviour had altered. Overtly attentive, he appeared to dominate her and his light-hearted banter seemed layered with intimidation.

Before she met Jacob, Nancy had been opinionated and free-willed, but now she had become subdued and withdrawn. She had put on weight, wore no make-up and did nothing with her hair, which was now its natural brown colour, and hung, long and lank, down her back. She said very little and when she did speak he pilloried her and she became wary, unnerved by the man who demanded her individual attention. She accepted his public belittlement and ridicule as him being 'playful', and did not put up the spirited fight she would have previously. She had changed. No longer was she the brash, obnoxious, intelligent girl who was always in control. She had turned into someone who was frightened by what she had become. And it took a lot to frighten Nancy.

The family sensed it, but none of them, other than Sebastian, were sure enough of what they were witnessing to speak out. Jacob was very clever.

The night before Nancy's birthday, she and Jacob went for a walk after dinner and when they returned, they had an argument outside the house, an argument that went on into the night even after they had gone to bed. When they came down in the morning, Nancy's face was ashen. Again, dumbness struck the family and no one said anything; they all sat looking at each other, their silent eyes searching for answers. Watching the way she acted, Sebastian felt sorry for her because she looked so pitiable. He had never seen her so downcast and subdued. Jacob, unabashedly, behaved as if nothing had happened and Nancy sat, not saying a word.

After breakfast, to escape the atmosphere, William went to a neighbouring farm to help with a cow that was in difficulty whilst calving, and Elspeth took Henry to the supermarket, leaving Sebastian, with Nancy and Jacob, at Taligth. While Nancy was in the shower, Sebastian seized his opportunity and, fuelled by naive, brotherly adrenalin, took it upon himself to confront Jacob, to ask him what had happened to cause Nancy such obvious distress.

Reliving it, Sebastian wished he hadn't. He wished he had left it alone.

~

Checking on William every fifteen minutes, Henry was becoming increasingly anxious. He could see his father leaving, and he knew time was short; Sebastian needed to be back at Taligth. William's breathing was laboured, and he was crying out incoherently. Henry was doing his best to make sure he was comfortable, but other than sitting and watching him, there was nothing he could do to make his passing any more bearable for either of them. Phoning Sebastian, Henry left an urgent message.

~

Deep in thought, Sebastian recalled the feeling of the sweat that gathered in his palms that day, and the nerves that ran cold down his spine as he stood in the kitchen, looking out of the window, watching Jacob in the backyard. Jacob was standing, squarely, legs apart, staring out over the fields, casually smoking a cigarette. Sebastian remembered talking to himself, deliberating over what to do, trying to summon up the courage to go out. He remembered backing away, thinking not to do it, before becoming emboldened once more. He remembered puffing out his teenage chest and flexing his undeveloped muscles like a gladiator about to enter the arena into which a lion had already been released. He would never come to terms with what made him go out into the yard that day and never regret more the course of his actions. He had witnessed Jacob's behaviour towards Nancy, he had felt the atmosphere that followed Jacob around the house but still... As soon as he stepped out of the door he knew he had made a dreadful mistake. Jacob noticed him and had turned around. Seeing the defiance in Sebastian's eyes, he stubbed out his cigarette and walked straight towards him. Sebastian hadn't said a word.

Sebastian would never forget the smirk on Jacob's face, and how petrified he felt, bracing himself for a really good thumping as Jacob came right up to him, his face within an inch of his own. He could feel Jacob's breath and smell the smoke from his discarded cigarette. But Jacob did not thump him, and, confused, Sebastian dared to raise his eyes. Slowly, Jacob came even closer, a hair's breadth away from Sebastian's face and, as he stared into his eyes, he moved his right hand low, placing it between Sebastian's legs, cupping him, gently. Unfathomably, disturbingly, horrifyingly, Sebastian was instantly aroused. Shocked, he took a sharp breath and froze, paralyzed with fear as Jacob slowly moved his hand, feeling Sebastian's excitement. Before Sebastian had time to think, Jacob's mouth was pressing violently on his own, kissing him, rough and passionate. Sick rising in Sebastian's throat, Jacob forced his lips apart, plunging his tongue deep into Sebastian's mouth, searching, their teeth clashing. Jacob was kissing him in a way Sebastian had never been kissed before and touching him in a way he had never been touched. This was it, Sebastian thought, panic disabling him; this was what Jacob wanted. Then when Jacob's hand moved to Sebastian's belt, Sebastian was suddenly terrified. Despite a desperate, animal-like struggle, powerless against the larger man, he was quickly and roughly turned around and slammed hard against the wall. With Jacob's hand on the back of Sebastian's head, pressing his face against the pantry window, Jacob pulled at Sebastian's clothes, exposing his soft, innocent flesh... and he raped him, brutally, thrusting into him again and again, ripping Sebastian's insides.

Unable to breathe, coughing against the acid from his stomach, in excruciating pain, fearful that Nancy might hear, Sebastian did not cry out. But as Jacob violated him and the pain intensified, he stared wide-eyed through the glass, with tears streaming down his face, praying for it to be over, and he suddenly saw her, standing in the darkness, looking straight out at him.

In the shadows of the pantry Nancy stood, numbly, watching Sebastian's face as Jacob did what he did, violent and urgent. She could see his unbearable pain and Sebastian could see Jacob's face reflected in the glass, smiling as he stared at Nancy. The face of a man showing her he could have whatever he wanted, whenever he wanted, with whomever he wanted and as he carried on brutalising Sebastian, he whispered in his ear, 'smile, you fucking prick. Pretend you're enjoying it, 'cos if you don't, I'll do the same to her.' Petrified, Sebastian did as he was told; he smiled through his tears and the horrendous pain because, despite everything, he did not want Nancy to be hurt. Even in the darkness of the room he could see she did not react. She just stood, stone-faced and watched Sebastian's agony. Why didn't she help him? Sebastian asked himself. What stopped her? He was seventeen, just a child.

When Nancy turned and walked coldly out of the pantry, Jacob instantly stopped what he was doing, withdrew and went back inside the house, casually buttoning up his jeans, smiling his warm smile, acknowledging that he had won the fight. Grabbing at his clothes, Sebastian ran as fast as he could, injured and bleeding, into the woods at the top of the farm and did not come back until the next morning, by which time Jacob and Nancy had left and William and Elspeth, on the verge of calling the police, were frantic with worry. Sebastian was so traumatised he would not talk, other than to make up a weak, ridiculous story about drinking too much at lunchtime and wandering off, sleeping the night in the woods. William and Elspeth were so preoccupied with Nancy's disappearance that they did not question his excuses. They were furious with him, but he didn't care. There was nothing his parents could do to make him feel any worse than he already did.

From that fateful day, everything changed for Sebastian. He made a promise to himself never to tell his parents or brother what had happened. How could he tell them? What would he have said? That he had been raped... by a man? That he had brought it on himself? It was all too awful. When he returned from the woods to find Nancy and Jacob gone, he thanked God. How could he ever look at them again? How could he ever look at himself again? No one talked about the real reason why Nancy left. Had he spoken out at the time, perhaps he would have discovered the truth.

If he could, he would tell them what happened now, now that he was older and able to understand. He would tell them that thirty-two years ago, a thirty-one-year-old man had raped him in the yard, and that it was not his fault. Jacob had taken his innocence, destroyed his confidence and made him hate himself. Since that day, he vowed he would never let anyone make him feel that vulnerable again.

Sitting in Verity Ellsworth's waiting room, he suddenly became terrified that he was about let his guard down. Other than Meggie, no one would ever know what had happened. This was his secret, his shameful, horrific secret, and he would take it to the grave, keeping hold of it tightly enough for it to be buried forever.

When Verity Ellsworth opened her office door, the waiting room was empty.

~

Listening to his father's rasping breath as he drifted in and out of consciousness, Henry knew that time was short. He had left a message on Sebastian's phone and was relieved when, finally, he received a call back. Sebastian was on his way.

'Seb's on his way,' he told his father, lying next to him on the bed, cradling him in his arms. A weak smile crept across William's face and he patted Henry's hand gently. Henry prayed Sebastian would make it in time. 'Just hang on, Dad,' Henry whispered, kissing his father's head.

Unable to wait for the slow opening of the gates, Sebastian left his car outside and ran the length of the gravel driveway to the front door. The damp weather had made the front door swell and he kicked it open sending it smashing against the wall. He ran through the hall and up the wooden stairs three at a time, stopping at the top to catch his breath and compose himself. Panting heavily, he crept into the bedroom to see Henry now sitting by their father, his face cupped in his hands.

'See, I told you, Dad,' Henry whispered, 'Seb's here,' he said quietly, kissing his father and moving out of his chair to allow Sebastian to sit. With his eyes closed, William turned his face to Sebastian. His hand now enveloped in his eldest son's, William took a deep breath, opening his eyes a fraction, and mouthed, 'I love you both,' before closing them for the last time.

William's smile was weaker now and his life was ebbing away.

'I need to tell you something, Dad,' Sebastian said. Henry moved to stop him, but Sebastian shrugged his brother's hand away. 'I'm going to find Nancy,' William's eyes flickered and he gave the slightest of nods. 'She lives in Switzerland and I will find her for you...' and, as Sebastian and Henry watched, William took his final breath.

Day Twenty-Seven

Tuesday

Into the dark hours of early morning, the brothers sat stunned, looking at their father's lifeless body, hardly believing that just over a week ago he had bravely walked behind their mother's coffin, whilst unknowingly dying himself. Perhaps that had been the plan all along. Perhaps that was what he and Elspeth had arranged, and now she had come to get him. No lingering, no hanging around...'come on old man,' she would have said, 'time ye were off; time tae go.'

After the doctor had come back to the house to certify William's death, Sebastian called Angus Stewart, but he was attending to another bereaved family and was unable to get to Taligth straight away, giving Sebastian and Henry time to be alone with their father, to watch him sleeping peacefully with no more pain and no more calling out.

Sitting in silence, Henry thought about the tears he was sure he had seen in Betsy's eyes and how he was going to break the news to her; he thought about how they were going to break the news to everyone, even Nancy. 'Can I ask you something?' he said to Sebastian, quietly. 'The promise you made to Dad earlier, about Nancy, I didn't realise you'd found her address.'

'I haven't,' Sebastian murmured, 'but I know someone who has it...' And with no pressure of time, in the stillness of their parents' room, Sebastian told Henry what he had found out about Nancy and how Meggie had encouraged him to contact her before their mother's funeral. He did not tell him why he resisted, but apologised to Henry for keeping it to himself, secretly sorry that his

314

fearfulness of dragging the past into the present had made him impuissant.

Motionless, with his head down, Henry listened. 'Why do you hate her so much?'

Sebastian thought about how to answer Henry's question. He did not just hate her; he despised her. He despised her for her weakness at a time when he most needed her to be strong, and it repulsed him. How could she have stood and watched and not protected him from the monster she had brought into the house? The further away he got from it, the more he loathed her and, looking at the scar still visible on his brother's face, and the lifeless body of his father lying in front of him, he answered. 'I hate what she did to people,' he said, reaching out and stroking the soft skin of his father's hand, colder and paler now. 'I think we should leave Dad in peace now. He will start to change, and we don't want to see that. Come on, let's try to get some sleep. Angus should be here before light.'

Sebastian waited for Henry to leave the room before taking one last look, and then he closed the door gently behind him.

Shattered, the brothers slept the few hours before the cockerels crowed in the dawn and the sun seeped into the house filtered by the condensation gathered on the panes of cold glass.

At 6 a.m. Angus Stewart and his colleagues arrived to take William to the mortuary. Angus, who had been so kind a few weeks before, was in shock at returning to the farm so soon. He offered kind words of condolence and an apology for taking so long to get out to them; it had been a busy night, he told them.

Standing in yesterday's clothes, Sebastian and Henry watched their father being brought steadily down the wooden staircase on a stretcher and taken through the hall and out to the waiting car; the damp, autumn morning making the walk across the wet gravel difficult.

Closing the swollen front door, the house seemed to settle, feeling quiet as they moved through to the kitchen.

Henry went straight into the back yard hoping Betsy was awake and snuffling at her gate in search of scraps. As he approached her with a bucket full of beet, her button eyes lit up, her mouth opened into a strange toothy grin and she pranced around. Henry could not bring himself to tell her about William. She might wonder, but she would never know. Sebastian brought out a cup of tea and he and Henry stood together looking out at the morning mist ebbing and flowing along the top of the grass and the sun making the dew glisten. Although everything looked the same, it suddenly felt very different.

After so many years of noise, Taligth sat quietly, respectfully. The house had lost its life so quickly and even the old farm cat, having slinked in as William had left, wandered forlornly from room to room, in search of its owners.

The day passed in a mix of telephone calls and silence and, as evening approached, Sebastian chose to stay another night with Henry while he could still sense the presence of his parents, no matter how distant.

Although neither he nor Henry were especially hungry, they had not eaten since the day before and, after hours of difficult telephone conversations, where they had recounted the same sad story over and over again, they needed to eat.

With the radio playing in the background, Henry set about making something out of the unrelated contents of the fridge, whilst Sebastian went to the pantry and to the last few bottles of his father's wine collection. Walking into the darkness, he looked to his right, towards the small window. Letting in little light, it was more or less obscured by ivy and cobwebs giving the room a gloomy, haunted feel.

William's wine collection had diminished, due, in the main, to Sebastian's own consumption, but as he rummaged, he remembered spotting a couple of bottles hidden behind some boxes and eventually emerged out of the pantry and into the kitchen clutching a bottle of unknown red and a bottle of champagne.

'What do you think?' he asked, holding them up to show Henry.

'My god! As if Dad still has that champagne!'

'Do you recognise it?' Sebastian asked, surprised by his brother's reaction. 'It's unlike Mum and Dad to buy champagne.'

'That's because I bought it. In fact, I bought two bottles, the one you have in your hand and the one we drank.'

'Why did you drink champagne?'

'To celebrate your 'Entrepreneur of the Year' award.'

'Bloody hell, that was years ago,' Sebastian said, thinking about the round, glass paperweight on his desk. 'I don't remember celebrating it,' he said, examining the bottle to see if he could find a date.

'You didn't. That's why they still have one bottle left; you didn't turn up.'

'I don't remember any of that.'

'No, you were too busy climbing ladders to celebrate with mere mortals like us,' Henry said with a smile on his face, as he chopped slimy, week-old mushrooms and tossed them into a pan of sizzling onions.

'Really?' Sebastian said, looking worried.

Henry laughed. 'It didn't matter, we understood. Mum and Dad were so proud of you that we celebrated in your absence. Now I come to think about it, I seem to remember Dad saying he would save the second bottle for when you made your first million. I guess he forgot about it. Imagine if we'd opened a bottle for every million you'd made, we'd have been pissed for years.'

Over dinner, and both bottles, the brothers talked more about Nancy.

'I was going to write to her this week,' Sebastian said, 'to tell her about Mum. Dad asked me to.'

'Are you still going to?'

'Well, Dad wanted her to know about Mum, so I'm presuming he'd want her to know about himself as well.

What do you think?' Sebastian asked, pushing his food around his plate.

'I think you're probably right. Do you want her at Dad's funeral?'

'No more than I wanted her at Mum's,' he replied. It was late and he'd had too much to drink. 'Actually,' he said suddenly, 'I'm going to go to Switzerland! I'm going to go and see her...'

'When did you decide this?' Henry asked, putting his fork down and pushing his plate away.

'Just now...' Sebastian replied. '*If* I can get her address off Meggie,' he added, raising his eyebrows.

'What's brought this on?'

'I can go on Thursday and come back Saturday,' Sebastian enthused, ignoring Henry's question. 'I've got to be here Monday for the completion meeting, but that's all.'

'Okay, okay,' Henry muttered, shocked by Sebastian's decision. 'Are you going to tell her you're going to be turning up?'

'No. I'll take my chance; surprise her so she doesn't have time to prepare.'

'What if she's not there?'

'Then I'll come home.'

'I didn't think you wanted to see her.'

'Neither did I, not until a minute ago. I need to ask her a question.'

'What question?'

Sebastian did not answer, but the events of the past few days had focused his mind, and he had found an inner determination that had previously failed him.

'Whatever you want,' Henry sighed, knowing Sebastian would not be forthcoming. 'I've been thinking I might cancel the production.'

'What?'

'Does it not seem insensitive to carry on? We're setting up next week.'

'Don't be stupid,' Sebastian protested. 'Mum and Dad loved your productions. Dad was only talking about it the other day. Imagine how disappointed he'd be if his last engineering project on earth didn't get off the ground, literally. And anyway, I've bought tickets.'

'Oh well, if you've bought tickets,' Henry laughed weakly. 'I just feel this play's been doomed from the outset.'

'Even more reason why you shouldn't cancel it.'

Sinking back into silence, Sebastian thought about his sudden decision to go to see Nancy, remembering back to his school days, and to a quote he learned in history: 'If you know the enemy and know yourself, you need not fear the result of a hundred battles' – Sun Tzu. It was time Sebastian faced her again.

Day Twenty-Eight

Henry awoke, fleetingly forgetting where he was before the weight of grief settled itself upon him once more. Lying in his bed he listened to the sounds of the house creaking awake after a cold, damp night.

Sebastian, unable to sleep, had been up for hours working and booking flights and accommodation. Once again, he messaged Meggie asking for Nancy's address. She had gone very quiet.

Before going to bed, Sebastian and Henry had agreed that their father's funeral should take place as soon as it could be arranged. Neither of them wanted an agonising wait. In an appointment at the funeral director's first thing, they agreed to a week on Friday for William's cremation, the same day as Henry's opening night. Although this initially worried Henry, on reflection he decided that getting ready for the production would be a welcome distraction.

Back at Taligth, the all too familiar list of things they needed to do was waiting for them. Henry started on it while Sebastian, reluctantly, went into work. Alone, Henry spent the morning making appointments, and the afternoon in his mother's potting shed, searching. He did not know what he was looking for; he was just looking, maybe hoping to find something from his childhood; a lost ball, a toy cricket bat, a little red car. Lifting up an old, dented metal bucket, he discovered the skeletal remains of a mouse, which probably having survived the murdering jaws of a cat, had thought it had made it to safety only to be trapped and unable to find its way out. The poor little creature had undoubtedly died a slow and painful death and for that reason, Henry buried it in the back garden.

Holding a small, dust covered cardboard box containing the mouse's remains, Henry looked up towards the house and thought about the enormity of the task he and Sebastian faced in dealing with over fifty years of life in one place, fifty years of weather damaged windows and slipping tiles, all of which had had promises of repair.

~

Matilda was waiting for Sebastian when he arrived home from work, late and shattered.

'How was Henry when you left this morning?' she asked, as Sebastian dragged himself wearily into the kitchen. Still in his coat, he slumped at the table.

'He was okay,' he said, sighing. 'He was very close to Dad... and Mum.'

'You both were,' she said, joining him at the table.

'I know. But he had something special, didn't he? Don't get me wrong, I'm fine with it,' he added, looking at her sad expression. 'Mum and Dad had to protect him more than they did me.'

'I suppose they did,' Matilda replied, remembering what Sebastian had told her about Nancy.

'He's going to stay at Taligth for a few days,' Sebastian said. 'The theatre company move up at the weekend, Sunday I think, so there's not much point in him going back to Newcastle.' As he spoke, his phone, which was lying on the table, lit up and a message from Meggie appeared on the screen. Sebastian's reaction gave him away.

'Who is it?' Matilda asked, looking at him.

Hovering over his phone, Sebastian considered saying 'no one', but it was too late.

'Who is it?' Matilda asked again.

Sebastian stared at the phone, considering what to say. Life was short and he and Matilda were on the brink of change. He did not want to go into the next part of his life without her, but he needed to be honest.

No matter what they faced during their marriage, Matilda had been his constant. She had always been able to find the right words and give the right advice and knew to stand back when he wanted to kick walls. When he wanted her, she held him close, and when he pushed her away, she let him. She deserved a medal for years of service, nurturing the seeds sewn when they had exchanged wedding vows.

Looking up from his phone and straight at Matilda, he answered her question. 'It's Meggie,' he said calmly.

~

Henry sat in his father's chair in the front room. He was tired and had made the error of opening a drawer full of photographs. Although he had been through each one when his mother died, he sat on the floor and looked at them again. Many he remembered, but some he looked at with fresh eyes, tiny black and white prints of his parents when they first met; grainy shots of them at dances and weddings, in the woods and on the beach, and hundreds of them at Taligth. Engrossed, he lost himself in the years and before long, the evening arrived and the light in the room began to fade. After tidying away the photographs, he went into the kitchen in search of something to eat. The fridge and freezer offered up little more than a packet of peas and some frozen chips along with some sorry looking vegetables which would be heading Betsy's way, and a couple of baking potatoes lurking in the bottom drawer. In the pantry there were plenty of tins. Tonight's meal would be interesting, Henry thought.

Putting the potatoes in the aga, Henry sat at the table and picked up his mother's book. Opening it, he idly thumbed through the pages and, as he did so, something escaped and fell onto the floor. Not immediately recognising what it was, Henry picked it up and looked at it.

~

Sebastian took a deep breath. With two glasses and an unopened bottle of red wine, he asked Matilda to sit with him on the sofa. Panda followed them and nuzzled her face into the rug, laying perfectly still, watching them, her eyes moving from one to the other as they talked.

Seldom spoken about, Meggie had been an invisible presence in Matilda and Sebastian's life from the moment they had met. In the early days she had been a comparison, sometimes a distraction and occasionally an excuse. Reluctantly, Matilda had accepted it, believing that one day Meggie would disappear, but she never did, not completely. The power of the 'first love' was too strong and Matilda always had the uneasy feeling she was close by.

'Why is Meggie messaging you?' Matilda asked, suspiciously.

'Because I asked her to,' Sebastian replied. Matilda said nothing, forcing him to continue. 'After Mum died, I bumped into her.' Matilda still did not speak. 'In the café on the hill. She works there.'

'Does she?' Matilda asked stiffly, 'I've never seen her. It's run by a girl, an artist.'

'Yes. Meggie's daughter. She's had a baby and Meggie's been helping to run the place.'

'Why did you go in?'

'Panda dragged me in. She went there with Henry, apparently. It's not relevant.'

'It is to me!' Matilda snapped. 'Why didn't you tell me?'

'I don't know.'

'Yes you do,' she said bitterly. 'You gave her your number!'

'So that she could send me an address. Here, look,' Sebastian said showing Matilda his phone, all previous messages deleted.

'Is that *her* address?'

'No, it's Nancy's.'

'Nancy's? Why has Meggie got Nancy's address?' Matilda asked, confused.

Matilda listened as Sebastian told her how Meggie and Nancy had got to know each other. Meggie and Nancy were a part of Sebastian's life Matilda had no access to. Whenever she asked about them, he either ignored her questions or, with shortened replies, refused to answer in any detail. Out of fear of his reaction, she had learned not to push. But today she was tired of it.

'What was it like when you saw her again?' Matilda asked, fearing the answer. 'Do you still have feelings for her?'

Looking at the darkened face of his phone, thinking what to say, Sebastian lifted his eyes to meet Matilda's, hoping she would understand. She always had. 'I lied to you yesterday...' he said. Matilda looked at him sharply. '...when I said I had seen the counsellor. I didn't go in,' he added.

'Right,' Matilda said, confused by his comment, desperate for him to answer her question.

'I couldn't face talking about it, not *any* of it...' Sebastian continued, '...and I can't answer your question, because it's all mixed up together and I don't know the answer.'

Shocked, Matilda held her breath. She couldn't help him, after all the years she had stood by and supported him, she couldn't help him because she couldn't reach whatever it was he had with Meggie. He was so tightly bound by his past that she didn't stand a chance, and for the first time, she didn't have the strength or desire to find a solution. Without saying a word, she got up and left the kitchen.

Sebastian let her go. Numbed by grief and the combined effects of red wine and little sleep, he gave up. 'You did ask,' he whispered to himself.

Finishing the wine, he eventually went to bed. Matilda was asleep by the time he went upstairs and he quietly repacked his overnight bag ready for an early start. Being allowed a rare opportunity, Panda joined them in the bedroom and she slept between them, tucked into Sebastian's back.

~

Picking up and examining the photograph that had fallen from his mother's book, Henry was glad Sebastian was going to Switzerland. Not using it to keep her page, his mother must have moved the photograph from book to book over the years as it travelled with her through her reading journey. A photograph that did not contain herself or William, a photograph that did not contain Sebastian or Henry, but a photograph of Nancy, sitting on the bonnet of a car on a hot day, dressed in shorts and tee-shirt, with Jacob pulled in close next to her, his hand gripping her waist tightly. It was a photograph in which Nancy was not smiling. Standing away from her, not holding her hand, was a little girl.

On the back of the photograph in Elspeth's writing, 'Florence, aged 6 years 9 months.'

Day Twenty-Nine

Thursday

At 4.15 a.m. the shrill call of the bedside alarm drew Matilda from her fretful dreams; she had not slept well. Not opening her eyes, she reached out to shake Sebastian, but her hand met with the soft, warm underbelly of Panda. Once Sebastian had relinquished his place, she had rolled over and purloined his still warm, vacant space. Unable to fight off her malaise, Matilda lay awake.

As the taxi pulled up outside the front door, Sebastian went back into the dark bedroom to say goodbye. 'Can we talk later?' he whispered, leaning down to kiss Matilda's cheek. Not replying, she turned over. 'Please, Til,' Sebastian said, sitting on the edge of the bed, his hand resting on her side. 'I should have said last night that there's nothing going on between Meggie and me. I promise you. You asked whether I still had feelings for her, and if I'm honest, I don't know what I'm feeling right now, but we're not having an affair, sweetheart. Please believe me.' Still Matilda did not respond. Sighing, Sebastian stood up and walked towards the door. Taking one last look into the room, he left, closing the bedroom door softly behind him.

Heading downstairs, he made sure his passport and check-in details were in his pocket. He grabbed his coat and bag and quietly let himself out of the front door and down the steps to the waiting car. Darkness hung in the windless sky and he was starting to feel nervous.

'Morning,' he said, getting in.

'Morning,' came the taxi driver's reply, the extent of his conversation for the entirety of the journey, which suited Sebastian as it left him to stare out of the window and think about what lay ahead. Looking back at the house as they pulled away, he saw the bedroom light was on.

Five in the morning in Edinburgh was an ungodly hour enjoyed only by all-night revellers and urban foxes, but the advantage of an early flight was that the roads to the airport were clear and the taciturn taxi driver dropped Sebastian outside the terminal doors with time to spare before check-in opened. Grateful for his silent ride, Sebastian tipped him generously.

Other than a few staff wandering around with bin liners and litter pickers, and some eateries with shutters half open, the airport was very quiet. Sebastian sought out the only open café and ordered himself a black coffee, accompanied by a dubious looking croissant, hoping that having something to eat might settle his stomach.

Watching the comings and goings of busy airport staff and a few weary travellers, he thought about Matilda, her disturbed night and the bedroom light being on as he left. It was the first time he could not feel her by his side. He wondered why he could not answer her question, and why, in all honesty, the fear of losing her was not strong enough to force him to. Perhaps the thought of what faced him was clouding his judgment; perhaps, when he was home, he would be able to talk. He hoped Matilda would understand.

Looking up at the departures board and seeing check-in open, he made his way to the departure lounge, gate 6, where he sat waiting alongside a small number of business travellers all sporting briefcases and overnight bags similar to his own. They looked like members of the same club heading to the international championships of a sporting event. Just before boarding, Sebastian messaged Henry, making sure he was prepared for the day ahead. He worried about him being at Taligth on his own.

~

Perturbed by the discovery of the photograph, Henry woke with it playing on his mind and he was up and about getting breakfast for Betsy and the goats when he received

327

Sebastian's message. He had been tempted to telephone Sebastian and tell him about what he had found hidden between the pages of their mother's book, but there was something about the little girl in the photograph that was unsettling and he wasn't sure he knew exactly what it was he was looking at; he did not want to risk complicating things.

Nancy looked to have been in her late twenties, thirty perhaps, but not much older, when the photograph was taken. She was wearing shorts, so it was clearly taken before her accident.

Knowing that his mother had kept the photograph preserved like a pressed flower, moving it from one book to another, saddened Henry. Why she had never mentioned being in touch with Nancy bewildered him. He wondered whether this was the only 'recent' photograph his parents had of her or was there a stash of them hidden somewhere, yet to be discovered? He drew a blank and now there was no one to answer his questions – other than Nancy.

Contemplating the day ahead, he got ready for his appointment at the registrar's office. This time, there would be no giggling.

~

Having slept for the majority of the flight, Sebastian landed in Geneva just before noon, local time.

Walking out of the airport and into the cold, damp, Swiss air, he started to feel his nerves rising once more. He had been reasonably relaxed on the plane, his mind occupied. But standing in the same country as Nancy felt too close. He was breathing the same air as her, and he didn't like it.

He looked up at the dull, grey sky as he waited in the taxi queue, made up of the same passengers who had accompanied him on his flight. With the weather not as expected, he drew his coat around him. According to the pilot prior to take off, Geneva at this time of year was 'a pleasant 14 degrees'; standing outside the airport in the rain and wind it certainly did not feel like it. On take-off the pilot had informed them it was currently sunny in the city but likely to be raining by the time they landed, 'such is the Swiss weather'. Sebastian could confirm that. During the flight, the pilot had gone on to explain, in detail, how the Swiss weather system worked, by which time Sebastian was asleep.

Ten minutes after joining the queue, he was in the back seat of a taxi, making his way across the city. It was his first time in Geneva and, from within a steamed-up car, it looked a beautiful place to visit, not that he felt much like sight-seeing. As expected in a big city, the drive through the centre was stop-start. It seemed controlled by unpredictable traffic lights, and the buses kept cutting into car lanes causing intense footwork by the drivers so that by the time they reached the address, Sebastian was feeling sick, regretting the croissant he had consumed earlier.

Trying to calm his nerves, he asked the driver to wait for a moment as he prepared himself. Looking out of the taxi window at the view, he breathed deeply before opening the door and stepping out onto the pavement. He paid the driver, and, grateful that the contents of his stomach had remained in place, he stood for a second. The taxi pulled away. Sebastian had considered going to his hotel first to drop off his bag and freshen up, but he feared he might not come back out again. He had come all this way to face Nancy, which was what he intended to do no matter how much he wanted to turn around and wave for the taxi to return.

From the top of the hill, he looked down on four luxury apartment blocks nestled into the hillside amongst well-established trees and beautifully manicured lawns, which led down towards Lake Geneva. His eyes sailed across the still water to the snow-capped Jura mountain range beyond. The view was breathtaking.

The apartment block Nancy lived in was at the bottom of the hill, closest to the lake and, although it looked newer than the rest, with its clean white exterior and modern architectural lines, it sat comfortably amongst three similar residences, each considerately positioned and secluded from the others by trees and mature shrubs. Walking down towards the lake, he noticed how the apartments, four in each block, enjoyed the spectacular scenery from large glass picture windows overlooking the rich and varied landscape. Arriving outside Nancy's, standing with his back to the building, Sebastian looked out at lake and the beautiful surroundings. It was exceptionally peaceful. With sweat settling on his forehead he took a handkerchief from his pocket and wiped his face before he turned around to face the apartment.

He approached the large glass entrance door. He communicated with the concierge who buzzed for him to enter. As instructed, he explained who he was and who he was visiting and, after an ID check, feeling like a guest at an exclusive hotel, he was pointed in the direction of a marble-floored corridor which sparkled under opulent wall lights that guided his way. The concierge followed him into the corridor and stood a little way back, watching, after Sebastian persuaded him not to ring through. He wanted to surprise his sister, he had told him.

By the time he reached the door to Nancy's apartment he could hardly breathe, and he stopped, pausing for a second. After a few whispered words of encouragement, he raised his hand to the door and knocked. '*Fuck!*' he mouthed, standing back, trying to calm his nerves. He examined the door, mentally preparing for whatever lay behind it. He took it all in, how it was wider than most doors, made from oak he thought, expensive looking oak. It was panelled with opaque glass, clear enough to see movement from within but little else. He stepped back, further away, glancing at the concierge who was standing to his right. He looked back at the door and the light that hung above it... waiting. As a figure approached, his heart pounded, and his breathing quickened. The heavy door slowly opened. Seeing her there, in front of him, stopped his breath short and he gasped, as did she, her hand raised to her mouth in shock. Eyes wide, mouths open, they stared at each other. Seconds passed.

~

It had been a sombre morning. The registrar's office appointment had taken just a short time and was solemn. On his way back to Taligth, Henry dropped his parents' prescription medicines into the doctor's surgery for safe disposal, visited the library to return his father's books and inform them of his parents' deaths, went into the opticians to settle their account and, finally, to the hearing aid shop to see whether they could find any use for both his mother's and father's hearing aids, all seven sets that he and Sebastian had found around the house. Everyone he spoke to was saddened and shocked by the awful news he shared; their day now tinged with a little of his melancholy.

Back at Taligth, he mopped the kitchen floor, cleaned the kettle and sat down to go through some papers from the case, which he and Sebastian had retrieved once more, from the top of their parents' wardrobe the night their father died; the case that they had hoped, after their mother's death, not to have to open again for a long time.

~

'Meggie!' Sebastian exclaimed.

'Who is it Meggie?' came a softly accented Scottish voice Sebastian instantly recognised. When Meggie did not answer, Nancy called again, more demanding this time, 'Meggie!' Sebastian peered into the apartment but was unable to see further than the hall.

'What are you doing here?' Meggie's curt voice whispered into the corridor as she stepped out, pulling the door closed behind her. 'You said you were going to write, not turn up!'

'I've come to see my sister, if that's all right with you?' Sebastian said abruptly. Looking to his right, he nodded at the concierge who nodded back before returning to his desk. 'Yes, I was going to write but I changed my mind,' he said, feeling confused. 'Why are you here?'

331

By the time Sebastian and Meggie caught their breath, Nancy had opened the door fully and was standing patiently watching the exchange between the pair.

'Well, well, well, look what the cat's dragged in,' she said tersely. 'Don't leave him standing out there, Meggie, show him in.' She turned away, leading them down the hall. She had wondered how long it would take for him to turn up; she knew he would, one day. 'You're lucky I'm home, I'm out of the country most of the time,' she said showing Sebastian into the vast, open-plan living room. 'You could have written or called, that would have been far easier. It's a long way for you to come when I already know the news about Mum. I hope you won't think this a wasted journey.' She stopped and turned to look at him, despite her estrangement from the family, he had never been far from her thoughts. Beneath her stiff exterior, she was pleased he had come; it was time they settled their differences. 'Please, sit down,' she said.

'You couldn't wait to tell her,' Sebastian said to Meggie who, still standing in the hall, had hung back.

'I didn't tell her!' Meggie protested.

'Then who did?'

'Now, now, you two,' Nancy interrupted, 'and there we were, getting on so nicely,' she said, walking towards the large picture window, looking out at the lake before turning to face Sebastian. 'If you must know, an old friend told me.'

'Who?' Sebastian asked.

'Just someone I used to know,' Nancy replied.

'Who?' Sebastian persisted.

'Would you like a drink?' she asked.

'Why won't you tell me?' Perplexed, Sebastian looked at his sister.

'Because it's not relevant,' Nancy replied, clearly ending the discussion.

Sebastian knew not to push, and thought about the last time he saw her; when she had looked, stone-faced, at him through the pantry window. With no emotion, she had been an empty vessel that day. Her torturer had taken the last of her fight away and Sebastian could see the lasting damage in her now soulless eyes. But in every other respect she was more like the Nancy he had known before Jacob, the old Nancy.

Looking at her face, he was reminded of how striking she was. Easily recognisable, the years had been kind. Her hair was cut short with a mix of natural colours highlighting the ends, and her flawless skin was still pale, with heavy eyebrows and sparse dark lashes with auburn tips. When he followed her into the living room, he had noticed how comfortably she walked. Had he not known about her accident and the loss of her leg, he would have been none the wiser.

'How long are you staying in Geneva?' she asked, moving to one of two cream leather sofas facing each other across an oversized, glass coffee table.

'A day or two,' Sebastian answered, turning to look out at the view.

'Stunning isn't it?' Nancy said. 'Do sit down. Meggie, would you be kind and get us a drink please? Coffee, Sebastian?'

Sebastian turned away from the window and looked at Meggie. 'Yes please,' he said.

Meggie went into the kitchen, glad of the opportunity to breathe. She had not expected to find herself in the same room as Nancy and Sebastian without warning. She was not prepared, and Nancy was unpredictable.

Taking his coat off, Sebastian looked around the room. The apartment was exquisitely decorated with tasteful furnishings and pieces of artwork placed on glass-topped console tables and carefully positioned shelves. Sebastian was drawn to the individually painted pieces of glass on the mantel above the fireplace, their colours spilling into the room. Nancy watched him.

'Do you like what you see?' she asked, as he sat on the sofa opposite her.

'How long have you lived here?'

333

'In this one, about four years.' Looking at Sebastian's confused expression, Nancy smiled at him. 'My husband is a property developer. We own these four properties and, as each one has been built, we have lived in it. Like hermit crabs, we have moved into bigger, more luxurious shells each time. The first block is over twenty years old now and considerably smaller than this one.'

'Will there be a fifth?'

'I hope so. I'm already feeling a little caged-in here. We have plenty more land and opportunity to build closer to the water. This is one of the more exclusive areas in Geneva and highly desirable. My husband, Stefan, bought the land cheaply when the area was not as well developed as it is now, and he sat on it, waiting to build at a time when people started to see its potential. You and my husband would get on well.'

'Do you rent the apartments out?'

'We do, although I keep a small, one-bedroomed place at the top of the hill, for visitors. Florence is currently occupying it. Most property around here is rented.'

'Florence?' Sebastian questioned.

'Meggie's daughter,' Nancy replied, dismissively. Sebastian looked at her, confused. 'If you build to a high standard,' Nancy continued, regardless, 'you can command high rent.'

'Do you have any more developments?' Sebastian asked, distracted by his thoughts, wondering why Meggie and her daughter were visiting Nancy.

'A couple. Stefan is on the other side of Geneva at the moment securing more land. Rather like you, Sebastian, he never stops. The Campbell empire must be quite a size by now,' Nancy said brusquely.

Sebastian did not comment.

'Would you like me to leave?' Meggie asked, putting the tray on the table.

'No, join us. I presume you're happy with Meggie being here, Sebastian?'

'Of course,' Sebastian replied, uncertain why Meggie was there.

'You're looking very well,' Nancy said, lifting her coffee from the tray and sitting back comfortably. Although it had been over thirty years since she had seen him, she had made a point of following his progress, and she felt she knew his aged face. 'I see your company is doing well; the business pages seem to like you. You have an impressive media profile,' she said, smiling coldly.

Not willing to get into discussion, Sebastian did not allow himself to be drawn in by Nancy's shrewd comments and, looking around the room, it was clear she had also done well for herself. 'What do you do?' he asked her.

'I'm an art dealer.'

'An art dealer?'

'Yes,' Nancy laughed, 'I realised it could make me a lot of money.'

'The pieces you have on your walls...?'

'I deal in fine art. This is not fine art,' she said dismissively. 'These pieces are Florence's.'

Sebastian looked at the familiar style of the pictures on the wall behind Nancy's sofa, reflecting on their similarity to the pictures in the café.

'So,' Nancy said, 'what are your ambitions now you've made a success of your business? Are you going to continue to grow your empire? Or sell it off and do something different?'

'I haven't made any plans, not yet.'

'You must have some idea, Sebastian. I can't see you not having a plan.'

'You don't know me anymore, Nancy.'

Raising her eyebrows, nodding slowly, Nancy agreed. Neither of them knew each other anymore. Both of their lives had been inextricably altered by the events of that weekend and she found it hard to go back to the last time she saw him and not see the terrified boy behind the man's face. So much time had passed that she had, more or less, erased her feelings of loss but, being close to Sebastian again could not mask the deep-seated love she once had for him. Suddenly, she felt terribly sad. Everything she had known and thought to be true was taken away from her on the day she left Taligth, determined never to return. But life away from the family had been far from easy and it had taken her a long time to work her way out of her pitiable, controlling, abusive marriage to Jacob. She had spent years preparing to leave, years building the strength, and then, just when she was on the cusp, she had the accident and lost their unborn child. What followed was a period of fiercely determined self-destruction. No longer able to control her, Jacob left and, having reached the lowest depths, Nancy changed her life.

'I was sorry to hear about Mum,' she said, suddenly. 'I thought about coming to her funeral.'

'I'm glad you didn't,' Sebastian replied.

'I realise that.'

'It would have been the wrong time to have difficult conversations,' he said.

Nancy stared at him, unmoved. 'Believe it or not, Sebastian, I'm sure I wouldn't have chosen Mum's funeral to rake up ill feeling, but I understand. How is everyone at home?'

'Are you interested?'

'Not really.'

'Then don't ask!'

'Okay,' she said, untouched. 'But I'm interested in Dad. How is he doing? I imagine it's been very difficult for him since...' Nancy stopped talking and looked at him. 'How many years has it been since we last saw each other?' she asked.

Surprised, Sebastian looked up. 'Don't you know?' he asked. 'Although it wouldn't surprise me if you didn't,' he added bitterly.

Nancy leant forward. So handsome, she thought, but so tormented. Sebastian's anguish was clear to see and she stared at him, her face softening, but still blank, unreadable.

'Of course I know,' she said, straightening up, her mood suddenly shifting. In an instant, the atmosphere altered as the unease in the room intensified. Where does one start? She thought.

Disconcerted by Nancy's change in manner, Meggie stood up. 'I think I should leave you two to it,' she said.

'No, Meggie, you should stay!' Nancy commanded, reaching out her hand and gripping Meggie's arm tightly, her eyes fixed on Sebastian. 'There's so much he doesn't know.' Panicked, pulling against her hold, Meggie stared hard at Nancy.

'I know how much you despise me, Sebastian, and believe me, I recognise your pain. Unfortunately, we cannot turn back the clock, but perhaps now we have an opportunity to put things right. What do you think?' she asked, suddenly turning her attention to Meggie, without letting go of her arm, knowing that what she expected Meggie to do would uncover thirty years of deceit.

'What are you talking about?' Sebastian asked, confused. It felt like battle lines had been drawn. He could see the fear in Meggie's face as Nancy manoeuvred her into position. Not sure what was happening, he felt distinctly uneasy. 'What's going on?' he asked.

'It's time to tell him, Meggie!'

'No!' Meggie cried.

'Tell me what?'

'Go on, Meggie,' Nancy insisted, malevolence in her voice. 'It's been a secret for far too long and I'm tired of keeping it.'

'No!' Meggie cried again.

'It's long overdue and you know it. Pull yourself together, Meggie!' Nancy snarled, looking at Sebastian with anguish in her wounded eyes.

Sebastian tried to read her. There was something behind her look that told him this was her final shot.

Nancy held the silence. Now that her mother was dead, everything had changed. Damaged, as a child she had hated her mother, detesting the way she had fawned over the boys, knowing that she loved them more than she had ever loved her. When she was older and found out the truth, she understood and she felt sorry for her father, caught between his wife and his family, desperately trying to do the right thing by them all, but getting it so terribly wrong. But now, in Nancy's eyes, they had paid their dues. It was time to let go.

As the tension in the room grew, Meggie knew there was no escape. 'Oh my god!' she said, so quietly she could hardly be heard. Nancy released her grip. Meggie rubbed her arm and swallowed hard. She looked at Nancy, but Nancy was giving nothing away as she unflinchingly watched her brother.

Sebastian waited for Meggie to speak...

~

Having retrieved them from the case, Henry looked at his parents' wills, bound together with tartan ribbon, and his father's handwriting on what appeared to be a letter, tucked in behind. It was the first time he had seen it. Addressed to himself and Sebastian, he hesitated for a moment, wondering whether he should wait for Sebastian to return before opening it. Deciding not to, Henry took a knife from the drawer and carefully slit the envelope.

The date on the letter revealed that it was written twelve years before.

Henry began to read...

Dear Sebastian and Henry

If you are reading this letter your mother and I will have gone. My outrageous side hopes we threw caution to the wind, sold Taligth and bought a yacht, sailed around the world and gambled away your inheritance, but I suspect we did none of the above and we will have sneaked off quietly, leaving you everything. I hope we have.

Before you read any further, we want you to know how much we love you both and how grateful we have been for the endless joy you have brought into our lives – every single day. But there is something we need to tell you, your mum and I, something we have kept from you, something which has eaten away at us and at times almost destroyed us.

In hindsight what we did was wrong, but at the time and under the circumstances, we had no choice.

I feel nervous writing this letter and terribly sad, especially for you, Sebastian. We should have told you whilst we were alive. We are such cowards. But we were sworn to secrecy and, as time passed and you started making your way in the world, we believed we would have lost you had we told you later and we could not bear that.

The reason this letter is to both of you, Sebastian, is that you will need someone to talk to and Henry has always been by your side, even when you weren't looking.

I am taking a deep breath as I write… here goes…

Sebastian, when you were at the end of your first year at university we got a phone call from Meggie, she wanted to come to see us….

~

Sebastian listened…

… Eventually, Meggie started to speak, slowly at first.

'I don't know where to start,' she said. 'I wasn't prepared for this…' She paused, looking at Sebastian, his eyes imploring her to continue. 'I loved you,' she told him, studying his face. 'I loved you more than you deserved,' she added, making him flinch and break eye contact. 'I don't know what it was about you that netted me, we weren't even together that long,' she said, 'but I was infatuated; so that when we ended, the *way* we ended, it broke me. I'd never felt anything like it before, and it was frightening. The pain of losing you and the betrayal I felt was so intense, I thought I'd never get over it, which was why I spent more and more time in the pub where Nancy worked.

I remember feeling scared. And I remember the feelings of loss and loneliness taking over, which made me paranoid. I stopped eating and looking after myself. I lost a lot of weight and fell ill. At first I blamed the drink until I realised...' she hesitated, 'until I realised I was pregnant,' she said, looking at him.

Shocked, he raised his eyes to meet hers.

Nancy smiled as she watched.

'At first, I was excited. I had something inside me that tied us together. So, stupidly, I drove to your university to tell you. I was drunk of course, constantly drunk, and I shouldn't have driven, but I just wanted to see you,' she said, looking at Sebastian's perplexed expression. 'I'm not proud of what I did, Seb, not proud of any of it, but I was nineteen and scared shitless and you'd pissed off!' She paused.

'You weren't in when I arrived, so I waited for you in my car, and when I saw you walking towards your flat with Matilda, the penny dropped. It hadn't crossed my mind, you see, that you had met someone else,' she said, recalling the feeling of devastation she felt at the time. 'God knows why. I remember watching you walk towards my car, praying you wouldn't see me. Luckily, you were too engrossed and you walked straight past; you were that close I could have reached out and touched you. I remember sitting there, like an idiot, crying, before eventually I pulled myself together and left, feeling utterly pathetic. So I never told you what I drove all that way to tell you and by the time I got home I'd decided what I was going to do, and that you were never to find out.' Meggie paused.

'It wasn't until I felt the baby move that I believed it was actually happening, by which time I was almost halfway through the pregnancy. Without you, there was absolutely no way I wanted your baby, Seb,' Meggie stated, shaking her head, 'and realistically, I couldn't look after myself let alone another human being. So I went to the pub, and whilst I pitied myself, I told Nancy I was pregnant with your child and that I was addicted to alcohol,' she said, pausing to compose herself. 'Nancy was kind to me, and we talked about what I was going to do. I had no one else to talk to, and there was no way I was going to tell my parents. I hid it from them by staying away. They never knew,' she said, quietly. 'It was Nancy's suggestion I should go and see your mum and dad.'

At the mention of his parents, Sebastian looked up at her sharply.

~

Henry read...

> ...*When she arrived, she looked terrible. And then, when she took her coat off, we could see she was pregnant.*
>
> *When Meggie told us what had happened and that the baby was yours, Sebastian, and that you had met someone else, we felt sorry for the situation in which she found herself. She was just a child and needed help.*
>
> *Initially she told us she was going to have an abortion. We didn't try to talk her out of it, whatever she did had to be her own choice, but when we found out how many weeks pregnant she was, we asked her to think very carefully before making a decision. We pleaded with her to tell you before doing anything, but she was determined you should never know. She did not want you to cloud her judgement and she didn't want two lives ruined or you in her life just because she was having your child. We had to respect her wishes.*
>
> *We begged her to tell her parents but she refused. She was adamant we were the only ones to know...*

~

Sebastian listened...

'...Your parents were unbelievably kind to me, Seb,' Meggie said looking at the desolation on his face, 'and they helped. I owe them a great deal. I know it was unfair, but at the time, I made them promise not to tell you, convincing them that I would tell you myself when the time was right. I can't believe they kept the secret. They are good people.'

~

> ... *After a lot of soul searching, she talked herself out of an abortion, thankfully. It would have been horrific for*

her. So, she was left with two options, either to keep the baby or have it adopted, and we knew she was too ill to keep it, but she went away to think.

The reason Meggie came to see us was because, by chance, she had met Nancy, and it was through Meggie that Nancy crept back into our lives, all-be-it, briefly. We didn't tell you because as ever, where Nancy was concerned, trouble followed.

Our wonderful boys, this is where we hope you will understand.

~

'... So, with their support I continued with the pregnancy, and thirty years ago yesterday, I gave birth, in Edinburgh, to a baby girl. Your parents were wonderful; they took care of us until the baby was ready to go. I called our little girl, Florence,' she said.

~

...When Meggie told Nancy she had decided to have the baby adopted, Nancy came up with an alternative solution which was that she and Jacob could take the baby and care for her until Meggie was well enough to care for her herself.

We knew why she suggested it, which I will explain later in this letter, but it was NOT a solution we wanted, far from it. However, as was Nancy's way, she worked on Meggie and persuaded her it was a good idea and no matter how much we tried, and believe me, we did, there was nothing we could do to stop them going ahead.

This was when we should have broken our promise to Meggie and told you. Perhaps then you could have done something, but we hoped once the baby was in Meggie's arms she might change her mind and not go through with the plan, but that was not to be. Please forgive us.

Meggie and Nancy arranged that when the baby was born, she would go and live with Nancy and Jacob whilst Meggie sought treatment and got herself well again. Then, when the time was right, the baby would go back to Meggie. To the outside world it would seem a gift on Nancy's part, but your mother and I knew Nancy all too well and we were unsure about Jacob.

Meggie had the most beautiful baby, Sebastian; 7lbs 6ozs. She looked like you when you were born but even more like Meggie. She called her Florence.

Of course, we were played like puppets because as soon as Florence was handed over to Nancy, things changed, and as you might expect, it wasn't long before she and Jacob came to us asking for money.

What could we do? We were so entrenched, we could not live with the idea of Nancy and Jacob not looking after Florence properly, and although we knew it was wrong, we were desperate and they called the shots, so we paid.

The money was the easy part. We gave them what they asked for, but once we paid the first time they kept asking, and by then we knew we would never be able to tell you. That has been the hardest thing of all.

At first, Nancy was true to her word and kept in contact with Meggie and we visited her and Florence, just the once, before she went quiet again. We met in a park. Nancy had not told Jacob we were visiting. By the time Florence's first birthday came, we had no contact at all and, despite countless attempts on our part to get in touch, we heard nothing and we did not see or hear from them for six years.

Then we had one final communication, when your mum got a birthday card, out of the blue...

~

'... My daughter, who runs the café, is *your* daughter,' Meggie said. 'Nancy and Jacob looked after her until I was able to.'

Hardly able to believe what he was hearing, Sebastian looked between Nancy and Meggie. He had told Meggie everything; thirty years ago he had bared his soul, trusted her and yet, when she was faced with betrayal herself she had retreated, schemed, joined the enemy.

'Why didn't you tell me, Meggie? I would have been there for you. I would have helped,' he said, before turning to Nancy. 'And you and that *fucking* bastard?' he said quietly.

'You'd gone, Sebastian! You'd left me! It was *my* choice,' Meggie argued.

'And Mum and Dad, for *fuck's* sake... They were in on it as well,' he said, lowering his head into his hands.

'That's not how it was, Seb...' Meggie said before Nancy interrupted.

'We took her against Mum and Dad's wishes, if that helps. We did it to save your child from being adopted or aborted.'

'You *fucking* bitch!' Sebastian whispered, lifting his head to look at her cold eyes.

'And if it's any consolation that 'fucking bastard' as you called him, didn't stick around long. He left after the accident when Florence and I became too difficult to look after,' Nancy said, and for the first time, Sebastian could hear a touch of emotion in her voice.

After a moment Meggie continued to talk, reluctantly...

~

... Inside the card was a photograph of her, Jacob and Florence, accompanied by a letter asking for more money, a regular payment this time, and as ever, a promise of keeping in touch. We agreed to pay, of course, in the hope we might see them again one day, but it was the last picture we received and the last time we heard from Nancy. Who knows why, perhaps her fortunes changed...

Henry read as he reached for the photograph that had fallen from his mother's book and looked at the little girl; Sebastian's little girl, *'Florence, aged 6 years 9 months.'*

... Today is Florence's 18th birthday, and hoping she will be grown up and independent, we have finally stopped the payments...

~

Sebastian listened as Meggie continued...

'... I couldn't care for a baby, Seb. I just wanted it out of me and gone and Nancy was very persuasive,' she said, as Nancy sat, smiling. 'I believed her when she said I could be a part of Florence's life, but it didn't work out, and I didn't see her for the first eight years. Then, after Nancy's accident, as you know, our paths crossed again and it's thanks to Stefan that Florence came back into my life.'

Nancy shifted her gaze away from Sebastian and towards the window, looking out at the wind-rippled water. It had been Jacob's idea to take the child, one that she had unwillingly gone along with. But as time passed and she failed to hold onto her own pregnancies, she grew to love Florence. She knew that one day she would have to give her back, but she couldn't let her go. When she lost her baby, so late in her pregnancy, the grief overwhelmed her and then, when she met Meggie again, she knew she had reached the end of the line. It was Stefan who made her look at herself and see what she had done to Meggie.

'It took almost four years to get to know her and to win her trust, but finally, when Florence was twelve, Nancy and Stefan came back to Switzerland to live, and Florence stayed in England with me and Aled, before going to study in Edinburgh. And now she runs the café and lives there and we come here once a year, on Florence's birthday.'

'Where is she now?' Sebastian asked, struggling to come to terms with what he was hearing.

'She's gone to meet a friend, she'll be back later,' Meggie replied.

Sebastian looked at her contemptuously. 'And she's been living in Edinburgh, right under our noses,' he said bitterly, 'so close to Mum and Dad.'

Meggie looked at him. 'I'm so sorry, Seb. Your mum and dad didn't deserve to be put in the position I put them in. I led them into the lion's den and they had no choice other than to follow,' Meggie confessed. 'I wish I'd kept in touch but...' Hesitating, she stopped speaking, following Nancy's gaze towards the mountains. She sighed. 'Despite not having touched a drop of alcohol since meeting Aled,' she said quietly, 'I am still an alcoholic. I struggle with it every day. When I needed help, your mum and dad were there. They tried to warn me about ...' she paused, looking at Nancy, '...but I wouldn't listen. Don't be angry with them, please,' she said finally.

Nancy turned to look at Meggie. It was obvious there was no love lost between the two women.

After meeting Stefan, Nancy had reluctantly accepted Meggie back into her life, but she found her naivety irritating. She was too trusting. Nancy believed her parents had been much the same and so easily manipulated. She believed they deserved everything they got and, with no intention of sharing her life with them, she took as much as they were prepared to give. When Florence stayed in England, she continued to take their money, justifying it as reparation for all the years she had felt sidelined.

~

... So there it is, that is all we know. I don't know how long we will outlive this letter but I guess, if things change, I will tear it up and write a new one, but if you're reading this one, nothing has changed and we will have not seen Nancy or Florence since a year after Meggie took her and placed her in Nancy's arms.

Meggie kept in touch for a while, as she promised she would, but Nancy soon shut her out and we lost contact. We hope and pray Meggie has found a way to come to terms with the choice she made and that she and Florence were reunited. We were all cheated, you especially, Sebastian.

Before we end there are a couple of things we want you to think about. Firstly, this letter is purposefully attached to our wills, which are identical. What is mine is your mother's and what is your mother's is mine, and what is left after we have both gone is yours to share. There's plenty of money. We invested wisely and Taligth and the land is worth a lot, unless, of course, one of you wishes to pick up the reins and take it on.

We know the money will not make things right, Sebastian. We just hope you have it in your heart to forgive us and perhaps find Florence and get to know the woman she has become. We hope she is happy. For you Henry, our money could change your life.

We have not included Nancy in our wills. As far as we are concerned, she had her inheritance over the years since she took Florence. However, if, after we have gone, you wish to give her something, then that is up to you, but we do not expect you to. Talk about it and agree between you but please do not fall out over it.

This letter has turned into a ramble. There was so much to say and it was difficult to get it right, but please take with you the following – we are eternally grateful we had the privilege of having you in our lives. We have loved you both more than words can say, and we will take that love to the grave with us and we will watch over you from afar.

I wonder which one of us went first. Hopefully it was me, I know I won't want to stick around once your mother has gone.

Isn't it strange how we know everything about our lives other than the very beginning and the very end? So, until we are together again...

With our deepest and heartfelt love,

Mum and Dad x

PS. There is one final thing we need to tell you, about Nancy...

Shocked, Henry read the letter to the end. No wonder their father had become a shadow after their mother died. Desperate to speak with Sebastian, he searched for him on his phone but, seeing he was still at Nancy's apartment, he did not want to call him there. It was getting late. He would keep checking and wait until Sebastian left. In the meantime, he grabbed all the papers from his parents' document case and dug amongst the certificates in search of evidence.

~

Looking from Meggie to Nancy, Sebastian took the advice he had given himself earlier and said nothing more. He sat in silence, processing what he had just heard.

With the two women opposite him, waiting, he tried to read them. Meggie was sitting forward, forearms on her knees, hands clasped, whilst Nancy was sitting back, relaxed, hands resting comfortably in her lap as she stared out of the window; they could not have been more antithetical.

Eventually he broke the silence. 'I'm going to leave,' he said, standing. 'I have heard everything you have told me, Meggie, but before I say anything, I need time to think.'

'Of course,' Meggie said softy, understanding.

'I think it's all fairly clear, Sebastian,' came Nancy's strident voice, as she sat up straight, returning her eyes to his. 'You got Meggie pregnant and I looked after your baby which meant you and Meggie got to live your lives. Looking back on it, I have to wonder who the mug was in this game. It was neither easy nor cheap bringing up a child. It cost a great deal, both emotionally and financially.'

'You were paid, Nancy!' Meggie suddenly announced, bravely.

'Who paid you?' Sebastian asked.

'Mum and Dad of course,' Nancy answered quickly, looking at Meggie, her eyes telling her to say no more. 'They supported your child, Sebastian. Ask Dad, I'm sure he will explain the financial arrangement to you.'

Looking at his sister, Sebastian could not help but loathe her. The child who had scratched her little brother so deeply across his face that he still bore the scar, was lurking just beneath her adult skin, smirking at the pain she always managed to inflict.

Picking up his coat and bag, Sebastian started to leave. Nancy made no attempt to move from the recline of her sofa. She went back to looking out towards the evening lights of the apartments surrounding the lake. By night, the view from the window took on a completely different atmosphere. It was her favourite time of day.

'Can we meet to talk?' Meggie asked, following Sebastian to the door. 'Not here. In town, tomorrow.' Meggie looked behind her to check Nancy had not followed them.

'The way I feel at the moment, Meggie, I can hardly bear to look at you,' Sebastian replied, opening the door, instantly feeling the cooling breeze of the corridor outside. Drawn to the welcoming space, he stepped out, relieved to be leaving.

'I'm sorry,' Meggie said, watching him walk away.

With his back to her he stopped. He did not turn around but carried on again, saying nothing as he heard her close the door behind him. His head ached and he wanted to get to his hotel. He had gone to Switzerland expecting to tell Nancy the news about their parents; he had wanted to talk about the day he was raped; he had hoped to find her a changed person; but she had denied him. She was still a monster. He had been so driven by his own desire to move on, to make peace and draw a line that he had been blinkered.

Calling a taxi, Sebastian walked up the sleepy road. It was exceptionally dark and wonderfully quiet and cold, and he was glad to be outside. As he turned away from the lake and walked up the hill, a car indicated off the top road and made its way towards the lakeside apartments. As it came towards him, Sebastian glanced at the driver, catching her eye for an instant as she looked directly at him and smiled.

349

For the briefest of moments, he thought he was looking back at Meggie.

Day Thirty

Waiting for Sebastian to return to his hotel, Henry fell asleep on the sofa and awoke hours later cold and stiff with his phone on his chest, the contents of the document case littered across the living room floor and the certificate he had been searching for held tightly in his hand. Sitting up, he forced himself awake, blinking against the bright light of his phone, trying to get his eyes to focus on the screen. It was 6 a.m. He pressed for messages; there were none. Certain Sebastian would be awake, Henry called his number, hanging on, listening to the rhythm of the phone's unanswered melody. He would try again later.

~

Sebastian took a long shower. Standing beneath the warm, pulsating stream, he let his head fall forward and the water flow down his back as his mind went over and over the events of the previous day again.

He found it remarkable that he had known nothing of what had happened and how difficult it must have been for his parents to keep their promise to Meggie until the day they died. He remembered staying away from Taligth after leaving for university, his childhood home having been infected by the horrific events of that day. He remembered that first summer, choosing to take off and spend it with Matilda, bumming around fruit farms, earning their passage across Europe before going back to university to continue their studies. If he had gone home, things might have been different.

Over the years, although scars remained, the wounds healed, and the pain dulled. After university, he and Matilda went back to Edinburgh to start their life together. Spending time with his parents at Taligth, which he had come to forgive, how had it stayed a secret? How had there not been a slip of the tongue, a misplaced letter, the drop of a name, something, anything to give it away? Perhaps over the years there had been many, but he hadn't been looking or listening for such things and any hints had gone unnoticed.

As the heat of the water rose and stole the air, he started to feel stifled; the image of Meggie crying disturbed him. And Nancy, her eyes so clearly full of resentment and sufferance, told him that she harboured terrible pain. What was it about her that was so commanding? That even after all these years of invidiousness, he felt pity for her. There was still so much he needed to say. Turning the water off, he opened the door, releasing the steam into the room to settle on the cold surfaces of the mirrors and grey slate tiles. He was hot and agitated and knew he could not leave without seeing her one last time.

Dressed, he packed his bag thinking about Meggie and the secret she had kept from him. He wondered how she and Nancy may have looked at one another when he had left, and what words were spoken. Sitting on the corner of the bed, rearranging his flight home for later that day, his mind turned to Matilda and the light he saw switched on in their bedroom window when he had left the previous morning. What damage he had caused, he thought. Would she be there when he got home? And then there was Henry.

~

Staying in the shower until it ran cold, Henry could not get the letter out of his head.

Turning the water off, he could hear the house telephone trilling through the walls. Hurriedly, he grabbed a towel from the hook and wrapped it around his waist. Pulling back the sodden curtain, he clambered out of the old, cast iron bath. He ran, flat footed, stumbling his way out of the bathroom and onto the landing, where, his parents having replaced the worn out carpet with smooth oak flooring a few months before, he lost his footing and aquaplaned across the shiny floorboards. Taking a sharp left turn down the first flight of unforgiving wooden stairs, he landed heavily on his bare backside. Grabbing his towel, he scrambled back up to answer the ringing phone.

'Sebastian?' he panted into the phone, water from his wet hair dripping down his face.

'Henry?'

~

With the sun rising over the city, Sebastian checked out of the hotel and walked onto the pavement where he waited for the taxi to arrive. It was a beautiful, bright start to the day and the sun, though devoid of strength, was welcome on his face. He telephoned Taligth… the phone was engaged.

Looking up and down the narrow street, he would have liked to be visiting the city under different circumstances. It was a city that had been on their list for when he and Matilda had more time to spend together. He was interested in its importance to the world economy and he would have liked to have seen the United Nations offices. But now the city was tainted and he no longer desired to spend any more time in it than absolutely necessary.

From the taxi he called both Henry's mobile and the house phone, which was still engaged. He left a message.

~

'Nancy!' Henry answered, her voice instantly recognisable.

'Sorry for the early morning call,' Nancy said, as if it were only yesterday when she and Henry last spoke, 'may I speak with Dad?' Henry did not reply. Trying to catch his breath he stood naked. 'Have I caught you at a bad time?' she asked.

'I was in the shower,' he stuttered.

'You're aware Sebastian came to see me yesterday I presume?' she asked, a little warmth in her voice. 'I was sorry to hear the sad news. How are you?'

'I'm okay,' Henry replied, covering himself up and moving into the bedroom, sitting on his bed.

'Did Sebastian go home last night, or has he stayed in Geneva, do you know?'

'He's due back tomorrow.'

'I thought he might have taken the first flight out of here. He left in a terrible state.'

'What happened?' Henry asked, feeling anxious that he had not spoken to Sebastian.

'Rather a lot I'm afraid. I should imagine he will have been exhausted. I certainly was. May I ask something, Henry? How was Dad after Mum died?'

'Why do you want to know?' Henry asked, defensive of his parents. He was not about to let Nancy denigrate them in any way. Unable to protect them from her when they were alive, the least he could do was protect them now they were dead. 'Why are you phoning?' he asked coldly.

'To speak with Dad. Is he there?' Taking time to compose himself, Henry said nothing. 'Henry?'

'Sebastian didn't tell you, did he?'

'Didn't tell me what?' Again, Henry went silent, the rawness of his loss searing through him as he fought against the constriction in his throat. 'Henry!' Nancy repeated, forcefully, 'what did Sebastian not tell me yesterday?' Henry pulled the damp towel tighter around his thin body. He remained silent. 'For god's sake, Henry!' Nancy snapped, raising her voice in irritation, 'stop being annoying! What did Sebastian not tell me?'

'He didn't tell you about Dad?'

'What about Dad? Oh, don't tell me he's gone and popped his clogs now as well? God! Leave you boys in charge of the olds for five minutes...' she said flippantly, laughing at the absurdity of her own joke.

Henry's silence ran down the line, answering Nancy's question.

'Oh!' Nancy said, abruptly. 'Am I right?' With his hand gripping the phone, Henry sat stock still like some kind of strange modernistic monument dedicated to Alexander Graham Bell. 'Are you still there, Henry?' she asked.

~

Giving the taxi driver more than he would earn in a week, Sebastian asked him to stay parked up on the top road so that he could make a quick getaway. Leaving his bag in the car, he walked down the hill towards Nancy's apartment. In front of him the morning sun reflected off the tranquil lake, rippling softly under the gentle breeze making the surface glisten.

Before entering the apartment he called Henry once more, but the line remained busy. He left another message. Then he switched his phone off and buzzed the intercom to alert the concierge of his arrival.

~

'Henry!' Nancy barked.

'Sebastian was meant to tell you yesterday,' Henry said, wishing for the line to go dead.

'I'm afraid I didn't give him much opportunity. We didn't part on very good terms. I'm sure he will fill you in when he gets home. Now tell me about...' she started to say, but she stopped speaking and, down the line, Henry could hear the faint sound of her doorbell ringing. 'I have someone at my door... sorry,' she huffed and, as he had wished, the line went dead.

'SHIT!' Henry shouted, launching the phone across the room, its batteries somersaulting out of their compartment as it rebounded off the wall and landed in pieces in the fireplace. 'SHIT, shit, shit!' he repeated, standing up from the bed, his towel collapsing at his feet. Reaching across to his bedside table for his mobile phone, he called Sebastian once more. The automated voice instructed him to leave a message, which he did, asking Sebastian to call him back before doing anything else. He needed to put him in the picture, though he sensed he was probably too late.

Once dressed, he retrieved the house telephone from the fireplace and reunited it with its batteries. Checking for a dial tone he heard the familiar beep of the answering machine and listened to Sebastian's message.

~

'If it's Meggie you're after, I'm afraid you've missed her,' Nancy said, leading Sebastian back into the bright sitting room they had been in a few hours before. 'She left last night.'

'She left?'

'I suppose there wasn't a great deal she and I had left to say to one another. What we once had, had come to an end. She and Florence weren't due to be flying back until tomorrow, but I guess after the events of yesterday, things changed and just as I was going to bed she left, just like that,' she said, clicking her fingers in the air. 'Florence is still here though. Can I get you a drink?' she asked, walking into the kitchen.

Sebastian stood looking out of the window towards the lake, wondering what words had passed between the two women to make Meggie leave, alone, without saying anything to him, no message, no phone call.

'I'm glad Meggie left,' Nancy called from the kitchen. 'I don't particularly appreciate the café being closed this long, but she does insist on coming over with Florence every birthday.'

'What have you got to do with the café?' Sebastian asked, bemused.

'I own it.'

'I thought Florence owned it?'

'No, Florence rents it from me. I bought it as an investment when she went to university. And then, when she decided to settle in Edinburgh, she needed a job and somewhere to live so it made sense. It makes her a decent living and she uses it to promote her artwork, so she doesn't do badly from it, and it keeps us connected.'

Sebastian thought about the prospect of meeting Florence; unsure of how he felt towards this person who was his but not his, and who Nancy had a closer connection to than he did.

'I've had a rather lovely conversation with Henry this morning,' Nancy said, bringing in the coffee. Sebastian turned towards her in surprise. 'Don't worry, I didn't say anything, I thought you'd want to talk things through with him yourself rather than him hear it from me.'

'Why did you call him?'

'I didn't, I phoned hoping to speak to Dad,' she said, placing the tray onto the low table between the two sofas. 'You don't take sugar do you?'

Sebastian watched as she pincered two tiny lumps of natural sugar into her coffee before sitting down. She was immaculate, he thought, as he examined her. The piercings from her teenage years healed, the rebellious tattoos covered up or removed perhaps, and her painted nails drew his eyes to her thin fingers elongated by rings housing weighty diamonds. She clearly paid meticulous attention to herself.

'I'm afraid I caught your brother rather unawares,' Nancy said. 'Still the same old Henry; he's not changed one bit, has he? I found him intensely irritating when we were children and for the few minutes we were on the telephone he managed to annoy me again,' she laughed. 'Luckily for me, you interrupted our scintillating conversation; the little there was of it. He's terribly awkward, isn't he?' Sebastian defended Henry with his silence. Looking at her brother, Nancy hesitated. 'Why are you here again, Sebastian?' she asked, sighing deeply. 'I would have thought we said all we needed to say last night. I appreciate you'll have had a lot to think about and perhaps some questions, but nothing Meggie cannot answer, unless, of course, there's something else you wish to discuss,' she added pointedly, watching Sebastian's face, the sight of someone who had been snared by his memories.

Sitting down, Sebastian wanted the conversation over. 'You know why I'm here,' he said, getting to the point. 'I need to talk about what happened... the day you left Taligth.'

'Right,' she said, preparing.

'And why you left.'

Gathering her thoughts, Nancy paused, looking out of the window first, then looking back at Sebastian. 'What is it you want to know?' she asked.

~

Henry went downstairs and into the front room. He collected up the strewn contents of the document case, putting the papers back where they belonged, his parents' lives housed in a case no deeper than his thumb. Birth certificates, marriage certificate, the deeds to the farm, insurance documents for the cars, bank statements, stocks and shares certificates and newspaper cuttings. Even his, Sebastian's and Nancy's little blue Post Office savings books they had opened when they were children, now empty, but at one time full of weekly 10p deposits.

Once again, he looked at the certificate he had searched out the night before and separated from the rest. Taking it with him, back in the kitchen, he felt exhausted. His head was foggy and he couldn't concentrate. But there was still so much to organise for the production, and Lorna and the team were due to arrive in a couple of days. There were also things he needed to sort out for his father's funeral. 'Two performances in one day,' he said to Betsy, looking at her through the window whilst filling the kettle. 'You couldn't write it, could you,' he sighed, thinking about the ridiculousness of it all. 'Perhaps one day I will.' Betsy lifted her snout and looked up at him, her jaw moving side to side as she caught his eye. 'Ah, so, you think it's a good idea, do you?' For the first time that morning, Henry smiled.

Wrapped in his father's coat, with his parents' letter in the pocket, he took his cup of tea and marmite toast out into the yard and, as his father had done, joined Betsy for breakfast. He wanted to read the end of the letter again. Betsy settled down on her fresh bed of straw, enjoying the feel of the morning sun as it flooded across her back.

~

'I need to understand why you didn't help me that day,' Sebastian said.

'As far as I can recall, you didn't need any help,' Nancy replied.

'You and I both know that's not true!'

Nancy sighed heavily. 'Have you let it trouble you all these years?' she asked quietly.

'I've learned to live with it.'

Moved, Nancy sat looking at Sebastian, remembering the unendurable sight of his eyes pleading for help. She sighed, and as she started to speak, she felt intense sadness for him.

'Having spent a small fortune on therapy, I am gratified to know I can put it to good use at last. So, let me tell you how it was,' she said, rare tenderness in her voice. 'Then perhaps you will leave me alone.' Sebastian nodded.

'As you know, I was not an easy child. I cannot excuse my precocious behaviour of course, but perhaps, as an adult, knowing what I now know, I can understand it. I can't remember much of my early childhood, obviously, but I know I was different. Looking back on it now, I suppose I thought that was just the way it was.' Nancy paused. 'They were making allowances, you see.' Hurt by her own words, she paused again. 'Then when you came along, Mum struggled to cope and, more or less, handed you over to me. I remember the feeling of love I had for you, and the joy that she trusted me to look after you. She must have loved me to do that, don't you think?' she asked. 'But then, Henry came along, and things changed and I was shut out. Which was why, from a very young age, I worked out that I had to up my game if I was to get what I wanted. I remember feeling intense jealousy for the attention you and Henry received. I was desperate for the love I didn't get,' she said, stopping and looking at Sebastian's confused expression. 'That's just a bit of background which might help you understand my subsequent actions,' she added, the tiniest chink in her armour opening. 'Unfortunately for you, I found out a lot about myself on my birthday which blew my twenty-one-year-old mind.'

Sebastian looked up.

'I have known you all your life, Sebastian, but you have not known me all of mine. I watched you growing as our mother's tummy swelled, held you when you were a few hours old. You, on the other hand, had not witnessed the same, no fault of your own of course, but all the same you had not watched our mother's tummy swell, you had not been there when I was born or held me when I was a few hours old, and you did not look into my eyes. If you had, you would have seen they were not our mother's eyes, or our father's. It never, for one moment occurred to me, you see.' She paused. 'Have you looked at your birth certificate?'

'Of course.'

'It's got your name on, hasn't it? And the names of both of your parents.'

'What's this all about?'

'Have you ever looked at mine?'

'I came across a copy of it recently, but I didn't look at it. What's this all about?' he asked again.

'If you had looked at that certificate you would have seen a difference between yours and mine, other than the obvious. You would have seen that we have different parents,' Nancy announced. Sebastian froze. 'I'm glad you're shocked,' she said, smiling, 'I felt the same when I found out. You see, Jacob wanted us to go away and I needed a passport, so I asked for my birth certificate. In fact, I had asked several times before I took it upon myself to look in Mum and Dad's document case. Can you imagine Mum's face when I came down the stairs with my birth certificate in my hand? It ruined what could have been a very nice day. How they could ever have thought I'd never find out, god only knows. So, of course they had to sit me down and tell me the whole story,' she said.

Sebastian listened...

~

Taking the letter out of his pocket, shuffling the pages to get to the last one, Henry re-read his father's words...

>PS. There is one final thing we need to tell you, about Nancy...
>
>There is no easy way to say this, so I am just going to get on with it.
>
>Nancy is not our first-born, Sebastian, you are. Nancy is not your sister, she is your cousin, my sister's child.
>
>Had we known how she would have turned out, we might not have agreed to take her, but when she was brought to us, a babe in arms, so sweet, so innocent, how could we not help? And that is what we were asked to do, help.
>
>Back then, it was not acceptable to have a child out of wedlock, not like it is today. It brought disgrace to the family and shame on the girl 'caught out'. So, when my sister, Lily, got pregnant at fourteen, you can imagine the reaction of Granny and Grandad Campbell.
>
>She was sent away from our family home in London, to stay with our grandparents in Southend-on-Sea to have the baby before going back home and continuing school as if nothing had happened.
>
>Your mum and I had only been married a few months. We were living here, at Taligth, and were not planning to have children until we were more settled, but Granny could not bear the idea of Lily's baby being adopted, so she asked us if we would take her, just for a while.
>
>We agreed, on the understanding that she would go back to Lily when we had our first child. By the time she

could crawl, we rather hoped that day would come sooner rather than later, but then Lily fell ill.

Sadly, when she was seventeen, Lily was diagnosed with leukemia and died when she was eighteen and Nancy was four. Of course, it meant Nancy was left with us. It was hoped one day she would live with Granny and Grandad and they had promised to tell her about her mother, but as Nancy's behaviour worsened that day never came.

She couldn't go to her father because Lily had refused to tell us who he was, some schoolboy we suspect. Lily took his name to the grave with her so where her father's name should have been, Nancy's birth certificate was left blank.

Nancy found out the truth on the morning of her twenty-first birthday. She did not take it well and said some very hurtful things to your mother, which could never be unsaid. I wish I had been at home at the time. Your mother was very upset, which is why she took Henry out to the shops. Whilst she and Henry were out, Nancy and Jacob left. Nancy never returned to Taligth.

We believe Jacob was behind a lot of what Nancy did (or didn't do) around that time and we were terribly worried for her, but what could we do? She made her feelings very clear.

We have always believed that what was done to her was one of the reasons why she took Florence, but we will never know.

We tried to do right by her, but ultimately, we failed. We have always felt guilty for not loving her the way we loved the two of you, but she made it very difficult.

So that's the lot, you know everything now.

X

Folding the letter back into its envelope and sliding it into his pocket alongside Nancy's birth certificate, Henry sighed.

~

'So, there you have it, you know now,' Nancy said. 'As you'd imagine, I didn't take it well, and I remember Mum, sitting there, calmly taking the abuse I gave her. But I'm glad I found out, it explained so much. Jacob was very upset for me.'

Taking in what Nancy had told him, Sebastian swallowed hard. 'And he took it out on me,' he said, looking at her. Nancy did not respond. 'I cannot pretend to understand how you must have been feeling that morning,' he continued, 'but I need to know...'

'What is it you need to know?' Nancy interrupted sharply.

'I need to know, *seeing* what that *bastard* was doing to me, why you didn't *stop* him?'

Nancy did not answer straight away but stood up from the sofa and walked to the window. Looking out to the lake, she spoke deeply, slowly, articulating every word. 'I knew exactly what he was doing to you,' she said. 'I saw your face, your tears, the sick... and I saw *his* face too, his eyes boring into mine as he took away your innocence, the innocence of my brother, who I had just found out was not my brother, and who, inside his head, was crying for his mother, the *pathetic* woman who had looked at her first born with *such* love in her heart, in a way she had *never* once looked at me. It was all so very clear.' She looked across the water to the freedom of the mountains, a reluctant tear falling down her face. 'I couldn't help you, Sebastian, because I was too damaged to fight for you. All I could do was walk away, hoping he would stop, which he did. Then he forced me to leave.'

'I was seventeen for *fuck's* sake, just a *boy!*'

'You were a *man!*' Nancy suddenly snapped, spitting out the words.

'A *boy!* A seventeen-year-old *boy* being *raped* by *your* boyfriend in front of *your* eyes and you did *nothing* to stop him. What sort of a person does that?'

'I was *scared!*'

'Yes, and you sunk back into the darkness of the room and hid, you *fucking*, *cowardly bitch*!' Sebastian said, standing up.

Nancy began to laugh. 'It wasn't up to me to protect you, Sebastian.'

'Why are you laughing? What the hell is there to laugh about?' he yelled, going over to her and turning her by the shoulder so she was facing him. 'He was hurting me, *ripping* my insides so badly I bled for days after and you think it's *funny*!' Sebastian snarled, his head pulsing with anger.

'OF COURSE I DON'T THINK IT'S FUNNY!' Nancy shrieked, inches away from his face. 'But I was scared stiff of losing him!' she shouted, swiping angrily at her tears with the back of her hand. 'I would have done *anything* to keep him!'

'SHIT!' Sebastian exclaimed turning away and lashing out at his coffee cup, sending it flying across the room, smashing it against the clean white wall leaving coffee dripping down to the floor.

Nancy screamed.

'YOU'RE AS BAD AS HE IS!' he yelled. 'I did what he told me to do to *protect* you, but you were *ALLOWING* him. You were standing there, watching him do that to me and you *turned your back*...' Nancy did not react. 'You *fucking*, heartless *bitch*! How could you?' Sebastian spat, 'and as if that wasn't bad enough, then you took Florence!'

'What has Florence got to do with it?' Nancy retorted. 'What did I do that was *so* wrong you had to take her?'

'Taking on Florence was Jacob's idea and I went along with it,' she snarled, 'and we didn't take her away from *you*, you'd never have had her. We took her from Mum and Dad,' she said bitterly.

Stunned silence slammed into the room and hung, stretched between them for a few drawn out minutes.

Sebastian was done, spent, ready to go, happy to leave, but before either of them had chance to speak again, the doorbell rang.

Nancy did not move at first. Then, sighing, she walked casually to the mirror and, her demeanour changing, checked her face, smiling, before walking to the door. 'Unless I am mistaken,' she said, calmly, the words trailing behind her, 'you are about to meet your daughter.'

As if in slow motion, Sebastian watched as Nancy walked away from him. Answering the door, she opened it wide, revealing the image of a younger Meggie standing in its threshold.

Sebastian saw that Florence had noticed him. She'd been about to step inside but had stopped herself the instant she saw him, a stranger in Nancy's sitting room. He could tell she had noted the smashed cup on the floor and the coffee stain, like a modern art installation, adorning the wall.

'Have I interrupted something?' she asked, looking from Nancy to Sebastian and back again.

'No, you're fine,' Nancy replied coldly, walking back into the room. 'He's about to leave.'

Sebastian struggled to know what to do. This stranger standing in front of him was his and Meggie's child, and he did not know her. Given the situation and the argument he had just had with Nancy, he could either make his excuses and leave, allowing himself time to come to terms with everything he had heard, or he could speak and let the situation play out.

'Hi,' he said, 'I'm Sebastian, Nancy's brother.'

Nancy sighed. 'Sebastian is the one who owns Tatch-A and those hair bobbles you used to love so much,' she added.

'Oh,' Florence said, 'yes, I had rather a lot when I was younger. It's nice to meet you. Are you staying long?'

'I'm not,' Sebastian replied. 'I'm just leaving, actually. I'm booked on a flight back to Edinburgh this afternoon,' he said, studying Florence's face.

'Ah, well that's what I came to tell you, Nancy. Mum messaged me to say she's gone?' she said with a quizzical look on her face. 'Have you two fallen out again?' Nancy did not answer. Lightheartedly, Florence rolled her eyes and sighed. 'Anyway, I've decided to go back today, if that's okay with you? I've booked us on the five-twenty. Would you mind giving us a lift?'

'Why didn't you check with me before you booked your flight? I'm busy this afternoon. You'll have to get a taxi.'

Sebastian stood thinking about the taxi he had waiting at the top of the road. 'I believe we might be on the same flight,' he said.

'Really?' Florence asked.

'Unless there's another one going to Edinburgh at the same time?' Sebastian said, smiling at Florence. 'I have a taxi waiting for me, you're more than welcome to share it.'

'Oh no, thank you, it's fine, we have a lot of stuff,' Florence replied, courteously.

Nancy turned to look at the two of them standing in front of her, speaking so politely. How tempted she was to take the pin out of the grenade and lob it, but she resisted.

'Allow him,' Nancy told Florence. 'I presume we are finished here?' she added coldly, looking at Sebastian.

'We are,' he replied emphatically, having heard enough. 'I'm sure the taxi's big enough to fit everything in,' he said to Florence. 'I'll wait for you at the top of the road. Take as long as you need.'

'Well, if you don't mind. That's very kind of you. Thank you,' Florence replied.

'Enjoy getting to know one another,' Nancy said.

'I'll go and get Nellie sorted,' Florence said, heading to the door.

'Where is she?' Sebastian asked, following her.

'She's having a nap in my apartment. Don't worry, I have a monitor,' she said, waving her phone. Opening the door, Florence walked into the corridor before turning to say goodbye to Nancy.

'Oh, Florence, before you go,' Nancy said, walking up to Sebastian, who was standing in the doorway. She rested her hand on Sebastian's arm. 'Be kind to my brother. Both our parents have just died. That's why he came to see me,' she said, smiling insincerely, perfectly aware of the impact of her words.

Florence looked at Sebastian. 'I'm so sorry to hear that,' she said kindly. 'Listen, I'll leave you two to say goodbye. I'll meet you at the taxi,' she said to Sebastian, as she walked away.

Sebastian turned to Nancy. 'How did you find out?'

'I guessed, when I was on the phone to Henry and he was being *pathetic*,' Nancy sneered.

'God, you're horrible!'

Nancy laughed. 'I don't disagree with you, Sebastian,' she said. 'Do enjoy your trip back and, just so you're aware,' she said, leaning on the open door frame, her arms crossed, 'Florence knows everything, other than who her father is, so it's up to you whether you want to tell her or not. Matilda need never know,' she whispered, moving to close the door. Sebastian looked at her incredulously. 'Oh, and another thing,' she said quickly, 'you wanted to know how I found out about Mum. Well, just to clear things up, it was your friend, Paul...'

'Paul?' Sebastian interrupted, shocked to hear his name mentioned.

'Yes, Paul. He telephoned and told me. Take care,' she said, closing the door abruptly.

Dumbstruck, Sebastian stood in the corridor, staring at Nancy's front door. Desperate to know more, he knocked hard, demanding her return. 'Nancy!' he shouted. 'Nancy!' When Nancy did not come to the door, he knocked again, harder this time, drawing the attention of the concierge who moved to see what was happening. Nancy did not answer and eventually, reluctantly, with his head once again full of unanswered questions, Sebastian left.

Why would Paul contact Nancy? He asked himself as he walked away. He had no idea that Paul and Nancy still knew each other, and if they did, why had Paul never mentioned it? He knew that Paul had once had an adolescent crush on her, but that was just a schoolboy fantasy. Or was it? He thought that the last time Paul had seen Nancy was thirty years ago. Had he been wrong?

Florence was already loading the taxi by the time Sebastian reached it. The ride to the airport was cramped. Along with Florence and the baby, came bags, bottles, toys, nappies and a pram. With his mind still racing, Sebastian was more than happy to sit amongst the chaos, relieved to be getting away. However beautiful the place was, it had been poisoned.

During the flight he and Florence talked comfortably, as strangers who had an unexpected connection might. With Nellie grizzling and fidgeting in Florence's arms, they talked about Scotland and the Scottish art scene and where Florence saw herself in five, ten, fifteen years' time. They talked about the café and the people who went in and her friends who dropped by to see her. And they talked about Nancy. Florence described how she had been brought up for the first eight years of her life believing Nancy and Jacob were her parents. It wasn't until after Nancy's accident when Jacob left, leaving Nancy struggling, that Nancy met Stefan and things changed. It was then that Meggie came into her life and she found out the truth. It had taken Florence a long time to come to terms with it and to trust Nancy again, and even longer for her to get to know Meggie and to understand why she had seemingly abandoned her.

'But life's very short,' she said, 'and I grew to understand its complications. I'm still close to Nancy. She's an acquired taste but that's what I like about her. She taught me to be independent, which is why she didn't freak when I said I was pregnant with no intention of telling the father. She loves me, secretly, in spite of her telling me all the time I should be grateful she took me on.' She talked a lot about Nancy.

'That sounds like Nancy.'

'She can't cope with being loved, can she? How come you lost touch with each other?'

'Has she never told you?'

'Other than telling me you own Tatch-A, she's never talked about her family.'

Sebastian did his best to be honest. Thankfully Florence did not delve and he was able to avoid unanswerable questions. 'Do you know your mum's family?' he asked, intrigued she didn't mention them.

'No. I know her mum and dad got divorced and then her mum died, but she doesn't keep in contact with her dad.'

'That's a shame,' Sebastian said, remembering back to a time when he knew Meggie's parents.

As they prepared for landing, Sebastian asked one final question. 'Do you ever wonder who your real father is?'

'Never!' Florence answered definitively, handing Nellie to Sebastian as she packed Nellie's bag. 'I asked Mum once, when I was a curious teenager trying to work out who I was, and she told me he was just someone she'd known for a few months in her first year at university. That was all, no one special. A bit like Nellie's dad,' she said with a wry smile.

'So, you've never wanted to find him?'

'Never.'

'Will Nellie ever know who her father is?'

Florence shook her head. 'No, because I don't know who he is,' she whispered, smiling cheekily.

The plane taxied along the runway and the 'Welcome' sign of the terminal came into view. Sebastian helped Florence with Nellie as they disembarked, reuniting her with her pram at the bottom of the steps. It was early evening and despite having been fed for the majority of the journey, Nellie was unsettled. During the short walk to the terminal building, the jostle of the pram wheels over the tarmac soothed her and she finally fell asleep. Sebastian had enjoyed the feel of a baby in his arms. It had been a long time since he had held one so small.

'I'm getting a taxi home,' Sebastian said as they entered the arrivals lounge. 'We're going in the same direction. Would you like a lift?'

'If you wouldn't mind? Thank you so much.'

In arrivals, Florence disappeared into the toilets with Nellie whilst Sebastian waited. He switched his phone on for the first time since silencing it outside Nancy's apartment. He was faced with a screen full of messages. He looked forward to the day when he could switch on his phone and the only message was from his service provider, telling him he wasn't taking advantage of his monthly allowance and he might wish to consider a cheaper option.

Since the death of his father and in the few days he had been away, Sebastian had relied heavily on Niamh and Matilda to keep things going in the office, but there were some questions only he could answer. The final days before completion would be critical. Some messages needed quick replies while others warranted proper attention and answers he could not give sitting in Edinburgh airport. Those would have to wait until he could get into the office.

At the end of the list, a message from Matilda appeared on his screen. Prior to going into Nancy's apartment, he had messaged her. It was the third message he had sent without getting a reply, until now, when she said, unexpectedly, that she was waiting outside arrivals. How he was going to explain why Florence and Nellie were with him was something he was going to have to think about quickly.

Before Florence returned, he called Henry.

'Hal, how are you doing?'

'I'm okay,' Henry replied, relieved to hear his brother's voice. 'Where are you?'

'I'm at Edinburgh airport.'

'How come? What happened?'

'Too much!' Sebastian replied. 'Listen, I've only got a few minutes. How about I come over to Taligth in the morning?'

'Yeah, okay,' Henry replied.

'By the way,' Sebastian said, 'did you know that Paul was still in touch with Nancy?' he asked, hoping Henry might know something.

'Paul? No, how come?' Henry asked, as Sebastian, seeing Florence walking in the wrong direction across the concourse, quickly wrapped up the call. 'I'll explain tomorrow. Listen, I've got to go. Night, Hal...' he said and, lowering his phone to end the conversation, he called out to Florence, who had lost him in the crowd. 'Florence!' he called out, waving his arms in the air frantically trying to get her to see him, 'Florence!' He closed the line and Henry heard no more.

'Florence?' Henry said to himself. What the hell had gone on in Geneva?

~

At risk of being moved on by the officious attendant patrolling the area, Matilda was parked illegally outside the terminal doors. Florence and a pram bought her valuable, un-ticketed minutes to get the car loaded and Nellie safely in, unchallenged.

'I can explain. Let's just get home,' Sebastian said uneasily as Matilda stared at him when he got into the car after helping Florence. Recognising her from the café, Matilda did not respond. 'You'd better get a move on before the fun police see you,' Sebastian said, feeling the tension between them

'I really appreciate the lift, thank you so much,' Florence said, getting into the back and securing Nellie's car seat.

'You're welcome, Florence,' Matilda said, smiling weakly into her rearview mirror.

'Sebastian's told me a lot about you.'

'Has he?' Matilda replied, looking across to her husband as she negotiated her way out of the airport. Sebastian avoided eye contact.

'So, you're Meggie's daughter?' Matilda asked.

'I am.'

'What's your little girl's name?'

'Nellie.'

'Nellie,' Matilda repeated, looking in her rearview mirror at the baby sleeping in her car seat. 'That's a pretty name,' she said, looking across to Sebastian.

'It's a long story,' he said.

'I'm sure it is,' Matilda said stiffly, continuing to drive, looking in her mirror, examining Florence's face.

With the unease in the car palpable, Sebastian talked about how beautiful Geneva was and how the city sat so comfortably at the foot of the mountains and he talked about the contrast between the old and the new town. 'You'd love it,' he said, 'though I never want to go back, so you'll have to go on your own,' he added, laughing to himself nervously, but Matilda was not listening and the car settled into silence. 'Have you spoken with Henry?' he asked, eventually.

'Once, why? Haven't you?'

'Not really.'

'Sebastian!' Matilda said sharply,' I didn't need to hear from you, but *Henry* did.'

'I know. I'm going to see him in the morning.' Again, Matilda did not reply and, sighing, Sebastian went quiet. It was going to be a long night.

Other than cooing from Nellie in the back, the car was silent for the rest of the journey. Matilda couldn't help looking at Florence, trying to determine what she could see: the shape of her eyes; the way she moved her lips; her smile; the colour of her hair. It was not difficult to work it out; Meggie was no longer an invisible presence.

Parking outside the café, Matilda helped Florence with Nellie, while Sebastian got the pram out of the boot. 'I like this place,' Matilda said, as Florence handed Nellie to her to hold whilst she organised her bags.

'I thought I recognised you,' Florence said.

'I've not been in for a while.'

'You must come, I make a mean honey and lemon cake,' Florence replied, smiling at her, leaving Matilda in no doubt who she was.

'I like the sound of that,' she said slowly, handing Nellie back to her. Sebastian helped Florence carry everything into the flat above the café before saying goodnight and returning to the car.

'Looks like we've got a lot to talk about,' Matilda said curtly, getting back into the driver's seat.

Sebastian looked out of the window and up at the rooms above the café seeing the shadow of Florence moving about. 'I know,' he sighed.

Walking back into the house, Sebastian was greeted by Panda who had shot out of her bed in the kitchen and was skidding down the hall, buffeting into the wall before scrambling back across the shiny tiles and jumping up at him, weeing all over his shoes in excitement.

'And I've missed you too,' Sebastian said, grappling with her in his arms.

Taking a bottle of wine from the fridge, Matilda sat at the kitchen table, waiting for Sebastian to join her. It took several glasses for him to explain what had happened in Switzerland. She listened without speaking and, whilst it was painful to hear, she took it in without questions. When Sebastian found it difficult to talk, she instinctively wanted to comfort him, but she knew she couldn't, so she just sat opposite him and watched. He had been through so much that she was no longer angry with him, but she was left empty; their future did not look like something she wanted.

'You knew, didn't you?' Sebastian asked her.

'I had to look hard, but yes.'

'How do you feel about it?'

'I don't know, Seb. I need time to think. How do you feel?'

'I don't know either.'

'Have you heard from Meggie since she left?'

'No.'

'Have you messaged her?'

'No.'

'Do you want to?'

Sebastian did not answer straight away. 'I don't know,' he said eventually.

Day Thirty-One

Saturday

Matilda was glad to be alone.

Sebastian had got up before dawn and had headed into the office, taking Panda with him. With the completion of the sale just a few days away, he needed to reassure himself that things were running smoothly, but he was struggling to concentrate. The revelations over the two days he had spent in Switzerland were constantly running through his mind. Meggie. Nancy. Florence. And then, just when he thought he had heard it all, there was Paul.

~

Outside Tatch-A UK's offices, Paul sat in his mother's car, parked in his usual spot, watching. He had spent the past few days on his phone, following Sebastian's every move. He had watched as Sebastian had flown to Switzerland; seen he had visited Nancy, not once, but twice. He had tracked him as he had arrived back in Edinburgh and returned home. Unsure of how much Nancy would have told Sebastian, he would bide his time. Wait for his opportunity. Now he was no longer tied to their friendship, he saw no reason why Sebastian should not know the truth.

~

Still in her nightclothes, Matilda sat at the kitchen table mulling over the conversation she and Sebastian had had the night before, trying to work out what the future might hold. She had spent the whole of their marriage by his side. Working full-time, she had supported and guided him as he grew the business; she had raised their children almost single-handedly whilst he spent night and day beneath machines or in his office. She had kept their house clean and their bed warm, seldom asking for anything in return. When he doubted himself, she reassured him, and forgave him when he shut her out. They had been married for so long, they were best friends and she felt desperately sorry for what he was now facing. He had lost his parents as well as his life-long friend, and he was about to say goodbye to his company, all whilst his past was playing catch-up. Heading upstairs to get dressed, she came to the conclusion that until she knew what she wanted, she should do nothing.

~

It was still early when Sebastian left the office and drove back across town to Taligth. On his way, he called Niamh to tell her that there were a few things needing her attention. He would be back in the afternoon and would, no doubt, see her there. In fact, there had not been a weekend over the past few months where Niamh had stayed at home, and today was to be no different. There was a lot to go through in preparation for Monday's meeting.

Driving over the cattle grid, he looked up at the farmhouse with fresh eyes, the house where he had spent so many happy years before it had been defiled by one event. With its windows illuminated by the morning sun, it looked back at him as if to say, 'it's been a long time,' and he could feel the warm pull of his parents as he parked behind Henry's car and released Panda onto the grass. He looked around, enjoying the stillness of the morning, while Panda snuffled along the edges of the lawn, racing across the wet grass, leaving trails in her wake like those left by night-time snails across damp floors.

Henry, having woken up when he heard the distant sound of the gates opening, quickly got dressed and rushed downstairs. 'When you said 'first thing',' he panted, playing tug of war with his sock as Panda did her best to prevent him from putting it on, 'you meant it.' Panda ran playfully down the hall flipping Henry's sock into the air and catching it again, then settled in the kitchen to gnaw a hole in its heel. 'I hope you're enjoying that,' he said to her. 'Coffee?'

'Yes please,' Sebastian replied, looking around the kitchen to see what had changed since he had last been in it. Lifting the blind, he smiled at Betsy who was scratching herself against the gate. 'How are you doing?' he asked Henry, glad to see his brother was in one piece and looking okay.

'I'm all right. You know how it is,' Henry sighed.

'I know,' Sebastian agreed, 'although luckily for me, PMaC is a distraction, but fingers crossed, in seventy-two hours, it'll all be over.'

'How's it going?'

'Well, there's bound to be few last-minute hitches, but so far it's all looking good. I'm meeting Niamh this afternoon. When's Lorna coming up?'

'Monday morning.'

'Do you want to come over to our house later, for a change of scenery?' Sebastian asked, thinking Henry's company might defuse the tension between himself and Matilda. 'We could take Panda to the park for her weekly cesspit swim, and there's something I want to talk to you about.'

'Florence, by any chance?' Surprised, Sebastian looked at Henry. 'I know who she is, Seb,' Henry said handing him his coffee. Going outside into the yard, they sat on the bench facing Betsy who was being pestered by Panda. 'I read the letter attached to Dad's will.'

'Did you?' Sebastian reacted, surprised Henry had opened the letter without him. Ignoring Sebastian's tone, Henry nodded. 'What did it say?' Sebastian asked.

'It explains everything. Meggie, Florence, Nancy. Did Nancy tell you she's not our sister?'

'She did,' Sebastian said, shaking his head, still coming to terms with the things he had heard.

'No wonder you didn't get a chance to tell her about Dad.'

'No, *you* did!'

'No I *didn't!*' Henry protested, 'she made some crass remark, and I wasn't quick enough to brush it off and she guessed.'

'It's fine, Henry.'

'It's all in the letter anyway.'

'I think I need to read it.'

Going into the kitchen, Henry took his father's coat off the peg and reached into the pocket, retrieving the letter and Nancy's birth certificate. He returned to the yard giving them to Sebastian to read whilst he went back into the kitchen to make breakfast. 'Yes, and I'll make some for you too, you greedy pig,' he said to Betsy, who snorted loudly.

Henry had been to McGregor's the day before and had replenished the fridge. A full fry up was the only thing their father had learned to cook and he was a master at it. Every Saturday morning after he came in from the fields, he would set about preparing breakfast for them all, giving Elspeth the rare opportunity for a lie in. Saturday mornings in Taligth's kitchen were magical.

~

Pleased to be back, Meggie unlocked the café. Being closed for a week meant the steamers on the coffee machine needed descaling and the fridges needed restocking before she could open. Usually, her niece would cover when she and Florence took their annual trip to Geneva, but this year she hadn't been able to, so they'd had to shut. With the gathering of post and unwanted flyers at the bottom of the door, and the lack of daily window washing, it looked to all intents and purposes like they had closed down. There was a lot to do.

She knew Florence was home, back upstairs, safe in her flat. She was pleased.

The night Meggie left Nancy's had been awful, one of her worst and not one she was proud of. She had let herself down in so many ways over the years and, once again, she had surrendered all too easily.

After Sebastian left, Nancy did not say a word, or look in Meggie's direction when she walked back into the living room. Meggie felt sick watching Sebastian walk away from the flat, a broken man. Had she been given the choice, he would have never found out. But as ever, Nancy couldn't resist. When she tired of her 'toys' she threw them out, discarding anything that no longer interested her. One apartment after another; artwork bought for a fortune and then sold for more; a friend short-lived; and Florence, a means to an end. Now the truth was out, there was no reason for Meggie to remain in Nancy's life; a message conveyed loud and clear following Sebastian's departure.

'Why did you do that?' Meggie had asked, coming back into the room where Nancy sat lounging on her sofa reading a magazine. 'Why did you make me do that when I wasn't prepared?' Not lifting her eyes from the magazine, Nancy did not speak. 'So, what now?' Meggie asked.

'I don't know, Meggie. What now?'

'What sort of a person are you?'

Nancy put her magazine to one side. Standing up, facing Meggie, she started to speak, slowly at first, getting quicker and louder until she was screaming in Meggie's face. 'I am the person you *willingly* handed your baby to so that you could carry on looking into the bottom of a bottle,' she said, keeping her eyes fixed on Meggie's. 'I am the person, who, for *thirty* years has kept my mouth shut! I am the person who brought *your* daughter up whilst you got on with your life, *that's* who I am,' she yelled.

'Your *brother's* daughter,' Meggie shouted back.

'No, Meggie, *your* daughter! *You* gave birth to her and *you* gave her to me, forcing my parents to keep your secret, and you never once thought to tell *him*,' Nancy screamed.

'Yes I *did*!'

'No you *didn't*! So the only person to blame is *you*! And now he knows, so I can finally get on with my life. Thank *god* for that!' Nancy shouted, walking away from Meggie. 'Close the door quietly on your way out,' she snapped.

Meggie stood looking at Nancy, thinking how much she had hated her all these years. Circumstances had forced Meggie into a corner when she was young and naïve, and, at the time, she had been too confused and scared to say that it was not what she had wanted. Nancy took advantage; broke her promise to her; kept her from seeing her own daughter; took money from those who loved her, long after Florence had returned to Edinburgh. But she was right; Meggie had only herself to blame.

Retreating into her room, Meggie put the few belongings she had into her bag and picked up her small flight case. Packed and 'ready to leave', was Nancy's condition when Meggie first asked if she could stay. 'In case you and I fall out,' Nancy had said. Nancy had always been Nancy.

Pulling the door closed behind her, Meggie stepped into the corridor. She stopped, thinking Nancy might follow her, but after waiting, she walked away. The taxi she had booked took an hour to arrive and she stood on the top road looking down at the lights glistening on the lake, knowing this was to be the last time she would see them. Waiting, she booked a seat on the last flight to Newcastle.

By the time she got to the airport, her head was pounding. It was hours before her flight... and the bar was open... the devil won the battle that day; the battle Meggie had fought every day since her last drink. Until now, she had always won, but tonight she succumbed.

Attempting to board the midnight flight, Meggie was so intoxicated that she was turned away at the gate and had to spend the night sleeping on the hard plastic seats in the airport. Airport staff avoided her and the large pool of vomit she had at her feet.

Sober enough to get the first flight the following morning, she ignored the looks from strangers when they worked out who it was that smelt rancid so early in the day. In her 'heyday' she had been used to that 'look', the turning away, the comments whispered behind hands. With the past catching up with her, she buckled herself in. She slept the whole way to Newcastle, getting a taxi back home in time for lunch and a sympathetic hug from Aled. On Saturday morning, Meggie, still nursing a slight hangover, was driven to Edinburgh by Aled, who helped her to get the café ready in time to open for the mid-morning rush.

So now she was busy mopping the floor, cleaning the windows and descaling the coffee machine, reflecting on the past two days.

~

Sebastian had continued to read his father's letter over breakfast. Finishing, he put down his knife and fork. He had grunted and commented all the way through his slow mastication. Henry had watched his brother as he stopped eating once or twice to re-read a paragraph. He had made the odd comment, but not given much acknowledgement to Henry as to what additional information the letter gave.

'That was delicious,' Sebastian said, pushing his plate away and bringing his coffee forward. 'Thank you'.

'How does the letter compare to what Nancy told you?' Henry asked, clearing the plates away.

'It's much the same. The thing that gets me most is what she took from Mum and Dad. Not just the money; all of it,' Sebastian said heavily. 'What a bloody mess!'

'Have you told Matilda?'

'I have.'

'And?'

'As you'd expect,' Sebastian sighed.

Henry looked at Sebastian, trying to understand what he must be feeling. 'Why did you ask about Paul?' he asked, eventually.

'How about we go for a walk and I'll fill you in,' Sebastian suggested, needing some fresh air.

Wrapped up against the wind, the brothers ambled across the fields with Panda, talking about Paul and then Matilda, Florence and their father's letter.

Henry remembered Nancy's twenty-first well: the awkward breakfast; the sudden trip to the shops; no one home when they came back. He remembered his mother calling, 'Nancy!' 'Sebastian!' through the house, and her finding the note, not in Nancy's writing, saying, they had left, no reason given. He remembered his mother crying and his father on the verge of calling the police, debating with himself as to when was the right time, and he remembered Sebastian returning home and the huge argument it caused, followed by days of telephone calls trying to find out where Nancy might have gone. And he remembered the blame his parents put on themselves. 'Tis all oor fault,' his mother had said over and over again. 'We should hae told her,' though she never said what and Henry never asked.

'I always thought it was because of me that Nancy left,' Sebastian said, walking back into the kitchen, Panda's feet caked in muddy 'boots'.

'Why?' Henry asked, not understanding.

'Just the way things were,' Sebastian replied, reticently. Henry could never know the full extent of the events of that day. 'Are you okay?' he asked, pulling off his father's boots and leaving them in the sink. 'It's been crap, Hal.'

'I'm fine.'

'As long as you are,' Sebastian replied, looking earnestly at Henry. 'Right, I need to go and do some work, this business won't sell itself. I'll see you in a few hours. Are you all right if I leave Panda here with you?'

'Of course,' Henry replied looking down at Panda who was sitting at his feet, wagging her tail, listening to the conversation. 'I think perhaps a shower might be in order,' he said to her. Her tail stopped and her ears went down. Panda did not like showers.

Much to the delight of Betsy who squealed with excitement, Henry hosed Panda's muddy paws off in the yard. Panda ran circles around him and by the time he had finished all three of them were soaked. Betsy had enjoyed the show so much she regurgitated her breakfast all over her clean straw, giving Henry another job to do before he left.

On his way to Sebastian's, Henry rang Lorna.

'You should write your parents' story into a play one day,' she said, at the end of the call.

'Funnily enough, Betsy and I were talking about that yesterday,' Henry said, as if it were the most natural thing in the world to discuss his ideas with a pig.

'And what did she say?'

'She agreed, as long as she's in it.'

Lorna and Henry were looking forward to seeing each other. The crew had packed the van that afternoon, ready for an early start on Monday morning, and Lorna was trying to contain her excitement, ever conscious of what Henry was going through. Henry was happy to be swept along. Mabel would be coming too this time. They could not bear the idea of putting her in kennels as they had for Edinburgh and Paris. She was so sad; having not eaten for days, she had come home skinny and withdrawn.

Arriving at Sebastian's mid-afternoon, the two brothers and Panda turned right out of the gate, walking down to the park. By the time they had encouraged Panda out of the pond, it was dusk and, walking back up the hill towards home, Sebastian could just make out the lights of the line of shops in the distance. Seeing no gap in the illuminations, it was clear the café was open. As they walked past, Meggie suddenly appeared at the door, sweeping the step before closing for the night.

'Meggie!'

'Seb!' Meggie said, surprised. They stood for a moment, looking awkwardly at each other. 'Can I have a word?' she asked, eventually.

'How about I meet you back at the house?' Henry said, carrying on up the hill.

Seeing Aled's car pull into the road, Meggie paused uncomfortably. 'We need to talk,' she said, the car drawing up alongside them. 'Could we go for that meal you mentioned? I've spoken with Aled. Do you think Matilda would mind?'

'Does Aled know about..?'

'He's always known,' Meggie interrupted.

'Am I the only one who's been in in the dark?'

'It's not like that.'

'It feels like it is. What happened after I left Nancy's?'

'That's what I want to talk to you about,' she said, switching off the lights and locking the café door. 'I'm so sorry,' she whispered, getting into the car.

Watching them drive away, Sebastian tried to work out what he was going to tell Matilda. Things were a long was from being right between them. Walking slowly up the hill with Panda trotting along beside him, he looked down. 'Thank god I've got you,' he said as she smiled up at him.

~

In spite of the underlying conflict between Sebastian and Matilda, they and Henry had a lovely evening. It was good for Henry to get away from Taligth and laugh, and it was good for Sebastian and Matilda to put their guns down and enjoy each other's company.

Despite Matilda's insistence that he stay over, Henry decided to drive back to Taligth. Sebastian and Matilda stood on the doorstep saying their goodbyes, watching the clear skies above Edinburgh and the rare abundance of stars unusually bright above the city lights. It had turned cold, and the evening dampness had settled on the metal railings running down the steps. Henry watched his footing as he walked to his car.

'Try and take it easy tomorrow,' he called back to Sebastian.

'You too.'

'Fat chance,' Henry replied, getting into his car.

'Oh, Henry,' Sebastian called, coming up to the car as Henry cleared the windscreen, 'I keep meaning to say, we need to talk about the farm. Can we have a chat about it after I've got Monday out of the way?'

'Of course,' Henry replied. 'Are we still going to see Dad on Thursday?'

'I'd like to.'

'Good, and good luck for your meeting on Monday.'

'Thanks, and you too, I hope... what do you luvvies call it? Get in, goes okay, break a leg, or whatever it is they say in the theatre world.

'That's the one – just don't mention the Scottish play.'

'What? Macbeth, you mean?' Sebastian said naughtily, falling about laughing as Henry swiped at him from his car window.

'You shit, Sebastian Campbell! Now you've put a curse on it. You'll be laughing on the other side of your face when the curtain falls down,' he shouted, joining Sebastian in his laughter as he started down the drive. 'Not that we have a curtain,' he yelled as he disappeared out of sight.

Day Thirty-Two

Sunday night was one of the most stressful nights Sebastian had experienced since starting Tatch-A UK. With a lot of wine and a few laughs the night before, he had slept without dreaming and had spent the majority of Sunday getting ready for his meeting with Patrick McCarthy and his team of lawyers.

To the best of his knowledge, everything was in position; they had all but shaken on it. The Sale and Purchase Agreement was in place, the warranties and indemnities were all agreed and preparations for the meeting were complete. Then at 10.30 Sunday night came a last-minute request to change the wording to an indemnity. There had been robust arguments over the indemnities throughout the negotiations and there were some pretty onerous clauses required by PMaC Inc. Now, with less than 12 hours to go, PMaC's lawyers wanted to change the wording to the clause relating to Paul that had been there since the first version of the agreement. Receiving the email, Sebastian was floored.

It was apparent that PMaC's lawyers had made a mistake, and although they readily put their hands up and were apologetic, they were not about to back down. The indemnity was as narrow as Sebastian could have hoped. He could just about accept it as it was, but changing the wording now meant it would leave them wide open and forever responsible should anything else regarding Paul come out of the woodwork. The lateness of the change felt like a gun to his head, leaving him little time to consider his options. Had it been there from the beginning, he might have been able to accept it, but not now, not like this.

After he received the email, he tentatively asked Matilda to be his sounding board. 'If we say no to the change, will they pull out?' he asked, sitting with her in his study, 'and if they pull out, is that because they know there's more to come and we don't? How would they know that though? Unless they've spoken with Graham, but there's nothing he's held back, is there?' he asked rhetorically. 'I can't imagine Graham saying anything to them he hasn't said to us,' he said as Matilda listened. 'If there is more to come out then we shouldn't go ahead and sell the business, should we? I mean, I'd prefer to pay for any liability out of fresh money we'd be earning rather than out of our lump sum. Who knows how much that could be? It could be huge. Graham always said we were only scratching the surface.'

'Knowing what you know,' she said, giving it some thought, 'you must have a gut feeling about Paul. Do you honestly think there's more to come out?'

'Until an hour ago I'd have probably said I don't think so, but getting that email we just don't know do we? I mean, he got away with so much for so long, who knows what else he might have done.'

'Have confidence in your judgment, Seb. You know Paul better than anybody.'

'Do I? Do I *really*?' he asked, looking forlornly at Matilda. 'That's not how it feels. I don't think I know him at all. What if he is in cahoots with one of the clients and he's still stealing? We've an obligation to take responsibility for that, but for how long?'

'Come on! Do you really think that? Graham would have found out.'

'I don't know, I don't know anymore. I just don't see why we will have to keep paying for it for the rest of our lives when we've done nothing wrong, but equally why should PMaC have to pay if more stuff comes out. It's not their fault either. I get it, I understand what they're asking for, I do, but it's just we'd all metaphorically shaken hands when I spoke to them on Friday, which I thought meant we were on the home straight. Now here we are, about to wrap it up and it feels underhand, which doesn't seem Patrick's style, at least I didn't think it was, or have I got him wrong?'

'Stop it, Seb!' Matilda said firmly, forcing him to stop going around in circles. 'You have not got him wrong; he's a good person but a very astute businessman as well. He probably doesn't even know anything about it. It'll be the lawyers going over the papers on the plane, suddenly realising their mistake and quickly trying to rectify it before the morning. Unless they really are sharks and you've got them all wrong, then you're stuffed, and if that's the case, pull out. But that's not the feeling you've got, is it?'

'It makes me nervous.'

'Of course it does, but it'll be something the lawyers are used to. They'll deal with these things all the time. You need to call Richard, he will advise you well. Listen to what he has to say. Perhaps there's a compromise position that can be agreed.'

'Perhaps,' he said, thinking. 'The only thing I can think is we extend liability specifically related to Paul for, I don't know, a year maybe. That would seem fair. Then at least it's not hanging over our heads forever. We can't have that bastard sitting on our coffins, laughing, as they lower us in.'

'That sounds a good solution,' Matilda said, smiling sympathetically at Sebastian's hangdog expression. 'You said there was bound to be a last-minute hitch,' she added lightly.

'Yes, but I was hoping I was wrong.'

'Unfortunately, for once, you were right,' she said, smiling wryly at him. 'But try not to panic. Try to look at the bigger picture. There have been so many hurdles, Seb, and you can jump this one just as well as you have jumped the hundreds of others over the last six months. Don't let it trip you up, not now. What would your mum say? 'Ye'v eaten th' donkey, dinnae choke on th' tail',' she said, making Sebastian smile.

'Very good. I almost thought you were her for a minute,' he said, laughing weakly.

Matilda laughed. 'Right, go and call Richard. He'll have had the email as well and will be able to sort it out. He knows better than you how to talk to the lawyers. Whatever you decide I will support you,' she said looking at his defeated body language. He was shattered and he needed the strength for one final push. 'You've been through hell this last month. I don't know how you're still standing, but you are, and you've got to keep going. Do not let Paul win; he's done enough damage,' she said, drawing him into her arms and speaking into his ear. 'We will work it out... everything,' she whispered before she pulled back. 'Now go and wake Richard up. You've paid him enough money over the years, make him earn it.'

Watching him walk away, Matilda wondered what energy either of them had left inside to keep up the fight. The process of selling the business had taken its toll and the final few days had been no exception.

Contacting Niamh first, Sebastian explained what was going on. Then just after midnight, he made the call to Richard, telling him to look at his emails. It was not the call a lawyer wanted to take in the early hours of the morning prior to an important meeting, but Richard knew what he was doing and offered reassurance, giving Sebastian an element of hope that they should be able to sort the wording of the indemnity to suit both parties.

It was 1 a.m. and Sebastian could not contemplate going to bed, but instead, lay down on the kitchen sofa and drifted in and out of sleep. In his wakeful moments he thought about how he and his father had once sat for hours in his and Matilda's tiny flat in Edinburgh, bent double, pouring over designs, making plans. He thought about how the company name had been born out of the way his father said, 'tatcha', 'if you 'tatcha' wire onto this part, that would work,' he had said. Sebastian started using the word himself and it stuck. The company name, 'Tatch-A UK', was created. He wished that his father was standing next to him at the end, as he had been at the beginning.

Standing and stretching, Sebastian looked out of the kitchen window as Monday morning dawned and the sun spilt over the wall, beaming its weak orange rays onto the lawn. The clock on the kitchen wall showed there were still a few hours before they needed to leave. Having dragged her lead across the floor, Panda sat with it in her mouth, patiently looking up at Sebastian and he decided some fresh air would do him good. Seeing him get his shoes on sent Panda into a twirling frenzy of excitement. Sebastian called up to Matilda and struggled not to trip over Panda as they headed out of the door.

Listening to Sebastian leaving the house, Matilda wondered in which direction he would go when he got to the bottom of the drive.

~

Having spent Sunday alone, Henry woke up in a melancholy mood on Monday morning. Rather than jumping in the car and going to the supermarket, he walked down to McGregor's; Dougie would have what he wanted.

'Morning Dougie,' he said, entering the garage shop making the bell above the door ring loudly.

'Mornin' Henry, 'how urr ye daein?' Dougie asked, kindly.

'Not so bad, thanks. How are you?'

'A'm braw, cheers.'

'Good. Have you got any candles?' Henry asked, searching the shelves.

'Candles? Aye, whit sort urr ye wanting? We hae tea-lights, pillar, birthday...'

'Have you got any of the tall ones, for the dinner table?'

'Och na, I'm sorry, we haven't git any o' they.'

Henry looked at Dougie in disbelief. There was a chance he would be leaving McGregor's empty handed. 'Really?' he asked. Dougie shook his head, looking around the jumble of items on the shelves.

'Okay. Well, never mind,' Henry said, going to leave. Just as he reached the door, Dougie called him back.

'Wid these be any guid?' he asked, holding up a box containing two red, battery-operated, dining table candles.

Henry laughed. 'They'd be perfect, thank you,' he said, and he left McGregor's with the battery-operated candles, a homemade chocolate cake, a 'good luck' card and a packet of dog chews for Mabel.

~

Panda knew exactly which way they were going, and it was not to the park. Try as she might to pull against the lead, Sebastian was having none of it, and she lost the fight. 'This way, Panda!' Sebastian commanded. 'We don't have time this morning,' he added, tugging her back. Looking up, her deep brown eyes pleaded with him. *But the café's boring*, she conveyed through her sorrowful expression. *I don't want to go to the café; I want to go to the park*. 'We can go to the park later,' Sebastian told her. *But I want to go to the park now*, she grumbled, lowering her head and letting her ears droop. 'How about we bring your ball?' Sebastian said absent-mindedly. On hearing the word ball, Panda's demeanour changed. *Ball?* she thought, her ears pricking up, *did you say ball? Where is it?* She looked around in excitement, jumping up at him trying to sniff it out. 'Not now Panda, later,' Sebastian said, realising his error as Panda carried on searching for her little, yellow friend. When she realised there was no ball, she went back to walking loosely behind him. *It's not fair. How come I never get what I want?* she thought.

Reaching the café, forgetting she was in a huff, Panda jumped up at Meggie as soon as they walked in. Meggie crouched down and ruffled Panda's fur. 'Hey, you smell good,' she said, standing and going behind the counter to find her a dog biscuit. 'Do you have time for a coffee?' she asked Sebastian as Panda munched noisily at her feet.

'I'm not stopping, I have a meeting this morning...' he trailed off. 'I was wondering whether you're free tomorrow evening? We need to talk. I was thinking perhaps we could meet at Lastrata's. Do you remember it?'

'Of course,' Meggie replied, remembering the restaurant she and Sebastian had gone to whenever they were in Scotland. 'What time tomorrow?'

'I'll message you,' he said turning to the door. He stopped and paused, looking back as Meggie snuggled into Panda, saying 'see you later, little one'.

'It's hard to believe,' he said slowly, 'that a month ago my mum and dad were alive, I hadn't seen you for over thirty years and I'd only got two children.' He sighed heavily and walked out, leaving Meggie standing in the doorway, lost for words.

~

Paul stood out of sight, watching as Sebastian left the café.

Earlier, he had sat for hours, parked on the road at the bottom of Sebastian's drive and then, when he had seen Sebastian walk out with Panda, he had followed him on foot. Paul had guessed where they were headed.

The compulsion that drove Paul to stalk his former friend, day and night, had heightened over the weeks since they had last spoken, to such an extent that, with little care or self-respect, he had camped out in the car for days on end in the hope of catching sight of Sebastian.

Despite knowing that what he was doing was madness, he felt powerless to control his overwhelming urge, and like an addict, he hated himself for being so weak.

Unwashed and unshaven, his hair slicked back away from his face, highlighting gaunt features, remaining hidden, he stood across the road from the café.

On previous days he had watched the early morning customers come and go and had even contemplated going into the café himself to buy a coffee just to see whether Meggie recognised him. But he had thought better of it, biding his time for the right opportunity to make his move. He would have his moment, he thought, his chance to put the record straight.

As Sebastian left, Paul followed.

~

By the time Sebastian dragged a reluctant Panda back to the house, Matilda was downstairs and ready. With her hair pinned neatly into a bun, she wore a fitted, black crepe dress with matching jacket, and black, stiletto shoes. She looked beautiful, Sebastian thought as he watched her sitting at the kitchen table, preparing for the meeting.

The espresso maker was warming on the Aga and, like witches waiting on ducking stools ready to be lowered, four thick slices of artisan bread were poised over the toaster. Before sitting down to breakfast, Sebastian dashed up the stairs to have a shower and get ready. He was feeling nervous. Taking advantage of the warm water running down his back, he tried to regulate his breathing and gather his thoughts. By the time he was dressed in his best suit, with white shirt, and the tie he wore at Ewan's wedding, he was feeling better. Back in the kitchen, he lent over the table and kissed Matilda on the cheek before joining her.

'Are you okay?' she asked, smiling up at him. Sebastian nodded. 'Any news from Richard?' she added, buttering her toast and cutting it neatly into squares.

'Not yet,' Sebastian replied, glancing anxiously at the clock on the wall.

'There's plenty of time,' Matilda said, reassuringly.

The taxi pulled onto their drive forty minutes later, and as it did, Sebastian finally received the confirmation he was waiting for. Their revised wording had been accepted, making them liable for just one year, should anything else come out relating to Paul. He and Matilda breathed a sigh of relief.

Meeting Niamh and Richard in the foyer of Makison-Stritch Global Law Firm, they struggled not to be intimidated by the prestigious building in which this world-renowned company sat. Tatch-A UK batted hard, but it was no match for some of the companies served by this organisation. After a team-talk outside the doors, they straightened their suits, picked up their briefcases and walked into the meeting at 11.55 a.m. The room was large and cool and, in the centre, an impressive, oval-shaped, oak table dominated the floor. Along one side sat executives from the law firm whose UK offices they were using, plus representatives from PMaC Inc. with Patrick sat comfortably amongst them. Sebastian caught his eye and the two men smiled at each other warmly.

On the table there were hundreds of papers in plastic wallets, numbered and laid out neatly, each representing a part of Tatch-A UK Sebastian needed to let go and, for a brief moment, he hesitated, feeling overwhelmed by the finality of it all, wishing his father was with him. 'It's never too late to change your mind,' he would have whispered.

'Sebastian,' Patrick said, standing and moving forward to shake hands, 'Matilda, Niamh, Richard, it's good to see you all again. Come, let me introduce you,' he said, gesturing to the individuals sitting formally in front of them. 'You know Anthony of course, our FD, then we have Anisah, and this is Jane,' he said, standing behind a young, dark haired woman, dressed in a light pink suit, 'and then we have Matthew and Phillip. These guys are all from Makison-Stritch who have been working on the acquisition whilst I have been improving my golf swing,' he said, everyone laughing politely. Sebastian found it difficult to look at the two immaculately attired lawyers who had given him another sleepless night. Patrick introduced each person in turn as the Tatch-A UK team moved around the table, shaking hands with people they were unlikely see again, until they finally ended up at seats opposite the PMaC Inc. team.

'Right...' Matthew said, starting proceedings.

After detailing what was going to happen in the meeting, they quickly got down to the task of transferring company ownership. Every document needed to be signed and witnessed, and as he and Matilda received each paper, Sebastian felt his energy wane. Once they had signed all the documents, there was time to recover over a break of coffee and biscuits. Patrick took Sebastian to one side. 'I hear we almost had a last-minute hitch?'

'We did,' Sebastian replied, sighing deeply.

Patrick laughed. 'You should have called me, I'd have put your mind at ease. As you know, I've left everything to the suits and although they're pretty smart, they don't always get it right. When is your father's funeral?'

'Friday.'

'Take as long as you want afterwards. You'll need time to recover. I don't expect to hear you're in the office and, whenever you're ready, Sangfroid will be waiting for you. All you have to do is head out and saddle her up.'

Remembering the heat of the Arizona sun on his back and the feeling of the mare's gentle movements, Sebastian smiled. 'I might just take you up on that,' he said.

With the finances settled and the paperwork boxed up, the deal was sealed and, although Patrick McCarthy was not one for lavish gestures, he marked the occasion with champagne. Sebastian appreciated the sentiment.

Joining in the celebration, Niamh felt a tinge of sadness to see the family-run company pass into new hands. Inevitably it would change. Before the final papers were signed, she had resisted looking too far into the future, to the task ahead of her. She would, from this moment, have much more responsibility and it felt a little daunting. Later, she would discover the round, glass paperweight, tied with a red ribbon, placed on her desk, and would feel reassured. The accompanying note saying, 'you might need this one day, though heaven help the poor sod you launch it at,' would raise her confidence and bring a small smile at Sebastian's oblique reference to her bowling skills on the cricket field.

They all raised their glasses to the future of PMaC Inc. and Tatch-A UK before they packed their briefcases and laptops away, shook hands and departed.

From now on Sebastian would endeavour to be a model employee until his contract ended and then he would take the last of what he was owed, and leave. 'Whit a thing!'

his mother would have said. 'We are sae proud o' ye our wee clever laddie.'

~

Late in the afternoon, having waited nervously all day for a message from Sebastian, Henry picked up the home phone on its first ring. 'Well?' he asked.

'Signed, sealed and delivered!' Sebastian announced.

'Excellent!' Henry replied, relieved. 'So, are you off to celebrate?'

'We are, and being the flash bastard I am, we're heading to The Duck on the Water for a white bread shrimp sandwich, washed down with a Guinness.'

Henry laughed.

'Has Lorna arrived yet?'

'She's in Scotland, but she's gone straight to the theatre to help unload the van and then she'll be back here for dinner later.'

'Good, and good luck for your get in tomorrow. I'd offer to help, but I intend to sleep all day. Sorry.'

'Wouldn't want you breaking a nail, office boy. Now go and get pissed.'

Henry placed the phone back on its holster. Although pleased, he felt nervous for his brother, imagining it being difficult to watch someone else remodel the company he had created. Henry gave him six months before he would be tearing his hair out and asking to be released from his contract.

Lorna and Mabel arrived just as dinner was being served. With candles 'lit' and the lights down low, Henry had made an effort to make the kitchen warm and welcoming like his mother would have done. They enjoyed a quiet night in with chicken stew followed by chocolate cake, half a bottle of sherry and the small bottle of malt whisky Dougie had given to Henry for William. As the evening progressed, they moved into the front room and sat with Mabel in front of the open fire and talked about what lay ahead. Henry allowed himself to feel excited. After such an awful time, it was good to have something to look forward to.

Day Thirty-Four

Betsy was looking very sorry for herself, standing in her pen, wet and covered in straw. During the night, she had got excited over some beet she could smell beneath her bedding and, in a frantic search, she had inadvertently knocked her water bucket over. 'Honestly, Betsy!' Henry moaned, raking out the damp straw, 'as if I haven't got enough to do today, without you playing silly buggers... and you look ridiculous,' he laughed, looking at her as she blinked up at him, pieces of straw caught in her coarse white hair. 'You are a silly pig,' he said affectionately, giving her a brush down and a hearty breakfast, making sure her water bucket was in a better place.

Settling Mabel in the kitchen, Henry and Lorna attempted to set off for the theatre. It was a cool, damp morning and the mist hung low over the fields surrounding Taligth, giving it a ghostly, Dickensian feel. The dank weather was too much for Henry's old car, which refused to start. It's going to be one of those days, Henry thought to himself as they transferred everything they needed into his father's Land Rover, which had sat cold on the drive for five weeks. After a nervous wait for the glowplug light to go off before the battery weakened, the engine rattled into action. The heater did little more than fog the windscreen, so they drove, with the windows down, making for a chilly but enjoyable, bumpy, forty-minute journey across unmade country lanes. As they drove they talked over the plan for the few days ahead of opening. This was the most ambitious of Henry's productions yet and it would take two full days to erect the set, which gave them one day for both the tech and dress rehearsals before they would need to leave the team to do a final run-through without them on Friday morning. It was going to be tight.

Parking up in a lay-by half a mile from the theatre, they were just in time to meet up with the crew who were already tucking into sausage and egg baps with tomato ketchup and brown sauce, accompanied by steaming tea poured from a huge brown industrial-sized teapot. The crew had spotted the 'Early Risers' van as they arrived the day before and thought they would try it out for breakfast. It was an impressive set up; a large, shiny, American-style trailer, with an awning and small round metal tables covered in red and white chequered plastic tablecloths gripping on tightly against the relentless Scottish wind.

Their breaths floated in the cold air as they talked and laughed, and Henry felt good being back in the real world. It was a welcome relief not to hear mention of funerals, and, with the sun chinking through the mist and massaging his back, he relaxed. It augured well for a good day.

With a promise to return, they drove in convoy up the hill to the theatre. Seeing the building again brought a rush of emotion for Henry. The only time he had been there before was with his father. 'This is where it all begins,' William had said that day. 'It's time to give up teaching.' Henry had not expected to feel his presence, not today. But here he was, standing right beside him.

Henry quietly entered the auditorium whilst the others busied themselves at the back doors unloading the van. Replaying his father's words, he stood alone, enjoying the peace of the empty stage. Looking around, he imagined the seats full of people and the expectant faces of the audience as they gazed up at the set hanging above their heads. He imagined them peering down at the stage and across and around at the other audience members wondering what view they would get from another seat.

'I want the audience to feel immersed,' Henry had said to Lorna when he first described his vision. 'I want them to leave desperate to turn around and come straight back in, sit in a different seat and see it from a different angle. Does that make sense?' To Lorna it made perfect sense. Having lived every one of Henry's plays, she understood.

Hearing people behind him, Henry turned and focused his attention on the task in hand. Whilst the actors rehearsed in the studio, today's job was to get the main parts of the set erected. Consisting of two large, open, cube-shaped frames with furniture fixed permanently to them, each was a mirror image of the other. One represented 'heaven' which was suspended from a circular track running beneath the lighting gantry; the other, 'hell', was on the stage and was able to be lifted and turned and reshaped. With the audience in the round, they would be able to see inside the cubes from different angles as they moved. Access to 'heaven' was tricky and not for the faint hearted.

Stepping up into the back row, Henry watched the construction team busying about the stage. It was going to be a lot of hard work, late nights and early mornings. By noon the place was buzzing.

Although Henry was reasonably practical, he was not as skilled with the power tools as some of the others, so he headed off into the sound and lighting box where the techs were setting up the boards in line with the script. He was still in the gallery when Sebastian turned up mid-afternoon.

'I thought you might welcome an extra pair of hands,' he said, after Henry rushed down to meet him. 'You've come in Dad's Land Rover?'

'My car wouldn't start,' Henry said, rolling his eyes.

'I'm amazed the Land Rover did. Why didn't you come in Lorna's?'

'It's too small. We had too much stuff.'

'Do you want me to get someone out to yours?' Sebastian asked as they walked onto the stage.

'If you wouldn't mind, yes please. I thought you were going to sleep all day.'

'How could I sleep knowing this was going on?' Sebastian said, smiling as he looked around. 'Is this the thing you and Dad were pouring over?' he asked, referring to

400

the cube-shaped framework that was taking shape on the stage floor.

'It is. It's going to be suspended from that track up there, see?'

'Really?' Sebastian said looking up.

'I know, Lorna's brainchild.'

'How does it work?'

'Pedal power. I'll let Lorna explain. Lorna...!' Henry called loudly, his voice circling the gods.

A small voice called back. 'Yes?'

'There's someone here to see you,' Henry's voice echoed. Within a minute Lorna could be heard running along the upper level, then, appearing at the top, she thundered down the steps. 'Seb!' she called, delighted to see her brother-in-law, 'it's good to see you. How are you?' she asked, hugging him tightly. 'Are you here to help? Because if you're not, you can bugger off, we've got too much work to do,' she joked.

'I am most definitely here to help if I can be of any use.'

'Actually, you've come at just the right time. I could do with your engineer's eye...' Lorna talked quickly, dragging Sebastian up the steps so that they could get a better view.

Unable to hear what they were saying, Henry smiled, watching them talking excitedly, Lorna pointing and shaping her ideas in the air.

Later in the afternoon, under the guidance of the theatre's construction manager, the cube was lifted. Everyone held their breath, watching it slowly ascend. Weeks before they arrived, Lorna had produced detailed drawings with estimations of weight, which had been passed onto the construction manager for agreement, but despite him confirming that the gantry was more than strong enough to support the combined weight of the frame, the bike and the actors, it didn't stop him sweating. Beneath the noisy commotion, Henry grabbed Sebastian to help him paint the stage floor whilst they had it to themselves.

'I can't stay long,' Sebastian told Henry, picking up a long-poled paint roller.

'Why, what are you up to?'

Sebastian hesitated. 'I'm meeting Meggie,' he replied, not making eye contact.

Henry stopped and looked at him. 'Just the two of you?' he asked.

'Don't, Hal.'

'Does Matilda know?'

'Let's not, shall we.'

'Are you going to tell her?'

'Please, Hal!' Sebastian said. 'Things aren't good between us.'

Henry sighed. 'It'll work out,' he said, unconvincingly, as he started to paint. 'How are you feeling about Florence? Are you going to tell her who you are?' he added.

'No.'

'Why not?'

'Because I don't see what good it would do... are we doing the whole of this floor?' Sebastian asked.

'Only this bit for now, I'll do the rest later,' Henry said, looking at the enormity of the job. 'I've been thinking,' he said, after a moment's silence, 'you mentioned the farm the other night.'

'Yes.'

'I've been thinking about what Dad wrote in the letter, regarding Nancy and inheritance.'

Sebastian stopped painting and looked at Henry. 'Nancy's not getting *anything* from Mum and Dad.' He said, his tone suddenly cold.

'It's not just your decision.'

'You don't know her, Hal. She doesn't give a toss. The only thing she would be interested in is their money and as soon as she got her hands on it, we wouldn't see her for dust. Mum and Dad left everything to us, to be split equally. That's what Dad wrote.'

'I know, but Mum kept that picture of her all those years.'

'It doesn't change anything.'

'Dad mentioned it in the letter.'

'Yes, so that Nancy didn't lay claim. That was why. She's not a beneficiary in their will. You read the letter. This could make a real difference to your life; the farm itself is worth a lot of money. You could give up teaching; you could do 'this' full time,' Sebastian said gesturing. 'Just imagine.'

'Just imagine,' Henry laughed, unsure.

'This is what you want, isn't it? It's what Mum and Dad wanted for you. If you let Nancy get her hands on their money, this will become a pipe dream. I know it doesn't come cheap.

'It doesn't,' Henry said with a wry smile. 'I'll never make my fortune doing this.'

'So, Mum and Dad's money will help.'

'Of course, greatly, but it's not just that,' he said, uncertainty robbing his voice of volume.

'What is it then?'

'This will sound ridiculous to you because you're a risk taker... but, what if I'm not good enough? It's all well and good 'playing' at it as I have been, but what if I can't make a go of it?'

'Then you go back to teaching.'

'That would be such a misuse of their money, I don't know if I have it in me.'

'It would be a *good* use of their money, Hal. You've got to believe in yourself. Your plays are brilliant... you could buy your own theatre.'

Henry laughed.

As they painted, the brothers continued to talk for the rest of the afternoon until Sebastian looked at his watch and put his paint roller down. 'I've got to go,' he said, rolling his sleeves down. 'But just so you know, there's no way Nancy's stopping you from living your dream. Absolutely no way, I'll not allow it,' he said, retrieving his keys from his jacket pocket. 'Now get on, you've got a lot to do.'

'Let me know how it goes with Meggie.'

'Will do. Speak later.'

'Thanks for your help,' Henry called after him as Sebastian headed out. 'That's stage left by the way, you'll end up in the changing rooms if you go down there.'

'Which way do I go then?'

'That way, stage right,' Henry pointed.

'How do you know what's left and right in this place?' Henry laughed as Sebastian crossed the stage. 'If I don't see you before, I'll see you on Thursday, at Angus Stewart's. I'm guessing you'll be busy here for the next couple of days,' he added, walking away.

'Sure will. See you Thursday,' Henry called after him.

'See ya,' Sebastian shouted back, laughing as he left to an array of voices, calling 'see ya' from around the building. Henry laughed, returning to the arduous task of painting the stage floor.

~

Meggie was sitting at the bar, waiting pensively, as Sebastian rushed in. 'Sorry I'm late,' he said, 'I've been helping Henry at the theatre. This place hasn't changed much,' he added, looking around at the packed, noisy restaurant. It looked much the same as it had the last time he and Meggie had been there as teenagers. It was still painted the same colour with the same pictures hanging on the walls and the same set-up of non-matching chairs and wobbly tables squashed into the small space.

'How's it going?' Meggie asked.

'Well, I think. It never ceases to amaze me what comes out of Henry's head.'

'When are you seeing it?'

'We were booked for Friday, but I bought the tickets before my dad died, so we'll go another night.'

'I was sorry to hear about your dad. Florence told me. That's a lot for Henry to handle in one day.'

'Seems to be the way with us Campbell brothers; nothing happens for years and then when it does, it happens all at the same time,' he said, looking at her. An embarrassed silence descended between them as the noise in the

404

restaurant took over. 'Shall we grab a table?' Sebastian asked. Taking menus from the bar, the restaurant owner showed them to the only unoccupied table, tucked away behind the stairs leading down to The Cellar, a wine bar housed beneath the restaurant. Menus in hand, they sat for a moment without speaking. Eventually Meggie broke the silence. 'About Friday...' she said. Sebastian put his menu down. 'I'm sorry you found out like that. I wasn't prepared.' She took a deep breath. 'It was my fault. I played straight into Nancy's hands... again... and then, when you turned up, I knew exactly what she would do – it's all a game to her.'

'Would you ever have told me?'

'Probably not,' Meggie replied, honestly. 'How do you feel about it, now you know?'

'How do you expect me to feel?'

'Please!'

'I don't know how I feel.'

'Perhaps given time, you...'

'No!' Sebastian interrupted, looking at her. 'I don't think so,' he said sharply. Picking up his menu he looked blindly at the choices. 'I can't believe I didn't know.'

Meggie resisted the urge to cry. 'I'm sorry.'

'Sorry for what?' he said abruptly. 'Sorry I found out?' Meggie did not answer and they slid back into silence. Sebastian looked at her. 'Why did you leave on Friday?' he asked after a moment.

'Nancy and I argued and she told me to go.'

'What was said?'

'Things that can't be unsaid. Hurtful things I don't want to talk about. But I do want to talk about your parents. Hate me as much as you like...'

'I don't hate you.'

'... you need to know your parents only did what I asked. Please don't let your dad go to his grave with you blaming them.'

Sebastian looked at the tears pooling in Meggie's eyes.

'Of all people, I understand how all-consuming it becomes to keep a secret, desperately wanting to bury it, hoping it will go away. But to put other people in that position, Mum and Dad, how could you have done that to them, knowing what they were like? Every day they had to live with their decision not to tell me.' A tear escaping, Meggie did not speak. 'They knew I'd find out one day. They wrote a letter.'

'A letter?'

'Full of remorse, telling me everything.'

'So you already knew?' Meggie asked, defensively.

'No!' Sebastian snapped. 'Henry found it while I was away. You have no idea the pain they were in.'

'I'm so sorry, Seb. If I could turn back the clock...'

'Would things have been different?'

'I would like to think so,' Meggie replied, tearfully.

There was little more to say. Watching Meggie cry, Sebastian could not work out what he was feeling. Resentment? Pity? Love? 'I'm sorry you got mixed up with Nancy,' he said, reaching his hand out towards Meggie. He opened it, and instinctively Meggie placed her hand in his, and, for the briefest of moments she was lost. 'She's poisonous...' he said, his voice trailing off, not finishing his sentence. Lifting her eyes, Meggie found Sebastian staring over her head, out into the restaurant. Turning around, she looked to see who it was who had caught his attention. A man was standing at the bar, staring back. Sebastian pulled his hand away.

'Sebastian!' Paul said loudly, making his way towards the table.

'What are you doing here?' Sebastian snarled.

'I just happened to be passing.'

'You lying *fuck*!'

'Maybe,' Paul said, laughing drunkenly.

'Did you follow us?'

'You're not very discrete.'

Sebastian shook his head. '*Fuck* off!' he said.

'My parents told me about your dad...'

'Don't talk about my dad!' Sebastian cut in, looking up at Paul standing, unsteadily, behind Meggie.

'Can we talk?' Paul asked.

'What about?'

'I made a mistake,' he slurred.

'A mistake?' Sebastian echoed, incredulity in his voice. 'You're drunk.'

'I know.'

'Then shut up and *piss* off!'

'You got your money back!' Paul said, raising his voice, making the noise in the restaurant hush. Sebastian looked at him. 'Every *fucking* penny you asked for,' Paul mumbled, leaning on the table.

'Keep a little bit back for yourself, did you?' Sebastian asked.

Paul laughed. 'I never spent it,' he said. 'I've had it all the time.'

'What?' Sebastian said. 'You don't know what you're talking about, you drunken shit! *Fuck* off!'

'I bet you're desperate to know why I did it,' Paul said, turning to leave, before alcohol-fuelled bravado brought him back to the table.

'Go away Paul!' Sebastian commanded.

'Aren't you going to introduce us?' Paul asked, looking intently at Meggie.

'*Fuck* off Paul!' Sebastian hissed.

'This looks very cosy, the two of you sitting in the corner, hand in hand,' Paul said, grinning.

Tension building, Sebastian did not respond.

Paul laughed drunkenly. Looking at Meggie again he was momentarily taken back to a campsite in France. 'Of course I know who you are, Meggie,' he whispered. 'I saw you both at your mother's funeral, Seb. Hardly respectful,' he added, tutting loudly.

'You weren't at my mother's funeral,' Sebastian spat.

'Yes I was.'

'I didn't see you.'

'But I saw *you*, the two of you. It doesn't take a genius to work out what's going on,' Paul laughed triumphantly.

'You bastard!' Sebastian retaliated.

Paul suddenly bent down, making Meggie jump. Speaking closely into Meggie's ear, he held Sebastian's eye contact. 'When I leave, your boyfriend here will tell you what I've done,' he said, his warm, alcohol-laden breath hitting Meggie's cheek. 'You might remember he and I were very good friends, but not anymore. I stole a *shit* load of money from his company, you see. It'd make your eyes water if you knew how much... He doesn't know the half of it.' Smiling, he stood up, holding the table to balance himself, not taking his eyes off Sebastian. 'Oh, and whilst I've got your attention, let me tell you something else Sebastian *doesn't* know,' he said, bending down again, getting so close to Meggie's ear he was almost touching her. 'All those years ago, whilst you and he were playing happy families, and he was screwing Matilda on the side, I was shagging Nancy! She'd come to me,' he whispered, 'when her little brother had pissed off and Jacob was being less than kind to her. And whilst I was in her knickers she told me everything... *everything*,' he said, standing unsteadily, staring intently at Sebastian. 'The *disgusting* secret you've kept hidden all these years, that I've *never* shared. And *you*...!' he said, suddenly turning his attention towards Meggie. 'Nancy told me all about *you* and your love-child that *she* brought up so that you could carry on getting *pissed!*' he slurred, spittle escaping his mouth. 'I loved Nancy. I mean, *really* loved her. So much so, that I was going to call off my wedding,' he said absently. 'And I *thought* she loved me, which was why I started taking the money, so that we could be together... but I was wrong... once a Campbell, always a Campbell... they all *piss* on you in the end...' Paul scoffed, turning and walking away.

Enraged, Sebastian could not speak. Paul spun back round to face them again. 'Oh, and one last thing,' he said, 'you might like to ask your boyfriend here about his university days and whether his *wife* knows what he did! I was thinking I might pay her a visit, what do you think?' Once again, he turned around.

Unable to control himself, Sebastian grabbed a pepper grinder from the table and launched it over Meggie, hitting Paul squarely on the back of the head, the grinder's winding arm gouging deep into his flesh before clattering to the floor and smashing into pieces, bringing instant silence to the restaurant. Paul stopped. He put his hand to his head as the blood fought its way through his fingers. He examined it before continuing to walk. 'You might just regret doing that,' he muttered, leaving.

'*Fuck*!' Sebastian spat. The restaurant owner approached their table. Hands up in defence, Sebastian pre-empted the request for them to leave. 'Yes, we're leaving. Here,' he said, emptying the contents of his wallet onto the table, 'for the pepper mill, and the trouble. Sorry,' he said, quickly gathering his things and grabbing Meggie's hand, dragging her out of the restaurant into the cool October air.

'What was that all about?' Meggie asked, hurrying to catch him up.

'He's just a pissed-off shit!'

'What did he mean?' she asked, breathlessly.

Not answering, Sebastian buttoned up his jacket against the cold. Paul knew everything, he thought. He knew everything and he'd never said a word? Why not? He quickened his pace, making Meggie run alongside him.

'What did he mean about your university days?' she asked again, pulling at his arm. Sebastian stopped abruptly.

'Is that all you're bothered about?' he asked her, sharply. 'What did I do that was *so* wrong?' he said, exasperated. 'I am not proud of the young man I was, *you* know that better than anyone. With what happened to me and the way I treated you, I didn't give a shit, and after the first flush of romance I wasn't particularly nice to Matilda either and I did things I regret, but I wasn't any worse than any of the rest of you; *all* of you!' he said, angrily.

'What *sort* of things did you do?' Meggie persisted, determined to get her answer.

'*All* sorts of things, Meggie!' he said looking away, 'things I never told you, and I've never told Matilda either, but like a *dick*, I told my best friend.' Catching his breath, Sebastian paused and looked up at the cloudless sky, searching the stars for the brightest. He spoke more calmly. 'Not long after we were married, Matilda met someone else. She didn't have an affair, but she was tempted,' he said, 'and it made her question everything about us and about me, and I don't blame her. I was so focussed on forgetting my past and forging my future, that I didn't see what was going on around me,' he said bitterly. 'She felt guilty enough that she confessed. That's the difference between her and me.'

'You haven't told her you're with me tonight, have you?'

Sebastian shook his head. 'No,' he admitted, coldly.

'Why not? What is it you want?'

Sebastian did not answer.

'Do you think Paul will tell her?'

'I reckon Matilda knows what I was like back then.'

'But does she know what you're like now?'

Stunned, Sebastian held his breath and watched as, not knowing what to say, Meggie walked away. This wasn't what she wanted; she didn't want clandestine meetings with a man she no longer knew, a man lying to his wife so that he could meet her in a restaurant she last went into when she was a teenager. She did not want Matilda to find out so that he could justify ending his marriage and pursue her instead; she did not want to rekindle a relationship or even a friendship, or to share her daughter with a father who Florence had never known. She wanted to go home.

Day Thirty-Six

Thursday

Angus Stewart's Funeral Directors was sadly too familiar, and this time, Sebastian and Henry were walking in without their father by their side.

Exhausted after two long days in the theatre, and remembering the way his father had smiled at the teddy bear sitting, welcomingly, on the chair when they had visited their mother, Henry was lost for words as they entered the chapel of rest. He had always known what to say to his father when he saw him, but today he could not speak even to say goodbye. In silence, he and Sebastian stood and looked into their father's coffin.

Although they knew it was him, without life, their father's body was no more than a vessel from which his unyielding spirit had been released. His face was drawn, his cheeks sallow, his sunken eyes, closed. If only there were a giggle, a laugh to say that this was all a big joke.

In reply to his parents' letter, Sebastian had written his own. The words had been difficult to find. Hidden away in his home office all of Wednesday, still reeling from the night before, four pages had taken him the best part of the day to get right, writing it over and over again until it said what he wanted. He had written it by hand; it was important his father should know that the words were his own. Having put the letter in an envelope, together with some family photographs and a picture of Betsy, he tucked it into the top pocket of his father's jacket; the one jacket he owned and wore on special occasions. Feeling desperately sad, he left the chapel of rest just in front of Henry.

Henry also had something to leave behind and, as Sebastian left the room, he took the little red car, with no wheels or doors, out of his pocket. When he was a child, Nancy had all but destroyed it and he remembered mourning for his precious toy. Having drawn a blank in the shed, he had thought his parents must have thrown it away once it had been broken and rendered useless, but they hadn't, and he had found it, carefully wrapped in newspaper and placed in an old soap box at the back of his father's bedside table.

Making the discovery had brought Henry to his knees and he had curled into a ball on his parents' bedroom floor, holding the little red car tightly to his chest. Growing up, he had often thought about it and when he found it he realised that, knowing how much he had cherished it, they had kept it, hidden away and safe from danger. Perhaps they had hoped that one day he would find it and understand. Henry placed the little red car in the cup of his father's hand and closed his cold fingers around it.

Leaving Angus Stewart's, the brothers walked the short distance along the canal towpath to The Lock Keeper's Arms, a pub they had often gone to with their parents. With a lovely sunny garden, which sloped down towards the water, in the summer months it was a popular place for walkers and cyclists to stop and rest, sitting outside and enjoying the barges chugging past. In the winter months, patronage was mostly inside, away from the unforgiving Scottish weather, although there were still a few hardy cyclists who preferred to sit on the damp garden benches watching over their precious bikes. The drizzle persistent, there would be no sitting outside for Sebastian and Henry, and the warm fire inside was very welcoming as they walked in. The publican, who had known the family for years, was delighted to see them and after a cheery 'hello' and 'how are you' naturally asked after their parents. The news came as a blow and Sebastian and Henry's first drinks were on the house.

'So, are you ready for tomorrow?' Sebastian asked, taking a sip from his beer and lowering his glass onto the small, round table.

'I think so. Are you?' Henry said, sitting down.

'No, I mean opening night?'

'Oh right, yes. Well, I've not heard anything from Lorna this morning so I'm assuming no news is good news. They should have done the first tech run by now,' he said looking at his watch, 'and then we'll do another one when I get over there later and then I'm hoping to do a full run before finishing.'

'Did you manage to get the bike working?'

'Eventually, last night,' Henry said shaking his head. 'It's a bit 'Heath Robinson,' but it works. I meant to ask, did you get my speech for tomorrow?'

'I did, I've sent it over to the celebrant.'

'Thank you. Then I think we're ready aren't, we?'

'I think we are,' Sebastian agreed. 'This time tomorrow it'll be all over.'

For the next hour, Sebastian filled Henry in on his and Meggie's encounter with Paul at the restaurant. Over the past twenty-four hours Sebastian had had time to think about what Paul had told him, and the look on Meggie's face as she walked away. He had come to the realisation that he hadn't known either of them the way he thought he had. He had taken the long route back to his car, thinking 'I haven't changed'. He had thought he was a better person, a different one from that seventeen-year-old who arrogantly believed he could puff out his chest and take on anyone, but perhaps not. Perhaps he had just been shaped by Jacob and, what he was then, he still was. He did not go as far as to tell Henry everything, but told him how, when he got home Tuesday night, he had intended confessing to Matilda where he had been and who with, but the wind had been taken out of his sails by Paul's final blow, when he walked into the house to find Trish sitting at their kitchen table with Matilda, crestfallen, as one betrayed wife told another something she had just found out. Honest Trish, who had known nothing of her own husband's deceit, knew that Matilda would not thank her for sharing her knowledge but felt a renewed compulsion to save others from the same misfortune she had suffered. She left as soon as Sebastian arrived and he and Matilda sat and talked. He was not sure Matilda believed him when he told her there was nothing going on between him and Meggie, but in truth, that was not the problem. Matilda had told him she was finding it increasingly difficult to live with a man who harboured secrets that he could not share with his wife, and, after their unresolved conversation turned heated, Matilda refused to speak to him anymore, and they slept apart.

On Wednesday morning, Sebastian got up early, trying to outrun his feelings in the gym before taking Panda along the river where she played in the cold water, retrieving stones. By the time Matilda came down for breakfast, he was back and waiting for her with tea and toast and the hope that they could talk once more: a little more calmly this time. They did, and it was there, in the kitchen, that Matilda asked him a question.

'Can I ask,' she said, 'this thing that happened to you when you were younger, that you've never felt you could share with me. Does Meggie know?'

Sebastian did not need to speak for Matilda to know the answer. She was at a loss to know what she wanted or where to go from there. They agreed to wait until Friday was over and talk again.

Sebastian spent the afternoon in the cinema room with Panda whilst Matilda went out alone. The papered-over cracks in their relationship were getting wider and the sale of Tatch-A UK only served to mask them no matter how hard they both tried to stay connected.

Leaving the pub, Sebastian continued talking as he and Henry walked back along the towpath. It was all such a mess in Sebastian's head. He struggled to think straight. But, recounting what had happened, he knew in his heart that it was not Meggie he wanted. Reaching their cars, the brothers said goodbye.

Just before getting into his, Henry asked Sebastian whether he had heard from Nancy.

'Nothing at all.'

'That surprises me. I thought she'd have been in touch to ask about Dad's funeral.'

'She doesn't give a shit, Hal.'

'Do you think she'll turn up tomorrow?'

'I don't think so because she'd be here by now, insisting on getting her place at the front. And anyway, I've not given her any details, so unless Meggie has, which I doubt, I don't see how she'd know.'

'Is Meggie going?'

'I hope not.'

Day Thirty-Seven

Friday

The last thing Henry needed was for something to go wrong. So, whilst busily getting the farmhouse ready to receive friends and relations, he did not need the phone call from Abbi, his stage manager, saying the bike was broken and the cube wouldn't move. Abbi had worked with Henry for years and, although in her late forties, she had an innocent, youthful look, which deceived people. Having never settled down, she was happy to go wherever Henry's productions took her and he trusted her wealth of experience. Resigned, he knew today was not going to go his way.

'I'm sorry,' she said, 'I really didn't want to bother you or Lorna this morning, but we've been at it for ages and we can't get it to work.'

'Do you know where it's stuck?' Henry asked, desperate to get the problem solved over the phone. It was only Lorna who really understood the mechanics of it, but she had left Taligth to go and collect Lilith from the station. The construction manager, who they had subsequently found out also worked behind the bar, had been scratching his head all morning with no joy. Their last resort was to contact Henry.

'We know it's something to do with one of the chains and not the connection to the runners on the track,' Abbi explained, 'which is good, because, if it was, we wouldn't stand a chance. From what we can see, and it's not easy because you have to virtually swing from the frame to get a good look, it just keeps slipping and then jams. So, when Ben rides it, it'll move a bit and then stop. With a bit of footwork it'll move again but then it'll stop again. It's so frustrating.

Other than to take the whole thing down and dismantle it, we don't know what to do. We just can't get at it.'

'We haven't got time to take it down,' Henry said looking at his watch, 'and we've got a full house tonight,' he added, thinking that if they could not get the cube to move, they would have to postpone the opening performance, which would be a disaster.

'We've got a full house every night,' Abbi pointed out.

'Listen, keep trying and I'll call Lorna to see whether she has any ideas. It'll be something simple. But if nothing works, one of us will have to come over.'

It was always the way; a last-minute problem threatening to scupper the production. If it wasn't one of the cast being ill or the lighting desk suddenly un-programming itself, it was famine, a flood, or a plague of locusts sent to test the nerves of the director. Although concerned, Henry was not panicked. He called Lorna.

'Hi, listen, Abbi's been on the phone. Apparently, there's something wrong with one of the chains on the bike.'

'Damn!' Lorna cursed. 'We were having trouble with it yesterday.'

'Were you? It was working fine last night.'

'We thought we'd fixed it. Obviously not.'

'Can you think what it might be so we can tell them what to do?' Henry asked, gathering crumbs off the kitchen table as he spoke.

'Not without seeing it. If it's the same thing as yesterday, one of the chains kept slipping. I shortened it but it's obviously doing it again.'

'Do you think it's knackered?'

'It could be.'

'I've got some spares in my boot. Where are you now?' Henry asked as he emptied the crumbs from his hand into the bin.

'Miles away. I haven't got to the station yet.'

The remoteness of the farm meant it was a forty-minute drive to one of the two train stations that served the area, forty minutes in the opposite direction to the theatre.

Waiting for the train to arrive and Lilith to get to the car laden down with her cello, and then driving back to Taligth to drop her off, would take Lorna at least an hour and a half, so, although he desperately did not want to, it was down to Henry to go to the theatre to see what could be done. He phoned Abbi, telling her he was on his way.

Before leaving, he went into the yard where he could see Sebastian in one of the far fields, breaking hay bales open for the cows. Henry was not surprised to see him amongst them, in much the same way as he had been on the day they buried their mother.

Trudging across the mud, Henry called out. Knowing there was little chance of his voice carrying against the strong headwind, he leapt onto one of the quad bikes. He stopped at the edge of each field to open and close gates, sheep scattering skittishly as he raced through.

'Sebastian!' he called, getting nearer. Opening the final gate, he could see Sebastian with his face nestled into the forehead of his favourite heifer. 'Sebastian!' Henry called again, pulling his bike up and walking through the long grass to get his brother's attention. Walking up behind him, Henry tapped Sebastian on the shoulder, making him jump.

'Shit! You scared the life out of me,' Sebastian said, taking his earphones out.

'I've been calling you and calling you,' Henry said, out of breath. 'Are you okay?'

'I'm fine, I just needed some time by myself.'

'It's nice up here,' Henry said, looking around. 'I don't blame Dad giving up the city for all this. Who wouldn't?'

'Which is why I want to keep it.'

'Keep the farm?'

'Before Mum died, I'd not worked out here for years. Yet nothing's changed. The animals are the same, they still need feeding, the cows still need milking every day and the fields need to be turned. It's the same as it ever was. We're treading the same earth our parents have trodden and our mother's parents before her and the ones before that. Now that I'm not tied to Tatch-A as much, I could have the best of both worlds and it might help me and Matilda. Who knows? It seems wrong to get rid of it.'

'If that's what you want, then great, let's talk about it. But, in the meantime, I'm really sorry, there's an issue at the theatre and I need to get over there.'

'What, now?'

'Yes. I really don't want to go but there's no one else. The bloody bike won't work and unless I can get it going there's no way we can open tonight. It's your fault, you jinxed it when you mentioned the Scottish play the other night, you bastard,' Henry laughed.

'Do you want me to come?'

'No, you stay here. I'm going to take everything with me for later, in case I don't make it back in time to go with you in the car. Are you okay with that?'

'Of course. Go and do what you need to do.'

'If I don't make it back here, I'll meet you at the crematorium,' Henry said, walking backwards against the wind towards his quad bike. 'See you later,' he called, turning and running, tripping and stumbling over the divots hidden beneath the grass.

'Don't be late,' Sebastian yelled, waving his hand in Henry's direction as the mud kicked up from beneath the wheels.

'Never am.' Henry's voice trailed behind him like a scarf in the wind as he sped off, bumping and lurching his way back towards the farmhouse.

An hour later, he was walking into the theatre.

'Thank god you're here,' Abbi said, relieved to see him. 'We've tried everything and now it won't budge at all. I hope we haven't broken it.'

'Don't any of you ride bikes?' Henry asked, looking round at their blank faces. Abbi looked down at her feet, uncomfortable at needing Henry's help on the day of his father's funeral. 'It's okay, I was joking, you useless bunch of luvvies! Right, let me have a look,' he said, rolling up his sleeves and ascending the steps to the gantry. Holding on firmly to the rails, he lowered himself onto the frame.

Lying on his stomach on a makeshift floor the construction manager had built for them so they could work on the bike without fear of falling, Henry finally located the source of the problem. 'Okay,' he called down, 'it's simple really, once you get to it. It's the second chain, the longer one. It's not meeting the sprocket right and it keeps jumping off. The derailleur might be knackered... which it could be actually,' he muttered to himself, leaning further over the edge. 'I got most of it second hand, so who knows what condition the bike parts are in. Can someone get Ben for me please? I could do with him up here.'

Within a minute, Ben, the smallest and most acrobatic member of the acting team, was climbing into the cube. Not needing to rely on the makeshift floor, he swung onto the bike seat.

'Right,' Henry said, 'I've put the chain back on for now but I'm guessing it'll jump off straight away. Can you pedal really slowly? I need to see whether it's the chain or whether we need to replace the derailleur. Hopefully, it'll be the chain, but if it's the derailleur, someone will need to go to a shop. Abbi...!' he called down, 'can you do a search and find somewhere that sells bikes.'

Hanging off the frame, his head millimeters from Ben's feet, Henry wriggled into position to watch carefully as he instructed Ben when to start and stop pedalling. At slow speed, it took all Ben's effort to get the cube moving, but he managed until the chain slipped off the sprocket again and Henry shouted 'stop, stop, stop!' and everything ground to a halt. 'Okay, thanks Ben, you can stop now. I can see it,' Henry said, relieved. 'I know what the problem is. Trudy, can you grab my keys out of my coat pocket. It's over on the seats, there, and go to my car. In the boot there's a cardboard box and in the box there are spares, including some bike chains and tools. Can you bring them in for me please?'

Trudy rushed out of the theatre, whilst Henry and Ben waited on the frame. Henry looked at his watch. It was 1 p.m. There was no chance he was going to make it back to Taligth in time to leave with the rest of them. Feeling a rising panic, he messaged Lorna and Sebastian.

'What's the matter with it?' Abbi called up.

'The derailleur's bent and some of the chain links have gone stiff. I should be able to bend the derailleur back and replace the section of the chain. It won't take long and then I'll have to run.'

'Can any of us do it for you?'

'Not unless one of you can replace a bike chain whilst hanging upside down.'

~

Looking out of the living room window, Sebastian saw the hearse and the two black limousines pulling up the drive, each coming slowly, respectfully, towards the farmhouse. The small family, including the children, Lilith, Isla and Ewan and his wife, gathered quietly on the top step, shivering against the cold, waiting for the vehicles to get into position. A chill wind cut through them, but it was dry. There was no need for black umbrellas this time.

As if Elspeth's funeral had been the dress rehearsal, they each sat in the same seats they had before, other than in the first car, where Sebastian sat alone, no William or Henry alongside him. Matilda and Lorna sat behind. They pulled off the drive and Sebastian looked ahead at the beautiful autumn flowers that filled the hearse's windows, obscuring William's coffin from the outside world. He was pleased no one could see inside; his father had been a private man and he would not have liked people gawking.

Sebastian watched the flowers tremble and sway as the cars made their way down the uneven road. He wished Henry was sitting next to him to share his silence. Henry was the only one who knew how he felt.

~

Having fixed and tested the bike, Henry hurriedly got changed into his suit with a white shirt, grey and black tie and his best school shoes, which could have done with a clean after he had played football with some year eleven

421

boys the last time he was in school. He spat on them and rubbed them with his sweatshirt. They would do. No one was going to be looking at his shoes.

Checking he had his speech in his pocket, that his hair was brushed and he didn't have bike grease plastered across his face, Henry got into his car, praying it would start. Relieved, as the engine roared, he made his way out of the car park. He was later leaving than he had hoped and was feeling anxious. He had forty minutes to do a twenty-minute drive. 'Plenty of time,' Henry assured himself.

Driving along the country lanes, Henry thought about his father. Smiling to himself, he recalled his and Lorna's wedding day. They had married in Lorna's hometown. The night before the wedding, Lorna had stayed at her family home, whilst Henry and his family had stayed in a small hotel nearby. The hotel was difficult to find and the taxi, taking Henry and his family to the church, got lost and was late picking them up. Henry despised being late and William was all for jumping into the Land Rover and taking them, but Elspeth had scolded him for making such a ridiculous suggestion, so they had waited. The taxi driver eventually found them, having passed the hotel a number of times, as William's Land Rover had obscured the sign. Elspeth scolded William again. The taxi arrived after the bride, who had been driven around the block whilst the congregation waited nervously, thinking perhaps the groom had changed his mind.

Looking at the time, Henry started to feel that taking the back roads had not been a good decision. They were slow and winding and the pot-holed surfaces meant he had to take greater care. At the first opportunity he diverted onto the main road, which ran straight through the middle of town. Within minutes of turning, he hit horrendous traffic and, instantly regretting his move, came to a virtual standstill. With his anxiety rising, he could sense he was going to be late and made a frantic call to Lorna.

'I'm stuck the other side of town. Where are you?' he asked, sweating.

'Don't panic. We're not there yet either. How far away are you?' Lorna asked.

'Twenty minutes, but it's carnage.'

'That's okay. We can wait for you, I'm sure.'

'I can't believe this!'

'Don't worry, Hal. You'll get here.'

'I can't be late.'

'You won't! We'll wait.'

'BLOODY HELL!' he suddenly shouted, slamming his hands on the steering wheel. 'How can I miss my father's funeral?'

'Henry! Stop it! You're not going to miss it. You'll get there.'

'Tell him to stop panicking. We'll wait for him,' Sebastian said calmly, turning to Lorna.

'Did you hear that, Hal?'

'Yes, okay, I'll stop panicking but this traffic is doing my head in!'

'Henry!'

'Hang on, we're moving again!' Henry said gleefully, 'COME ON YOU BASTARDS!' he shouted, clearly audible to the driver of the limousine who winked at Sebastian through his rear-view mirror. Sebastian smiled. It was weird to hear Henry getting so angry. Had it been him in that car, he would have got out, abandoning it where it was, and walked.

'Sorry,' Henry said when Lorna told him everyone in the car had heard his outburst. 'I'll get there as quickly as I can.'

'Poor Henry,' Lorna said, 'he hates being late.'

Finally crawling through town, the road opened up and Henry was able to put his foot down. With his heart pounding, he prayed for no more holdups.

~

Turning left off the road, the funeral cortège made its way slowly up the long drive to the crematorium. A crowd of friends and relations were gathered at the top outside the chapel, shivering under the grey October sky. Getting out of the cars, the family greeted them warmly. It was so kind of people to come and pay their respects and Sebastian was pleased to see so many familiar faces. To his relief, there was no sign of Nancy or Meggie and, spotting Paul's parents standing together, he looked around praying Paul was not close by.

'Do you want me to stay outside and wait?' Ewan asked, interrupting his father's thoughts as they walked into the chapel.

'What?' Sebastian asked.

'For Uncle Henry.'

Sebastian looked at his watch and then again behind him, towards the open door as they took their places. 'Thanks, but he's only a few minutes away. He'll be here,' he said reassuringly, checking his watch again.

~

Now on an open stretch of road, Henry was caught behind a large and very slow white van. He contemplated overtaking, but the opposite carriageway was running fast with a constant stream of on-coming traffic preventing him from sticking his nose out to see whether the coast was clear. A large 4x4 behind him was getting equally impatient, dashing from side to side, pushing close to Henry's car then drawing back, seeking any opportunity to overtake. Distracted, and feeling pressure from behind, Henry decided to make a move. When a gap appeared, he pulled out to see beyond the van. The screaming of horns forced him back into line and a finger held firmly in the air by a startled van driver told him exactly what he thought about Henry's attempt to overtake. Henry's heart was racing.

'Shit...! Shit! Shit! Shit! Shit, *fucking* shit!' he shouted, slamming his hands on the steering wheel, angry that the van in front of him was travelling so slowly. 'Trust me to get behind the only white van driver in the whole *fucking* universe who drives under the speed limit,' he yelled. The 4x4 nudged ever closer, filling Henry's rear window with its

424

toothy grill. He felt sandwiched and intimidated. 'Come on,' he said under his breath. 'Come on you *bastard*, get a *fucking* move on!'

~

Looking at the time, unable to hold off any longer, the celebrant approached Sebastian and spoke quietly to him. Understanding, Sebastian nodded, standing up. Matilda reached out, gently squeezing his hand. Lorna and the children looked across.

'Don't worry, he'll be here,' Sebastian mouthed, moving towards the lectern.

Standing to face his family and friends, he kept his eyes fixed firmly on the large doors at the back of the room, listening, in hope, for the sound of car tyres on gravel and running feet. The empty space on the pew in front of him, devoid of Henry's comforting smile, stared back. The silence inside the room was palpable. Nerves overtook tears as he read his speech from the page, word for word, not daring to deviate or improvise in case he lost his way.

~

In the far distance, Henry could just make out the distinctive green and gold sign of the crematorium. He was five minutes away. Anticipating the right-hand turn coming up, he decided to pull back and wait, but just as he did, the 4x4 behind him pulled out, and started to overtake both his car and the white van. Seeing his opportunity, Henry followed, but the junction was closer than either he, or the driver of the 4x4 had anticipated, and the 4x4 suddenly turned sharply right in front of an oncoming lorry onto the driveway leading up the hill to the crematorium. Again, Henry tried to follow, but the gap was too narrow and he almost overshot the junction. '*Fuck!*' he yelled, booting the accelerator and pulling hard right on the steering wheel, flinging the car across the path of the oncoming traffic. Again, vehicle horns blasted in the air as he misjudged the space and an articulated lorry, unable to stop, clipped his rear left side, sending the car spinning down the road.

Within moments, the lorry hit him again, this time catching the edge of his bumper, sending him into the path of the line of traffic he had just tried to escape and he was hit once more, this time by a van travelling too fast to apply the brakes in time and Henry's car was propelled from the road. The sheer power of the thrust was too much for his small but faithful 'friend' and he was tossed into the air. Weightlessly, the car rotated before returning to earth. Crashing on its side, it came to rest, concertinaed on its roof in a field across the road from the entrance to the crematorium. Smoke billowing. Wheels spinning.

~

After Lilith played her cello, it was Henry's turn to speak. Members of the congregation turned at any sound they thought they heard behind the closed doors, hoping he would come through them. Looking at the celebrant, who nodded, Sebastian checked his phone to see where Henry was; he was close. Sebastian smiled, reassuringly touching Lorna's hand.

~

Adrenalin flowing, Henry did a quick body check. He moved his feet from beneath the pedals to free his legs and although the door was caved in, he could move his arms. His eyes were open and his face was moving, he was breathing; he was alive! Suspended upside down by his seatbelt, he knew better than to just unbuckle it, having heard stories of poor unfortunates in similar situations who, having survived the crash, had fallen to their deaths, breaking their necks after clicking themselves free. With all the strength he could muster, raising his arms to the roof to slacken the tension on the belt, he prepared to release.

~

When Henry had still not appeared, the celebrant moved, reluctantly, to speak with Sebastian and, handing him a copy of Henry's speech, asked him whether he would like to read it in his brother's absence. Looking down at the paper

426

in his hand, Sebastian hesitated. The celebrant, although understanding, was insistent that they needed to continue.

Sebastian stood and moved slowly to the lectern. At least Henry's words would be heard and his message of love for their father, shared. Henry had written his speech in the form of a letter and slowly, controlling his breath, Sebastian started to read...

'Dear Dad...'

~

It wasn't until he raised his arms and pain seared through him that Henry realised that his effort to free himself was futile. Despite being able to move, he was unable to get out. With the car on its roof and him lying crumpled against the broken glass of the door's window, he could smell the sweet aroma of the newly mown grass as he moved his head slowly to look across, tracing the length of the fence post with his eyes. The car had landed on it after it had flipped, and like a javelin, it had penetrated the door. Travelling through the car, it had entered Henry's side, its momentum pinning him to his seat.

As silence filled the air and drivers from stopped vehicles rushed to his aid, Henry imagined he could hear the resonating sound of 'Yesterday', the Beetles classic that his father had loved so much and which he and Sebastian had chosen to play during the funeral. He smiled at the irony and, closing his eyes, hummed breathlessly.

~

Folding the paper containing Henry's words and without looking up, Sebastian started to make his way back to his seat. Then, something caught his attention and he stopped and looked towards the doors as the congregation turned to share what he was seeing. Hearing the sound of approaching footsteps, his heart quickened.

Thirty-Seven Years After the Unimaginable

Thirty-seven years after burying his father, Sebastian was in Switzerland once more. At eighty-six, he hadn't visited the country in almost four decades and, as he walked, a little slower than he once had, towards the car waiting for him outside the hotel where he had been staying for the week, he was reminded of the feelings he had when he last saw Nancy. There would be no such feelings today.

A week ago, he had attended Nancy's cremation. The last time he had seen her was at their father's funeral, when her footsteps outside the chapel had heralded her entrance.

A conversation with Stefan had convinced her that she might regret not going to the funeral and that perhaps it was time to make peace with the dead. After Sebastian's visit, she had spent time thinking about the years she had stayed away from Taligth, the years she had resented her parents for not telling her who she was and for not helping her understand the feelings of detachment she had grown up with. Once her parents had died, she could no longer hold on to the anger and the energy it gave her to justify her actions. Acting on Stefan's advice, the night before her father's funeral, she had booked the last seat on the only flight into Edinburgh that day. Time was always going to be tight so Stefan had organised a rental car for her. But, along with a delay at the car rental booth and heavy Friday afternoon traffic, precious minutes were lost. She was late, just as she had been the day she was driving to the hospital for her antenatal appointment twenty-two years earlier.

As she accelerated hard and overtook the old car and the slow white van, her attention was focused on taking the right hand turn of the junction before the oncoming lorry closed the gap. Had she looked to her left as she passed, she might have seen her brother, wracked with tension. Had she looked in her rear-view mirror, she might have seen him pull out behind her and follow her path. Oblivious, she had left carnage in her wake.

It wasn't until they all came out of the crematorium that they could hear the sirens and see the lights of emergency vehicles flashing in the distance. Instinctively, Sebastian knew Henry was in trouble; instinctively, he knew that Nancy had been involved, and he ran the length of the drive and across the road to be confronted by utter devastation. Henry's car was unrecognisable. Sebastian would not forget the despair he felt that day, and despite her future attempts at reconciliation, he never spoke to Nancy again.

When she had walked into the chapel where her father was lying, she had been surprised to see so many people turn and face her, but that was not the case at her own funeral. Fewer than ten people attended the service, such was the consequence of being a very old lady who had outlived the few friends she had managed to keep. Sebastian only attended because he wanted to make sure she was finally gone.

Today, as her next of kin, Sebastian was taking the short trip across the city to collect his sister's ashes from the funeral directors. He would then fly back to London where he had arranged for Nancy to be buried alongside her birth mother, his father's sister, Lily.

Lily had been asleep when, one night, at just a few days old, Nancy had been lifted out of her cot and taken away. Lily never got over the heartache of her loss and, feeling desperately sorry for her, William and Elspeth did everything they could to allow Lily time with her child. Lily spent weeks at a time at Taligth looking after Nancy, playing with her, until the pain of her own illness ravaged her body so much that she could no longer make the journey. She was buried with the blanket that Nancy had been wrapped in on the day she was born. Despite his estrangement from his sister, thinking about Florence, Sebastian felt compelled to do right by Lily and to give Nancy back, so that she could rest alongside the one person who had loved her unconditionally.

It was good to see Florence at Nancy's funeral. It had been a long time since they had met, but through Christmas cards, they had kept in touch over the years. In the months following their unexpected introduction, Sebastian had thought about the possibility of getting to know Florence and the potential of playing a part in her life, but too much time had passed for both of them. Sebastian's mix of apathy and lack of desire to complicate things any further led to him not seeing Florence again other than for the odd wave through the café window when he passed. Much to Panda's disappointment, he never went back in.

After a couple of years, the café changed hands; Nancy having sold it after Florence met and married a sculptor. The newly-weds moved down to the Cornish coast to open a B&B and raise a second child, another daughter, Polly. Florence kept sending Christmas cards and Sebastian enjoyed reading her letters in which she chattered about what she had been up to during the past year and what Nellie and Polly - and eventually, their children too - were doing. With neither Ewan nor Isla having had any children of their own, Sebastian enjoyed hearing the news of his grandchildren and great-grandchildren, albeit from afar. Her Christmas cards always included photographs and a promise of return to Scotland one day but, although Sebastian would have liked to see her, they both knew it would never happen. It was just something people wrote at the end of a letter. Florence never did, nor did she ever want to, find out who her real father was.

Through Florence Sebastian kept up with news of Nancy and Meggie.

Little changed in Nancy's life other than that Stefan left her when he met someone he unexpectedly fell in love with, finally understanding the true meaning of happiness. Although she would not admit it, least of all to herself,

Nancy was bereft, and refusing a divorce, did not make life easy for him. Happier without her, he did not care. Stefan died suddenly when he was sixty-eight having contracted meningitis for a second time. His innate kindness never failing, he made sure Nancy was financially secure for the rest of her life and she remained living comfortably, but alone, in her Swiss apartment, until her death.

In one letter Florence included a line about Jacob. Seeing his name written in her soft, round handwriting, had made Sebastian shudder, but he was relieved to find out that, after years of being the perpetrator in a controlling and abusive, second marriage, Jacob had had his comeuppance and had spent the rest of his life in one of the country's toughest prisons. How he had died, Sebastian neither knew nor cared about.

Florence wrote very little about Meggie, but reading between the lines, Sebastian sensed she was happy. She and Aled stayed on the farm in Hexham and continued to breed Alpacas and produce exceptional fleece, which Florence learned to knit into jumpers, scarves and hats, adding artisan crafter to her artistic talents.

Meggie returned to Edinburgh only the once after Florence left – to visit Taligth.

~

Following the accident, Henry spent weeks in intensive care, battling with death. It seemed determined to take him, but against the odds, he won the fight. Although his injuries were horrific and life-changing, it took him less than a year to recover his strength and start to learn to walk again. The trajectory of the fence post had damaged his spine and, although he had movement in his legs, he did not regain full control and was unable to support his own weight for long periods of time. He would only ever manage a few steps before sitting back down in his wheelchair, but it was enough for him to be able to walk Lilith down the aisle when, at twenty-seven, she married a French violinist, Didier, whom she met during the time she was in Liverpool.

Fifteen years older than her, he was divorced and had a son from his first marriage who Lilith loved as much as she loved their own three children. Lilith, Didier and their children spent the majority of their time in France when they were not travelling and playing in some of the world's most prestigious venues. She returned to England when she could, to visit home, but was never back for long, the call of the concert hall always dragging her away again. Lorna and Henry enjoyed the precious, short time they were with her.

In the immediate aftermath of his accident, whilst in and out of consciousness, Henry gave strict instructions from his hospital bed that the production should still go ahead. With Lilith by his bedside, Lorna made sure that it was every bit the success Henry could have hoped for and, with outstanding reviews, it launched his playwriting and production career firmly into the spotlight. As soon as he could master a wheelchair, he was back in the theatre once more, working on his next production. With the generous support of his parents' money, he and Lorna took his work all around the world, even, at times, into the same country where Lilith was performing. For the last three decades of his life, Henry was able to say goodbye to teaching.

It took him a long time to come to terms with his accident and he suffered many dark days, filled with remorse at letting his brother and family down the day they buried their father. His regular nightmares became more vivid and were added to with ones where he was drowning in oats stored in oast houses. Having trained herself to sleep more lightly than she did before Henry's accident, Lorna learned to wake him from his dreams and bring Mabel to him when he needed comfort.

After a short illness, Henry died peacefully in his dreamless sleep when he was eighty-three and was buried alongside Lorna and Mabel.

~

Henry had been right when, the day before their father's funeral, he had laid a £20 bet with Sebastian that he would not see out the end of his one-year contract to remain with Tatch-A UK after the company was sold. Not being at the helm dampened Sebastian's motivation and drive, and although his experience in running the company was invaluable, it soon became clear that the people who had taken over wanted to do it their way and it was time for Sebastian to move on, which, with Patrick's blessing and Niamh's support, he did.

Tatch-A UK continued to be a successful, vibrant company, thriving in countries Sebastian could never have imagined taking it to. He and Patrick remained close friends and Sebastian spent many happy holidays in Arizona honing his riding skills. Patrick offered good advice when Sebastian talked to him about Matilda and how they were trying to repair their damaged marriage, but he confessed to perhaps not being the best role model. Patrick continued to work right up to the end and, as requested, was laid to rest on his ranch to enjoy the afterlife in the searing heat of the dessert sun beneath the shadows of the saguaro cactus.

Eighteen months after leaving Tatch-A UK, Sebastian moved out of his and Matilda's home and back into Taligth, taking on the farm. By this time, he and Matilda, unable to resolve their differences, had separated. On the morning he left, he had received a phone call from Ade to tell him that Betsy had died. Devastated by her death and the connection she had to his father, Sebastian had packed his bags and walked away from his marriage. Matilda, unable to live with his secretiveness and the devastation it had caused, did not stop him. She had stood, looking out of their bedroom window, watching as he drove away without looking back. Until he could live with himself, she did not stand a chance of helping and she was exhausted from trying.

Taking over Taligth, and investing money in the house and the farm and the community around it, gave Sebastian a new purpose and, after many years of counselling, he grew to realise that all he needed were the fields and the simplicity of the animals that roamed them. He loved the physical, hard work and grew the farm back to the size it had been in its hey-day, giving employment to locals and something back to the community that had been so supportive to his family over the generations. It was whilst he was out in the fields one day that he got a call from Sam telling him there was someone to see him.

It had been almost ten years to the day since he last saw Meggie and, as he made his way around the side of the house, the same rush of emotions he had felt when he bumped into her in the café a decade before flooded him once more and he invited her in, eager to hear her news. Meggie had come back to Taligth to return something to him that Elspeth had given her the day Florence was born. It was a gold locket that once belonged to Elspeth's grandmother, a locket in which Elspeth had placed a tiny curl of Florence's hair. She had given it to Meggie in the hope that one day she would be reunited with her daughter. Meggie wanted Sebastian to have his great-grandmother's locket, which contained a lock of his daughter's hair on one side and locks of his granddaughters', Nellie and Polly's, on the other. That was the last time they saw each other.

~

Now, thirty-seven years after the death of her father-in-law, Matilda was waiting for Sebastian at Edinburgh airport. It had taken her fourteen years to walk back into his life and several more for them to learn to live together again. But now, almost twenty years later, they were happy. Sebastian had finally been able to share with Matilda what he had only ever shared with Meggie and, although it meant they could move on without secrets, Matilda understood why he had kept it from everyone. Their love for each other ran deeper than the events which took place on Nancy's twenty-first. As an old man, Sebastian learned to find peace and to accept the actions of others. For a while he reconciled with Paul, although it was short lived. Fifteen years after Tatch-A UK was sold, Paul took his own life when the breakdown of his marriage and the crushing weight of his best friend's forgiveness became too much.

Driving back to Taligth, Sebastian filled Matilda in on what he had seen in Switzerland and the places he had visited. On their way through the village, they dropped into McGregor's to buy some painkillers for Sebastian who, having been diagnosed as in the early stages of cancer, was suffering a little stomach pain. Dougie McGregor, as active as ever at eighty-seven, still ran the shop, now helped by his son and grandson. Although the petrol pumps had been replaced and the till computerised, the garage shop remained a treasure trove for anything and everything anyone could want. Dougie extended a warm welcome to Sebastian, and Sebastian left with a packet of painkillers, a bottle of his father's favourite whisky, a box of soft toffees for Matilda and a dog chew for Noodle, their twelve-year-old golden cocker spaniel they had bought many years after losing Panda.

Saying goodbye to Dougie, Sebastian walked back to the car. They needed to get home to change as they were meeting Ewan, Isla and their partners, along with Lilith and her family, for a special dinner before they went to the theatre that evening to watch the premiere of one of Henry's plays being performed at The Sheep Shed by a group of well-known, talented actors. Although Henry had written the play from his hospital bed, thirty-five years before his death, he had never brought it to the stage. The reviews claimed it to be one of his best.

Henry had kept his promise to Betsy and had written her a part in a play dedicated to his parents' lives, telling the story of thirty-seven unimaginable days.

Acknowledgements

There have been many people involved in writing this book. To these people, I would like to extend my thanks. You may, or may not know who you are, but I know who you are, and that's all that matters.

Many thanks go to my editor, Anthony Wootten, who not only encouraged me, but more importantly, guided and educated me.

I would like to thank Penny, Sue and Emily for reading the book when it was in its infancy and for giving their opinions and advice.

I would also like to thank my family, friends and neighbours who have listened to me talk about my book for the past eighteen months. They have helped me bring the story to life. And to Adam, a big 'thank you' for emptying the 'recycle bin' and saving Minus 10.

I would like to extend my deepest thanks to my wonderful sister, Clare, who has not only been by my side everyday of my life, but has also read the book more times than any human should. She offered brilliant editorial and content advice when the book was in its raw form and, for having the courage to be honest, I will be forever grateful.

And to my husband, Michael, without whom this book would still be in my head. He encouraged and supported me and I can never thank him enough for putting up with my belligerence and unreasonableness, and for arguing his point when I disagreed with him. Thank you, Mike.

Finally, I would like to thank my parents. They always believed in me. I think they would be proud.

About the Author

Dominique Darley was born in Buckinghamshire, England, in 1966. She now lives in a small village in Staffordshire with her husband, Michael, and has two grown-up children.

After studying drama at St. Mary's University in London, Dominique started 'The Drama Class' and has worked as a teacher of speech and drama for many years. She has produced, directed and written a number of plays for The Blue Suit Theatre Company. As a playwright, her works include OH GUMTREE, When Cows Dance, and Cabbages.

Thirty-Seven Days to the Unimaginable is her first novel.

dominiquejdarley@gmail.com
Twitter: @DarleyD_Author
Instagram: dominiquedarley_author

Printed in Great Britain
by Amazon

69323497R00262